A MAZE FOR THE MINOTAUR
AND OTHER STRANGE STORIES

By the same author

Plays
Imaginary Lines
Put Some Clothes on, Clarisse!
The Music Lovers
Winner Takes All
Once Bitten
Love Unknown

Biography
Out of the Woodshed, the Life of Stella Gibbons

Story Collections
The Dreams of Cardinal Vittorini and Other Strange Stories
The Complete Symphonies of Adolf Hitler
Masques of Satan
Madder Mysteries
Mrs Midnight and Other Stories
Flowers of the Sea
Holidays from Hell
The Ballet of Dr Caligari and Madder Mysteries

Collected and Selected Editions
Dramas from the Depths
Shadow Plays
The Sea of Blood
Stages of Fear

For Children
The Hauntings at Tankerton Park and How They Got Rid of Them

Novels
Virtue in Danger
The Dracula Papers
The Boke of the Divill

A MAZE FOR THE MINOTAUR
AND OTHER STRANGE STORIES

Reggie Oliver

Tartarus Press

A Maze for the Minotaur and Other Strange Stories
by Reggie Oliver
First published 2021 by Tartarus Press at
Coverley House, Carlton-in-Coverdale, Leyburn,
North Yorkshire, DL8 4AY, UK

This paperback edition published 2021

All stories © Reggie Oliver, 2021
All illustrations © Reggie Oliver, 2021

The publishers would like to thank Jim Rockhill
for his help in the preparation of this book.

CONTENTS

The Old Man of the Woods	1
Coruvorn	25
The Wet Woman	49
A Maze for the Minotaur	73
Shadowy Waters	105
A Fragment of Thucydides	135
The Crumblies	151
Monkey's	175
Collectable	193
Via Mortis	219
A Cabinet of Curiosities	251
The Armies of the Night	269
A Tartarean Century: Author's note	339

For Rosalie Parker and Ray Russell
with thanks

. . . tum Tartarus ipse
Bis patet in praeceps tantum tenditque sub umbras
Quantus ad aetherium caeli suspectus Olympum.

Then opens Tartarus down to depths of night,
Twice further than Olympus up to heaven's height
                      VERGIL *Aeneid* VI 577-579 (trans. R.O.)

THE OLD MAN OF THE WOODS

THE OLD MAN OF THE WOODS

Besides myself and M. Chanal, the *Notaire*, five people were in his office that morning for the signing of the documents. There were two middle-aged married couples and a rather younger single woman, more *soignée* than they, who stood apart from them smoking a cigarette in a holder, like a vamp in a 1930s film. She intrigued me. The married couples looked like typical French country people, though one pair was better dressed (and presumably richer) than the other. Their figures were thick set, their skins were tanned and lined; there was something dogged, forbidding, deeply respectable about them. The single woman, on the other hand, had an elegant figure and wore make-up. Her clothes were simple but *chic*, as was her coiffure. Despite this, I got the impression that the four others looked on her with some disdain.

The five of them were, or rather had been, the joint owners of an ancient farmhouse called *Les Bosts* on the outskirts of the village of Montpeyroux in the Dordogne. They inherited it from an uncle, M. Gaston Durand, who had died some ten years before; and they had been endeavouring to sell it ever since. That they had hitherto not succeeded was partly due to family disputes and the complexities of the *Code Napoleon* in matters of inheritance, but mainly, I suspect, to the fact that only an eccentric Englishman, such as myself, would want to buy a derelict sixteenth century building in a small rural village with barely half an acre of land attached to it. Yet this was exactly what I wanted, and could afford; so here I was at the *Notaire's* in the little nearby town of Villefranche, fearfully, excitedly committing myself to a new life in the Dordogne.

During the course of the lengthy and elaborate process of signing the documents of transfer M. Chanal was, for some obscure Gallic legal reason, obliged to ask me about my marital status. I replied that I was single, having been divorced some three years previously. The two couples looked away from me and at each other, but the single woman seemed enlivened by the news.

'*Ah! Moi aussi! Je suis divorcée,*' she said. At this the two couples frowned, while *la divorcée* and I exchanged the wry smiles of fellow sufferers.

When the sale was at last completed to the *Notaire's* satisfaction we all shook hands very formally, the two couples without warmth or so much as a smile. The *divorcée*, however, not only shook hands but kissed me on both cheeks and pressed into my palm, as she did so, a small visiting card.

Mme Adeline Pelissier, it read and there was a telephone number and the address of an apartment in the nearby town of Sainte-Foy-la-Grande. What was I to do with it? Was it some kind of amorous overture? I put it in my wallet and decided to forget it.

A year previously, I had retired from the Civil Service with a handsome pension. I was by that time living alone in a flat in Muswell Hill and there was nothing to hold me in England. I was separated from my wife, and our one child, Beatrice, married with children, was running a successful textile design business in Suffolk. Beatrice had taken her mother's side over the divorce so that our relationship, though not now acrimonious, was distant. I had little to hold me in this country where, despite a not unsuccessful career, I felt something of a failure. I was looking, I suppose, for a new life, and I had always loved France. The friends I had left in England, far from discouraging me from living abroad, seemed enthusiastic about the idea. Perhaps invitations to stay were in their minds, but that is to take too cynical a view. So I made several trips into rural France in search of property, and, by the end of the third, I found *Les Bosts*.

Though not exactly a ruin, the house showed signs of considerable neglect. It was bare but for a few sticks of worm-eaten furniture, a couple of huge dark armoires, like miniature wooden mausolea, and a formidable old *lit bateau*. The stone flags on the ground floor were uneven and the wooden boards on the upper ones creaked and bowed. Beyond running water and some electricity, whose *puissance* was badly in need of elevation, there were few modern conveniences, not even a bath, but the rooms were large and well-proportioned and the location delightfully rural.

It stood at the foot of the hill of Montpeyroux on which a picturesque château and a small Romanesque church, a town square and a few dwellings were situated. The land about my house—hardly to be described as a garden—was dominated by a great oak tree. I could picture myself, even on the hottest days, sitting and reading contentedly beneath its generous shade.

A MAZE FOR THE MINOTAUR

Renovating *Les Bosts* would be, as they say, 'a challenge', and might even restore to me a sense of achievement. That is what I told myself.

I will not bother to tell you about my adventures with builders, decorators, electricians and the like over the year following my purchase. If you have an appetite for such things, there are countless books by Britons with titles like *We Bought a House in Gascony,* or *A Little Property on the Gironde,* which will satisfy it. I will only say that I found the process as absorbing, frustrating, and sometimes rewarding, as no doubt did the authors of those books. I will concentrate only on what made my experience differ from theirs.

In the first place my French builders, though perfectly amiable, honest and hard-working, had a habit of fading away from the job after a week or so. No real explanation was given for this, other than that they had commitments elsewhere. Though I was regularly on site to supervise their handiwork, I don't think I was a particularly exacting taskmaster. In the end I had to hire a team of English builders who lived and worked in the Dordogne, to finish the work. They were no better at the task than their French counterparts and were considerably more expensive, but they did at least stay the course; yet even they, by the end, seemed anxious to depart.

I can find no satisfactory explanation for this. The house did not have 'an atmosphere', not that I am particularly susceptible to such things. Quite the contrary, for such an ancient building, it appeared to be singularly empty of any mood or tension. It was, you might say, *tabula rasa,* a clean slate onto which I could imprint my own personality and style, and I was glad of that. When, eventually, I allowed my books and pictures from London into it, I believe it did begin to seem like a part of me, though not, perhaps, as much as I had hoped.

A few small events that occurred during the renovation process need to be told.

One morning, a week or so after I had taken possession, there was a letter in my post box, the first to be addressed to me at *Les Bosts*. *M. Egerton, Proprietaire, Les Bosts* read the envelope. I felt a ridiculous involuntary surge of pride. It was from M. Chanal, the *Notaire* and contained the various deeds and documents relating to my purchase of the house. It was early and the builders had not arrived so I took the documents indoors to study at my leisure. On going over them meticulously I was surprised to see that I was not only the owner of *Les Bosts* but also of the little wood that stood opposite my property.

It was situated on the other side of the road that led up to the château and opposite the front entrance of *Les Bosts*. It was one of those dense, seemingly accidental areas of woodland that you find dotted about that part of rural France. The trees were high; the undergrowth appeared impenetrable. It did not look inviting and it annoyed me that I, all unwittingly, had been saddled with it. I rang up M. Chanal. Why had I not been informed about this wood? I did not want it. Could I not sell it?

M. Chanal, perhaps literally, certainly metaphorically, gave a shrug of the shoulders on the other end of the line. He was *desolé*, but he thought I knew about it. It was a part of the property. No, he did not think I could sell it. No-one would want to buy it, because permission to build upon it would almost certainly be denied by the authorities. In any case, would I want a new house directly opposite my front entrance? Besides, he had heard that the little wood was just the place to find cepes. Did I know cepes? They were a most delicious wild mushroom, best served simply *à la Bordelaise*, fried with chopped parsley, shallots and breadcrumbs. I cut M. Chanal off shortly, but I made a note of the recipe.

At that time I was not actually staying at *Les Bosts,* but at a small pension in Sainte-Foy-la-Grande. The facilities in my future home were still too primitive, and many of the windows had fallen out due to a termite infestation. Most mornings I would drive up to *Les Bosts* to supervise and sometimes assist any labour that was going forward. One morning, shortly after I had received the documents from M. Chanal, I had decided to take the morning off in Sainte-Foy-la-Grande. It was market day.

There is something festal about market days in French provincial towns, particularly during the summer months. Fruits and vegetables of every kind and colour on sloping stalls, chickens clucking, rabbits snuffling in cages, Africans selling leather goods, bright garments and chiffon scarves fluttering gently in the breeze, fresh, iridescent fish on little fields of ice: to me it was a delight to the eye, so gloriously distant from Grey Britain.

I had no plans to buy anything because I was taking all my meals out at that time; I merely wanted to wander and gaze. Then I caught sight of a familiar figure in the crowd, dressed, as before, with considerable *chic* in an elegant black and white polka-dotted summer dress and a wide-brimmed black straw hat. It was Madame Pelissier, *la belle divorcée,* and she was haggling very hard with a grocer over some aubergines. Finally the deal was concluded to her satisfaction and she bore them away triumphantly in her string bag. Even the string bag, black of course, looked *chic.*

I suddenly felt an urgent need for company. I ran after her, but when I caught up, I tried to appear as casual as possible.

'Hello! *C'est Madame Pelissier, n'est ce pas?*'

'Ah! Monsieur Egerton!' She seemed pleased to see me. I invited her to take some refreshment with me and she graciously consented. At that moment we were passing a suitable establishment, so we sat down at an outside table under a striped awning and ordered coffee. For a while we remained in a companionable silence, watching the crowds drifting to and fro along the street in the sun, then Madame Pelissier turned to me and said:

'So, how do you like your new French home?' I had been prepared to converse with her in my very serviceable French, but there was no need. Her English was excellent, almost idiomatic; her accent, which was light, added piquancy to what she said.

'On the whole, very much.'

'You know you have chosen a very historical part of France.' I nodded. 'You are interested in culture?' I indicated that I was very interested in culture. 'Very good. Then I suppose you have visited *Le Château de Montaigne?*'

As a matter of fact, this was one of the few expeditions I had made in my time off from renovating my new home. It is only about eight miles away from Montpeyroux.

'The wine of the château is very pleasant but a little overpriced, but the tower is most interesting. You know the *Essais*?'

'I studied them at University.'

'Ah good! Michel de Montaigne was *un vrai humaniste*, and in a day when it was even more dangerous than now to be so.'

'*Homo sum, humani nihil a me alienum puto.*' I had seen these words carved on a beam in the tower where Montaigne wrote. A quotation from Terence, the African: 'I am a man; I count nothing human alien to me.'

'Excellent! You know that Michel de Montaigne's brother Bertrand lived at the Château of Montpeyroux?'

'I did not.'

'Go stand beneath the walls of the Château de Montpeyroux and look across the valley. You can just see the Château de Montaigne from there. Michel and his brother were—how you say?—very close, true brothers. When they were in residence Bertrand would put a candle in the highest window of his tower, and Michel would do the same in his so they could be assured of each other's presence, though miles apart. *C'est sympathique, n'est ce pas?*'

'They must have had bloody good eyesight.'

'Perhaps it is only a legend. But remember, in those days there would have been no other lights in between to interfere.'

'It certainly is a very delightful legend.'

'But all history is legend, and all legend history, do you not think?'

I did not want to get into a philosophical discussion, so I broached the subject of the wood.

'Ah! The wood!'

'You knew about the wood?'

'But of course! Why did you not?'

'That's a very good question.'

'But what is your complaint? There are good cepes to be found in that wood.'

'So I have already been told,' I said irritably. Madame Pelissier seemed amused.

'I have not found any there myself, but . . .'

'You've been into the wood?'

'Once, I remember, when I was a little girl. My father and his brother my Uncle Gaston were not good friends like Michel and Bertrand, but one time we did go to see Uncle Gaston at *Les Bosts* and had lunch there. After lunch my father and my uncle had business to discuss, so Uncle Gaston told me to go into his wood opposite and look for cepes. For some reason my mother was not with us, and men are careless about such things, so I went as I was told. It was a bright sunny day like this one, but the wood, it was very—' She searched for a word. '—dense. I was only seven and small for my age. Everything was taller than me, even the grass it seemed. There were no paths, but I pressed on in search of the cepes, thinking how pleased my papa and uncle would be if I found some. Then all of a sudden I realised I was lost. I looked around me. No path. Nothing! Nothing but trees and grass and bushes in every direction, the sky above very distant, and now it seemed darkening with cloud. The heat oppressed. I became terrified. I ran in all directions; I screamed very loudly. At last my father and uncle heard and came to find me. They took me into the house and gave me some Cognac with a little water and told me not to breathe a word to my mother, and my uncle gave me five francs to make sure. Gradually I stopped weeping, but I had been deeply frightened, not simply of being lost: I had been terrified that I might see *Le Vieux des Bois*.'

' "The Old Man of the Woods"? What is that?'

'It is a local legend. A fable perhaps. It had been told to me by the nuns at my first school not long before my visit to Uncle Gaston and it was still fresh in my mind. Those nuns, they thought it was a very moral tale and perhaps they imagined it would frighten us little girls into being better Christians. But if that was so, then they were foolish. You can be frightened into evil but not into goodness, do you not think?'

I had my doubts about her proposition, but I was in no mood to be sidetracked by metaphysical speculation.

'The story?'

'Ah, yes! Well, there is this man. He is young, he is beautiful, he has money, he can do anything. In consequence he does many wild and terrible things, but always he is haunted by the shadow of his conscience. So one evening when the sun is low and the shadows are long he enters into a young green wood and he cuts off his own shadow. The shadow dances off and hides itself in one of the trees. Now the young man is free from his conscience and he can do what he likes without remorse. The years roll by and the man without a shadow becomes very corrupted and old. Then he realises that his pleasures are hollow and he is without feeling. The life he once loved has lost all flavour, and he understands that this is because he has no shadow, no conscience. So he returns to the wood to find it again, but the wood is now dense and overgrown and he cannot recognise the tree into which his shadow fled. And there he remains for ever in that wood, perpetually searching for his lost soul among the trees.'

'A very pretty story.'

'No. Not pretty, I think, but it made a great impression upon my young heart. I was a timid little girl and very pious. You find that hard to believe?'

'Not at all . . . Tell me more about your Uncle Gaston.' Madame Pelissier glanced at her watch.

'*Ah, zut! Je suis en retard!* I must go. Thank you so much for the coffee, Monsieur Egerton. My apologies but I must fly, as you say.'

'Perhaps we could have dinner together one evening?'

'Perhaps! That would be delightful. *Au revoir*!' And the next minute she had disappeared into the bustling market crowds of Sainte-Foy-la-Grande.

Soon after that, partly for reasons of expense, partly for convenience, I abandoned the *pension* in Sainte-Foy and hired an old camper-van which I parked in the grounds of *Les Bosts*. There was nothing wrong with the camper-van. It was reasonably comfortable if cramped, but I spent there the most unpleasant and troublesome two weeks of my life.

I could never settle or rest properly in it. I was constantly going over to the house to see if there was something that I could do in it. I suppose I was getting impatient for my new home, but there was more to it than that. At night, when I was trying to sleep in the van, I was besieged by a whole battery of unaccountable noises. It sounded as if twigs and branches with leaves were scraping and swishing against the sides of the vehicle, and yet I had deliberately placed it out of reach of any vegetation. Often I would hear a bird (or something) walk across the van's roof. The steps it made were slow and deliberate, almost heavy, not very like any bird I knew. Then I would get out of bed and step outside to look, but I never saw anything, except once when I thought I sensed something scuttling away towards the wood. It did not fly, and it was too dark to tell what sort of an animal it was.

I avoided going into the van as much as possible, except to cook and sleep. In the evenings I would sit outside it in the 'garden' for as long as possible, but even then I was conscious of disturbance. On the stillest nights some breeze or other would appear to be fumbling with the bushes that surrounded my domain. If I looked over towards the wood, the trouble was even greater there: the trees shuddered in the wind, the undergrowth stirred.

One evening, as dusk was approaching, I walked to the edge of the road to observe this phenomenon. I had still not ventured into the wood; in fact, I chose, whenever possible, to ignore this part of my property altogether. Still, there were times when it could not be overlooked and on that occasion I was standing on the side of the road staring rather irritably into the wood when I became aware of someone watching me.

I have not said anything about my neighbours in the little hamlet that surrounded me. They were all French country people, pleasant enough, but incurious and not very forthcoming. The exception was the local farmer, M. Bobelet, a squat middle-aged man who had a large cage outside his front door in which he kept an alsation that barked and snarled at you as you went by. I must admit I had a slight prejudice against M. Bobelet on account of that dog which I never saw him let out, though I am sure he must have done. On the wire fence that bordered his land was a notice which read *Chien Méchant*. I did not blame the *chien* for being *méchant*, I blamed M. Bobelet.

He would often come round to my house while the renovation was in progress and sometimes talk to the workmen. I could not make out what he said because he spoke very rapidly with a thick Southern French twang which was quite impenetrable at a distance. When I approached him he would always shake hands with me very formally and ask questions, which I would do my best to answer. They were always about what I was proposing to do with the building. He seemed to regard himself as some kind of informal inspector of works which also did not endear him to me. He had piercing blue eyes.

It was M. Bobelet who stood on the road watching me as I peered into the wood. I had no desire to speak with him but I thought it only polite to do so, so I greeted him with a wave and a friendly *'Bon soir!'*

This he took as his cue to approach me. I cannot record our conversation exactly as I only understood half of what he said. He was asking me questions about the wood and what I was proposing to do with it.

'Rien!' I said. Nothing! And this appeared to satisfy him. I then asked him if he would like to buy the wood. At this he looked very shocked and shook his head. He glanced at the wood and said 'Non!' several times very emphatically. After he had muttered something which I could not understand he addressed himself to the subject of a large millstone which stood on one corner of my land, half obscured by a box hedge. What was I proposing to do with *that*? I shrugged. I had not given the object any thought other than to wonder what it was doing there. He told me that the millstone should be respected as it was a very historical stone. Apparently, his father and some friends in the Resistance had, shortly after the Normandy Landings in 1944, rolled that stone into the middle of the road *'pour arreter les Boches,'* to stop the Germans: but stop them from what? His reply was vague. I became interested. I knew that during the war this part of the country had been a border land between German occupied territory and Vichy France, and that strange, wild things had gone on during that period. M. Bobelet seemed disposed to instruct me on the subject but I could follow little of what he said. Finally, I asked him how well he had known M. Gaston Durand, the previous owner of *Les Bosts*? This stopped his flow. He looked at me, mumbled something and shook his head; then, very deliberately, he spat on the ground. After which he quite unexpectedly shook hands with me, wished me *bon soir* and walked off.

Over the next few days, the floors were finished, the stairs restored and, most importantly of all, a man came to certify that *Les Bosts* had been cured of its termite infestation and we were safe to put in new windows. I decided to move into the house as soon as possible, despite the fact that there was still much to be done, but, before I could, I had a telephone call from England.

It was my daughter Beatrice informing me that my ex-wife was seriously ill and had not long to live. I said I would come back at once. I think Beatrice was rather surprised by this decision, but she seemed to approve.

On the evening before I left for England the new windows were finally fixed into the ancient stone walls, making my house at last truly habitable. They gleamed in the sun which, as it set, turned the panes into little plates of gold, flecked and dappled by the branches of intervening trees, making of them dark gilded mirrors of their surroundings. As I was admiring them from a distance, I noticed a strange anomaly: something appeared to be reflected in the glass which was not there in reality.

It was more like a shadow, though it was quite clearly delineated and it was moving to and fro across the window panes and the glass of the French doors. At first I thought it was some trick of the light brought about by the slight unevenness of the glass panes, or that something was moving about inside the house, but that could not be because I was unable to discern anything else of the interior. I could see myself mirrored in the glass and at one point the thing passed between me and my reflection obscuring my image for a moment.

It moved so quickly and mercurially that it was hard to make out at first, but it looked like the shadow of a man, slightly bent, head thrust forward, walking to and fro. I watched it for a minute or so, trying to clarify my impression of it, then I began to move towards the house to get a closer, perhaps a clearer view. I think I was hoping that my change of view might dispel the vision altogether and reveal it, after all, as some kind of optical trick.

The figure remained only a shadowy outline, but I thought I could now tell that it was a man, elderly but not completely decrepit. It moved too fast for that.

The reflected shadow changed direction again as I approached and moved now steadily in one direction towards the entrance to my property and to the wood beyond. Now it was gone and I could see nothing reflected in the windows except myself, the sunlight and the trees in the garden. It was a relief. Almost unbidden, anxiety had been building up inside me; now it was dispelled. Nevertheless, I was glad that a car was about to pick me up from here and take me to Bordeaux airport. By midnight I would be in England.

I spent longer there than I expected. I visited my wife regularly in the hospice where she spent the last weeks of her life. It would be an exaggeration to say that a reconciliation took place, as she was almost constantly under heavy sedation for the pain and coherent thought was difficult for her, but peace of a kind was established. When she died, I took it upon myself to manage the funeral and all the other arrangements that surround a death. The whole experience had been hard on my daughter who was finding it difficult to cope. So, when the service was done and we were all standing, as one does, rather listlessly outside the church, Beatrice came over and took my arm.

'Thanks for doing all that, dad, with the funeral and all,' she said.

'I only did what I had to.'

'Yes, but you *did* it. Are you going back to France now?' I nodded. 'Aren't you going to get lonely out there?'

'I don't think so. In the summer why don't you and the family come out and stay.' I outlined the various attractions that were on offer in that part of the world.

Beatrice said: 'Maybe we will.'

It was spring when I returned to France and I was glad to do so. By that time *Les Bosts* was fully habitable, though I had yet to arrange furniture and pictures to my satisfaction, and unpack all my possessions, in particular my books. This task should have been a pleasant one, and was, occasionally, but I was plagued by restlessness. It was understandable, I suppose, after my emotionally exacting time in England, but there was more to it than that. I would go for long walks in the countryside, mostly along the by-roads, past rolling vineyards and patches of dense woodland like my own. I did it to soothe my anxieties, to tire myself out so that I could sleep at night. I had committed myself to a strange life in a foreign country and I was now beset, all too late, by doubts about it. I did sleep much better at night in my own home than I had in the camper van, but I was still, if more dimly, conscious of those strange, irrational nocturnal sounds. Then I saw him again.

One afternoon I was in the kitchen preparing some vegetables at the sink. Above the sink is a window which looks out on a patch of rough ground at the back of the house. Though my head was bent over my task I caught a glimpse out of the corners of my eyes of a shadow passing across the window. I looked up but the shadow was gone. I had had the impression of someone walking round the house to the front, yet this was improbable, if not impossible. The back of *Les Bosts* was an area full of rubble interspersed with clumps of bamboo and patches of nettles. I had yet to do something about it. No-one would want to go walking there.

I left the kitchen and went into the dining room at the front of the house. There, through the window, I saw him again, this time a little more distinctly. It was the same figure that I had seen reflected in the glass of the windows on the evening before I set out for England. The head was thrust forward, the steps rapid, the figure that of a man not exactly old, but past the prime of life. He was making for the entrance to my property and the wood across the road.

I called to him, but he evidently did not hear me. I ran to the door, opened it and looked out. The figure, now dwindled to a shadow, was disappearing in the direction of the wood. I went to the entrance of *Les Bosts* and stared after it into the trees. There was a disturbance in the young green undergrowth, a shiver among the leaves and leaf buds. I felt I was being urged to walk into the wood, but the urge was overmastered by reasonable doubt and unreasonable fear. I looked around me, almost hoping to see M. Bobelet. He might give me the requisite courage, or perhaps offer sound advice, but he was not there. His alsation, though, was barking violently in its cage.

The following morning I rang Madame Pelissier. She seemed delighted to hear from me and I invited her to come out to *Les Bosts* and have lunch with me there. I would fetch her and take her back by car if necessary. The pause on the other end of the line after I had issued this invitation was enough to indicate that it had not met with her approval. Then came a number of excuses and prevarications. I then suggested lunch at a restaurant in Ste-Foy, but no, she had another idea.

'Come to have tea at my apartment tomorrow. I know how you English love your afternoon tea. We French once called it 'le five o'clock' in your honour.'

'When shall I come?'

'At about four, I think.'

Madame Pelissier's apartment was smaller than I had expected and much less lavishly appointed. Her elegant appearance had led me to expect that divorce had left her well provided for. Evidently it was not the case, but there were sufficient indications that she was a woman of taste and culture: the well-stocked bookshelves, the framed posters from art exhibitions on the walls. The tea service was of modern design, very stylish, not mass produced.

She received me graciously and listened with sympathy to an account of my recent stay in England. When I started to talk about *Les Bosts* I thought I detected a slight lessening of interest, so I switched to more general topics. I tried gently to probe her own circumstances and gathered that she worked part time as a receptionist at the local doctors. She seemed not too keen to go into details about her existence which I understood. Finally our conversation dwindled and, after a pause, Madame Pelissier looked at me searchingly and said:

'Monsieur Egerton, I think you have come to see me not simply for the pleasure of my company. Am I not right?'

I assured her that the pleasure of her company was very considerable, but she was right. I wanted to know about her Uncle Gaston.

She asked why. Was it just curiosity?

No, I said. It was to do with the attitude of my neighbours in the village, and I told her about M. Bobelet.

'That pig!' she said. 'But I think it is more than that. No?'

'Perhaps . . . Yes . . .' I said nothing more, but she seemed to understand. I saw her gathering strength to fulfil an unpleasant obligation. The story came out hesitantly, prompted by many questions from me. When it was done, she seemed relieved but drained.

Gaston Durand had been the brightest of the four sons of a prosperous Dordogne farmer. Before the war Gaston ran several businesses in the Bordeaux area and they all prospered. He married a beautiful girl called Francine who had been a *mannequin* in one of the dress shops that he owned. The relationship was passionate but troubled from the beginning. Then came the war. Francine formed a *liaison* with an SS Colonel in Bordeaux which was just over the border in German Occupied France. Gaston was at first devastated by this, but he and Francine somehow managed to maintain cordial relations. Gradually Gaston began to take advantage of her liaison with the Colonel. His business ventures were favoured by the Nazis. It was said that he managed to acquire several houses in Bordeaux which had belonged to a deported Jewish family, and sold them again at a considerable profit. Soon after the Normandy landings, however, his fortunes suffered a reverse. His wife Francine disappeared: some said she had fled with the SS Colonel, others that she was killed. No-one was sure, and if Gaston knew he kept silent. After the war various accusations were made against Gaston for collaboration, but none stuck and he managed to hold on to his businesses. Increasingly, though, he became reclusive and began to neglect his work. He retreated to *Les Bosts* and spent most of his time there, in spite of the fact that the local inhabitants shunned him because of his wartime associations. Eventually he sold his businesses and lived off a dwindling capital. When he died his relatives were shocked to find that he was practically destitute. He could be seen occasionally taking long solitary walks in the district of Montpeyroux. In particular he was frequently observed wandering into his wood where he would spend hours shooting small birds and animals, or looking for cepes. It became his only pastime.

'It is my belief that my Uncle Gaston imagined he had lost something during the war,' said Madame Pelissier, '—apart, of course, from his wife. Maybe he had. His soul perhaps? If you believe in such things. Are you a *philosophe*, Monsieur Egerton?'

'I suppose I try to be.'

'Ah! *Moi aussi!* That is good!' She leant over and patted my knee. It was a gesture of affection, but more maternal than amorous. Just then I heard the front door of her apartment being opened. Madame looked momentarily disconcerted. The door of the sitting room opened and a young man in blue overalls came in.

He must have been in his twenties, with the body of a fully grown man but the soft-featured face of a teenager. He had black curly hair and large brown eyes like those of a young calf. His features were even, if a little lacking in definition, but he was decidedly good-looking. You might say pretty. Could this be her son? If he was, why had she not mentioned him before?

Madame and I rose from our seats together and she introduced the young man to me as Fabrice. We shook hands formally, Fabrice eyeing me with a blatantly sulky and suspicious expression on his face. Madame Pelissier observed this and immediately engulfed him in a flood of talk of which I could only gather fragments. Still talking volubly, she hastened Fabrice out of the room as if she were packing a recalcitrant child off to bed. I heard the conversation continuing in another part of the flat, Fabrice replying to her mostly in resentful monosyllables. After a few minutes, Madame Pelissier returned smiling.

'I have told Fabrice to take a shower. He is *mécanicien* at the garage by the bridge, and he always comes home smelling of oil.' I looked at her interrogatively, as I thought it would offend if I asked her outright if Fabrice was her son, but she understood.

'Non! Fabrice, he lives with me,' she said. 'My—how do you say now?—"partner". A good boy: he has no culture, but he is a superb lover.' She looked for my reaction, and I must have given one, for she laughed. It was a charming laugh, if a little studied.

'Ah! You English! Always the respectability!' I laughed too; it seemed only polite.

'I think I should go,' I said and thanked her profusely for my 'five o'clock'. She escorted me to the door. I could hear Fabrice singing a pop song in the shower.

'But you must come again,' she said, smiling.

'Really?' I said, glancing in the direction of the singer.

'Nothing in this life is permanent, *mon ami*. We should know.' Fabrice in his shower hit a wrong note and Madame Pelissier winced, then laughed.

'One more question, Madame.'

'Yes?'

'How did your Uncle Gaston die?'

There was a pause.

A MAZE FOR THE MINOTAUR

'He shot himself.'
'In the wood?'
'But of course.'

During the next few days, I spent most of the time arranging my books in all the shelves that had been made for them. It was a deeply satisfying activity, and I even began to devise a scheme of reading for myself in the future. I would start by re-reading and finally finishing Proust: that, I was sure about. And then? One shouldn't think ahead too far. Nothing in this life, as Madame Pelissier said, is permanent. *Tout passe, tout casse, tout lasse.*

Knowledge, they say, is power. That is not always the case, but it does invariably change things. The information I had been given about Uncle Gaston never left me. I found myself at odd moments looking out for him passing the window: or rather the apparition that I had supposed to be him. I reflected on his life, and began to experience a fellow feeling with a man who, like me, had become a kind of exile in his own country. No doubt he had done terrible things during the war, but we were beyond that now.

One lovely evening in June when the longest day of the year was almost upon us, I sat reading in my salon with the French windows open. The air was warm, the sky cloudless. Birds were singing and the nightly chorus of frogs was just starting up from behind the hill of Montpeyroux. I was utterly absorbed in my book when quite suddenly all these pleasant little noises stopped. I looked up, startled, shocked. It was so unnatural. In the garden was the man, head bowed, walking across my line of sight in the direction of the wood. He seemed darker than his surroundings, as if he existed in a different light from the rest of us, dimmer and more crepuscular.

It was instinct more than reason which made me put down my book and get up to follow him. Reason and caution told me to go back to my reading and ignore this psychic interruption, but instinct prevailed. Without looking to left or right he crossed the road and entered the wood. Though he was perfectly solid in appearance he made no sound and the undergrowth did not move as he passed through it.

I was directly behind him and about twenty feet away, as I too entered the wood. It was my first time in there and I noted that the feeling of enclosure and oppression was strong. I was perfectly aware of the strangeness of what I was doing, but I felt detached from it. I registered dread, bewilderment, extreme anxiety but almost as if these emotions were being felt by someone else, albeit close to me.

The figure—I suppose I should call him Gaston—walked on further into the wood, I following until I had no sense of where we were. We inhabited a pathless jungle of thick undergrowth, waist high ferns and myrtles, lush grasses, dense stands of beeches whose leaf canopy almost shut out the sky above. Green was everywhere; the scents of warm earth and vegetation were overpowering.

Gaston stopped and so did I. We were now little more than a dozen feet apart. This, I knew, was the moment. He began to turn round to face me. It was a slow turn, timelessly, all but infinitely slow. I heard my heart thumping and recognised that I had a choice of whether to run or stay. It was a very pure decision, the forces on both sides being strong, perhaps in some ways stronger on the side of flight, but balanced. I chose to stay.

Now he was fully facing me. I saw a ragged hole where his head and the upper part of his chest should have been, as if blown away by a shotgun blast. Yet within the hole there was no tangled confusion of blood and sinew and bone, as there should have been, just a blackness. A tunnel into the void had been drilled through his body. The fear I felt was not that of physical danger but of something far greater and more perilous, yet still I held my ground.

I sensed something reach out to me from Gaston's darkness, as if hoping to engulf me in its misery and despair. It wanted me to share its fate and become a companion. I felt it pulling at my thoughts and twisting them, as sleep sometimes does before you submit to it, but I held on. I would not receive it, but at the same time I would not reject it. Words from my late wife's burial service about rest and peace came to me; and, without exactly believing in them, I said them to myself, as if they were a mantra, or a magic spell.

The figure of Gaston began to change. He became more indistinct, and at the same time the blackness of his upper body was beginning to heal. I started to see features on his face, grey and smoky, yet recognisably those of a person. He was no longer trying to envelop me; there was more of a sense of communication. The grief and anguish were still intense, but they had assumed human proportions. I waited as he became whole, if insubstantial, then while he dissolved quietly into the night air like smoke from a dying fire. It was almost dark when the process was complete, but there was just light enough for me to see my way out of the wood, following the tracks that I had made on entering. Slowly the birdsong and the frog choruses were restored to my ears.

It was a clear but moonless night when I emerged from the wood. I felt I needed a walk before returning to *Les Bosts,* so I took the road that leads up to the main village of Montpeyroux to the church and to the château which had once, according to local legend, belonged to Montaigne's brother. It was, like the rest of the village, silent and dark, but not quite! Far up in the topmost window of the château's main turret there gleamed a small steady golden light, like that of a candle flame.

CORUVORN

CORUVORN

It is three years ago now since Dennis Marchbanks became a god. Of course, he did not know this immediately; the realisation came upon him slowly as such things do and he was decently reluctant to believe it in the beginning. Dennis would have been the first to admit that he is an unlikely god. Do I believe it? Well, that is unimportant; I must simply record what happened, as far as I can.

Dennis and I had been contemporaries at the same Oxford college. We had both read classical 'Mods and Greats', and belonged to the same dining clubs and societies. Dennis was highly intelligent, but not very imaginative and, though conventional in most of his attitudes, he liked the company of unconventional and artistic people; hence, I suppose, our friendship.

I graduated from Oxford with a modest second and went into literary journalism while Dennis who had got a first in 'Greats' stayed on to take a law degree and studied for the bar. In time he became an eminent Q.C., dealing mainly with commercial cases, hence a rich one. We kept up with each other through college reunions and I would often see him at the first nights of plays when I became a drama critic. We occasionally dined together at Brummell's in St James's of which we were both members. I would not say that our friendship was really close, let alone intense, but it was of long standing and invariably cordial. We were able to share confidences from time to time, partly because our worlds did not impinge on each other's too much. Dennis was unmarried and, though he had met my wife once or twice, he had never visited my home.

One Friday night we happened to meet and have dinner at Brummell's. (My wife, incidentally, was away visiting relatives in Yorkshire for the weekend in case you are wondering if I had callously abandoned her for this still exclusively male preserve.) We ate together at the long table in the Coffee Room. There were several others dining at the table but they were down at the far end, so we could be fairly sure of not being overheard or interrupted. Dennis was not quite his usual genial self and I asked him what was the matter.

He told me that he had just lost a case in the appeal court. He had been representing Centaur, the online retailers, whom their employees on zero hours contracts were suing for better rights and conditions. Centaur and therefore Dennis had lost both in the High Court and on appeal. Representing the workers on both occasions was Dame Maggie Standish Q.C. the well-known human rights lawyer and campaigner.

'No, Jack, it's not what you think,' said Dennis, taking note of my raised eyebrow. 'It was not being bested by a woman or anything like that that irks. As a matter of fact, I think she probably had the better case. Their Lordships certainly thought so. It was the way she treated me. She obviously saw me just as some sort of boss's lackey, a—what is the term they use?—a "lickspittle"? But, dammit everyone needs legal representation, even criminals, even bosses. It's a human right, after all.'

'No doubt Centaur paid you well.'

'Well, yes. If you want the best you have to pay for it. But that's not the point. There is such a thing as professional courtesy, professional respect. As far as she was concerned, I was "less than the dust beneath her chariot wheels". I think she sees herself as some sort of champion of virtue and anyone who opposes her must therefore be contemptible.' There was a pause. 'But I am sure she is a genuinely good and highly principled person.'

I smiled at his reluctant gesture of magnanimity and he, eventually, smiled back.

'Just unbelievably arrogant,' he added in an undertone. We both laughed. Dennis was not without a capacity to see the funny side of himself. We moved on to more benign topics, and though he relaxed a little, I could tell there was still something on his mind.

After dinner Dennis asked me back for a drink at his apartment in Albany, that exclusive and discreet domain of the wealthy and well-connected off Piccadilly. The usual procedure at Brummell's was to have after dinner-drinks in the little snug under the stairs at the club, so I sensed that Dennis was anxious to confide in absolute privacy. I just hoped it was not to be any more railing against Dame Maggie Standish Q.C.

We took a cab to The Albany. I would have been glad to walk, but Dennis was never an exerciser and thirty years or so of doing well for himself had expanded his figure considerably. He was, like me, in his mid-fifties. He had a pleasant round face and thinning sandy hair and, if I had been asked about him at the time, I would have said he was the epitome of contented prosperity and success. He was, as he had put it to me once, 'not a man of strong urges where human relationships are concerned', so bachelorhood suited him.

We were silent in the cab, and, when we arrived at Albany, barely a word was spoken until we had seated ourselves with a large brandy apiece in armchairs on either side of the fireplace in his drawing room. Coming to Dennis's Albany 'set' was like stepping back in time a hundred years or more. The lighting was subdued, the furniture antique but comfortable. Georgian silver gleamed on the sideboard and a faint lustre of gold emanated from the tooled backs of Dennis's antiquarian book collection. An illuminated glass-fronted cabinet glowed with a small but impeccable collection of *famille verte* porcelain. Family portraits hung on the walls, a couple dating back to the eighteenth century, and one to the seventeenth. The atmosphere was steeped in wealthy, cultured bachelordom.

'Do you dream a lot, Jack?' asked Dennis when we were settled and had taken our first sip. I was a little taken aback: it was not a familiar conversational gambit of his.

'Yes. No more than most, I suppose.'

'I hardly do at all. Or if I do, I remember practically nothing of my dreams when I wake up. At least, I used not to. It all changed a couple of weeks ago. But then, I am not at all sure if it's a dream I am talking about.'

He then began to tell me his story. One night he had returned to the Albany rather later than usual having attended one of those legal banquets in Lincoln's Inn. He had given a speech— 'rather a good one, though I say so myself'—and was feeling exhausted from his efforts. He could barely remember undressing and getting into bed, but once in bed he fell into a deep state of unconsciousness of this world.

'I found myself in what I can only describe as *another* world. I was walking on a hillside towards evening. The sun was setting and I carried a long staff and wore a blue hooded cloak. The landscape was clothed in peace and the colours were deep umbers and greens and azures, such as you see in a landscape by Claude or Poussin. You may think this all sounds very dreamlike, but it wasn't. It was as vivid as you and I in this room now, if anything more vivid, and, unlike a dream world, it was utterly solid and consistent.

'One thing that appears in retrospect most curious, though not at the time, was that I seemed to see myself standing on that hillside and yet be inside the person on the hill simultaneously. It could be compared to being in a TV studio and being aware of yourself on a TV monitor at the same time, except that I *was* the monitor if you see what I mean. There was no effort involved in this double perception, no sense of a "divided self": quite the contrary.'

The image of himself that he saw was different to the one he presented to me. He saw not a plump, middle aged lawyer but a tall gaunt figure in a long blue cloak with a hood, carrying a staff. He was shod in boots of soft leather and underneath his cloak he wore a closely-fitting tunic of dark violet velvet. As he walked, the earth seemed to give way slightly under his feet. 'It was like,' he said, 'walking on water, though naturally that is something I have never actually done, but it's how I imagine walking on water to feel like.'

Dennis's descriptions of his experiences were full of these precise and pedantic qualifications. At times it was like listening to Henry James at his most delicate and tentative, so I shall continue in third person précis.

The sun was sinking, salmon pink, below the horizon, as he walked down the hill towards a cottage from whose roof came an aromatic plume of grey blue smoke. The feelings he had were those of immense calm coupled with that of purpose, though to what end? That he could not say, though he tried to at considerable length.

The cottage, perched on the hillside, was surrounded by a small garden, fenced and gated. Dennis opened the gate and went up to the door on which he knocked with his staff. He noted that the lintel was only just high enough to let him in without his having to bow his head.

The door was opened by a pleasant looking elderly woman in a brown, homespun dress who welcomed him into a low whitewashed room. Beside an open fire sat an old man, white haired but still hale. When he saw Dennis, he rose, greeted him and told him that he was most welcome under his roof.

Dennis tried to convey to me the extraordinary gratification he felt on being received so courteously. His whole being was suffused with benevolence towards this elderly couple and with this goodwill came a sense of power. The old couple—they were husband and wife—asked him to share their simple meal. Dennis told me that he had rarely tasted anything so austerely delicious. It almost persuaded him to eat less elaborately in future, to order only one plain dish at Brummell's, even to try his hand at cooking for himself occasionally. I took these raptures on the simple life with the scepticism that they perhaps deserved, but he was on fire with enthusiasm when he spoke.

One incident of interest and importance occurred at the end of his stay with these good people. They had finished the meal and the woman of the house was offering to make up a bed for him. Dennis politely refused their kind offer. He told me that he felt not tired in the least. A kind of calm energy was passing through him.

As he was explaining his need to set forth again and his gratitude for their kindness, he noticed a small niche in the wall beside the fireplace. It appeared to be some sort of shrine. In it was a lighted candle and a small figure of a cloaked man bearing a staff, carved in wood. It had been carefully painted in muted bluish colours. The image struck him as vaguely familiar.

'Who is this?' he asked.

'That is our God,' said the woman, touching her forehead with her right index finger and bowing to the statuette. 'It is Coruvorn, the Wanderer, Lord of the Hills.'

At that moment, Dennis told me, he knew that he himself was Coruvorn, and that the image that they were worshipping was an image of himself. 'It appeared at the time,' he said, 'the most natural thing in the world. It was only later and on reflection that the implications seemed rather problematic.'

He turned towards the elderly couple, a golden light shone from him and they fell on their knees in adoration.

'This made me feel slightly awkward,' Dennis told me, 'because, while I seemed perfectly confident that I was—or rather *am*—a god, I was still conscious of being myself, that is Dennis Marchbanks. It's a complicated business. Since then, I have been subject to these visions almost every night. Time is different over there and weeks, months even seem to pass during the time that I am asleep in this world.'

I asked him why he was confiding all this in me.

'I couldn't think of anyone else. You are the only person I know who might remotely understand. You are literary, after all: artistic, imaginative. You've even had a novel published.'

'I gave you a copy, if you remember.'

'Yes, I know. I actually read it. It's really not at all bad, in its way. That's why I thought you might be sympathetic.'

'To tell the truth, I don't know what to make of what you've told me.'

'That's all right. As long as you don't dismiss it out of hand.'

'*I am a man; I count nothing human alien to me.*'

'Nor nothing divine too, I hope!' He smiled rather complacently at this little joke.

'But isn't there some more "professional" advice you could seek?'

'Not really. I wanted a lay person. Someone without an ideological axe to grind; someone with no real metaphysical opinions of their own. As you know, I am a Catholic, so this is very disturbing for me. I can't exactly go to confession at the Oratory and tell Father O'Hare that I'm a sort of god. He'd be most offended. We've been friends for ages. I might even be excommunicated.'

'Surely an exaggeration.'

'Perhaps, but it would be very embarrassing for us both.'

'Why not go and see a shrink?'

'Well, you know my views about psychiatrists.' I didn't. Dennis had a habit of assuming you knew all about his habits and opinions, most of which, it must be admitted, were extremely predictable. 'They'd say it was all due to a mother fixation, or being taken off the breast too early or nonsense like that. It's no such thing. I'm perfectly sane. It's just a—a phenomenon, I suppose. I am an eminent Q.C. in this life and a god in another.'

I don't think Dennis was a vain man but he was one of those people who, thanks to a trouble-free passage through public school to Oxford and beyond, had a calm and confident sense of his own worth and place in the world. A friend of mine once said of Dennis that he had in life 'taken the smooth with the smooth'. But everyone has their own particular struggles and difficulties which most of us don't appreciate, being preoccupied with our own. And I suppose you could regard being a god in another life as a peculiar problem: Dennis certainly did.

It was very late, but I asked Dennis to go on with his story.

Dennis, or rather Coruvorn, raised his hand in benediction and then pointed to the figurine in the shrine. It was turned on an instant from wood into gold except for the blue cloak which was now of pure lapis lazuli. The ancient couple gazed at their new treasure in delighted astonishment. The next moment Coruvorn was standing on the hillside in the moonlight. The moon was full and low, a pale peach colour. It was beginning to sink below a dun-coloured belt of trees before Coruvorn stretched out his hand and raised it a few inches to see it better, then he let it fall into its original position. The earth gave a little shudder, but otherwise there was no disturbance.

Coruvorn took to the air and floated over hills, forests and cities. He visited many homes, answered many prayers, righted many wrongs until he descended once more upon a hillside and stretched himself under a great oak.

'The next moment I was in Albany again in my own bed. My alarm was ringing and I was due for a conference in chambers in an hour. My experience hadn't exhausted me: in fact I felt thoroughly refreshed.' He looked at his watch. 'Good grief! It's two in the morning! You'd better come back tomorrow and I'll tell you the rest. It's a Saturday. Would you be free for lunch?'

During the course of that weekend Dennis told me much more about his life as a god. Some of it was not that interesting in the way that other people's dreams are always less enthralling than your own. He seemed to spend his time wandering his world dispensing arbitrary and unsystematic benevolence and receiving homage in turn. Not everyone in his world believed in Coruvorn, but he seemed to bear no grudge against the unbelievers. If his acts of random kindness favoured those who acknowledged his existence that was only to be expected. I thought it was genuinely magnanimous of him that he expected no servitude towards him, nor even credence.

I asked him if he regarded himself as omnipotent in his world. Dennis pondered this, genuinely intrigued by my question.

'Well, I suppose in theory, yes,' he said. 'That business with the moon for example. But I don't exercise it. I want people to be free to worship me or not as the case may be. I must be adored by free spirits or there would be no point in being a god. The same, *mutatis mutandis*, I suppose applies to human relationships.'

I agreed that this applied to human relationships as well.

'I see myself, I suppose, as a tutelary deity in the old classical sense. One who stands guard over his people and his planet.'

A MAZE FOR THE MINOTAUR

'So you don't command a galaxy, or a universe?'

'Well, I don't think so. I may do, of course, but that understanding has not been vouchsafed me.' I found his complacency rather irritating and was beginning to feel that it was my duty to puncture his illusion. Because that was what it was, make no mistake about it. At least, I suppose so. You must judge for yourselves.

I asked him for details of his planet and its people. Did they all speak the same language? Were they all of the same race? In what state of technological and political development did they exist? Were their animals and plants similar to ours? In this way I was hoping to convince him, and myself, that the world over which he presided was simply the product of his rather infertile imagination.

In a way, I was proved right. The world that he described could have been dreamt up by him. Its culture and state of technological development was a mixture of classical and medieval, its language was a version of Latin that Dennis was well equipped to understand. There were cities and city states and kings. There was no established religion, but in small shrines on hillsides or in homes, people paid homage to Coruvorn, the Wanderer, Lord of the Hills. Libations of wine were poured to him and small cakes, not dissimilar to the *madeleines* so beloved of Proust, were placed before his statue in the shrines.

The flora and fauna were similar to those in our world except that in his certain beasts existed which we regard as mythical. There were centaurs, hippogryphs and unicorns. There were also dragons, fire-breathing flying reptiles, but they were no bigger than ostriches and easily tamed.

The world of men and women on his planet was, according to him, peaceable and mercantile. The city states and petty kingdoms rarely had disputes, so there were no wars to speak of. If a crisis threatened between two powers Coruvorn always contrived to have it stopped before it went too far. There was no printing and though there were some books in manuscript, literature was mostly disseminated orally, consisting in long epics or shorter lyrical pieces sung to the accompaniment of an instrument resembling a lyre. The visual arts were on the whole decorative and abstract.

It all sounded very conventional and a little dull, just the sort of world that Dennis's rather staid imagination might have created. When I pointed this out to Dennis, he nodded as if he had considered this already.

'Yes, of course,' he said, 'I am quite aware that it might well be what you call an illusion, or is *delusion* the word you are looking for? But what exactly do you mean by delusion? If I were to say to you that I was a jar of marmalade, then you could quite easily say I was deluded. I am self-evidently not made of glass and filled with boiled-up Seville oranges; I am not an inanimate object. But when it comes to my experiences as Coruvorn to which I have access mostly at night in some kind of trance-like state, you cannot either prove or disprove their reality. They might appear to *you* to be just a dream, but they are quite unlike any dream I have ever had. They seem to me to be real. Now of course it might be possible that I am suffering from an acute mental illness, but you must admit that I show no signs of it, other perhaps than my so-called "delusion". I don't drink to excess; I certainly don't take drugs or imbibe strange herbal concoctions. I am at the top of my profession. You see? You might just as well apply the C. S. Lewis argument to me. You remember. . . . Jesus claimed to be the son of God. To do so one must either be a lunatic, a knave or the real thing. He was self-evidently not the first two; ergo he must have been the latter.'

'There are flaws in that argument. In the first place—'

'But I am not really claiming to be a god; merely that I have experience of godhead.'

'A distinction without a difference.'

'Possibly. Possibly.' He lapsed into deep thought and seemed to be no longer in need of my company, so I left him.

After that he would frequently phone me and tell me of his recent adventures as Coruvorn. I would occasionally take notes and once or twice recorded our conversations, even though what he had to say was not always very interesting. It was the concept that remained intriguing. I confess, I had thoughts of making my friend's strange aberration into a book or a series of articles.

According to Dennis, Coruvorn went about his business in his benign way, pardoning, resolving difficulties, often healing, generally looking after his planet. Dennis would occasionally ask my advice about whether he should intervene in some particular issue. I always told him that it was his decision: he was the god, after all and ought to know better. On one occasion he contemplated resurrecting an infant girl from the dead for the sake of her distraught parents. After some discussion, we decided against it, but for what reason I forget. Then something of significance happened.

He rang me at six one morning. My wife, to whom I had said nothing about Dennis, other than that he confided in me, expressed understandable irritation and went back to sleep. I went down stairs in a dressing gown and took the call in my study.

'What on earth is all this about? Do you know what time it is?'

'Jack, I'm most terribly sorry about the early hour, but this is important. And time really has no absolute meaning where I have come from. I have just woken up, so to speak, or returned to this world might be a more accurate way of putting it, and I must tell you while it is still fresh in my mind.'

Coruvorn had been, as was his wont, wandering the hills towards dusk. The sun was setting in its usual luxuriant way behind a belt of pale violet-coloured cloud into the gilded tops of an oak forest. A nightingale was singing in a nearby brake and a faithful rustic was turning his flock homewards towards lower and safer pastures. The god was surveying this gentle crepuscular scene with satisfaction when his eye caught a gleam of bright orange through the oak woods that crowned the hills.

Was it a fire? If it was Coruvorn must hasten to contain it or warn his people in a dream to come and put it out. In an instant he had lifted himself above the trees in the guise of an eagle and was winging his way over the tree tops towards the blaze.

He alighted on the topmost branch of a great elm tree at the edge of a large clearing, roughly oval in shape. Almost in the centre was a great bonfire of felled logs and around it was grouped a large number of men and women standing very still and solemn. In front of the fire at one apex of the oval was a raised wooden platform upon which stood about a dozen women dressed in long white robes. One of the women, older than the rest, appeared to be their leader. She stood in the middle holding a banner which fluttered in the ripples of heat emanating from the fire. On it in silver thread was embroidered the figure of a winged woman holding a sword.

Coruvorn flew down from the branches and assumed the shape of an old man on the edge of the crowd. The white women on the platform began to sing and the congregation was enraptured.

'The words,' said Dennis, 'as far as I can remember went like this—' And he sang, somewhat tunelessly:

Hail, Thora, our Lady of Wind!
Harbinger of Change, bringer of Purity!
Blow through our hearts, cleanse us with your breath!

'The music sounded to me a little like one of those Soviet anthems that Shostakovich and Prokofiev were forced to produce, but I can't really put my finger on it.'

While this chorus was being repeated countless times, according to Dennis, first by the ladies in white then by the congregation, Coruvorn moved among them, picking up their thoughts and murmured conversations. This was a new cult, apparently, that had sprung up and the people were worshipping a deity called Thora, Goddess of Wind.

'Thora, Goddess of Wind?' I interjected. 'Are you sure about this?'

'Yes, of course I'm sure!' said Dennis irritably. 'I was there, wasn't I? So there was another god being worshipped apart from me. It was rather strange that I wasn't aware of it until now, and really I wouldn't have minded . . . After all, I suppose, two gods are better than one. (Three even better, if you count the Trinity which you shouldn't really.) The trouble was, the chief priestess was requiring exclusive adulation for Thora. Thou shalt have no gods other than Thora, that sort of thing. And I found that her devotees were actually going round and destroying my shrines. Well, naturally this sort of thing has to stop, but I can't use force. Violence is simply not in my nature; besides I felt my powers subtly weakening. I still had plenty of devotees but they began to live in fear of these Thora fanatics who were taking over whole towns and cities, setting up their own political institutions and demanding exclusive allegiance to Thora. Severe penalties were being exacted from those who refused to comply. My faith went underground. I wanted, of course, to get in touch with this Thora but she proved elusive. Sometimes, standing on a hilltop, I felt her pass by in a gust of wind that nearly pushed me off my feet. I tried to stay her and speak to her but she ignored me. She must have known I was there but she would not stop. I am perfectly prepared to come to some sort of amicable arrangement with this goddess, but I am being swept aside. What am I to do?'

Never having faced a remotely comparable situation myself I was unable to help. When I tried to make a joke of it and told him that I was sure 'it would all blow over', he slammed down the phone.

I didn't hear from Dennis for almost a fortnight, and I must admit I was rather relieved. I had begun to feel responsible for him. Should I alert some authority—the Bar Council? The Law Society?—that one of their most distinguished Q.C.s was off his head? If Dennis had severed all communication, then it was someone else's problem.

Not wishing to burden her too much I had given my wife Jane a heavily expurgated version of the facts, merely telling her that he was subject to some 'strange delusions' and unburdening them on me. Jane suggested I had nothing more to do with him. I sighed as a friend; I obeyed as a husband.

Then he rang again, at three o'clock one morning. Jane advised me to tell him to go to hell. I said I would do my best though I am not a great believer in hell and took the call in the study. Dennis was in a state of high excitement and spoke as if there had been no hiatus at all since our last conversation.

'Jack, I know who she is!'

'Who?'

'Thora, of course.'

'Yes. You told me, the Goddess of Wind or something.'

'No, no no! Don't be an idiot. I know who she is in *this* world. Just as Coruvorn has an identity here, namely me, so does Thora. You're not going to believe this.'

'As you have strained my credulity to breaking point already, I don't think I am going to be that surprised.'

'It's Dame Maggie Standish! You know, the Human Rights lawyer.'

'Good grief! Really? How can you possibly know?'

'I just do. It would take too long to explain in detail. Suffice it to say that there exist things called astral corridors which link different worlds in space—'

'You mean like . . . black holes?'

'Yes, something like that. Please don't interrupt. Well once on my planet I managed to catch sight of her goddess form as she streaked across the sky. Incidentally the weather there has taken a marked turn for the worse since her arrival on the scene. Well, at once I set off in pursuit, hoping to have a conversation with her of some sort. She fled from me down an astral corridor but I was close behind. We travelled light years in a few earthly seconds and several times I nearly caught her. The next moment I was standing, still in my divine form as Coruvorn, in a strange bedroom. I was just in time to see the faint silvery form of Thora fly through the open mouth of a sleeping female in the bed. There was enough light for me to see that the female in question was Dame Maggie Standish. The next moment I was in my own bed in Albany.'

'I see.'

'Well, now I know, I can do something about it.'

'What do you propose?'

'Well, I shall just have to confront Dame Maggie with what I know and then we can have a reasonable discussion about it all. One just hopes she will prove to be amenable.'

'I'm not sure that's a good idea, Dennis. She could be tricky.'

'Oh, I'm aware that this is not going to be easy. Maggie of course is a big cheese in the Labour Party and I, as you know, am a lifelong Conservative.' I did not know, as a matter of fact, but I might have guessed. Coming as he did from an old Catholic family, his ancestors had probably been Tories since the days of the Old Pretender. 'As you are aware, she almost certainly disapproves of me. You know how priggish and censorious these Socialists can be.'

'All political zealots of any persuasion are prigs.'

'Exactly. That's the problem. She's a zealot. I'm not and never have been.'

'But what if she just says "you're mad", and tells you to go to hell?'

'I can only hope that she has enough personal integrity not to do so.'

'But what if—? What if you are simply mistaken about this whole business?'

'Jack, we have been into this. I know it's hard to believe, but I am not mistaken. I simply am not.' The tone of his voice was, I have to admit, level and sane. He told me that he would be encountering her 'in the flesh, so to speak' at a Law Society banquet in two days time, and would 'beard her' there. I once again advised caution and rang off. There was nothing more I could do.

My next news of Dennis was through a short piece in the *Daily Telegraph*. Dame Maggie Standish had accused Dennis of sexual harassment and stalking: he was about to appear in court and probably 'bound over to keep the peace'. He was being investigated and in disgrace. I couldn't imagine what his state of mind was like but I felt guilty about him even though Jane insisted that I had done all I could.

I rang the Albany and was told that Dennis was recuperating at a private sanatorium in Kent called The Cloisters. The man who answered the telephone, an Albany concierge, also told me that I was one of the few people to whom he had been allowed to give this information. The very next day I drove over to The Cloisters.

It was a fine June day. If Dennis needed a refuge from his difficulties, he could have done worse than The Cloisters. Though the building itself, a red brick Edwardian sprawl attached to some monastic ruins—hence the name—was not very impressive, the grounds were extensive and serene. Smooth lawns fringed with deciduous woodland and views of the Kentish Weald beyond might have been vaguely reminiscent of his planet. A nurse showed me to the back lawn where I found him seated on a bench with a plaid rug over his knees contemplating the scenery.

I had expected to find a distraught wreck of a man, for Dennis's reversal of fortune had been dramatic, but it was not like that. Dennis had lost weight dramatically and he had a haggard look, but he was not in any obvious distress. He greeted me with warmth and said he was pleased to see me.

'How are you?' I asked lamely.

'Dying,' he said cheerfully. 'Inoperable cancer. I've had it for some time apparently, but it's only just been diagnosed. And, no, that does not explain anything at all. The brain has not been infected.'

'But you admit that you shouldn't have gone after Dame Maggie in that way?'

'Not at all. I have exposed her for what she is: a ruthless dissembler and a fraud.'

'So you accused her to her face of being Thora, Goddess of Wind.'

'It was not an accusation, more an assertion.'

'Which she vigorously denied, no doubt.'

'Not exactly. She told me I was off my head and should see a doctor.'

'So why didn't you leave it at that? Why did you persist in harassing and stalking her.'

'Because I couldn't stop there. I had obviously rattled her. I was sure I could break down her defences and make her see sense.'

'But you didn't. And now you are facing a trial and complete humiliation. I'm sorry; you're ill and I shouldn't be talking to you like this.'

'That's quite all right. I know you mean well. As a matter of fact, this case will never go to court. I will either be dead or too sick to plead long before it comes to trial. I am going, as the Bible says, "to my long home". I shall be resurrected as Coruvorn, in my own world.'

'And what about Dame Maggie?'

'I have exposed her. I have got her on the run. Mind you, I will have to rethink the whole of my religious position. I can't be quite as easy going as I used to be. It will be, if you'll excuse the vulgar expression, *No more Mr Nice God.*'

He seemed positively serene. Our conversation drifted pleasantly into other topics and though he responded amiably and intelligently I could tell that his mind was not fully on them. The things of this world were no longer his concern. I was relieved of guilt.

One morning, barely a week after that conversation a doctor rang me from The Cloisters to tell me that Dennis had died in the night. She said it had been very sudden and unexpected, but it was more of a surprise to her than to me.

As it happened, that evening I was due to attend, in my capacity as literary editor of *The New Observer*, the launch party in the House of Commons for a book by Dame Maggie Standish entitled *Human Rights and Human Wrongs—the Future*. It sounded like one of those books which is destined to be more talked and written about than read; 'an important contribution to the debate' no doubt, but probably not a page turner. I had been debating whether to go but Dennis's death decided me.

I had not encountered Dame Maggie in the flesh before, though I had seen her countless times on television. I was impressed. The fluent and passionate address she gave before signing copies of her book was enthusiastically applauded. It was some time before I could get to talk to her, but I managed it eventually.

She was a tall handsome woman and exuded a personality that was certainly forceful but not unattractive. I had been prepared to dislike her, for my friend's sake, but I could not do so. She had a way of fixing her full attention and considerable charm on whomever she was with. It may have been developed for professional purposes but it had a natural origin. I told her that I represented *The New Observer,* a journal for which she expressed courteous enthusiasm. When I casually mentioned my name, I saw a slight bewilderment come into her eyes.

'You're a friend of Dennis Marchbanks, aren't you?'

'How do you know?'

'He mentioned you to me once or twice in his ramblings. You're not going to ask me to drop my charges against him, are you?'

'No. There would be no point. He died last night.'

'What! Good God! I didn't know that!' It seemed to me a slightly strange reaction.

'Why should you? I only just found out myself.'

'Did he . . . ? Was it suicide?'

'Cancer. He'd had it for some time.'

'Ah . . .' She gave a sigh which I thought expressed relief but also a certain irritation. 'Well, that's very sad,' she added in a flat voice. 'If you'll excuse me—' and she left abruptly.

Two days later Dame Maggie was standing outside the Royal Courts of Justice in the Strand talking to a film crew about her latest Human Rights case when a freak accident occurred. A sudden gust of wind blew up and must have dislodged one of the stone finials on the Gothic arches of the façade. It was a heavy piece of masonry and it fell some sixty feet onto Dame Maggie's head, killing her outright.

Dennis Marchbanks's memorial service at the Brompton Oratory under the direction of his confessor Father O'Hare, was a subdued business, but a surprising number of his colleagues were present. His recent aberrations went unmentioned in the eulogy. Death, both his and Dame Maggie's, would appear to have expunged those egregious embarrassments.

After the service, I approached Father O'Hare and asked if I could speak to him about Dennis. He invited me back for a cup of tea in his rooms at the Oratory, and it was to him that I first related all that Dennis had told me. To begin with, Father O'Hare seemed hurt that Dennis had confided in me rather than his true

Father Confessor. When I told him that he had been fearful of offending an old friend, Father O'Hare softened a little.

'The poor foolish man!' he said. In the utterance of that phrase I caught for the first time a hint of O'Hare's Irish origins. 'Did he think I hadn't heard things like that before? Did he really suppose I was so hidebound and censorious? In my time I've had to cope with much worse delusions from members of my flock. I had terrible trouble once with a young man who thought he was an egg. Well, you can imagine.'

As it happens, I could not. 'So you think it was just a delusion?'

'Oh, lord, yes! It was all a lot of nonsense.' His tone was brisk, dismissive, almost irritable. 'Mind you,' added Father O'Hare after a long and thoughtful pause, 'if one *must* have a god, one could do a lot worse than Dennis Marchbanks.'

I was going to conclude there, but only last week I was informed that I had been left a small bequest in the will Dennis had made shortly before his death. I was touched. It consisted of several choice items from his antiquarian book collection, including a complete original set of *The Yellow Book*. There was one other item which was the reason why I had been informed so late, as there had been considerable difficulty in establishing its value for probate purposes. Several experts had been consulted and none could agree as to its date or origin.

Dennis had named it in the will simply as 'my gold and lapis lazuli figurine' and there was no mistaking it. It stands about six inches high, the figure of a tall gaunt man in solid gold holding a staff. He has on a cloak of brilliant deep blue, fashioned somehow out of pure lapis lazuli. The experts could agree only on one thing: it is a work of astonishing beauty.

THE WET WOMAN

THE WET WOMAN

If you are a consumer of tabloid revelations you may have heard of Woodlands. Woodlands, or Woodlands Hall to give it the correct title, is a health farm in Suffolk about a hundred miles from London. Some journalists have called it a 'Rehab Clinic' but I prefer not to: I dislike the word 'rehab'. Let's just say that Woodlands is where jaded celebrities in the artistic and sporting worlds go to become healthy again or, as some like to put it, 'detox'. That's another word I hate, but perhaps an appropriate one in my case.

Not that I'm a star, or pretend to be, just a fairly successful actor who had been through a lean patch both personally and professionally. When I managed to land a role playing the villain in a big Hollywood thriller called *Hard Man Returns with a Vengeance*, (the third in the successful *Hard Man* series) my agent noticed that I was out of condition and more or less ordered me to go to Woodlands. It would have offended his professional pride if I were not in the right shape for filming a month hence. To judge from the script, some of the action sequences were going to be demanding, and there is only so much a stunt double can do, so I suppose he was right. He even advanced me the money to go there. I was wary, but not entirely reluctant.

Woodlands Hall had been bought by an American millionaire towards the end of the nineteenth century, razed almost to the ground and rebuilt in a grandiose neo-baroque style, with pillared porticoes, grand staircases and vast marble-floored rooms. An Astor, a Vanderbilt, or a Jay Gatsby might have felt at home there, I suppose. Its most attractive features are the extensive grounds in which it is set, where deer drift in dappled herds under the generous shade of ancient oaks and cedars. That had a kind of tranquillity about it, or so I thought.

The facilities are excellent, though they are geared, naturally enough, toward physical improvement rather than pleasure: saunas, massage rooms, swimming pools, gyms, that kind of thing, all with their attendant instructors and staff. The food and drinks are of the lettuce and carrot juice variety, and the general regime strict and intensely supervised.

After I had checked in at the front desk, and a white-coated member of staff had taken the bags to my room, I was shown into the office of Dr Max Belkin. He ran the place and liked to be known by all as 'Dr Max', though it would be unwise to infer from this form of address that he invited any degree of warmth or familiarity from his subjects.

Dr Max's office was on the ground floor. It was part of a suite which he occupied, one of several with private terraces looking out onto the grounds, the others being for particularly wealthy or favoured guests. The office was painted a pure brilliant white and illuminated by long tubes of neon lighting so that even on the darkest day you were dazzled and intimidated by the glare. As I entered, I was faced with a desk at which sat Dr Max. He wore a white coat and was hunched over some papers.

All I could see of his head was a shiny pink cranium on whose margins a few greyish white curls of tightly-cropped hair clustered. Without looking up, he raised his left hand with which he beckoned me forwards and then pointed to a wooden chair in front of the desk on which I was meant to sit.

I was conscious of a certain theatricality about his actions which I resented. Professional actors prefer such devices to be confined to their proper domain: the stage. Was I really meant to believe that Dr Max's papers were too important to be abandoned for the sake of courtesy? Nevertheless, if his intention was to humiliate me, he had succeeded.

He looked up. I saw a smooth, pink face, curiously bland, and a pair of pale blue eyes behind rimless spectacles. He was looking at me with detached curiosity, as one might look at a specimen on a slab. Without getting up or leaning further forward he stretched out his right hand to be shaken. I obeyed, rising from my chair to do so. The hand was cold, damp, and bony.

'So,' he said. 'You are here, your agent tells me, because you are out of condition. Your wife has just left you and you are drinking too much.' I was about to protest against my agent's betrayal of confidence when he stopped me. 'I could have told you that just by looking at you. What particular tipple is it? Gin? Whisky? Red wine?'

Against my better judgement, I told him. He wrote something down on a notepad and without looking up again, he said: 'And when did you last have sexual intercourse?'

I told him it was none of his business.

He did not seem offended, he merely said calmly: 'But it *is* my business, Mr Johnson. That is why your agent paid for you to come here. That is why it is my business and your business to put you back together again because otherwise you will be wasting my time and your agent's money. It's not going to be easy, but if you are prepared to co-operate I think we can get results. Do you understand?'

I gave him a rough date.

'With a man or a woman?'

After a few more questions of a similarly personal nature, all asked with clinical coldness, Dr Max began to outline the regime he was prescribing for me. It involved massages, saunas, a strenuous program of exercise, colonic irrigation, yoga and a vegan diet of repulsive austerity. No alcohol, of course, but I was expecting that.

My time at Woodlands proved initially to be purgatorial rather than infernal, thanks to one compensating factor: my fellow patients. All were interesting, some positively congenial. By the end of my second day there I had teamed up with an ageing rock star called Garth (lead guitarist of *Rectal Thermometer*), and an old theatrical colleague of mine, Sir Benjamin Arthur. Their companionship helped to take the curse off an otherwise dire experience. We laughed a good deal, when we had the energy. A dish of brown rice and steamed broccoli tastes less noxious if you have someone with whom you can complain about it.

There were women around too—several of them very attractive—but mingling of the sexes was generally discouraged, especially by Dr Max.

One afternoon all three of us were sweating away in the sauna and feeling pretty low because we knew that the next 'meal' at five o'clock would consist of nothing more than a cup of milkless blackcurrant leaf tea and a dry, sugar-free biscuit. We tried to think of something else.

'Did you know we have a new inmate,' said Sir Ben. 'You'll never guess who.'

'Yes?'

THE WET WOMAN

'Stuart Edge. Arrived this afternoon.'

'Blimey,' said Garth. 'You mean the director?'

'None other. World famous. Of stage and, lately, screen.' Sir Ben turned to me. 'Have you ever been a victim, Charles?'

'A couple of times.'

'He's supposed to be brilliant, isn't he?' said Garth.

'He has established that reputation very successfully,' said Sir Ben. 'Actually, his ideas are either second-hand or second-rate and he has been saved time and again by the quality of his actors and designers. His real talent is for exercising power.'

'But isn't that what directing is all about?' Garth, I noticed, had a taste for provoking Sir Ben, who did not always rise to the bait.

'Up to a point, Garth. Up to a point. Stuart has this technique of building up actors with flattery and encouragement, then crushing them with scorn and obloquy half way through rehearsals, then building them up again from nothing in his own image. It can be very effective, and the actors who respond to the treatment tend to become his devotees. Others are destroyed. The rest of us just survive.'

'He wrote a book about it called *The Naked Stage*,' I added.

'A classic, I am told, and required reading in all bad drama schools.'

'What intrigues me,' I said, 'is why he is here at all. I mean, whenever I see him, he always looks the picture of health.'

'Perhaps because he comes here so often,' said Sir Ben. 'And that nice boy who brings in our mint tea and dry toast in the morning told me that Stuart is apparently an old friend of Dr Max.'

'Good grief. I wouldn't think those two have very much in common.'

'Well,' said Sir Ben, 'They are both power junkies, and power junkies are like millionaires and paedophiles. They may not get on but they stick together.'

'Come to think of it,' said Garth, 'in my experience millionaires and paedophiles usually *are* power junkies.'

An attendant came in to announce that we were to move on to the cold plunge bath, after which that cup of blackcurrant leaf tea would be waiting for us in the library.

While we were making our move, Garth said: 'As a matter of fact, I know rather more about your pal Stuart Edge than I was letting on about.'

'Oh, do tell! I am all ears,' said Sir Ben.

'I know you are, you frightful old gossip. I'll spill the beans in the library.'

After the cold plunge, I went up to my room to change. As I was coming down the stairs to go to the library, I saw Stuart Edge in the hall talking to Dr Max. Edge was wearing a grey track suit and trainers; he seemed poised and relaxed. In some ways he and Dr Max were very different specimens; Edge being of middle height and stocky, Dr Max tall, bony, cadaverous. Both, however, had regular, slightly blunt features, their heads round and almost hairless. More importantly, they seemed to exude an air of effortless authority. I would have recognised the will to power in both, even if I had not known what I did. I waited till they had gone before proceeding downstairs to have my tea.

When I reached the library—no books to speak of, but plenty of health magazines—I found Garth already settled at a table by the window with his blackcurrant leaf tea. I could see at once he was in a bad mood, and the reason was not hard to find. At the end of the room one of the attendants, in his regulation white coat, was seated on a dais strumming an acoustic guitar. He was playing a selection of vaguely folk-like melodies, the intention being, I suppose, to create a soothing atmosphere. I found it pleasant enough, but that was not the effect it had on Garth. All the cold rage that the professional feels for the presuming amateur was welling up inside him.

'Folk songs! God, I loathe them, even when they're played competently.'

'At least he's not singing . . . So tell me about Mr Edge.'

'Let's wait for Ben, shall we?'

Just then Sir Ben appeared, very red in the face and puffing. Having flopped into a chair, he said: 'He saw me. I'm positive he recognised me.'

'Edge?' Sir Ben nodded.

'Well, of course he would. Why shouldn't he?'

'I don't know. We've had several run-ins. He always rubbed me up the wrong way.'

'I didn't know he was that way inclined.'

'Oh, don't be so childish, Garth! He was always trying to undermine me somehow. I think he resents my knighthood.'

Garth said: 'Doesn't everyone?' Sir Ben glared at Garth for a moment, then, recognising the tease, giggled.

'Oh, you are awful, Garth! So, dish me the dirt about Edge.'

'Well, it's not exactly dirt. Ever knew an actress called Janet Wendice?'

'Oh, yes!' said Sir Ben. My heart also missed a beat. 'As a matter of fact—'

'Beautiful girl. She was a model when I first knew her. We had a thing going; I might even have married her, though that was not the sort of thing rock stars did in those days: certainly we were in love, whatever that may mean. Well, she got into a couple of films, mainly on the basis of her looks, I suppose, but she started to take acting seriously. Took acting classes, did rep; it was all fine by me. We were still seeing each other, but I was touring a lot; then she was in a show that this man Edge directed and she suddenly just cut me off completely. I'm not even sure whether they were having an affair, but he had a hold on her, that's for sure. Once I rang her up and he answered her phone. I can't remember the conversation exactly, but there were some very nasty vibes. Basically, he was telling me to back off, because

I wasn't any good for her, but there was something else going on. Maybe it was to do with that power thing. Well, that was the year *Rectal Thermometer* did our first big American tour and by the time I got back she had just gone. Later someone told me she was dead, or I may have read it somewhere. Some sort of accident, I think.'

'Yes, she died,' said Sir Ben, 'but it was no accident. It was hushed up at the time, but she drowned herself. She was found at the bottom of a swimming pool with her pockets full of pebbles. I was very fond of her myself. Not that—I mean, ours was a purely professional association.'

'Yes. I realise that, Ben,' said Garth.

'I've never had a better Ophelia.'

Sir Ben, to my knowledge, had only played Hamlet in two different productions, but his words implied a great many more. That sly piece of self-aggrandisement was typical of the man: I was both irritated and touched by it.

'It was at the Vic and luckily Edge was not directing, but she was still very much under his thumb. She was living with him at the time and he used to try to alter her performance. In the end someone had to ring him up and tell him to back off. I didn't dare, I'm afraid. He made a tremendous fuss and tried to sabotage the whole production. In spite of which, Janet gave a wonderful performance and pulled away from him for a while but he was too strong for her. She tried several times to escape from his clutches and was constantly drawn back. In the end she went for the only sure method of escape and, sadly, succeeded. She booked herself into a hotel on the south Coast and drowned herself in the pool. The rumour was that Edge was on his way to get her when she did it; but someone who should know told me he was already there. The whole story is not widely known, and it has done nothing to stall Edge's career. Far from it.'

'We ought to do something about it,' said Garth. 'That bastard needs to be shaken from his pedestal.'

THE WET WOMAN

'All very well to say that, but how?' I said.

'It's coming up to Halloween: let's trick or treat him.'

'Oh, for heaven's sake, grow up, Garth,' said Sir Ben. 'We're supposed to be mature adults; not nine year olds.'

I said: 'He treats his actors like nine year olds.'

'Right on, man,' said Garth. 'Anyway, it could be fun. Take our minds off all that brown rice and raw eggplant we get for our dinner. Meet you again, then. In the meantime, I must do some research.'

At that moment, the guitar playing attendant began to play 'The Streets of London'. Garth looked up, rage in his eyes.

'God, I loathe that song with a passion! That sanctimonious, sock-and-sandal-wearing shit!'

He rose. Sir Ben plucked feebly at the sleeve of his shell suit. 'Garth! Please! Don't do anything stupid!'

Garth broke free and began to march towards the guitarist who ceased playing when he noticed his approach. Garth's stride slackened slightly and when he reached the player much of his initial fury seemed to have evaporated. Garth spoke and the guitarist responded emolliently. I could not hear what they said but the conversation appeared to develop along friendly lines. Finally, they shook hands and Garth returned to us.

'Not a bad bloke after all,' he said. 'Turns out he's a big *Rectal* fan, though why he goes in for that folk crap is beyond me. Anyway, he told me something rather interesting. Apparently, Edge is occupying one of those suites on the ground floor; you know like Dr Max's with French windows and a terrace and all. Could be useful.'

Sir Ben asked what he meant.

'Tell you later, over the brown rice.' And he was gone. Sir Ben studied me for a moment.

'You knew Janet too, didn't you?'

'How do you know?'

'Just the way you looked when Garth mentioned her.'

'Dundee rep. Her first theatre job, though not mine. We had a thing going. A big thing, I thought. Then it went nowhere. Something happened.'

'Edge?'

'Possibly. I never found out. There was something very special about Janet.'

'There was. Do you believe in coincidence?'

Sir Ben required no answer.

When we three came together for the evening meal Garth was taciturn and preoccupied. He appeared mildly irritated by the show business gossip in which Sir Ben and I indulged, and confined himself to a few trenchant comments about the food.

As our painfully inadequate meal was coming to a close, Garth's guitarist friend called for silence and announced that in half an hour there was to be an event in the Gurdjieff Suite. (The public rooms at Woodlands were all named after modern mystics and sages.) Dr Max would be delivering a lecture on 'The Science of Holistic Health'.

'It sounds excruciating,' I said. 'We should give it a miss.'

'Oh, no. We're going,' said Garth. 'It will be very useful and instructive.'

Sir Ben and I looked at him in astonishment but did not demur. Garth had a strong will to power himself, though it was, for the most part, exercised benignly.

The Gurdjieff Suite was a long room, with a platform at one end, and various other ancillary rooms opening off it. On the platform was a lectern with a screen behind it. Rows of chairs had been set up to face the lectern; the walls were white and unadorned. When we arrived, rather late, we were surprised to find quite a number of our fellow guests were gathered to hear Dr Max. Several of the staff in their white uniforms were standing against the walls. Garth found their presence irksome.

'What are *they* doing here? Are they expecting a riot, or what?'

The three of us seated ourselves at the back, as far away as possible from the dais. One of the staff indicated that we should occupy some of the vacant seats further forward but we merely smiled and shook our heads.

Presently Dr Max entered. There was a spatter of applause from some of the audience which he waved away imperiously. Behind him came Edge who, instead of taking a seat in the auditorium, was shown by Dr Max to a seat on the platform behind the lectern and facing the audience. There he sat, scrutinising us and smiling enigmatically.

'What the f—?' said Garth.

Dr Max stood shuffling his notes at the lectern. He did not look round at Edge or make any reference to him in his opening remarks to explain his privileged position. I looked at my friends enquiringly.

'Power Games,' said Sir Ben.

'I'll give him power games,' said Garth.

Dr Max's lecture was as dull as we had expected it to be, if not duller. I was surprised that Dr Max was not even *trying* to make it sound interesting. At one point Sir Ben yawned. It was a big noisy yawn, a stage yawn you might say. Dr Max looked up and stared at Sir Ben for a moment with utter contempt, then he continued reading his lecture in exactly the same tone, at exactly the same pace. Clearly he did not care whether we were bored or not, and Edge appeared equally indifferent. He maintained his enigmatic smile and occasionally nodded, keeping his eyes on the audience rather than the speaker.

The talk lasted about three quarters of an hour but seemed much longer. At the end of it he called for questions and was favoured with a few obsequious inquiries. Despite their sycophancy, Dr Max seemed irritated by his questioners; his answers implied that what he had said in his lecture needed no further explanation and that you were a fool for requesting it. Then Garth put up his hand.

'Max, has anyone drowned in the swimming pool here?' There was a stunned pause before Dr Max responded.

'I am sorry, but what has this got to do with my lecture?'

'Oh, absolutely nothing. I was just wondering that's all.'

'Why?'

'Just that there was no one about when I went for a swim this morning. I was surprised that the place was totally unsupervised. Isn't that potentially rather dangerous?'

'You should have informed someone that you were going for a swim. Why did you not do so?'

'You haven't answered my question, Max. Has anyone drowned in the swimming pool?'

'No, they have not! Thank you, ladies and gentlemen. That concludes this evening's lecture; you may all now retire to your rooms for rest.' And with that he left hurriedly, by a side door, Edge following.

When he had gone Sir Ben rounded on Garth: 'What the hell was all that about?'

'I just wanted to see how Edge would take it. You know, drownings, swimming pools and that. And he definitely reacted.'

'Well it wasn't exactly Claudius in the play scene, if that's what you were looking for.'

'I wasn't expecting effing Claudius, Ben; I didn't want effing Claudius! I just wanted to rattle his cage a bit, and I did.'

'So, what now?'

'Follow me.'

The following night there was a full moon in a cloudless sky. The silvery light gave the grounds and house the look of an old steel engraving. An owl hooted. In the distance deer moved slowly and silently under the trees.

THE WET WOMAN

Garth, Sir Ben and I had managed to get out of Woodlands unobserved, despite there being a sort of unofficial curfew at ten o'clock. We had found a door at the back by the kitchens which was always left open and had slipped out with the 'equipment' we had prepared under Garth's supervision. Once we had made our arrangements, we placed ourselves behind a clump of laurels at a convenient distance from the house. Garth had his mobile at the ready to take videos.

From our vantage point we had a clear view of Edge's rooms. The light was on in one of them, which had French windows opening onto a small private terrace. The curtains were drawn, but were thin enough for us to see beyond them the shadow of Edge pacing up and down. Occasionally he gesticulated. Was he with someone?

'Perhaps he's dictating one of his excruciating books about "Theatre",' said Sir Ben.

'We must rouse him,' said Garth. He crept forward and picked up a handful of gravel which he threw at the French window and then darted back to join us behind the laurel bush.

'This is terribly childish you know,' said Sir Ben, 'do you think we really—?'

'Ssh!' Garth said, taking out his mobile.

Edge drew the curtains, opened the French windows and strode out onto the terrace. He was wearing nothing but a white towelling bath robe and a pair of flip-flops. A similarly clad young woman could be seen peering out of the French windows behind him.

'My God! That's Fiona, our Yoga teacher!' said Sir Ben. 'She's a dam' nice girl. What's she doing with *him*?'

'Ssh!'

Edge stared indignantly around him. For a moment he seemed to be looking directly at the laurel bush where we were hidden before he continued with his survey, and then he saw it. Propped up against a stone urn on the terrace was a figure like a life-sized doll, its limbs splayed, its head hanging loosely to one side. It was crudely female in shape with pendulous breasts and the head looked as if it had been made partly out of an old mop head, partly from an eviscerated pumpkin. The object was swollen and soaked in water. It looked, as it was meant to look, like the grotesque representation of a bloated female corpse dragged from the water after drowning.

Edge stared at the thing without moving a muscle. I could not clearly see his expression but his chest was heaving. He was not happy, and I felt both shame and pride. We had made a damned good job of our little dummy.

Fiona put her head out of the French windows and, with a puzzled look, said something to Edge. He turned around and snapped at her furiously, then he went up to her, grabbed the collar of her robe and put his head within inches of hers. I heard him ask: 'Do you know anything about this?' in a terrible voice. She shook her head and tried to retreat indoors, but he held on to her while issuing instructions in an urgent undertone. Having done this he shouted: 'Do it! Now!' and shoved her, sobbing with fright, through the French windows.

Then he looked around once more, his gaze finally fixing itself on our laurel bush. 'I think,' said Sir Ben, 'the time has come for a hasty retreat.' Garth snorted with suppressed laughter.

'Right on!' he said, and we ran.

Behind us we could hear Edge bellowing with rage. Had he recognised us? I didn't think so. We had taken the precaution of giving ourselves crude disguises. Dark glasses and the appropriation of some wigs from the hairdressing salon had been my idea.

In retrospect, I can feel nothing but shame and embarrassment at what we had done, but as we ran through the moonlit park, three dissolute professional artists in wigs and shell suits, I felt only exhilaration. We had succeeded beyond our wildest imaginings in pulling off an absurd prank and, so far, getting away with it. We had made the dummy out of a pair of tights and a Lycra body suit which we had found in the dance studio, some surgical gloves pinched from the dispensary while Sir Ben was distracting the nurse's attention with a complaint about his knee, a pumpkin and a mop head from the kitchens while I was employing similar diversionary tactics. These we had stuffed with newspaper and sewn together into the strangely horrible thing that had so alarmed Edge. (Sir Ben proved remarkably handy with a needle and thread; Garth had carved the pumpkin expertly; I had lent moral support.) Then we had smuggled the thing out via the kitchens, set it up, and doused it in water to enhance the macabre effect. Now we were flitting under the trees and moon, not knowing quite where we were going or what we were doing, and giggling uncontrollably.

We were all pretty out of condition, but Sir Ben, the oldest, was the first to flag.

'Hang on! Slow down! Look, chaps, we've got to decide what —Ah!'

Suddenly Sir Ben was on the ground, and something was bolting away from us at high speed.

Sir Ben said: 'Bloody deer! I bumped into one of those bloody deer!' Garth and I nearly collapsed with laughter. We got Sir Ben to his feet, all of us gasping for breath. 'Seriously,' said Sir Ben, 'What do we do now?'

'We circle the park, keeping out of sight,' said Garth, 'Then, when we can see that the coast is reasonably clear we sneak in through the back by the kitchens. Let's get rid of these bloody wigs for a start. They itch like hell.' We cast them off.

'But what do we do if they catch us or see us?' said Sir Ben.

'What *can* they do? The worst is they can chuck us out of Woodlands and that would be no great loss. Come on, Ben!'

'Look! They're out there searching for us!' said Sir Ben pointing to where a number of white-coated Woodlands staff were flashing torches through the trees. We could just see Dr Max, who had joined Edge, directing their searches in a loud, angry voice. One of the torch beams swept across us.

'Come on,' said Garth. 'They may have seen us. Let's make ourselves scarce. Follow me.' He set off at a jog and we followed him.

They *had* spotted us and had fanned out in the way you see police do on a manhunt in films. We dodged behind trees and changed direction several times in an attempt to throw them off, but they were beginning to catch up with us. One of our pursuers in a loud voice began to urge us to give ourselves up, assuring us that 'no harm' would result.

'I say,' said Sir Ben, panting heavily, and coming to a halt under a great oak, 'don't you think we ought to give ourselves up. This is getting ridiculous. I can't go on running away like a schoolboy who's been caught scrumping apples. I'm too old and too bloody distinguished for this caper. Dammit, the Queen's knighted me for my services to acting!'

'We're not giving up yet,' said Garth. 'We've still got a chance of getting away with it. Let's give them a run for their money.'

'But I *can't* run any more,' wailed Sir Ben.

For all Garth's cunning tactics, the white coats had located us and were rapidly gaining on us while we, and especially Sir Ben, had almost exhausted our resources of energy. Then something strange happened. We were still recovering our breath behind the oak while the line of flashlights—six of them—advanced inexorably towards us, when something ran very fast across the space between our tree and them, but much closer to us, so that we felt the wind as it passed. We also felt, or thought we did, some drops of water spray off it. The water was cold and smelled slightly stagnant. I say we *thought* we felt it because when we discussed it afterwards, none of us could be absolutely sure, or wanted to be.

'Another of those bloody deer,' said Sir Ben.

'Don't be an idiot, Ben!' said Garth. 'Deer go on four legs, not two!'

THE WET WOMAN

That much we could be certain of. The something was a biped and roughly human in shape. It was greyish in colour, with a strange furry kind of head, and wet, very wet. It glistened in the moonlight, and seemed to stumble rather than run, as if, in spite of its amazing speed, it was unused to movement. But whatever it was, it saved us from capture and humiliation. The white coats had picked it up with their torch beams and all of them veered off to chase it. We watched in astonishment as they disappeared from view, their flickering torches throwing grotesque shadows through the trees, in pursuit of something, we had no idea what. Cautiously, we made our way back to Woodlands through the park and let ourselves through the back door by the kitchens.

Inside Woodlands there was an atmosphere of mild confusion. Our fellow patients had come out of their rooms to investigate what was going on. The staff were urging them to return to their beds with the assurance that 'everything' was 'under control'. We had no difficulty in mingling with our distracted fellow inmates and making it back to our rooms unnoticed.

The following morning, when we three met at breakfast, we fully expected some sort of retribution to descend on us, but it did not. Everything went on as normal, though I did notice that the mood of the staff was subdued, and perhaps more easy-going. Dr Max, usually a busy and ubiquitous presence, did not appear. When Garth boldly asked after him, he was told by a tight-lipped masseur that the doctor was 'managing a slight crisis with one of the guests'.

The three of us met several times during the day to compare notes, but none of us had anything significant to report. That evening, after supper, we took a stroll in the grounds. We saw more white coats about than usual, but they paid no attention to us. Garth said that we were obviously 'home free'. Sir Ben, a born worrier, said he hoped Garth was right, but did not seem at all sure.

A MAZE FOR THE MINOTAUR

We happened at that moment to be passing Edge's French windows and the terrace where the main drama of the night before had taken place. The curtains were open, as was one of the French windows, and the room beyond fully lit. Curiosity drew us closer. At first the room appeared to be empty. It was a sitting room, furnished and carpeted in anodyne hospital colours: pinks and greys. That was why we did not immediately notice that a naked man was lying on the pale pink carpet. He was motionless and there was what looked like a large damp patch on the rug beneath him. It was Edge.

Something else was in the room. At first we took it to be a shadow because it was grey; but it was also shiny and slightly iridescent. It was bobbing about the room with odd, jerky movements. The shape was roughly that of a woman. For a moment it obscured our view of Edge while it bent over him, clumsily nodding its grey fuzzy head at the body, like a badly manipulated puppet.

Suddenly it turned and began speeding toward the open French window with that strange uncoordinated but rapid movement we had seen the night before. Instinctively we turned away, so we did not see it pass us, but we felt the stagnant wet wind it left in its wake. By the time we had dared to look again, the grey wet woman was some distance from us, shambling through the trees of the park and into obscurity.

'Good God!' said Sir Ben. 'Do you think we should inform someone about this?'

'Oh, no,' said Garth. 'We don't want to be mixed up in all that. It really is none of our business.'

We all agreed that it was absolutely none of our business.

Over the next few hours we watched dispassionately while events at Woodlands took their course: the discovery of the body, the summoning of medical help, its failure to revive Edge, the arrival of the police and some cursory questions asked, the general view established that though the death was sudden it was from natural causes, heart failure almost certainly. We saw Fiona weeping uncontrollably in the arms of Dr Max who looked not so much grief stricken as indignant.

At breakfast the following morning Dr Max entered the dining room to announce formally the sad passing of the great stage and film director Stuart Edge, and command a minute's silence. Other than that, the day went on like any other day at Woodlands, healthily, hygienically, dully. Sir Ben found this rapid return to normality somehow ominous and remained nervously on the alert. Garth and I tried to reassure him, but without success. The next day Sir Ben decided that he had had enough. Pleading pressure of work, he told Dr Max that he was leaving Woodlands without completing his 'course'. Dr Max had, according to Sir Ben, subjected him to a lengthy and harsh interrogation, but got nothing out of him. To give him his due, Ben could act. Garth and I saw him off that evening.

As his taxi was going down the drive. Garth said: 'Who's that in the back of the car with Ben? I'm sure it was just the driver and him when he got in.'

I looked at the receding vehicle and thought I could just see the back of a rather tousled head of damp, grey hair beside Sir Ben's immaculately combed silver coiffure.

'No,' I said. 'Can't really see anything. Don't blame him for going, though. God, I could murder a Scotch!'

Garth and I both stayed the course, but saw less of each other, exchanged fewer jokes, and dedicated ourselves quite seriously to the business of detoxification. When the time came for us to leave Woodlands, we swapped mobile numbers and email addresses, both knowing it was little more than a polite formality.

One morning, a few days after my return to normal life, feeling, I have to admit, in considerably better shape for Dr Max's regime, I happened to hear on the radio news that Sir Ben had died quite suddenly. The details were vague, but I gathered that he had had a heart attack in his bath. The news troubled and saddened me. For all his faults I had liked the man; there was no harm in him and he had been a fine actor.

Though I was about to start filming, I managed to make the memorial service where I saw Garth. We shook hands and embraced warmly, but somehow there was nothing we wanted to say to each other.

About a year later I was still on the film in Prague. At the hotel where they had billeted me, I picked up a three-day-old English newspaper and read about Garth's death. It was some sort of boating accident apparently. He was fished out of the Thames near Marlow where he had a house. I can't remember all the details, and I don't want to. On the day I read this we had finished filming reasonably early. Everyone else on the shoot wanted to go out on the razzle, but I felt too exhausted. In any case I was still theoretically on the wagon (agent's instructions), and there are few more tiresome experiences in life than watching other people get drunk while you are on tonic water.

I went back to my hotel, had a rather dreary meal in the restaurant there, and then went up to bed. My room was spacious and well appointed, but drab beyond belief. I took a shower and put on the hotel bathrobe to dry off on the large double bed. The air in the room was warm and stale, but I did not want to open the window and let in the noise of the Prague traffic. I closed the curtains to drown the noise still further, so that when I turned out the bedside light there was complete darkness. I took off the bathrobe and crawled under the duvet. Almost instantly, as I recall, I was in a heavy sleep.

When I woke some hours later it was through a veil of unease. My brain took some time to identify the source of the trouble. It was not my headache or the dry, lifeless air that surrounded me, it was something else, something unexpected: dampness. Had I been sweating? No, but there was something wet next to me in the bed. It was smooth and bulky. I could see nothing in the dark, so I stretched out a hand to turn on the light but something grabbed my wrist to prevent me. I was being held by a cold wet hand. I cried out, but another hand, cold and wet, covered my mouth. Someone damp and smooth and naked was climbing on top of me. My eyes, now accustomed to the dark, could discern the outline of a woman straddling me, thrusting at my groin with her thighs. She was heavy and cold, and drops of water were raining on my body as her lolling head bent over me. I say her head, but while I could see clearly her smooth female outline, with its rather heavy pendulous breasts, her head was less defined, more of a fog, a kind of furry mass. In spite of terror and revulsion, my body responded to hers. I had not had a woman in over a year. She was writhing on me wildly while I tried vainly to resist. She plunged down on me and my whole body gasped. A spasm of pleasureless pleasure that seemed more like agony than sensual delight was wrung from me. Now she was all over me and my nostrils were filled with the heavy damp odour of stagnant water. I could barely breathe with the weight and the smell and the water. My gorge rose and I began to choke. Then I was awake again, this time properly, truly awake. I lay there gasping.

I was of course wet and slimed from my nightmare ejaculation, but it was more than that. The space beside me in the double bed was soaking. I felt the sheets which were cold and wet.

In my restless sleep I must have spilled my glass of water onto the bed. I switched on the bedside light to look for the glass, but it was not there. This was strange, as I was sure I had a glass beside me when I went to bed. I went to the bathroom and there was the water glass on the shelf above the washbasin, empty. I must have put it back there during the night, but I don't remember doing so. I wanted to get back to sleep, but a stuffy room and a damp bed were not going to help.

A MAZE FOR THE MINOTAUR

I took two towels from the bathroom to put over the wet patch in the bed which did not look like the usual spill. It was long and thin and some of the water had splashed onto the pillow next to mine. You might almost have said that the dampness had a human shape. I covered it with the towels, but I couldn't get into bed and go to sleep. The traffic outside my sealed window was like the snore of a distant sleeper. I parted the curtains and looked out. Yellow street lamps shone on deserted boulevards; the alien city lay in a fitful doze. In the distance a motorcycle roared off to an unknown destination; a tram clanked past. I was wide awake and did not even know what time it was.

I couldn't find my watch so I switched on my mobile phone. It told me that it was three minutes to midnight on October 31st. Halloween.

Was it you, Janet?

A MAZE FOR THE MINOTAUR

A MAZE FOR THE MINOTAUR

From the *Marylebone Gazette* December 15th 1897

STRANGE DISAPPEARANCE OF LOCAL PHILANTHROPIST

Mr Frederick Cooper has mysteriously disappeared from his home in Melina Grove NW. A wealthy commercial gentleman of, we are told, philanthropic interests, he was chiefly noted in the district for driving a smart two horse phaeton, usually with a groom in the dickey. On the afternoon of December 10th, despite a mist having descended, he went for his customary drive, leaving the groom behind in the mews at the back of his house. A little over two hours later, he returned to Melina Mews. The groom, Laird by name, saw Mr Cooper descend from the carriage and signal to him to unharness the carriage and stable the horses. Then Laird saw him walk round into Melina Grove, apparently to enter his house by the front door, but he never arrived. It was some hours before it was realised that something was amiss, the alarm being finally raised by Mr Cooper's wife, but by that time it was dark and very foggy withal. Intensive searches and enquiries were instituted by the local Constabulary in the surrounding area the following morning, but to no avail. Not a single clue as to his fate has as yet been made manifest. Mr Cooper has the reputation of being a man of somewhat eccentric habits and is known by some, for reasons we cannot ascertain, as The Minotaur. We can only be sure that he has vanished into the mists of a most baffling labyrinth.

෨

'Does he come today?'

'I doubt it, my dear,' said Mrs Belling, 'the Minotaur rarely comes on Fridays. Surely you remember?'

'Oh, yes,' said Mabel with a little sigh of relief. 'I was forgetting.'

'But Lord Arthur is due at any moment.'

'Will he wish to see *me*, Mrs Belling?'

'Of course, my dear. He always does.'

Mabel seated herself in the window of Mrs Belling's 'drawing room', as she chose to call it (rather than a 'parlour'), and looked down onto the garden below. It was nothing very special in the way of front gardens, just a patch of lawn surrounded by a few disconsolate bushes, but Mabel viewed it with satisfaction. It was so different from what she had known before. It was a September afternoon in the year 1897 and the first sere notes were beginning to manifest themselves in the trees and shrubberies of St John's Wood.

A MAZE FOR THE MINOTAUR

The house, Number 2 Boscobel Place, stood in a street of similar white stucco houses, with small front gardens surrounded by high brick walls. The doors in the high brick walls were usually painted green and had in them small square metal grilles through which the visitor might see in and perhaps determine whether the occupants were at home.

It was a leafy, oddly secretive place, St John's Wood in those days: too grand to be called a London suburb, almost fashionable, but Belgravia or Mayfair it was not. It has been called 'a metropolitan oasis . . . with a peculiar moral and aesthetic character.'[*] Some successful artists inhabited 'the Grove of the Evangelist'. as the more artistically inclined among them would call it, and theatre people of the better class, a smattering of writers, and some others of more dubious standing. The gentry, the aristocrats, the purple of commerce (as Oscar Wilde would say) did not often dwell there, but they visited.

It was a quiet place too, before the traffic came. There were the visiting carriages, the grocer's van, the butcher and baker with their deliveries. Every month or so the secluded streets would echo to the cry 'Rag-a-bone! Rag-a-bone!' as the rag and bone man passed with his open cart drawn by a single, shambling old cob. It was a cry that for Mabel brought back the streets where she was raised, and she did not welcome it, but today the afternoon avenues, muffled by the leaves of early autumn were all but silent. She was at peace, as far as one could be while waiting for the first client of the day. Lord Arthur was not an unpleasant man, and, though on the wrong side of forty years old, still within hailing distance of it. Not like the Minotaur.

---

[*] From *St John's Wood, its History, its Houses, its Haunts and its Celebrities* by Alan Montgomery Eyre (Chapman and Hall, 1913). A very brief and incomplete account of the legend of The Minotaur of St John's Wood may be found therein.

Effie entered the room, young and high spirited. Many, herself included, would have said she was prettier than Mabel: certainly she dressed more flamboyantly; but, as Mrs Belling, said: 'Many of my gentlemen prefer the quiet ones.' Mabel looked up and smiled. She liked Effie's gaiety even though she could not always respond to it.

'Well, here I am,' she said, performing a little pirouette to emphasise the fact.

'So I should think,' said Mrs Belling. 'Getting up at all hours, and your gentleman expected any minute. Have you eaten, my girl? Go down to Mrs Mason and get yourself something. There's bread in the crocket and tea on the hob.'

'Oh, Mrs B, you have a heart of gold,' said Effie whirling Mrs Belling's stout form around in an impromptu waltz.

'Get along with you, girl!' said Mrs Belling, disengaging herself and puffing hard from the exertion. She did not seem altogether displeased, though. The quiet when Effie had left the room was palpable.

'Mrs Belling,' said Mabel, 'why do they call him the Minotaur?'

'Lord, what a question! Well in the first place, we don't know his true name, but Lord Arthur when I told him about his doings—he likes to hear about such things while he has his sherry—he says: "My word, he sounds like a proper old Minotaur." And then he says something in Latin. And every time after that, he asks after "the Minotaur". Maybe it's because of that mask he wears.'

'I don't like that mask, Mrs Belling. It gives me the shudders.'

'Well, he doesn't do no harm. Not really.'

'And I don't like being all sticky afterwards.'

'I know, dear, but you girls always get a good old rub down once he's gone.' The bell rang. 'Oh, gracious! That must be Lord Arthur. Make yourself presentable, my girl.'

Mrs Belling came over and pinched Mabel's cheeks to put a blush in them. She always did this before the arrival of a client and it did hurt a little. Mabel on the whole liked Mrs Belling who could be kind as long as you did as you were told, but there were occasions when an underlying harshness was evident. The cheek pinching was one such example, but never in her previous existence had Mabel been treated with such consideration, so she made allowances. Maybe Mrs Belling had not liked being asked too many questions about one of her most profitable clients.

'*I come from the haunts of coot and hern!*' said Lord Arthur Brook on being shown into the drawing room by the maid. It was a verbal sally with which he often made an entrance at Mrs Belling's, especially when, as on this occasion, he had just arrived from the country and was wearing tweeds.

'Oh, Lord Arthur, you are a one!' said Mrs Belling, her customary response.

Lord Arthur, a younger son of the Marquess of Martlesham, was not very distinguished in appearance: florid, balding, inclined to stoutness, but quite pleasant looking. Like many Old Etonians he gave the impression of having received an education more extensive than his capacity to do anything useful with it. Politics he had considered, but then, perhaps sensibly, had given up in favour of complete idleness. He was a man who had made no mark on the world beyond marrying a wealthy cousin and siring two sons, but he liked to think of himself as a bit of a character. He carried about with him the remnants of sound learning and a taste for the arts slightly in advance of the majority of his peers. The quotation with which he announced his presence was from Tennyson's 'The Brook', and the implied pun was of his own devising. He prided himself on it, but he would never have deigned to explain it to the likes of Mrs Belling or her girls. Their ignorance was all part of the fun.

Effie entered the room with a flourish.

'Oh, Lord Arthur, this is an unexpected pleasure!'

A MAZE FOR THE MINOTAUR

'Hello, Effie,' said Lord Arthur offhandedly before turning his attention to Mabel. 'Miss Mabel, how have you been keeping?' Mabel had risen and given Lord Arthur a demure little curtsey. 'Pining away in my absence, what?'

'Thank you, Lord Arthur, I have been very well.'

Effie gave a little pout and left the room. She could never understand why Lord Arthur preferred 'Mousy Mabel' to her. Effie would have liked to have added a titled gentleman to her retinue. Mrs Belling looked on and understood perfectly.

'Would you care for some refreshment after your journey, Lord Arthur?' she asked. Like so many things at Number 2 Boscobel Place this speech was a formality which received the anticipated response.

'Thank you, Mrs B, I'm much obliged but I'll take a sherry and a biscuit with you afterwards. And now, Miss Mabel, if you would be so kind as to lead the way?'

Mabel took the proffered oil lamp from the maid and led the way up to the second floor bedroom which was their customary place of assignation.

After the business was done Lord Arthur liked to dress slowly while Mabel lay stretched on the bed, naked. The dressing table mirror was so placed that he could adjust his necktie and watch her small languid movements on the bed at the same time. Lord Arthur flattered himself on the refined pleasure he took in these moments.

'You look like one of Mr Poynter's sea nymphs,' Lord Arthur had said to her on one such occasion. It was an apposite remark. Mabel possessed an exquisite figure, and had worked as a model, though not for Mr Edward Poynter R.A. She knew how to pose on a bed, and had for a while been a model at the St John's Wood Art School. It was while working there that she came to the notice of Mrs Belling who had offered her a more lucrative and less tiring means of employment.

'Lord Arthur, what do you know about the Minotaur?'

'Good gracious, girl what a question!'

'I beg your pardon, Lord Arthur.'

'No, no! No offence, little girl.' Lord Arthur was in an emollient mood. He had performed to his own satisfaction, if to no-one else's and was not indisposed to chat. He left the mirror and came to sit on the edge of the bed. His hand stroked Mabel's soft and perfectly shaped left thigh. It was another of those exquisite pleasures which seemed to him even more delightful than the act itself.

'I shouldn't trouble your pretty head over old s*emibovemque virum semivirumque bovem.*' He laughed at Mabel's puzzled frown. 'He's certainly a rum 'un and no mistake.'

'Do you know who he is?'

'I do, Miss Mabel. As a matter of fact I made some enquiries, but the results are not for the likes of you, lassie. I will only say that he is a man of much substance, but not a gentleman, I fear. Made his money out of jute, I understand. Though what one does with jute, I have never been able to grasp. Does one eat it? Does one weave it? Import it? Export it? Who knows? Perhaps you should ask the fellow next time he calls.' And with that he slapped her bare thigh and resumed his dressing. The rose-coloured imprint of his hand stung for quite some time. Mabel wiped away a tear and waited for the pain (and the mark) to fade before she asked another question, but she was ignored. Lord Arthur was trimming his moustache in the mirror.

Mabel had learned to disguise her passions well, but once they had been aroused she would doggedly pursue them until they were satisfied. She was not sure why her curiosity about the Minotaur had been so stimulated, nor why she hated him so vehemently, but somehow the hatred and the curiosity were connected. The other girls just thought it was a lark, 'money for jam', as one of them had rather wittily put it, but Mabel did not.

When Lord Arthur had gone Mabel told Mrs Belling that she would briefly go out for a walk, and to post a letter. Mrs Belling

A MAZE FOR THE MINOTAUR

nodded approvingly: she considered Mabel to be a good girl, because she behaved herself demurely with clients and never went absent without leave as some of her girls did. As for Mabel, familiarity had not yet worn away the charm of pleasant surroundings and an absence of money worries for the first time in her life. She was only just beginning to chafe at her employer's restrictions. As for the nature of her work, it had been a part of her life for a long while, long before Mrs Belling, and not always in the safest of environments. Mabel had learned to bury its ugliness deep inside her, and yet a man like the Minotaur could arouse the latent horror. Why exactly?

Mabel finished the letter to her cousin. To Cousin Margery, the poor but respectable wife of a country schoolmaster, Mabel presented herself as an artist's model and a dancer in musical shows, both of which she had once been. Cousin Margery was not to know that St John's Wood was a rather grand address for a mere chorine.

It was still light when Mabel went out but a London fog was descending in consequence of which the lamplighters were about their work. The street lights were surrounded by an aureole of bright mist, similar to that which Mabel had seen encircling the head of Christ in paintings. She reached the corner of Acacia Avenue where stood the pillar box and posted the letter. She felt a momentary pang as she committed her little budget of half-truths to the darkness beyond the scarlet lips of the post box.

'Hello, Mabel!'

The voice, immediately familiar yet not so quickly identified, made her gasp. She turned and saw a young woman, smaller than her and wrapped against the chill of the fog in a grimy plaid shawl.

'Lily! What are you doing here?'

'Ain't you pleased to see your little sister? My you're looking smart. We don't see you these days. Don't you want to know your own flesh and blood?'

Mabel felt cold. She knew how she must look to her sister. 'How have you been?' she asked.

'Very kind of you to ask, I'm sure,' said her sister putting on an absurdly genteel voice. It occurred to Mabel that Lily might be imitating her accent, acquired partly through natural absorption, partly from Mrs Belling's deliberate tuition. To return her voice now to its old ways would be to insult Lily still further; she would have to continue to sound prim and proper.

'You look well,' said Mabel.

'Ta very much, Mabel. I'm not so bad. Ma's the same. Maybe worse. I'm trying to look after her a bit, but everything I gives her goes on drink.'

'Oh.'

'Yes. That's all on yours truly now. Never a word from you, let alone a visit.'

'I didn't know where you were. We lost touch.'

'You could have tried to find out. I've found *you*.'

'Yes, but that's . . .'

'Easier? Well, it would be, wouldn't it? Ain't no excuse.'

'No,' said Mabel. She looked in her purse and found a half sovereign. 'Here,' she said, proffering the coin. 'It's all I've got just now. Could you use it, Lil?'

Mabel knew that if this were a melodrama, her offer would be greeted by an heroically indignant refusal; but, this being reality, Lily took the coin and said: 'Thanks. And don't think I won't be back for more. Are you going to show me where you live?'

'This way. I'm afraid I can't ask you in. We will be receiving callers shortly.'

'Not good enough for the likes of me, eh?'

'No, it's not that, Lil . . .' But perhaps it was. Lily was not bad looking, but her face and figure lacked Mabel's natural refinement. As for her clothes, Mabel could hardly bring herself to look at them, while feeling shame at her own fastidiousness. The two walked slowly up towards Boscobel Place, exchanging news. Lily was still 'at the game', 'like you are,' she added looking accusingly at her sister.

They were approaching Number 2 when a two horse phaeton with a groom in the dickey came round the corner and stopped in front of the house. The driver, caped and hatted was a large man in black who clambered awkwardly down from the driving seat, assisted by the groom, a swarthy little fellow who looked almost dwarfish by comparison. The big man threw the reins at the groom who proceeded to attend to the horses while his master rang the bell outside the gate of Number 2. Lily drew her sister against the high wall that ran along the street.

' 'Struth almighty, I know that old rotter.' So did Mabel. The big man was the Minotaur. Even in the thickening light he could be identified by his huge, barrel-chested bulk, and the leprous whiteness of his skin. 'Looks like you know him too.'

'I know he comes to us. He's known as the Minotaur. I don't know his real name or nothing.'

'Nor do I. But we call him the Beast.'

'Why?'

'You should know. A right nasty piece of work, that one. But he pays.'

'I must get back, Lil, now he's here.'

'Sooner you than me, Mabel love.'

'Quickly, Lil: when, where can I see you again?'

'Oh, so you're not too grand to know your little sister after all. Most evenings you'll find me at the Empire Promenade. If I'm lucky not after eight. Don't look so shocked. I'm the same as you even if I don't do it in a swanky St John's Wood 'residence'. Well, tata for now.'

The next minute Lily was gone, swallowed up in the deepening twilight and thickening fog. Mabel felt a peculiar revulsion at having to enter through the gate of Number 2 under the eye of the groom. She had barely noticed him before. He stared at her while he held the horses and breathed steam into their nostrils to calm them. Greying blackish curls sprang from under a greasy forage cap. His face was deeply lined; there was an old, hungry look about him.

When Mabel entered the house, Mrs Belling said: 'Where have you *been*? Come on, girl, he's here.'

'I know,' said Mabel and hurried upstairs to undress.

She came down stairs with the other girls. There were four of them: Effie, Mabel, Rose and Charlotte and they all wore thin robes of Chinese silk over their naked bodies. Effie, Rose and Charlotte were giggling but Mabel was silent. In the drawing room all the furniture had been moved to the edges of the room. Mrs Belling was sitting (fully dressed) at an upright piano. Candles in elaborate brass sconces illuminated the sheet music on the piano's stand. She was practising 'Ta-ra-ra Boomdeay' which was giving her some trouble.

'Quiet now, girls,' said Mrs Belling. 'I can't hear myself play with you giggling away like that.' There was silence while Mrs Belling launched into 'Ta-ra-ra Boomdeay' once more, at a very sedate pace, but this time all her notes were correct. Her cheeks glowed in the light of the candles that flanked her. The parlour maid entered with a large plate of jam tarts on a black lacquered tray and placed them on a side table. She paused for a moment as if she wanted to stay, but Mrs Belling looked up from her piano and nodded fiercely to dismiss her. Soon after she had left, the Minotaur entered the room.

His huge white body was naked save for a mask which covered the upper part of his face. The mask was black and fringed with woolly black hair, and two black horns shaped like those of a bull emerged from the temples. Above the mask a shiny bald cranium streaked with a few reddish grey hairs emerged. Beneath was a large sensual mouth with loose engorged lips whose ruby redness contrasted hideously with the almost dead white pallor of his skin. The aggressive chin was partly obscured by pendulous jowls which hung like dewlaps from his veined cheeks. The whole effect might have suggested the Minotaur to a classicist; to anyone seeing it for the first time it would have appeared merely monstrous.

The man lowered his head and peered round the room. There was something bull-like about this gesture, as if he were preparing to charge. He sauntered over to the plate of jam tarts and examined them minutely, then having selected one of them he retreated into the centre of the room. His long member, hitherto flaccid, began to show signs of arousal. With an impatient, imperious movement of his left hand he gestured to the girls who slipped off their silken robes and stood naked for his inspection. The Minotaur strutted before them, the jam tart poised on the flat of his right hand. Mrs Belling turned round from the piano and looked enquiringly at him. He nodded and she immediately launched into 'Ta-ra-ra Boomdeay'.

This was the signal for the girls to begin to dance about the room. Mabel was a better dancer than the others, and she deliberately showed off her skills while knowing that this was not what the Minotaur was looking for. The others followed her lead, and it did not please him. He stamped and growled, executing a few clumsy steps himself by way of example. He was looking for less refinement, more Bacchanalian abandon. Then, with one swift and surprisingly adroit movement the Minotaur hurled the jam tart at one of the dancing girls. It struck Rose on the left buttock with such force that she gave a little cry of pain which she rapidly converted into a whoop of abandon. That cry of pain seemed to jerk the Minotaur into full arousal. He gestured to Mrs Belling to play faster which she did, stumbling over the notes, this time of 'Daisy Bell' while the girls began to cavort around the room uttering shouts of mock ecstasy.

Meanwhile the Minotaur had picked up the plate of jam tarts and was hurling them in a frenzy at the passing girls. Then, quite suddenly, he gave a great roar, which was a signal for the music and the dancing to stop. For a space of half a minute nothing could be heard in the room except the exhausted gasps of the dancers and the Minotaur's stertorous breathing. Effie, involuntarily, let out a little giggle, and went pink with embarrassment and fear. She knew that any indication that their activities had been somehow a source of amusement displeased the Minotaur greatly.

There were three jam tarts remaining. Taking them from the plate which he unceremoniously dropped on the carpet, the Minotaur advanced towards Effie while she stood naked and now trembling in front of Mrs Belling's upright piano. Cupping one of the jam tarts in his right hand, the Minotaur came very close to Effie until she could feel his hot malodorous breath on her forehead. Then he pressed the jam tart hard into her left breast. Effie let out a scream of pain and stumbled back, almost falling over Mrs Belling as she did so. Mrs Belling rose and held Effie steadily from behind by the shoulders while the Minotaur, with even greater force, slapped a jam tart onto Effie's right breast. Effie cried out even louder at the pain and burst into a torrent of sobs.

Mabel, who had been standing next to her made an involuntary move forward to defend Effie from any further attack. The Minotaur turned upon her. He was almost a foot taller than her, and she could see his eyes staring down at her through the mask. She had never before seen his eyes so close to. The irises were a strange pale green colour, the whites bloodshot, the overall effect feral and malignant. Keeping his eyes on her he slowly and deliberately ground the last jam tart into the space between her thighs. Mabel stared back defiantly, determined to show no sign of weakness, suffering, or even loathing. The satisfaction of a mirrored hatred would be denied him. All the same, some satisfaction must have been achieved, and the resulting emission spilt itself on the carpet.

Another few seconds of complete silence followed before the Minotaur stamped out of the room. Mrs Belling who always kept her composure on these occasions, uttered a peremptory 'Shh!' as soon as the client had slammed the door behind him. Then, putting her index finger to her lips she rang for the maid who was close at hand and carried a dustpan and brush. Having commanded her to clear away the fragments of jam tarts and other spillages she sent the girls upstairs to wash and change without any further words.

In the upstairs room the maid had, as usual, filled a hip bath with hot water. All the girls crowded around Effie who was still in tears from the attack she had sustained. Tenderly they washed her bruised body before they attended to their own needs.

'That man must not come again,' said Mabel.

'Oh, yes? And who's going to tell Ma Belling that?' said Effie still sniffling.

'I will,' said Mabel. 'If you'll all back me.' There was a murmur of assent. It was not as wholehearted as Mabel had hoped, but she had to concede that their position was weak.

Mrs Belling frowned at their deputation, like a disappointed headmistress. She had always looked on Mabel as a favourite because of her good sense and genteel ways, and so, to find her leading what amounted to a rebellion saddened her. Perhaps it even enraged her, but Mrs Belling was a woman who kept her composure at all times. She told her girls that 'the gentleman'—she did not refer to him by his sobriquet, let alone name him—had acknowledged to her in private that he had been a little 'too rough'. Then she pointed to four sovereigns on the plate where the jam tarts had been and said that he had left 'a little extra present' for each of them, by way of recompense, and that he would be calling again as usual the following week.

Mabel was the last to take the gold and leave the room. She heard Mrs Belling call her back softly but she chose to ignore the summons. What else were they to do? The St John's Wood House was their home now.

The following Monday evening Mabel managed to get down to the West End. Monday was a day they often had off, because

Sunday was usually busy. Many gentlemen felt the need to escape from the oppressive domesticities of this 'day of rest'.

When Mabel arrived in front of the façade of the Empire in Leicester Square, she hesitated before she went in. She knew it to be foolish but she did not want to be associated with the kind of women, like her sister, who haunted the Promenade. As an unaccompanied young female she must arouse suspicion despite the stern respectability of her dress.

A broad staircase of some grandeur, flanked on both sides by globes of electric light upon elaborate wrought iron lamp stands, led up to the promenade which encircled the stalls, separated from it by waist high balustrades and Corinthian columns. It was a broad, carpeted space, sufficiently well-lit to give one a good view of the promenaders. The clock had struck six, but even at this early hour most of the men on the promenade or leaning against the bars that lined the back wall were clearly in search of company. Mabel avoided their glance.

A decorous ballet—the Empire was famous for its ballets—was proceeding on stage but nobody seemed to be paying it much attention. It was a woodland scene, painted in soft colours. Mabel allowed herself for a moment to be drawn into the landscape. Its utter unreality was what beguiled her, even its absurdity: it allowed her to believe for a moment in a better world.

She permitted herself only a moment of respite, then she was watching the promenaders. Some of the women were so well dressed that Mabel wondered how her sister could fare in such a company, but Lily did not lack boldness.

Mabel tried not to look at the women, or to attract attention, but she was searching for her sister. Guilt had been building up in her all through the week since she had seen Lily, the simple guilt of the more prosperous survivor.

'Hello, dearie, what you up to?' The woman who addressed her was tall and thin, her face heavily painted. Her evening gown was of red shot silk, not quite in the first blush of cleanliness, but still lavish.

'I'm looking for my sister,' said Mabel. 'Lily Jerome. You seen her?'

'So you're Mabel Jerome.' The woman seemed genuinely curious. 'Oh, yes. Lily talks a lot about *you*. "St John's Wood Mabel" she calls you.'

Mabel did not care for the sobriquet at all, but she did her best to conceal her distaste. 'And who are you?' she asked.

'You can call me Julia. Or Julian.' Julia laid her hand on Mabel's and she saw it was broad with strong well-formed fingers. She had no feelings of revulsion or even astonishment. The world she had entered was all mystery, and only the quest mattered.

'Have you seen Lil, today?'

'She was here earlier, dear. She found a customer.'

'Where does she live?'

'She's got a gaff off Windmill Street, but he's probably taken her to a hotel.'

'D'you know who? A regular?'

Julia bent down close to Mabel's ear. The breath smelt of gin and tobacco. Julia whispered: 'The Beast!'

'Him! What's his real name?'

'Oh, we don't know that, dear. Nobody's saying.'

The ballet was coming to an end but Mabel heard the music as in a dream. A man passing by made some remark to her but she did not hear it. Something in her had changed. Julia wandered off but Mabel pursued her and asked for further details of her sister's lodgings.

Julia's directions were vague but she found them in the end. A door in a dark alley in a cliff of dingy brick. The place reeked of bones and rubbish. Mabel found herself ashamed of her own fastidiousness. A woman in a red dress with a face to match and a jet black wig, set a little askew, opened the door and agreed reluctantly that Lily lived there but was not in at the moment and that she was behind with the rent. Mabel put a few coins into the woman's hand and followed her up a creaking wooden staircase. Other occupants looked out of their rooms as she passed and seemed troubled by her fine clothes and ladylike ways. Mabel felt equally uncomfortable, because she did not quite know what she was doing there.

The room was a shock to her, even though it was what she had expected. There was a mean threadbare rug upon the floor, a table and chair by the window, a washstand and a brass bedstead with a green tasselled silk shawl draped over the end. The gesture of flamboyance seemed curiously pathetic in these mean surroundings. Threadbare curtains of an indeterminate colour were drawn back from a grimy window. It looked out upon the alley in which someone was singing drunkenly. Mabel sat on the chair first to wait for her sister, then, when the discomfort of that became unbearable, on the bed. She felt at times as though she were staring into a mirror darkened by time, at a life that might one day be hers again.

She had waited for over an hour and the light was beginning to thicken into a foggy evening when she heard a noise upon the stairs outside. The footsteps staggered as they approached and sobbing could be heard. Mabel ran out onto the landing where Lily fell into her arms. Her face was streaked with blood and there was blood on her clothes. She had on a yellow silk shawl, tasselled, like the one draped over the end of the bed, but it was stained in several places with blood.

Lily was in such a state that she barely registered that it was her sister who was with her. Mabel laid her on the bed and gently removed her clothes. The wounds and bruises were hideous. She went down stairs and gave money to the woman in the red dress to go out and fetch bandages and hot water and a doctor if possible. When she returned, Lily was barely breathing, and it was a while before she could answer any of Mabel's questions.

Very little was coherent, but Lily mouthed the word 'Beast' and gripped Mabel's hand in hers. Mabel felt the chill of her sister's hand pass through her: it was enough.

A doctor came, a poor excuse for a doctor if ever there was one, with the blush of gin on his cheeks, and bandages were applied to the wounds. Mabel gave more money, but then had to go, leaving her address, somewhat reluctantly, in the hands of the woman in the red dress. She took her sister's bloodstained shawl with her, wrapped in brown paper.

When she arrived back at the St John's Wood house Mabel was chided by Mrs Belling for being late: Lord Arthur was waiting for her. Mabel said nothing but went up stairs to where Lord Arthur sat in an armchair complacently smoking a cigar. The smoke sickened Mabel. She contemplated Lord Arthur's soft, silly face for a moment, then smiled and moved towards him. The fact that he was harmless made her feel suddenly warm towards him. She knew her feelings had been on a knife edge since she had last looked at her bloodstained sister. She could have turned away from all men; instead she turned towards Lord Arthur, but with a purpose.

'Oh, how I've longed for you, Lord Arthur!'

'Have you? Have you, little girlie? Have you?'

She turned round and sat on his knee.

'Oh, please will 'oo undo us at the back?'

'With the greatest of pleasure, little girlie mine.'

Lord Arthur did not see her grimace as he applied himself to her laces. Almost tenderly he undid them while Mabel sighed softly and turned back to him to bestow kisses and loving glances. Lord Arthur planted kisses on the back of her neck. Mabel knew she was giving a performance but like a good actress she also to some extent felt what she was acting. It was a paradox which she had encountered before but not in such an extreme form. This time she gave herself wholeheartedly to the expression of a pretended passion, though she always kept in sight its purpose. Lord

Arthur responded with a gentler and more considered approach to lovemaking, less of the hearty rough and ready manner that he usually adopted. He slid off her bodice with a practised hand and let his fingers play gently with the nipples of her breasts.

The unexpected tenderness and fervour of Mabel's subsequent lovemaking had its desired effect. It put Lord Arthur in the mood for conversation, but she knew she must tread carefully and not make her intentions obvious. She allowed him to tell her the funny stories that he had told her before. She giggled and kicked her legs in the air which aroused his playfulness once again, but she never for a moment forgot the wretched bruised and bloody girl lying in the bare Soho bedroom. At last, as Lord Arthur was dressing, and she was helping him in the neat, fussy way that amused him, she said:

'I think I saw our friend the Minotaur in the West End, the other day.'

'Oh, really! Old *semibovem*! What was he up to, then?'

'On the Empire Promenade.'

'And what was a respectable little girlie doing there? You ought to be ashamed of yourself.'

'I'm friends with some of the dancers. Do you know, they call him *The Beast* there?'

'Do they by Jove?'

'But they don't know his real name.'

'Aha!'

'And you do.'

'Do I, girlie?'

'You said so.'

'Did I, Miss Mouse?'

'You did, Mr Big Black Pussycat. And you can tell your Miss Mouse because she won't tell a soul else.'

'But why does little Miss Mouse want to know?'

'Just because she's a curious Miss Mouse who likes to share a secret with her big brave pussy cat. He can whisper it in her ear.'

And he did, and she kissed him tenderly for it, but then wondered what it was she could possibly do with the information. The following morning a message was delivered to Mabel informing her that Lily had been taken to the poor hospital at St Giles's where she had died from her injuries.

Mabel told Mrs Belling merely that her sister had met with a fatal accident and was given time off to make arrangements for the funeral and attend it. Her mother was drunk at the grave side and Mabel spurned her when she attempted to beg a few shillings off her. She later sent her some money but her mind was all fire and ice. She spent her remaining free time in the local library with a gazetteer looking up a certain Mr Frederick Cooper whom she discovered to be living not far from Mrs Belling's in Melina Grove NW.

Mabel did not tell the police, knowing what a world of trouble to no good effect that would unleash, but she did confide in Effie. Effie, she knew, had conceived an almost equal hatred of the Minotaur and would faithfully infect the other girls. She made a suitably fervent and vindictive confidant, so much so that she became almost impatient with Mabel for the slowness and deliberation with which she matured her plans. Otherwise, business went on as normal. Clients came and went, but the Minotaur did not come. Effie acquired an admirer in an elderly Baronet. It was almost as good (in Effie's eyes) as Lord Arthur, but not quite.

One afternoon towards the end of October a very respectable-looking young lady carrying a brown paper parcel rang the front door bell of Number 1 Melina Grove. To the parlour maid who opened the door she presented a card bearing the legend;

Mrs L. Prentice
Society for the Reclamation of Fallen Women

A MAZE FOR THE MINOTAUR

When she asked to see Mr Cooper the servant replied that he was out for a drive, but would be back shortly. The lady looked a little flustered and said that an appointment had been made: perhaps she could wait? Was Mrs Cooper at home by any chance? Perhaps she could see her: she was sure that Mrs Cooper would be acquainted with her husband's most generous and charitable patronage of her little society.

The maid seemed dubious, but the lady appeared so earnest and respectable that it was hard to refuse such an innocent request. Besides Mrs Cooper went about so little, saw so few people that a little company might do her good. Those were the servant's thoughts as she ushered Mabel into the Minotaur's drawing room.

It was a pleasant enough room, lavishly furnished and decorated in a style which was now becoming distinctly unfashionable. Rich and sombre colours predominated. A profusion of ornaments decorated available surfaces. Oil paintings depicting cattle basking in sunlight or drinking from tranquil pools and other rustic scenes all but obliterated the heavily-patterned, sage green wallpaper.

In a corner, by the window in the sunlight sat a plump little woman doing embroidery. She looked up startled when Mabel entered. Mabel caught a smell of fear and smiled at a reaction which she might have predicted.

'I'm afraid my husband—'

'Mrs Cooper, how delightful to meet you at last. I have heard so much about you from your husband.'

'Oh, have you? Oh, really?' It would seem that this innocent remark had intensified Mrs Cooper's agitation.

'May I be seated?'

Mrs Cooper nodded nervously.

Mabel proceeded to explain very gently how Mr Cooper had been taking a great philanthropic interest in the Reclamation of Fallen Women. Mrs Cooper was very surprised at this.

A MAZE FOR THE MINOTAUR

'I am afraid, Mrs Prentice, I was not aware—'

'Ah! Such is the way of some philanthropists, Mrs Cooper. They are too modest for their own good; they hide their light under a bushel. Does not the bard say: "The evil that men do lives after them, the good is oft interred with their bones"?'

Mabel did not quite know why she had made the last remark. It just seemed appropriate to the occasion, and the genteel piety of her assumed character. She had picked it up from Lord Arthur who was fond of his little tags. At that moment the door opened and the Minotaur entered the room. As soon as he saw Mabel the pale, flabby face became suffused with spots of colour, the eyes were enraged.

Both women rose but Mabel advanced swiftly towards him extending her hand.

'Lily Prentice, the Reclamation of Fallen Women. So nice to meet you at last, Mr Cooper, on your "home territory", as it were!' She gave a genteel little laugh.

The Minotaur stood astonished, baffled, almost fearful. At last he said: 'Mary, my dear. Would you excuse us? This lady and I have some business to discuss.'

Mrs Cooper picked up her embroidery and hurried from the room. Several seconds of silence followed the closing of the door. The Minotaur went to open it and looked out. Only the parlour maid was standing in the hall and he shooed her away with an impatient gesture. Then he turned and bore down on Mabel who stood her ground.

The man's extraordinary pallor had restored itself. At a distance the Minotaur's face might have resembled a lump of dough with a gash in it for a mouth and above it two currants buried rather too close together, for eyes.

'What the devil is all this about?' He scrutinised her. 'Have I seen you before?'

'Oh, yes, Mr Cooper. At Number 2 Boscobel Place. Why do you no longer visit us?'

'What do you want, damn you?'

'Oh, Mr Cooper! That is no way to talk to a lady.'

'You're not a lady, you're a damned little whore!'

'And you are no gentleman, sir. You're nothing but a beast, a Minotaur!'

The Minotaur stared at her in silence as Mabel coolly turned her back on him and went to the chair on which she had laid her brown paper parcel.

'I have something for you,' she said. Turning again she held the parcel out to him. 'Open it!' She could see the hesitation, the stubbornness in his eyes. He was afraid of surrender. 'Open it, please, Mr Minotaur!'

He snatched the parcel from her, tore it open and drew out a yellow, tasselled silk shawl. It was smeared with the brown stains of dried blood.

'What the devil—?'

'It belonged to my sister Lily. Do you remember her? The Empire Promenade?'

'What is it you want, damn you? Money, I suppose?'

'No. I want you to have it cleaned and then return it to me.'

'What? Why?'

'And then I want you to start coming to Boscobel Place again.'

'But why, damn you? Why?'

'Why do you like jam tarts so much?'

By this time, the fury in him was eating him up. Mabel could see that he was longing to seize her and hurl her through the window, but the surroundings held him back. The slight fear that he might break into violence added something piquant to the pleasure Mabel felt at the sight of this twitching, defeated lump of a man.

'I will call for the shawl at this precise hour in a week's time when you will receive further instructions,' she said. 'And now, if you will excuse me?'

The Minotaur put his vast bulk between her and the door.

Mabel said: 'What would you like me to do? Shall I call for the servant? I am sure she cannot be far away.'

The Minotaur stepped aside. 'Be very careful, little girlie,' he said.

'Thank you, Mr Minotaur. I will be.' A pleasant fleeting smile and she was out of the door. As she had expected, the parlour maid was on hand in the hall to open the street door for her. Mabel told her that she had made an appointment to call on her master at the same time next week, and would be glad to see Mrs M—Mrs Cooper also. Then Mabel was out into the light misty air of autumn. She breathed heavily and fought back the spasm of hysterical laughter that threatened to overwhelm her.

During the following days Mabel barely ventured out of Boscobel Place. Mrs Belling noticed that she was even more docile and well-behaved than usual, but that if she ever entered a room when Mabel and some other girls were present, their conversation stopped or became more subdued. Fortunately Mrs Belling was not a suspicious woman. She remained confident of maintaining one of the most successful and 'respectable' houses of assignation, as she chose to call it, in London. Had they not been visited on several occasions by Royalty?

The following Wednesday Mabel rang the bell at Melina Grove at the hour appointed.

'Mrs Prentice to see Mr Cooper.' It was a fine, coppery autumn evening in the Wood. The parlour maid smiled as she let Mabel in and studied her curiously. But she knew nothing, surely: she could not.

'Mr Cooper is in the drawing room,' she said.

'And Mrs Cooper?'

'Upstairs, ma'am. Would you like to see her, ma'am?'

'No. I shall not stay long. But if you would remain in the hall to let me out.'

'Very good, ma'am.' and she opened the drawing room door and announced Mrs Prentice to its occupant.

The Minotaur stood with his back to the fire, hands clasped behind him. He had taken up a position where his gigantic frame might be seen to its best advantage. Mabel was so amused by this assumption of threat that she almost forgot her loathing of the man. Over these last days her mood had become steadier, less febrile.

The Minotaur pointed to a brown paper parcel on a low table before him.

'I have had it cleaned as you requested. Now take it and go.' The venomous contempt with which he spoke aroused Mabel's hatred again. Coolly, taking her time, she opened the parcel and examined the shawl.

'There are still traces of blood, here and here,' she said, pointing to them. 'Not good enough! Have it cleaned again!' She threw the shawl in his face and drew back two paces, knowing the risk she had taken. The Minotaur did not deign to catch it; the shawl fell from his face to the ground. For a brief moment it looked as if a monument were being unveiled.

He stood still, paralysed by the shock of her affront. Fiery threads of blood vessels pulsated in his cheeks. His eyes glistened darkly like two tiny shards of pure jet.

Quickly, before he could speak or move, she said: 'This time next week you will come to us in Boscobel Place. Bring the shawl, clean this time, and come alone. Do not bring the groom. We can mind the horses while you are with us if you choose to drive. Then we can bring this matter to a conclusion. Fail to obey these instructions and you know what the consequences will be. Good afternoon, Mr Minotaur!'

Mabel left the room without a backward glance, closing the door behind her. She was relieved to find the parlour maid in the hall.

'I am afraid I must leave. Will you give my very warmest regards to Mrs Cooper?'

The parlour maid dropped a curtsey. 'Yes'm!' And she led her to the front door. Just then both of them distinctly heard a howl of rage coming from beyond the drawing room door.

'Mr Cooper is much vexed,' said Mabel in a confidential undertone to the maid. 'One of our *protegées* has met with a most distressing fatality. I would advise you not to disturb your master for as long as possible.'

The parlour maid nodded her head and dropped another curtsey. Her hand was white and trembling as she opened the front door for Mabel.

Mabel informed Mrs Belling of the proposed visit of the Minotaur the following Wednesday. Naturally she was asked how this had come about, to which Mabel replied, with a certain cool politeness with which Mrs Belling had begun to be familiar, that she was sorry, but she was not at liberty to say. With the other girls she was more forthcoming about what was to occur. To Mrs Belling she only said that the customer would be arriving by carriage without a groom and that Mrs Mason the housekeeper could attend to the horses during his stay. Mrs Belling nodded, but made no comment.

And he came at his usual time of three in the afternoon. Mrs Belling smiled upon him and the girls smiled to themselves. One incident puzzled Mrs Belling. As he encountered Mabel in the hallway, he thrust a brown paper parcel into her hands with such an aggressive gesture and such a dark look that even Mabel's composure was shaken, if only for a moment.

When, having disrobed and put on his mask, the Minotaur entered the drawing room, he felt, as all did except Mrs Belling, a certain tension. She began to play 'After the Ball is Over' while the girls shed their silken robes. On the side table, as before, was the plate of jam tarts. The Minotaur clapped his hands and the girls began dancing slowly around him, nodding and winking at him as they passed by. He clapped again, a signal for the music and the dancing to become more abandoned. Mrs Belling changed to 'Ta-ra-ra Boomdeay'. The Minotaur threw his first jam tart. It hit Effie on the thigh and she let out a little shriek. This was enough to arouse the Minotaur who bellowed his satisfaction. He picked up another jam tart to throw but just then somebody behind him stripped him of his mask and blindfolded him. Before all went dark he could see the gold tasselled fringes of Lily's yellow shawl dance in front of him. He was about to raise objections when he found that a handkerchief was being stuffed into his mouth. Somebody clapped to increase the pace and volume of the music. Mrs Belling, oblivious to all else applied herself diligently to her tune while the girls surrounded the Minotaur pressing their naked flesh to his and leading his staggering body onwards he knew not where.

A strange sensation overcame the Minotaur, a mixture of bafflement, fear and arousal, but above all of a complete absence of power which almost seduced him. Soft hands caressed him; soft breasts pressed against him; a tongue was at work as he was drawn away from the music in the drawing room towards a wider, cooler space. The hallway? Then something struck him on the back of the head and he was tumbling down some stairs. There was a moment of bleak, intense revelation before the void swallowed his shrivelled soul.

The girls contemplated the great white body crumpled at the foot of the stairs.

'Do you think he's gone?' said Effie.

Mabel laid down the poker she had just wielded and said, 'I will go and make certain.' So, still naked, she walked down the stairs. On reaching the bottom she crouched over the body to feel for a pulse in his neck, pulling the handkerchief from his mouth as she did so, and removing his blindfold. Then she straightened up, nodded solemnly and said: 'He's gone all right.'

In the sitting room Mrs Belling had not ceased from hammering away at 'Ta-ra-ra Boomdeay'.

She only did so when one of the girls interrupted her playing to tell her what had happened: apparently the Minotaur had chased some of them out into the hall, then lost his balance, tripped and fell down the uncarpeted stone steps leading to the servants' quarters in the basement. Mrs Belling reacted at first with hysterics, but her agitation was alleviated by the fact that her girls, despite being still dressed only in their silken robes, were behaving so calmly. No suspicion entered her head at that moment. When it did later on, it was far too late to do anything about it and was quickly suppressed.

The idea of summoning the police was soon rejected. Mrs Belling's, as she insisted, was a 'respectable house', and such a discovery would do irreparable damage to her reputation and that of her girls. It was then that Mabel intervened.

She reminded them that the Minotaur's phaeton was still outside their house guarded by Mason, the housekeeper. She therefore suggested that Charlotte, the tallest of the girls, should dress in the Minotaur's clothes and drive the phaeton round to Melina Grove and leave it in the mews behind the Minotaur's house. Mrs Belling wondered for a moment how Mabel had come by the address, but discreetly chose not to ask.

Charlotte was not as vast in size as the Minotaur, naturally, but it was a misty afternoon, and she was a big girl. She could pass for Mr Cooper in the twilight. Moreover, she had the advantage of knowing something about horses, her father having been an ostler before the drink took him.

The rest of the girls, under the supervision of Mabel, would take care of the body. The servants would have to be informed, if they did not know already, for the body had fallen into their domain, but they would be discreet. It was in their interest as much as everyone else's. This, as Mrs Belling had so often said, was a respectable house.

The corpse was dragged into the pantry and lifted with much difficulty into a capacious butler's sink. Then the kitchen maid was sent round to borrow a saw from their local butcher's. She told the butcher it was to cut up some game presented to them by a noble client. The butcher offered to perform the task himself, but the kitchen maid, with a nervous smile, said that they were quite adequate to the task themselves.

It was Mabel who did most of the sawing. Mrs Belling, who never actually ventured down into the servant's quarters herself, was surprised that Mabel was so willing to undertake this sordid task, but she was becoming used to the girl's surprising qualities and even though Mrs Belling had not quite admitted this, to relying on them.

Parts of the Minotaur were then boiled or minced and fed to the kitchen cat. The rest of him was put piecemeal into the great stove which had recently been installed to heat the new hot water boiler for the house. The calcined bones were raked out and placed in a sack along with some mutton bones that also needed to be disposed of. The Minotaur's clothing was cut up and either made into dishcloths, or put into another sack for the rag and bone man. All this was conducted under Mabel's patient and untiring supervision.

About four days after the Minotaur's disappearance, the Police called to make enquiries. They spoke to Mrs Belling respectfully in the knowledge that the local Commissioner was an occasional visitor to her establishment. Mrs Belling, with Mabel seated beside her, had of course known of the man in the phaeton and had seen him pass by on frequent occasions, but not on the afternoon of his vanishing. The Police went away unsuspecting.

Then came the afternoon, bitter cold it was and misty as usual, when the rag and bone man called. His chant, heard from afar off, was to Mabel like a summons to the last rites or to a funeral. Rather to Mrs Belling's disapproval Mabel helped the kitchen maid take out the sacks of rag and bone which were the final remnants of the Minotaur and place them on the old man's cart.

A MAZE FOR THE MINOTAUR

To Mabel, this last act was a necessity, the curtain call to the drama in which she had played such a prominent role.

This done, she came indoors, poured herself a cup of tea and sat at the drawing room window to watch the light die in the street outside. When it is spent, a great passion—hatred or the other kind—leaves behind an emptiness. 'The evil that men do lives after them . . .' No. Lord Arthur, or Shakespeare, or whoever it was, was wrong. Nothing lives after them: good or evil: it is all carried away by the rag and bone man.

'Rag-a-bone! Rag-a-bone!' cried the man on the cart as he disappeared into the mist. Mabel turned away from the window. Her eyes were moist.

'Dry your tears, lovey,' said Mrs Belling. 'Look, there's Lord Arthur come to see you.'

'Give me a few minutes, and then show him up, Mrs Belling,' said Mabel. Mrs Belling was surprised, even a little indignant. Mabel's tone had not been imperious, but it was firm and indicated a certain authority. An irrevocable change had taken place. Mrs Belling hesitated for a moment, wondering whether she should reassert herself by pinching Miss Mabel's pale cheeks as she had done so often before, but she thought better of it. She merely nodded and went down to usher in Lord Arthur.

Mabel turned back to the window. The mist had thickened. Long after all sight of the man and his cart were gone, the chant of 'Rag-a-bone! Rag-a-bone!' echoed through the twilit Grove of the Evangelist.

SHADOWY WATERS

SHADOWY WATERS

Forgael: Where the world ends
The mind is made unchanging, for it finds
Miracle, ecstasy, the impossible hope
The flagstone under all, the fire of fires,
The roots of the world.
       W.B. Yeats, *The Shadowy Waters*

Returning to Alderness was both an end and a beginning. There a grey North Sea hurries to and fro over the shingle beach, and the wide skies offer bleak tranquillity. For some it is a holiday resort; but it is also a place to which people of a certain wealth and distinction retire. There they may sail, or golf, or play bridge. The more intellectually minded among them join book clubs, or choirs, and listen to string quartets in country churches on Sunday afternoons. There are plenty of activities here to fill the time between redundancy and death, but I had not come to retire.

Shortly after my wife Margaret died, an old friend, Nell Harkness, had written to me. She had seen the announcement in *The Daily Telegraph*. I was both surprised and touched because, beyond the odd Christmas card, we had not been in contact for many years; besides, I would not have considered the *Telegraph* to be Nell's newspaper of choice. I wrote a letter back expressing thanks for her condolences, but also indicating, politely I hope, a certain reserve. There were elements in her letter which reminded me why our relationship, ended some years before my marriage, had not flourished.

'I am sure,' she had written, 'that Margaret's spirit has not deserted you, but is still looking over you from the everlasting wings of the world's stage. All true love is immortal.' Someone quicker to take offence than I might have felt that Nell was being presumptuous; I just thought, 'typical Nell!' Though the notion that my wife's spirit was still around was one which I did not for a moment seriously entertain, her reference to it, I must admit, made me uneasy. Once or twice I caught myself, metaphorically looking for Margaret over my shoulder.

I was glad when, in the letter she wrote in response to mine, she said no more about watchful spirits; and I was relieved that she did not appear to have spotted the slight coolness in my words to her, as I was beginning to feel slightly ashamed of them.

She began to tell me a little about herself. She was unmarried—indeed she had never married which surprised me—and ran a little shop in the Suffolk coastal town of Alderness. The shop, called *Mandala*, sold mystic paraphernalia: packs of tarot cards, crystals, dowsing rods, astrological charts, yoga mats, books on occult subjects, that kind of thing. I could see it in my mind's eye, and her behind the counter with her long, curly golden hair (now almost certainly greying), wearing perhaps an embroidered kaftan, with an ankh on a silver chain about her neck. 'I don't do a roaring trade,' she wrote, 'but I make a living. The place has a favourable spiritual aspect.' That was her sole reference in her second letter to matters of spirit, and I was thankful for that. However, her mention of Alderness made me uneasy; because it was there, almost forty years ago, that we had first met and known each other.

Subsequent to this exchange of letters we communicated via email. Once or twice she suggested that I should come down to see her in Alderness. I riposted by writing that, if she ever ventured up to London, I would like to take her out to lunch. It was that kind of correspondence. Then came an email which told me, in her characteristic roundabout way, that she was seriously ill. It was only then that I realised I must see her. I suggested a date, but received no reply. Instead a letter came from a solicitor informing me that Nell had died suddenly. It told me in addition to the date and time of the funeral that I had been appointed one of two executors of her will.

Being her executor was an annoyance I could have done without. At the same time, I felt that the service I had failed to do in life, I could at least render her after death. It would be an expiation of sorts, as I was ashamed of my irritation with her.

I made an appointment to see the solicitor the day before the funeral and booked myself in for a few days at the Hotel Metropole, Alderness which looked, from its online profile, reassuringly old-fashioned and expensive. I saw no reason why I should not do myself well. I was a retired headmaster, a widower, childless with an adequate pension and no indecent habits, except for a certain idleness, the result of a lifetime of hard and mostly uncongenial work.

I had not been back to Alderness for nearly forty years. There are those who enjoy returning to the scenes of their youth; I do not. On the few occasions that I have tried, the experience has been curiously dispiriting, like viewing the corpse of a loved one. I suppose it is because such revisits inevitably disappoint expectations. The spell of nostalgic imagination is shattered by reality: it is only a location like any other, after all, not a magic realm.

Alderness had been the first place where I was completely and uninhibitedly happy, and perhaps the last. I am fully aware that memory has a way of creating extremes, of either blackening or gilding the past, but I think there is some truth in my statement.

In my hot youth, before I had reluctantly taken on the secure financial path of teaching, I had been an actor. For a brief while I had flourished, and one of my first engagements was in a summer season of plays at the Jubilee Theatre, Alderness. There was a young woman there, in her first professional job, assistant stage managing and playing small parts. I think she was the most beautiful person I had ever seen, and her name was Nell Harkness.

It had been early summer when I first came to Alderness over forty years ago; now in my second coming it was late autumn. The bay window of my hotel room overlooked the sea from the second floor, and as I unpacked before it, I consoled myself with the thought that at least my being here had a purpose. A gull screamed past my window and settled itself on a ledge close by. It was an unusually large creature which turned its head sideways on, so as to examine me through one bold eye. Its scrutiny was cold and inhuman but, it seemed to me, not unintelligent. I waved it away, but it did not move. The glacial stare persisted. I looked at my watch: I was due to meet the solicitor in half an hour.

Mrs Watson was her name, middle aged—younger than me—smiling and pleasantly formal. I am not usually sensitive about these things but I was faintly aware of her seeming rather relieved when she saw me. Perhaps she was reassured by my appearance which was distinctly conventional: a suit and a tie, spectacles, tidy hair (what there was of it). There may have been a connection with the first question she asked me.

'Have you met your co-executor, Mr Souter?'

'No.'

'Ah. Yes. It's a Mr Hamilton Souter. Slightly strange name.' She seemed pained that I should be subjected to an oddly named person. I liked Mrs Watson for her sensitivity, even though I wasn't bothered. 'I hope you don't mind: I told him you were staying at the Metropole. He seemed anxious to speak with you.'

'Well, that seems understandable.'

Mrs Watson made no reply; evidently, she was not so sure. Mrs Watson then explained the will to me. It was relatively straightforward. There were a few small bequests to local people and institutions. I was surprised to find that I had been left two thousand pounds and my choice of several items in her house by which I was to remember her. But the bulk of her fortune which, to my surprise, was considerable, including the proceeds of the sale of her shop and house (the same building), was to go to a Donkey Sanctuary, called Thelma's Haven, some miles inland from Alderness.

A silence followed the digestion of these facts. I had no comment to make. Then Mrs Watson cleared her throat, a sign of embarrassment, or possibly inner conflict.

'I must tell you, Mr Villiers,' she said to me, 'that shortly before Miss Harkness died, she rang me up to say that she had written and had witnessed another will which she would have delivered to me the following day. Unfortunately, she became very seriously ill that night. She was taken to hospital and never returned home. The will has not been found.'

'Does Mr Souter know about this second will?'

'I believe so, but we did not inform him.'

I recognised a world of professional discretion in this remark. My own late profession often demanded the same quality, so I accepted the inference and asked no further questions about it. Before we took our leave, I asked if she would be attending the funeral the next day.

'No, Mr Villiers. I'm afraid not. As a matter of fact, that reminds me. I should have told you before. The venue has been changed. It's no longer at St Jude's.'

'Why is that?'

'Mr Souter was put in charge of arrangements and he made the alteration in spite of Miss Harkness having communicated to me that a burial service at St Jude's was what she wanted.'

'I see.'

'He will inform you of the venue.'

Shortly after that we took our leave of each other. It was about a ten minute walk back to the Metropole which took me along the front. It was a bright day but windy, the kind that invites brisk movement, not contemplative loitering, but I stopped in front of the Jubilee Theatre with its ornate red brick Victorian front, designed by Matcham. It had long since passed out of the domain of actors and had become a night club of sorts with bars, discotheques and special nights of 'live music'. Had I remained on the stage I might perhaps have experienced a pang of sentimental regret at this point but I felt none. I had passed my life among the young long enough to know that everything has its day, or hour. That of the French window, the exit round and the gun shot that brings down the first act curtain had long gone. What replaced it was no better and no worse; and very soon something else would succeed it.

I paused again—reluctantly because the wind was decidedly chill—when I came close to the pier. It had been on the shingly sand beneath its black skeletal legs that Nell and I had first consummated our love. That is one way of putting it. It was late one night and a full moon, I remember. The wonderful corkscrew curls of her golden hair were silvered, but her face was in shadow.

I stood, leaning on the iron railing that bordered the esplanade and looked towards where it had happened. The tide was in and the waters were almost lapping the spot. Out of the corner of my eye a gull had come to perch on the railing. It seemed to be scrutinising me, perhaps in expectation of some titbit.

A part of me knows that the event had in reality been perfunctory, uncomfortable, and had left me emotionally drained, even a little mortified. There was anxiety that others might see us, even though it was the early hours of the morning and the beach was deserted. Yet the event was baptised by my imagination, spiritualised through romantic detail—shadowy waters under the moon, the susurrus of the waves, a distant cry of gulls; while close to me was the moan of ecstasy and the touch of silken flesh. All this remains as vivid and as true to me as the awkward reality. I have two memories of the same happening, and I reject neither.

The gull was edging towards me along the railing. Its eye was more human than the last that I had seen. Rather than cold curiosity it appeared to show concern. The head then turned away and the back of it looked for a moment as if it were a mass of tiny white curls, but it flew away before I could confirm the impression, so that could easily be dismissed as a passing illusion. I walked from the esplanade across the road to my hotel.

Upon arrival at the Metropole, I was informed at reception that there was a someone waiting to see me. A smallish, stout man rose from a sofa in the entrance hall and advanced towards the reception desk.

'Mr Villiers? Hamilton Souter. Pleased to meet you.' I shook a damp hand.

So, this was Mr Souter. A man in his late forties or perhaps fifties with sandy hair; he wore a tweed jacket, a mustard coloured waistcoat, and green trousers. The impression of a fogeyish dandy was enhanced by a pair of side whiskers, and a silk cravat of white spots on a red ground. I have no strong objections to unconventional attire, but I was wary. I asked Mr Souter if he would have tea with me in the lounge.

He said 'I won't have tea. It interferes with the chakras—the spiritual portals of the body, you know.'

'I am familiar with the term.' I had not been a headmaster for nothing.

'But I'll have a whisky and soda if I may.'

I ordered tea and a whisky and soda, and we went into the lounge which was pleasantly empty. We found ourselves a table and two chairs by the window overlooking the sea.

'Most people might say that whisky interferes with the chakras more than tea,' I said once we had sat down.

'I am not most people.'

The last remark was made without a smile, or a hint at self-deprecating irony. I was beginning to feel uneasy in Mr Souter's presence. He was quite well-informed about who I was—facts almost certainly gathered by a trawl of the Internet—but was anxious to find out how I had known Nell. Sensing that Souter was a man who gathers facts to use as ammunition, I was vague, merely saying that I knew her from 'way back' and we had got in touch again after many years. Before he could pursue me for more detail, I retaliated by asking about his relations with her.

'Oh, we were very close, you know. She had great spiritual gifts so we bonded on that. She was part of a small development group which I run.'

'You're a spiritualist?' He raised his eyebrows in surprise at my recognition of the term he used.

'Not strictly speaking as such. I have my own ideas, so I am not a member of any major organisation. We have mediumistic sessions, but not in the normal sense of the word. Our intention is to communicate with Higher Beings. You will meet some of our group tomorrow.'

'I understand you have changed the venue of the funeral.'

'Oh, yes. St Jude's was quite unsuitable. Nell never went in for that dreary C. of E. nonsense.'

'Mrs Watson said that was what Nell had requested.'

'She must have got it wrong. You know these solicitors . . . We are holding our little ceremony at the Unitarian Chapel in Nelson Street. Our group sometimes hires the place and has meetings there. The Unitarians are harmless, you know.' He paused, then added with a slight smirk: 'they barely believe in anything, as a matter of fact.'

I was tempted to ask what exactly *he* believed in as I would have liked to know more, but I kept my peace. It could have involved an argument. Instead we began to discuss the will and it was then that I made a slight *faux pas*.

I said: 'It appears from her will that she has left nearly all her money to one of those absurd animal charities. A Donkey Sanctuary of some sort.'

'—and Crematorium.'

'I'm sorry?'

'It is a Donkey Sanctuary and Donkey Crematorium. For those who wish to dispose of their beloved dead donkeys with dignity, and preserve the ashes as a memento. Very few funerary crematoria can cope with donkeys, you see.'

'You seem to know a lot about it.'

'I am in charge of the concern. You might say that I have dedicated my life to it.'

'Ah. My apologies.' Souter ignored them.

'We can do horses by special request. Dogs too, cats, the occasional guinea-pig. . . . No rats or rabbits, naturally. Definitely no parrots and that sort of thing. There is a "chapel" and we perform a simple ceremony—entirely non-denominational of course—suitable for most small and large quadrupeds. We were once asked to handle a dead circus elephant called Bruno, but, alas, that was beyond our capacities.' My silence was taken for suspicion. 'It is an entirely charitable and not for profit venture,' he added.

'I see.' I didn't.

The lounge window where we sat looked out onto the esplanade towards the sea. On the railing that bordered the esplanade on the seaward side, perched a row of six or seven gulls directly opposite where we sat. They appeared to be watching us, an absurd notion of course; but I noticed that when he spotted them Souter became uneasy.

'Well,' he said, 'I must be on my way. I will see you at our little funeral gathering on the morrow. Perhaps we can meet later at Nell's house. I believe Mrs Watson has given you the key?' I nodded, noting a hint of disapproval in Souter's tone.

He lowered his voice to a confidential murmur. 'I think it's best we go over the place together. Decide on the disposal of items and so forth. Or if you prefer, I am quite happy if you left it all to me.'

'No,' I said. 'I don't think that's what Nell would have wanted.' Souter gave a tight little smile at this.

'Right ho, then! I'll say cheery bye for now!' There was something distinctly forced about the jollity of these antiquated expressions. As he got up from his seat and we shook hands the row of gulls also rose from their railing and took wing in a fanfare of squawks.

I was glad to see him go. Had I found Souter congenial I might have invited him to dine with me; instead I ate alone in the quiet Metropole dining room with a half bottle of Burgundy. It soothed me, and settled the day's events. After dinner I decided not to go for an evening stroll: the memories I might evoke would be too strong for me.

I was one of the first to arrive at the funeral. I had had a restless night of abstract unease, but far from exhausting me, it had made me curiously awake in a way that I had not felt for a long time.

The chapel was, as I had expected, an aesthetically null brick box, as dismal inside as it was without. In the centre of the hall on two trestles was the coffin. It was made of wicker, no doubt an ecologically sound choice.

Souter, dressed exactly as he had been on the previous day, was standing near the coffin with a group of undertakers. He was instructing them and they appeared to defer, though once or twice I saw them glance at each other uncertainly. When Souter saw me, he came over to address me.

'Ah! Glad you could come, Villiers,' he said jauntily encircling my hand in the now familiar damp grasp. Did he really think I might stay away? 'It will be very informal. I will say a few words. There will be a reading. I will lead the company in a little meditation. Very much as the spirit directs, as we say. By the way . . . did you wish to say a few of the "well-chosen"?'

'Well, I have not been asked to.'

'You're very welcome, of course. It's all quite informal.'

'No. I don't think so.'

'Fine! Fine! Just as you like.' And he patted my shoulder, provoking a surge of anger in me, which soon subsided. Someone began to play a meandering succession of murmurs on the organ. About a dozen elderly people of both sexes trickled into the hall to attend the event. They all appeared to know Souter. One of them, a small woman with a hat like a crushed raspberry on her head came and sat beside me.

'Hello,' she said, 'I'm Betty Caker. Mrs. Have you come to hear Mr Souter?'

'No, I'm an old friend of Nell Harkness.'

'Oh, I see. I didn't know her that well.'

'Then why are you here?'

'She was part of our little group. Led by Mr Souter. You have to show willing. Not that I had anything against her.'

I said: 'I am glad to hear it.' She did not seem to notice the irony.

'You're not from round here, are you?' said Mrs Caker.

'No.'

'So, you don't know Mr Souter.'

'We have met.'

'Mr Souter is a very spiritual man. He is always in touch with the Higher Powers.'

'I am glad to hear it,' I said. This time Mrs Caker caught the note of dryness in my voice.

'You should hear what he has to say,' she said sternly.

'No doubt I will.' Mrs Caker said nothing, but gave an emphatic sniff.

The service, if it can be described as such, was uninspiring. Informality can be as drab as its opposite. Its main feature was an all but interminable address from Souter which I could have borne more easily if it had been about Nell and her life. But he uttered nothing beyond generalities and that: 'she was a valued member of our little company of seekers.' The rest consisted in portentously vague statements about life and death, with constant references to the 'higher beings' and their teaching. I did not find it very illuminating but Mrs Caker evidently did. Several times during Souter's speech she nudged me, nodding vigorously, as if urging me to attend to some especially important point of doctrine.

Then an elderly man in a heavy overcoat got up and stumbled through Canon Henry Scott Holland's: 'Death is nothing at all. I have only slipped away to the next room . . .' I have occasionally heard this piece read at funerals, and never cared for it, even when read less execrably than it was on this occasion. I had to admit, though, that given what Nell had written to me in her letter of condolence, *she* might have approved.

SHADOWY WATERS

Finally, the organ began its aimless mumblings again, while the undertaker's men picked up the wicker coffin from the trestles and bore it out of a side door of the chapel. The rest of us followed, Souter leading.

Behind the Unitarian chapel was a small burial ground surrounded by a high brick wall. It was not well kept. The grass was tall between the stubby grey-green burial slabs; tall nettles hung over the far corners of the plot. A cloudless autumn sky did something to mitigate the gloom of the scene. The coffin was placed across two planks which bridged an oblong hole in the ground.

I remembered the last funeral I had been to, that of my wife Margaret. How different! There the ceremony, in my local Anglican church, had been soothing, full of affectionate remembrance and consolation, almost cheerful. And yet, throughout that event Margaret had been conspicuously absent for me. The tributes, so kindly meant, seemed to me to be about someone not quite real, like a character in a book. My own memories were barren. I could barely even picture to myself what she looked like, and constantly throughout the ceremony I had stared at the photograph printed on the front of the service sheet to remind me.

But here, upon this bleak and dismal turf, without so much as a photograph to recall her, or a word of real recollection, Nell was present to me. In my mind's eye, I saw her dancing alone on the stage late one night after we had changed the set for the next production, her bright golden curls scintillating under the stage lights. A record of Mario Lanza singing Schubert's *Ave Maria* was playing on the panotrope, why I cannot remember. I did not think at the time that it was very suitable music to dance to, but Nell managed it. She had trained as a dancer and her movements were always graceful. The fact that there was something absurd, almost surreal about her impromptu performance only added to its charm.

That had been the night when, in the early hours of the morning, full of wine and laughter, Nell and I had wandered onto Alderness beach and consummated our love for the first time.

Slowly the group draped itself around the grave while the undertaker's assistants took hold of the straps to lower the coffin on which I placed a bunch of yellow roses, the only flowers that graced it. That morning I had suddenly remembered how Nell had had 'a thing', as she put it, about yellow roses, and had been lucky enough to find a florist that would sell me some.

Souter had stepped up to the head of the grave, preparatory, I supposed to giving another address, when a gull suddenly swooped out of the blue air and landed on the coffin. With its head cocked on one side it appeared to be scrutinising the yellow roses. Perhaps it was considering their suitability as food, but it made no attempt to peck at them. Its appearance caused Souter consternation and he began to whirl his arms around to shoo it away. The gull observed this rather ridiculous activity for a moment with scornful indifference, then flew off to perch itself on the cemetery wall and watch proceedings from there.

The planks were removed and the coffin was lowered into the ground. Souter picked up a handful of the orange sandy soil heaped up on the side of the grave and cast it with a hieratic gesture upon the coffin, now at rest in the hole. Then he raised both arms in the air and cried: 'Our sister has gone! Hail the goer!'

At which the rest of the congregation (but not me) raised their arms and lugubriously murmured: 'Hail the goer!'

Just then I heard laughter, the sweet, silly, joyous laughter of a young girl. I looked around me but nobody else appeared to have noticed. I observed that the gull on the wall had its beak open and it looked almost as if the laughter were emanating from it. The next moment it had launched itself off the wall and was soaring in circles higher and higher over the grave and uttering its familiar and reassuringly alien cries.

The funeral was over. Mrs Caker informed me eagerly that there would be tea and sandwiches in an ante-room to the chapel, but I was in no mood for them. I sought out Souter and we arranged to meet at Nell's house the following morning. He said that if it was too much trouble for me and I wanted to get back to London, I could hand the keys to him and he would 'sort it all out', as he put it. I merely smiled, shook my head, and took my leave.

My mind was full of Nell and I wanted to be alone with thoughts of her. It was strange that though I had lived with Margaret for over thirty years, and happily—mostly—she was only a shadow at this moment compared with Nell.

After that first night on the beach we had made love many times either at my lodgings or at hers. We had 'digs' in different parts of town and had to avoid the wary eye of landladies, so there had always been a frisson of danger. I was possessed by Nell: she was beautiful, she was sweet, she had a heart overflowing with kindness for everything and everybody, but she was, as my mother would have said—and I could hear her saying it—'a goose'. My mind was in almost constant rebellion against my heart. I knew, or thought I knew, she was wrong for me. Nell was taken in by every superstitious 'New Age' fad that was around, so her proprietorship of *Mandala* in later years had not surprised me. She had, I considered, little or no capacity for rational thought: all sensibility, no sense. As an actress she was erratic; sometimes intuitively right, more often than not merely undisciplined. There were times in company when she would say things which, at the time, I considered so foolish and lacking in intellectual rigour that I would be horribly embarrassed on her behalf. Now, having spent half a lifetime among the young, I think I am more tolerant, a little less of an intellectual prig. A little less, perhaps.

Oh, but she was beautiful and kind, and though I knew she was hurt when I reproved her silliness, she took it well. Once or twice, when I was particularly severe, she turned the tables by laughing at me. That was deeply annoying. Now I think she may have been wiser than I thought.

I remember one hot Sunday afternoon in her digs. We lay entwined on her bed, naked after love. The window was open and a slight sea breeze stirred the curtains, while gulls cried in the blue air, and a murmur of holiday crowds filtered up from the baking pavements below us. It was for me an idyllic moment, abandoned and thoughtless, but not for Nell. Her head began to move restlessly on my chest, the golden curls brushing my chin.

She said: 'You think we're very different people, don't you?'

'Well, yes. In a way.'

'Does it worry you?'

'I don't know.'

'It shouldn't,' she said, reading my true thoughts, as she sometimes did. 'You see, you're my antitype. It's like *animus* and *anima*. You know, *yin* and *yang*. That's why we're actually right for each other. It's like complementary. . . .' She told me she had been reading Jung or Yeats, or possibly both. Needless to say, she had got it all hopelessly muddled, I thought. Perhaps she had, but now I am not so sure.

When the season was over, we continued to see each other in London. She got a job in a shop; I did extra work for films and television. The work we really wanted to do in the theatre was not coming our way. In the end I got tired of it all and decided to take up my parent's offer to finance my training to be a teacher, and so the separation occurred. For me it was almost painless; I have no idea what it was for Nell, but I am ashamed I gave it so little thought. I wonder if, 'we drifted apart' is ever a wholly honest phrase.

The following morning, I was at *Mandala* on time, but Souter was there before me.

'Ah, there you are, Villiers,' he said, as if I were late.

He carried a clipboard onto which various lists had been attached. I unlocked the shop door and we entered. Its contents were as expected: crystals, dowsing pendulums, 'dream catchers', astrological charts, packs of tarot cards, scented candles and joss sticks, even ceremonial swords and wands, the whole panoply of neo-paganism. What surprised me was the immaculate order in which it was kept. The shelves and cupboards were painted pale green, the items in and on them meticulously arranged and labelled. I had expected such an array of nonsense to convey a strange, perhaps slightly oppressive atmosphere, but the effect was quite the opposite.

Souter was studying a list on his clipboard and was ticking off items on it in an important way, so I decided to venture into the private side of Nell's house. Souter stopped me.

'One moment! I think we should do this systematically, don't you?'

'By all means, but that doesn't mean we should not also do it separately. You carry on in the shop, I will continue in her private apartments.'

This did not please Souter. 'I think I had better come with you,' he said.

A small dark passageway connected the shop with Nell's home. Souter pushed his way past me into this, so that I had to reach over him to unlock the door. It was during this strange and awkward interlude while we were trapped as it were between one world and the next that Souter said.

'By the way, the solicitor, Mrs Watson, did she mention something to you about another will?'

'I believe she did say something, yes.'

'I wouldn't take all that too seriously. You know what these solicitors are like.'

'No. What *are* they like?'

'Nobody has found one, and even if it exists, it almost certainly isn't properly witnessed. I don't think we should worry about it.'

'I won't,' I said and opened the door to Nell's living quarters. 'I expect you've been here many times,' I added.

'Oh, yes. Nell and I were very close. That is why I don't believe all this nonsense about another will.'

'You mean she would have told you about it?'

'I would have known.'

We entered a small sitting room furnished with both comfort and taste in mind. Though we must have been the first people to venture into it for at least a fortnight, it gave the impression of having only just been quitted. I saw very little dust. Souter was looking around him searchingly.

'Hello,' he said. 'That's new.'

He pointed to a framed black and white photograph of a young man which hung on the wall next to the fireplace. For a moment, I did not recognise it. Souter darted over and plucked it off the wall; then he turned it over to examine the back of it.

'Looking for something?' I said.

'No. No. Just wanted to know who it was.' He studied the picture: the head and shoulders of a young man, floppy hair black as a raven's wing, looking at you sideways, half smiling. Souter looked at me, then at the picture again, then once more at me.

'This you?'

'It was.' I had forgotten that Nell and I had exchanged photographs of ourselves. They were those flattering 'ten by eight head shots' that every aspiring professional has made to send round to theatres and managements. I wished now that I could remember if I still had hers.

'Here,' said Souter, holding the picture out to me. 'You'd better have it.'

'I don't want it,' I said, very deliberately putting my hands into my pockets. It was true. I wanted no reminders of what I once was. My refusal annoyed Souter considerably and he tossed the picture petulantly onto a nearby sofa. Then he began, studying furniture and ornaments, looking in drawers and taking books off shelves. I could not endure being in the same room with him any longer, so I quietly slipped into the adjoining kitchen and up some back stairs to the floor above.

Under different circumstances I think I might have found Nell's house delightful. In contrast to her rather fey beliefs, I had to admit that Nell had a charming feel for interior design. Her fabrics and colour schemes were not, as I am afraid I had expected, too pretty for my taste. I wondered if Souter would notice that some of the pictures ('Modern British') were by recognised names and quite valuable.

Her bedroom was small and neat with an adjoining bathroom. I saw no signs of her having left for her final destination at the local hospice in any confusion. Clothes were neatly folded in drawers or resting on hangers. As with the sitting room downstairs I had the impression of a place that had just been vacated in good order.

The window looked onto a sloping roof and commanded a view of the sea. I sat down on the bed and tried to collect my thoughts. Just then I heard something tapping on the window. I turned and saw a large, pure white gull eyeing me through the glass. It tapped again with its beak.

Quite how I came to the absurd conclusion I do not know, but it seemed to me that the bird was pointing with its beak at something in the room. It tapped again, this time more insistently so that I was afraid it might break the glass. I followed the line of the beak and saw that it appeared to be indicating the bedside table on which stood a small wooden box.

I knew that box. One Saturday afternoon, late in the Alderness season, Nell and I had been wandering about the town. We

A MAZE FOR THE MINOTAUR

found an old bric-à-brac shop in a side street and passed some pleasant minutes examining the selection of oddments on display, most of which could be described, even by Nell, as 'tat'. Suddenly Nell gave a little exclamation of pleasure. She had found a polished wooden marquetry box. On the lid was an image, in various coloured woods of what I took to be a swan, wings stretched, flying over a mere fringed with trees. It was a lovely thing but there seemed no way of opening it, and there was no keyhole.

The owner of the shop who had been hovering near us, there being no other visitors, explained that there was a secret method of opening the box, by sliding various of the marquetry panels in a certain order. He demonstrated. Nell, rather injudiciously in my view, expressed absolute delight in the object and asked him the price. When he named it, her face fell. I think it was no more than about thirty pounds; still, that was a week's wages in those days and quite beyond her means. We walked away from the shop in low spirits because of it, but I went back to the shop on my own on the Monday and bought it for her. I had a little 'family money' put by and it was not going to break me. There were tears in Nell's eyes when I presented it to her. I never forgot the look she gave me.

This, I thought, would be the item that I would take as a memento. Idly I fiddled with it, trying to remember the location and order of the sliding panels which would open the box.

It did not take me long. Conscious recollection played no part, only some strange, atavistic muscle memory. The lid sprang open and the interior, lined with sandalwood yielded a soft warm fragrance that seemed to me both fresh and ancient at the same time. Lying in the box was a folded sheet of stiff paper.

Before opening it, I looked up at the window. The gull was still there staring at me intently. It was then that something happened which I cannot properly explain. My eyesight became blurred for a moment, then, as I continued to look at the gull its head began to change shape. The beak receded and became a nose; the eyes moved from the side of the head to the front; tiny golden-grey curls sprouted from the cranium. The body of the gull remained the same but the features of the head were now those of Nell. It was not quite the Nell that I had known: there were fine wrinkles on her face and the jaw line had loosened, but it was her. She was gazing at me with an intense, eager look, perhaps inviting a response. My own expression must have been one of astonishment and terror, not because it was Nell, but because, quite clearly, I was going mad. My late wife's terminal dementia had filled me with a horror of such things.

I rubbed my eyes. She was still there, and the head was nodding vigorously. I was meant to do something. Yes. I was meant to read the paper. So I took my eyes off the creature and concentrated on the document.

It was a will, typed, properly signed and witnessed, naming me as sole executor. There were some bequests as before, but Thelma's Haven, the Donkey Sanctuary was not mentioned. Instead the bulk of her property was left to me: 'to dispose of as he thinks fit', whatever that might mean.

I replaced the will in the box and turned my eyes once more to the window. The gull no longer had Nell's head. Once more, thank heaven, it was an ordinary gull, which gave me an ordinary gull's feral stare, then flapped its wings and flew off towards the sea.

'What's that you've got?'

I started violently and turned round to see Souter standing in the bedroom doorway. Quickly and surreptitiously I slid the secret panels of the box back into place.

'It's just a box,' I said. 'I thought I might keep it as a memento of Nell. According to the terms of the will. I gave it to her as a present long ago.'

'Can I see?' He held out his hand like a child eager for a sweet and I passed it to him. After a close study of the object he said: 'How does it open? There's no lock or anything.'

'It's one of those trick things. Mystery boxes, I think they're called. Lovely marquetry work, don't you think?'

'What's inside?'

'I'll attempt to open it when I get back to my hotel.' He tried to wrestle with its secret mechanism, but he had no idea where to begin. I said: 'Can I have it back please?'

Reluctantly he returned it to me. He was looking at me intently, and I was sure he had noticed my evasions. He said: 'I think it's easier if we go through things together, don't you?'

And so, for the rest of the morning, we did. It was a wearisome business. Souter was meticulous and pedantic, listing everything, asking my opinion about value with a suspicious air as if he doubted my expertise or honesty. I had little clue about furniture or china, but I had some knowledge of pictures, picked up from my late wife who had been an artist. When we finished at lunchtime, I noticed that he had appropriated 'as a memento' a little Clausen landscape (birds flying over a cornfield) which I had pointed out as being of particular value.

'Well, I think we might call it a day,' said Souter. 'You taking that back to the hotel?' he said, indicating the box under my arm.

'I thought I might.' There was a long silence during which he stared at me, his thoughts unfathomable. I tried to show the same lack of unease at this strange hiatus as he was demonstrating.

'Tell you what,' he said at last. 'As executor, I think you ought to see where all the money's going, don't you? I'll take you out to see Thelma's Haven this afternoon. How about that? Pick you up from your hotel in the old jalopy around three?' He spoke with that slightly old-fashioned jauntiness with which I was becoming familiar, if not altogether comfortable.

'Splendid!' I said, trying to respond in kind.

On the stroke of three I was in the foyer when Souter duly appeared, wearing a tweed cap in hound's tooth check, pigskin gloves, and a spotted silk scarf. I almost expected motoring goggles, but his car was not open topped, just a very ordinary saloon.

As we were driving out of Alderness he asked: 'Manage to open that box?'

'No. I felt so tired after lunch I fell asleep.' It was true.

'Ah.' The rest of the journey took place in silence until we got to the gates of Thelma's Haven some seven miles out of Alderness in gently undulating countryside. The name was carved in rustic lettering on a varnished board at the entrance to a drive.

'Who is Thelma?' I asked.

'It's an abbreviation of Thelema.'

'Ah, I see. "Do what thou wilt shall be the whole of the law"?'

'You are remarkably well informed for a pedagogue.'

'Retired pedagogue.'

Souter indicated two distinctly elderly and moth-eaten grey donkeys grazing in a field to the right of the drive down which we were proceeding towards a motley conglomeration of sheds and bungalows.

'Just at the moment we only have two donkeys on our books. We usually have a great many more: quite a few of them retired beach donkeys from Jagborough Sands. The rides are no longer popular.'

'What are their names?'

'That one's Esmeralda. That's Jesus.'

'*Jesus*? Unusual name for a donkey.'

'Any objections?'

'None whatsoever. Is this also where you live?'

'It is my humble abode.'

Souter showed me round the stables and the offices of his donkey sanctuary with some pride. Everything appeared to be very clean and in good order, perhaps a little too much so.

'Are you going to show me the crematorium as well?' I asked.

'Later! Later! But first, I think, a little tincture in my humble dwelling.'

'For the chakras?'

Souter laughed uneasily.

The humility on which Souter had insisted was, I suppose, reflected in the neat and Spartan lines of the decor of his bungalow. In the sitting room the walls were white and adorned with a few smallish pictures, one of which, I noted, was the Clausen Souter had expropriated that morning. There was one bookcase crammed with books, a leather clad suite, and, of all things, a bar behind which was arrayed a formidable collection of bottles.

'Now then, what's your poison, Mr Villiers?'

To my astonishment a figure suddenly emerged from behind the bar where it had presumably been engaged in cleaning glasses or some other menial activity. It was Mrs Caker in a floral overall and her crushed raspberry hat, looking like a charwoman from a mid-twentieth century farce.

Souter explained. 'Betty Caker comes and "does" for me, as they say.'

'I help out with the donkeys too,' she added.

'Yes. Yes. Invaluable. Salt of the earth and all that.' Mrs Caker seemed pleased by the accolade, but I noticed she strenuously avoided looking at me. 'I'll have my usual, Mrs C. Scotch. What's yours?'

I could not face whisky at this time of day, so I asked for a sherry.

'I believe we have a bottle of Amontillado somewhere, if not a cask, eh? Mrs C., will you do the honours?'

While Mrs Caker was attending to the drinks Souter drew my attention to the view from a large picture window at the end of the room. It was pleasant enough though not particularly inspiring, just a field of tussocky grass fringed by a line of horse chestnuts.

'I can meditate in front of that for hours, you know,' said Souter. I noticed that he kept looking at me as if waiting for a reaction. Mrs Caker brought us our drinks on a polished metal tray.

'Well,' said Souter picking up his whisky. 'Mud in your eye!' My sherry tasted strange.

The next thing I can remember was lying on a hard, rubbery surface. My head was aching and my eyelids felt so heavy that I could not open them. Somewhere behind me two people were talking. Slowly I began to identify Souter and Mrs Caker as the conversationalists.

At first my brain was so sluggish that I had difficulty in understanding what they were talking about. Mrs Caker was asking if he was 'sure about the box'. Souter replied that he was. Then Mrs Caker asked how he would get hold of it, to which Souter replied that he had 'found Villiers' key card in his wallet'. This baffled me for some time until I realised that he was referring to the key card of my room at the Metropole. Presumably Souter was proposing to go to my hotel and fetch the box from my room. But what about me? This was what Mrs Caker wanted to know.

'He's going in there, Mrs C.,' said Souter. 'Don't worry. He's well under. He won't feel a thing.'

While Mrs Caker was raising objections to this course of action, I finally managed to force my eyes open.

I had, fortunately, not drunk all of my sherry, but, suspecting the taste, had poured the remainder of the glass unseen into a convenient plant pot. Had I drunk it all, I would no doubt have been completely unconscious. As it was, it took all of my will to remain alert.

Looking up I saw a whitewashed vaulted ceiling and tiled walls. I was lying on a surface, I guessed, some four feet above ground level, but where was I? I tried to move my head to one side to look, but the effort was too painful.

Mrs Caker was saying: 'I have no objections to Mr Villiers being dead, but why can't you kill him in a more normal way?'

'What on earth do you mean by "normal", Mrs C.? Killing may be necessary, but it can't be normal. This way we will leave no trace, only ashes.'

'But I don't see why—'

'Oh, for the love of Mike, woman, will you just do what I tell you!'

'All right! All right! I'm not something the cat's brought in, you know.'

A mechanical device of some kind was set in motion and I felt the surface on which I lay begin to move. I forced my head up to look and saw that I was on a moving belt and that ahead of me two metal doors were sliding apart. Beyond the doors was a brick chamber from the floor of which burst great garnet and orange flames like pentecostal tongues. I was moving towards it inexorably, yet I could barely lift my limbs or utter a groan.

'Look! He's moving,' said Mrs Caker. 'I can hear him! We can't go on like this!' And the machine was turned off; I stopped moving, the tongues of flame subsided.

Souter was shouting: 'Put it back on, damn you! I'll see to this!' I turned my head enough to see Souter coming towards me with what looked like a poker in his hand. The belt began to move again. I felt my feet warm to the flame. With an effort which took all my strength and more I managed to roll sideways and fall off the moving belt onto the tiled crematorium floor, but this was of little help because Souter was on me, raising his poker to strike and stun. Then it happened.

The air around me was suddenly full of white wings. Souter cried out and staggered back; Mrs Caker screamed. I looked up and saw nothing but a great flock of gulls white and whirling round the crematorium chapel filling it with their harsh calls and clamorous wings. I saw them cluster round Souter's head so that it was nothing but a mass of white feathers bellowing with pain. As for myself, they appeared to pay no attention to me, so I began to crawl towards the open door through which gulls and yet more gulls were still flying.

When I was out in the open air I managed to get to my feet and, holding onto the wooden fence posts that bordered the donkey field, staggered up the drive. Esmeralda and Jesus brayed mournfully at me as I went by. I walked all seven miles back into Alderness, by which time my whole body was aching but my brain was clear. The receptionist at the desk of the Metropole was sympathetic in a rather condescending way about the loss of my key card and presented me with another. She advised me to 'have a lie down', assuming perhaps that I had had too much to drink.

I took her advice, hoping rather than believing that I had suffered from yet another unpleasant hallucination. However, a report in the *East Suffolk Gazette* the following day indicated, that I had not been completely deluded. Under the headline FREAK ATTACK BY SEABIRDS, it stated that 'local donkey sanctuary owner' Hamilton Souter had been the victim of an assault by a flock of gulls in his crematorium and was blinded as a result. His, 'assistant, Mrs Betty Caker', according to the report, suffered only minor bodily injuries, but had been the victim of a severe mental trauma. I visited her in a psychiatric hospital some weeks later. She greeted me with smiles and was still wearing her raspberry hat.

In the end Souter did not do too badly out of his injuries. He became an object of sympathetic local curiosity. In the months that followed his terrible accident he began to claim that his blindness had bestowed upon him clairvoyant gifts, in honour of which he adopted the *sobriquet* of Tiresias. Most people were of course as sceptical as I was, but a surprising number gave him credence. He made himself available for consultations, and people paid good money to attend his séances. Later I heard from at least two independent sources that he had predicted, with uncanny accuracy, the Great Polar Ice Cap Melt of 2023 and its attendant worldwide catastrophes. But I am getting ahead of myself.

On the afternoon following the events at *Thelma's Haven*, having delivered the new will to Mrs Watson, I went down to the beach at Alderness and sat on the shingle underneath the pier until dusk. I cannot say what I thought or why I lingered there so long, only that the events of the previous days were assuming a pattern; and, as the sun began to set, casting its gilded pathway across the sea, the gulls started to circle. One landed nearby and waddled towards me across the shingle. I stared at it in terror, fearing that my mind would begin again to convert its head into Nell's features, yet I couldn't look away. It was watching me closely, but its eye, to my great relief, retained a feral, alien stare, though the way it took slow, tentative steps towards me, as if provoking me to show fear, was uncomfortable. I may have flinched a little because it suddenly let out a series of squawks, like mocking laughter; then, with clamorous wings it took to the air and soared from me in ever widening gyres over the shadowy waters.

I was alone again.

A FRAGMENT OF THUCYDIDES

A FRAGMENT OF THUCYDIDES

Then it was proposed that Alcibiades be sent with twelve ships to the city of Koinonia in Oxon which had declared alliance neither with the Athenians nor the Spartans, that its citizens might subject themselves to Athens and send tribute and support. But a delegation came to Athens from Koinonia under the leadership of Euphellodes,[1] a man much respected for his wisdom and probity, who asked the Athenians to show restraint and be content with the friendly non-allegiance of the Koinonians, it being profitable to the Athenians, not only because it was in conformity with the justice of the gods, but because it demonstrated

---

[1] An unusual Greek name, the root "$\phi\epsilon\lambda\lambda\omega\delta\eta s$" presumably referring to the cork oak ($\phi\epsilon\lambda\lambda os$). The name must mean something akin to 'like a well grown cork oak' or 'fine grower of cork oaks', or 'corked well', but this has been disputed.

strength to show restraint in the exercise of power, and that destructive means, unless dictated by extreme circumstances, always produced destructive ends, deleterious to all parties. But the Athenians heeded him not, and the following spring Alcibiades went with twelve ships to lay waste Koinonia and enslaved its citizens, but Euphellodes he brought back to Athens as a man worthy of honour for his uprightness and wisdom.

It was Parsons who discovered the fragment, transcribed it, and offered the slightly stilted translation quoted above. He claimed it to be a hitherto unknown passage of Thucydides probably from the end of the fifth book of his history of the Peloponnesian War. The text had been part of a job lot of papyrus fragments found in an excavation at Alexandria. It had been thought that these fragments were part of the remnant of those books which survived the notorious library fire of 48 BC but this, like everything else, is disputed. The fragmentary text of Thucydides, of which this, according to Parsons, was a part, was extremely corrupt, even Parsons had to concede that. Many thought it to be the interpolation of a scholiast at best, but Parsons would have none of it and demanded that the next edition of the Oxford Thucydides should include the fragment, at the very least in an addendum.

The whole affair of 'Parsons' Thucydides' as it was called, and the bizarre and terrible circumstances that surrounded it, happened almost sixty years ago, and I had no hopes, when I began my researches, of finding anyone who remembered it, let alone anyone who was involved, but then at a Horatian Society dinner I happened to meet my old friend Rajasinha. He told me that Dr Corcoran was still alive and about to attain his one hundredth year and was moreover in full possession of his faculties. No sooner had I heard this than I wrote to Dr Corcoran and received a most courteous reply back. I knew he had been an actor in this strange drama but quite what his role had been I had no idea.

Dr Corcoran received me in his home in Moreton Road one afternoon with the stately courtesy for which he is (among other things) justly famous. His face looked more than ever like a finely chiselled mask of Greek Tragedy, a mask which somewhat belied the genial if austere love of humanity which was his leading characteristic. Once his carers had left us in possession of a good cup of tea and each other's company I was able to tackle him more directly on the subject. At first he seemed reluctant to tell me about 'the Parsons affair', but once I had convinced him that it was 'ancient history'—his subject after all—and that there was no-one now to be hurt, he told the whole story.

Parsons, who was at that time, like Dr Corcoran, a junior fellow of his college, published in the *Journal of Hellenic Studies* a piece boldly entitled 'A Fragment of Thucydides'.

'This was his first bid for pre-eminence in Thucydidean scholarship,' said G.C., 'and, I suppose, a pretty impressive one.'

'What was your opinion?' I asked.

'I wasn't entirely convinced, but I wasn't much concerned. What has always interested me is what Thucydides says about Athenian politics, and in particular his views on the use and misuse of power. Whatever the fragment says had already been expressed in the Melian dialogue in Book Five, the great debate about how strong communities should exercise power over weak ones. There is little doubt that this fellow Euphellodes, assuming for a moment he is genuine, holds the same sort of views as Thucydides, but we know what the man's views are already. That's not the point. The point is that this is where Simcox came in.

'Simcox was a fellow in Ancient History at New College: another young thruster. He wrote a piece which came out about a month later in the *Classical Quarterly,* a piece provocatively entitled "A Fragment of Thucydides?" In this, Simcox, with some academic rigour it has to be said, comprehensively took apart Parsons' claims. He said that the fragment was a mere gloss on the Melian dialogue by a later writer, but not an unskilful pastiche. He even suggested, perhaps not entirely in earnest, that the interpolation had been made by Xenophon.

'This especially infuriated Parsons who thought little of Xenophon: definitely an inferior being according to Parsons. But Xenophon was a sportsman in my view. Well, Parsons wrote a blistering response, and so the war of words began. It became rather nasty and quite personal but both Parsons and Simcox seemed to be obsessed by it. I believe that Parsons even used to go into New College on balmy summer evenings and stand outside Simcox's window. Then he used to taunt him, rather as Evelyn Waugh used to do to poor old Cruttwell. Not a sensible thing to do. I was slightly senior to Parsons and was also Dean of our college at the time so I thought it incumbent on me to try to introduce some kind of rationality into the issue, being, as you know, fundamentally a man of peace. These academic feuds may seem very amusing to some people but they do no good in the long run to anyone. They bring our profession into disrepute.

'Well, I tackled Parsons after hall one night and we had a long chat but I can't say I made a great impression on him at first. He seemed in some obscure way to be enjoying the war and he had this peculiar belief that Simcox was out to destroy *him personally*, not just his pet theory. Had I believed in such things I might have suggested Parsons see a shrink, it was that bad, but I didn't. Perhaps I should have done. Then I had an idea which I thought was something of a brainwave. I had begun a college dining club for philosophers in the college which I had decided to call the Bentham. After Jeremy Bentham, you know, the Utilitarian philosopher. When Professor Hart heard of my proposed name, he approved: "Very good," he said, "maximising pleasure!" That's by the by. But I decided that, as the next Bentham dinner was coming up, I should invite both Parsons and Simcox. It being a philosophical dining club, you see, they would be meeting on neutral ground as it were. A rapprochement might be effected. I put this idea to Parsons and, at first, he seemed shocked, then he looked thoughtful, finally he nodded his agreement. Well, I thought I had done a great and good thing. It is only late in life that you learn the law of unintended consequences and that very few good deeds go unpunished.

'Simcox accepted the invitation without hesitation, and all seemed to go well. I was sensible enough not to put them together for the main part of the evening, but at the port and nuts stage I contrived to have them sit next to each other. I calculated that the excellence of the food and wine would have mellowed them enough not to start a fight. I stayed close by in case a referee was needed, so to speak, but all seemed to go well. They were both hesitant and wary at first, but after a while they were talking away like fun. I began to congratulate myself, but I am, as you know, a man of caution. I knew we weren't out of the woods yet.

'Neither of them appeared to be great port drinkers and when, as the party was breaking up, Parsons suggested they repair to his rooms for "a proper drink", Simcox agreed with some alacrity.

'Parsons, I should say, used to cut something of a dash in his tutorials by offering his undergraduates cocktails after they had read their essays to him. I have always stuck to sherry for my people and there were never any complaints. Be that as it may, Parsons had the whole works in his rooms: cocktail shakers, special glasses, a battery of liqueurs and spirits; he even had a fridge installed in which to keep ice and other necessaries of that kind.

'Well the prospect of a post prandial cocktail seemed to excite Simcox. Personally, I can imagine nothing more foul, but off they went all smiles. I thought I had done my good deed for the day so I retired to my room in college to sleep what I fondly imagined to be the sleep of the just.

'The next thing I knew I was being shaken awake by Douglas, the college porter. Douglas was in a great taking and was using more colourful language than was customary even for him. I got dressed quickly and he directed me to Parsons' rooms where his scout was standing in the doorway, quivering like an aspen. Parsons' scout had come to wake him and so had been first on the scene.

'I'll cut to the chase and tell you what I saw. The room was in chaos with furniture and books thrown about. There were, in short, as the detective stories tell you, "signs of a struggle". Parsons was lying in the midst of all this, blood everywhere and his throat cut from ear to ear. The gash was horrible to behold, particularly as there were what looked to me like scorch marks surrounding it. His arms were outstretched and in his right hand he clutched a red handkerchief which was still damp. His left upper arm was cut, but it did not look like a recent wound. Beside the body lay two cocktail glasses, one smashed, the other with a residue of liquor and a slice of lemon still lingering in it. The room was overpoweringly hot and had an acrid smell which came from some sort of plastic substance which had melted on the two bar electric fire which I took the liberty of turning off. I made sure that Parsons was indeed dead, before telling Douglas to go down and phone for the police in the porter's lodge. Of course, that was what he should have done in the first place, but I wasn't going to tell him that and receive an earful of vivid invective for my pains.

'I dismissed the quivering scout after first telling him to hold himself in readiness for questioning, while I stood guard over the scene of the crime until the police arrived. I must say I took advantage of this hiatus to take a good look at Parsons' rooms. I do not fancy myself as a detective: as a matter of fact, I have little time for detective stories unlike some of my colleagues, but I had, I think, a brain, and an instinct. A scholar without instinct is a poor creature, you know. By that I mean what Keats called "negative capability", the capacity to take in impressions without immediately analysing them and then letting your feelings direct you to the solution. Well, my feelings told me that there was something odd about the scene.

'On the surface it would appear to be relatively straightforward. Parsons had struggled with an assailant. The assailant had slit his throat, presumably with a knife, and then left. But why? I searched for a weapon, but none could be found. Much of the furniture had been thrown about with the exception of a table on which reposed a recent copy of the *Journal of Hellenic Studies*. I looked inside it and saw, as I expected, that it contained Parsons' Thucydides article. On the floor beside the table was a copy of the Oxford text of Xenophon's *Hellenica* which had been wrenched apart with some fury and the pages scattered in fragments across the carpet. I noticed too that Parsons' fridge was turned off for some reason. By the window was a tape recorder, on which Parsons, in his vanity, was wont to record his lectures, even his tutorials, but there was only one empty spool on the machine.

'I went into the bedroom. On the bedside table were a few specks of white powder but nothing else; in the waste paper bin, however, I discovered an empty pill bottle. The label suggested that Parsons had been prescribed some sort of anti-depressant. Pretty crude, I should imagine, because we are talking about the very early 1960s.

'What did all this add up to? Well, I couldn't think, and besides, by this time, the police had arrived.

'The man in charge was an Inspector Morson. By no means a fool, but not exactly an alpha. Beta double plus perhaps and I may be being generous. I told Morson everything relevant about the Bentham dinner and he, naturally enough, sent off a couple of men to New College to bring Simcox in for questioning. I couldn't quarrel with that, though I thought it highly unlikely that Simcox had committed an act of violence against Parsons.

When I told Morson about their Thucydidean contretemps Morson nodded and sucked at his pipe—policemen actually had pipes in those days, you know—and said that I would be surprised. He had known a husband kill his wife over her disparagement of his football team. I said this was hardly the same thing, but he shook his head and smiled in that knowing, wiseacre way that people have.

'The policemen who went to pick up Simcox found him asleep in his rooms at New College. He had taken off his dinner jacket but otherwise had not undressed and was lying on his bed still unconscious. It took a while to rouse him. His recollections of the night before had been hazy but he remembered that he had been in Parsons' rooms for a drink and Parsons' behaviour had been "funny". In what way funny? He couldn't say. When informed that Parsons was dead, Simcox expressed shock and bewilderment. His shock was even greater when the pockets of his dinner jacket were searched and in it was found a small sharp bloodstained knife. The blood was proved undoubtedly to belong to Parsons; the fingerprints on the handle were Simcox's. Also found in his pocket was Parsons' key to the front gate of the college. Simcox was arrested and charged with murder. Morson's case against him would appear to be watertight.

'Further evidence against Simcox, if further evidence were needed, came from an undergraduate who was wandering through the Radcliffe Quad very late that night and heard sounds of a vociferous argument between two people coming from the open window of Parsons' rooms. This young man, Ingrams his name was, had made rather a habit of wandering about at night. Strange fellow, not a bad scholar, but a little over inclined to make smart remarks. I wonder what became of him. Anyway, when he came forward that rather put the seal on it.

'It was an affair that aroused widespread alarm and incredulity. It was not just me who believed that Simcox could not possibly have done it, not even in some kind of drunken brawl, but the others did not know what I did. I felt that I had been the instrument of this catastrophe, albeit an unwitting one, and that it was incumbent upon me to do something about it.

'I asked myself what Thucydides would have done in similar circumstances. You may think that absurd, but it's not really. Thucydides—*pace* Herodotus, for whom I have the greatest respect—was the first truly scientific historian. He took all the evidence at his disposal, laid it out and then tried to make a coherent pattern from it. Having eliminated the impossible, what remains, however improbable, must be the solution. I realise that Sherlock Holmes is the one to whom that maxim is attributable, but it's all there in Thucydides, and Holmes was of course a classicist. I had, naturally, taken as *a priori* that Simcox had not killed Parsons, but one must always begin with an *a priori* premise, even if, afterwards, you abandon it. The whole of Western metaphysics, religion, even science rests upon that.

'After some reflection I recognised that there were three questions that needed answering. The first was, what was the nature of the powder to be found on Parsons' bedside table, secondly what was the burnt substance on the two bar electric fire, thirdly what traces of liquid, if any, were to be found on the smashed cocktail glass. I got in touch with Simcox's solicitor and urged him to insist that the police supply him with answers to these questions and, if he would be so good, to pass the answers on to me.'

As Dr Corcoran spoke these last words he suddenly nodded off (Rajasinha had warned me about this). It was a tantalising moment, but I was not tempted to rouse him. His eloquence and clarity had been astonishing. I tiptoed out of the room and proposed to his carer a return at the same hour next day.

The following day, he resumed his narration without so much as a 'Where was I?' It was an astonishing feat, a testament to his mental discipline, and an example to us all.

'When the answers came, they were as follows. The powder on Parsons' bedside table was the same substance as his antidepressant pills which contained among other things a powerful narcotic. Evidently he had crushed some of these pills on his bedside table. The melted material on the electric fire belonged to a spool of magnetic tape. Unfortunately, the tape was too damaged to yield any useful information. The answer to the third question was, as I am sure you must have gathered by now, the most significant of all. There was no trace of any alcoholic liquid of any kind in the smashed cocktail glass, indeed of anything at all other than a few tiny drops of tap water.'

'I am afraid I don't quite see the significance . . .'

'Tarry a while and you will. Well, by this time Simcox had been charged and was on bail, but he was in a pretty bad way. I rang Morson and told him to drop the charges. He not unnaturally demurred, but he agreed to see me and hear my reasons.

'He came round to my rooms in college and I gave him a sherry. He seemed rather in awe of me, perhaps even afraid: I can't imagine why, but it was all to the good. I told him in no uncertain terms that Simcox could not possibly be Parsons' killer. In the first place it was not in his nature, secondly, he was no fool and however drunk he was he wouldn't have allowed himself to be found with a bloodstained knife in his pocket, thirdly, as I had ascertained from his solicitors, no signs of a struggle had been found on his person. Morson told me, though not in those words, that, like Hamlet, I needed "grounds more relative than this". So I explained.

'Now as you know, I am fond of the theatre. I have a great admiration for actors, even undergraduate ones as long as it doesn't interfere with their work. I have a feeling for it, and when I went into Parsons' room that morning, my immediate impression, though I couldn't define it at the time, was that something had been staged. It was like the set of a play. And, of course, when I put all the evidence together, I realised that my impression had been correct. The furniture had been knocked about, but a table had been left standing on which reposed the journal containing Parsons' famous article. There was the shredded copy of Xenophon's *Hellenica,* and in the midst of it all, beside two cocktail glasses, one shattered, lay Parsons' dramatically splayed corpse. The conclusion I had come to was that Parsons had committed suicide but staged it to make it look as if he had been murdered by Simcox.'

'But why?'

'I was hoping to answer that last of all, by way of peroration, but I may as well answer it now, with the caveat that it is only conjecture on my part. Parsons was young, ambitious, neurotic, paranoid, almost certainly what we now call "bipolar". He had convinced himself that Simcox, by rubbishing his Thucydides fragment, had destroyed his glorious academic career. He felt he had nothing to live for but was determined to bring down his arch enemy with him. That is the plausible explanation; whether it is the true one only God knows.'

'But how?'

'I was coming to that. It is my belief that Parsons began planning the thing almost as soon as I had invited him and Simcox to the Bentham dinner. There were three things he needed to do. The first thing was to collect a fair amount of his own blood which he did by cutting his left arm, and keeping the blood he collected in his fridge. He kept it in a small plastic bag which was later found in the shrubbery below his window. The second was to grind some of his pills into a soluble powder, and the third was to make a recording of his having a violent altercation with someone, incorporating samples of Simcox's own voice, some of which, it later transpired, had been recorded on his nocturnal expeditions to New College, during which he had provoked Simcox to respond to his taunts. He also borrowed a spare key to the front gate, from me as it happened, on the afternoon of the Bentham dinner. Then all he had to do was to invite Simcox back to his rooms, put the drug in his cocktail, take him to the main gate when no-one was looking, and let him out with his key. He slipped that into the already half-doped Simcox's jacket pocket, then locked the gate again with my borrowed key and returned it to my pigeon hole. It took me a while to work out the significance of that. Then he comes back, throws the furniture about, disposes of the blood bag, washes out the drugged cocktail glass and smashes it on the floor, plays the tape for the benefit of the night-wandering Ingrams whom he has watched for at the window and cuts his own throat.'

'But the knife! The bloodstained knife was in Simcox's jacket pocket!'

'Ah, there I think Parsons showed an ingenuity worthy of a better cause. The knife was not the murder weapon of course. Parsons got Simcox's finger prints on it by the simple expedient of getting him to slice up a lemon with it for the cocktails. Then he surreptitiously smears it with his own blood from the fridge and slips it into Simcox's jacket as he is letting him out of the main gate of the college, at the same time as he is also slipping the key into his pocket.'

'But now Parsons has no knife to cut his own throat with!'

'You will remember that in my scrupulous desire to lay before you all the relevant clues I told you that there were scorch marks around the incision in his throat. Note that I said they were *scorch* marks not *burn* marks. They were made by a knife which he had fashioned from ice and kept in his precious fridge. Ice at very low temperatures leaves scorch marks on the skin and Parsons' ice compartment was capable of freezing to very low temperatures indeed. That is why he turned the fridge off, presumably to divert attention from it and allay suspicions. But this had the very opposite effect where I was concerned. The damp handkerchief found in his right hand was used to wrap around the frozen knife's handle and give him a decent purchase on it, and also to prevent scorch marks on his hand. The electric fire nearby was used both to destroy the tape and to evaporate the knife swiftly and almost completely, apart from a residual dampness on the handkerchief. He must in his hour of death have taken considerable pride in his ingenuity. But *hubris* is always followed by *nemesis,* not to mention *anagnorisis*. As a Hellenist, he should have known that. I put all my ratiocinations to Morson with the hint that if he did not act, I was prepared to make my views widely known.'

'And was Morson convinced?'

'Not immediately. I told you he was only Beta double plus. Beta plus perhaps. But a good fellow. He did finally see the light and the murder charge was dropped. The coroner brought in a verdict of suicide while of unsound mind. And that was the end of the Parsons affair, and for that matter his fragment of Thucydides which none but sad fellows like you, and superannuated ones like me, now remember.

'Simcox went on to greater things as you know. He wrote that book about the Megarian Decrees. Totally wrong-headed of course, but it caused a flutter in the dovecotes. He and I had something of a dispute about those Decrees, as a matter of fact, but all quite amicable.'

'Did he know you had saved him from the hangman's noose?'

'Well, not quite that, as I think the death penalty had been abolished by then, thank heaven. And anyway, all I did was point Morson in the right direction, but Simcox never knew about my part in it and I didn't care to remind him. It would not have been the right thing to do. Besides, just as it is the offender who never forgives, it is generally the debtor who bears the grudge.

'I have to say though that Geoffrey Simcox and I never really got on. The fellow was a Marxist. I'm C. of E. myself, and thus immune to the primitive superstitions of the Marxomanni. But Simcox was worthy of respect because he valued scholarship for itself, and he was also a very passable leg spinner in his day. Parsons on the other hand was a fanatic, out for nothing but his own glory and prestige. An academic Widmerpool. Such people are always a little mad. The fact is, I had known that Parsons was a wrong'un from the start. You see, the fellow had spoken disrespectfully of Xenophon.'

THE CRUMBLIES

THE CRUMBLIES

It was, whimsically, but perhaps not unexpectedly, called The Crumblies. It had once been The Old Rectory, Bracton Magna, Gloucestershire, a dull if respectable name, but that was a long time ago, before the Foljambe sisters had had their great success.

Emma and Sebastian were in their mid-teens and of course far too old for The Crumblies these days, but they had fond memories of them as children, both the books and the television series; so they were amused to be moving in to the house where it all began. Emma and Sebastian's mother Stephanie was less amused, mainly because her husband had bought it without consulting her. She had feigned delight when Alan had made the announcement; and it was true, she had been longing for a place in the country—heaven knows they could afford it!—but it was the way he had exulted in the purchase. It seemed as if it was not for her that he had done it, not principally anyway, but because the house had been, as he said, 'a bargain' and 'a great investment'.

Stephanie, therefore, was not disposed to like The Crumblies when she first saw it, but had to admit to a favourable first impression. Alan and she had driven down, just the two of them, Emma and Sebastian being at their expensive boarding schools, one bright morning in May to view the place. It was approached by a winding gravel drive between trees which shed a pleasant dappled shade through their young green leaves along the way.

'House with a drive,' said Alan. 'Rather smart, don't you think?'

Stephanie smiled: Alan was not one of those men who cared nothing for appearances. The drive swept round an elegant oval lawn and came to rest in front of a long two storey house—early nineteenth century at a guess—with a white stucco front, long sash windows, and a little classical portico supported by sandstone Tuscan pillars.

'Oh, it's lovely!' Stephanie couldn't help herself. She hadn't intended her enthusiasm to be so unguarded, but it was her ideal: stylish, spacious, yet completely unpretentious.

'Didn't I tell you?'

Slightly, to Alan's annoyance Stephanie insisted on going round the house before entering it to see the full extent of the garden. It was over six months now since Alice Foljambe had put the house up for sale on the death of her sister Eleanor and taken up residence in a nearby home for the elderly; in spite of which the grounds were in remarkably good condition. Stephanie was inspecting them alone, Alan having gone into the house, and there seemed to her something familiar about the garden, a sense of *déjà vu*. Here was a sunken garden with a paved area, in the centre of which was a sundial, roses occupying the borders.

Beside it was a terrace with a lily pond in which she could see the scarlet flash of a goldfish or two. She somehow recognised the cedar of Lebanon that threw gigantic wings of shade over the surrounding lawn; then she remembered. Of course! The *Crumblies* books had been illustrated by Alice, the younger sister who had evidently used parts of the garden as background to some of the adventures recounted by her sister Eleanor, the senior literary partner in the venture. For some reason Stephanie had never much cared for the Crumblies herself, but Emma and Sebastian had adored them when they were young, and she had dutifully read them aloud to her children at bedtime. The illustrations, with their delicate wavering lines and pale, muted colours, had been marginally more palatable to Stephanie than the text. Yes, Stephanie had to admit, the garden had distinct possibilities, and it would not take too much work to make something rather wonderful out of it.

Just then, a sash window facing the terrace was thrown up and Alan thrust his head out rather irritably.

'Are you coming inside Steph, or what?'

She was shaken from her reverie. 'Yes! Coming!' The name, of course, had to go. Stephanie disliked the idea of living in a house, however lovely, with the stupid name of The Crumblies; The Old Rectory suited her much better. Just then, there came from the open window a distant muffled thumping sound as of a heavy weight falling.

'What was that?'

Alan appeared again at the window. 'What was what?'

'That noise from inside the house. Did something fall over?'

'Oh, I don't know! Come on in, for heaven's sake! Have a look. It's incredible! So much space!'

She went in and was again favourably impressed, at least initially. The rooms were large and well-proportioned; there were discreetly elegant plaster mouldings on the ceilings. No trace of damp could be seen or smelt, though the atmosphere in the rooms had a dusty feel to them, but that was only to be expected. One thing Stephanie did notice was that, though the windows were big enough, and it was a bright summer's day, strangely little light seemed to penetrate within. The rooms remained rather dimly illuminated even when the electric lights were switched on.

The hall was particularly dingy, and the staircase leading to the floors above was of dark polished oak, the newel posts topped by finials in the shape of grinning heads. It looked to Stephanie, who took an interest in such things, like a late Victorian addition. The original early nineteenth-century stair would have been of stone with wider, shallower treads; it might have curved elegantly instead of going straight up and then taking sharp right-angled turns on the landing. The stairs too looked uncomfortably steep, and Stephanie remarked on the fact.

'I know,' said Alan. 'It's not ideal. Mind you, it's thanks to that staircase that we got the place at such a bargain price.' It needed no bewildered looks from Stephanie to elicit an explanation.

The Foljambe sisters had been in their seventies, both increasingly infirm, with Eleanor, four years older than Alice, the frailer of the two. Still they refused to quit the beloved house where they had been brought up and, as neither had married, lived almost all of their lives. Then, one night, Eleanor had a fall down the staircase, and, a few days later in hospital, died from her injuries without recovering consciousness. It was only then that her sister Alice decided it was time to go. She put the house and its contents up for sale and moved into 'Meadowview' an expensive residential care home only a dozen or so miles away. The haste with which she did so was remarked upon. Had she not been in such a hurry she might have got a lot more for the house, though the contents, with its fine antique furniture, not to mention its Crumblies memorabilia, sold very well.

'We'll have to do something about those stairs,' said Stephanie. 'A decent stair carpet for a start would help.'

'Just as you say, Steph,' said Alan who was not an unreasonable man.

The following weeks were taken up with furnishing and decoration for which Stephanie had an aptitude and a liking. Alan meanwhile, who was earning the money to pay for it in the shadowy world of investment banking benignly approved from a distance. It was only when Emma and Sebastian came home for the summer holidays at the end of June that all of them travelled down together to Gloucestershire, by which time the house was habitable.

Not everything, of course, was as Stephanie would have wished, but the curtains (pale pink chintz) had, she thought made all the difference to the sitting room, though it was still not as bright and airy as she would have liked. Emma and Sebastian were delighted with the place, even if they did appear to be rather more quarrelsome than usual in their new environment.

Emma at seventeen was three years older than Sebastian and was strongly inclined to dominate her brother who was equally determined not to submit to her rule. Matters first came to a head over the issue of bedrooms. Before their arrival Stephanie had assigned them, taking the best (Eleanor Foljambe's) for Alan and herself and assigning the next largest, which had belonged to Alice to Emma. Oddly enough it had been Emma who had objected to her prescribed room without giving a coherent reason, vaguely complaining about its north facing aspect and the view from her window. Sebastian, who had at first been more than eager to swap rooms, then suddenly turned against the idea out of perversity or even spite. No-one was happy, and a general undercurrent of discontent rumbled on.

There were plenty of rooms in the house, but none of the others would have suited Emma, and Stephanie had done nothing yet to make them usable. All the same she felt guilty that she had not worked harder to make the place more accommodating. Still, there was general approval for the place as a whole, its elegance, its spaciousness and a sense of potential, and everyone was pleased with the garden, even though Stephanie had barely begun to work on it.

With regard to this, a gardener had been found. His name was Jack Woodard and he had worked for the Foljambe sisters. Though now in his seventies he seemed quite hale and amiable, though rather set in his ways. He rarely set foot in the house itself and when he did it was always and only into the kitchen. Stephanie, who unlike Alan, disliked any sign of feudalism, was made uneasy by this, but accepted it. They would sit at the kitchen table with their tea, making plans for new plantings and old restorations. She noticed that whenever she mentioned the Foljambe sisters Jack would veer off the subject as quickly as possible. Stephanie felt mildly aggrieved and frustrated by this. She was naturally curious, and besides, had, at the back of her mind, vague plans for a book about the house and its former inhabitants: before marriage to Alan had sealed her fate, she had been in publishing.

Barely a week after they had moved in two disconcerting events occurred. It was a fine evening at the beginning of July. Alan and Stephanie were on the terrace drinking a bottle of chilled Sancerre before dinner; Emma and Sebastian were somewhere in the garden having been reconciled temporarily to each other. It was a moment of contentment. Alan was in his most emollient mood, having selected the wine and cooled it in the fridge for just the right length of time.

'Pretty decent bottle, I call this,' he said, squinting at the sunlight through its glass green depths.

'Delicious, darling.'

'Goes down very nicely, I think. Fruity but subtle. I bought a case from Berry Bros. Good price too.'

Stephanie was spared the necessity of commending her husband's taste and thrift by the sound of tyres on the gravel drive.

'Not expecting anyone are we?' said Alan who disliked surprises.

'No, darling.'

They rose and walked round the corner to the front of the house. Half way up the drive a car, evidently a taxi, had stopped. The driver got out, went to open the passenger door, and helped an old lady with a stick onto the drive. She wore a floral print summer dress, a straw hat, and, over the dress, a long white summer coat of some elegance and antiquity.

Stephanie murmured to Alan: 'I do believe that's old Alice Foljambe. You know, the surviving sister.'

'We must make her welcome. Ask her up for a drink or something.' He called to her: 'Hi! Miss Foljambe, isn't it?'

Alice Foljambe—for it was she—stood staring at the sudden apparitions, then raised her stick and began waving it threateningly in front of her.

'Hello! I'm Alan Markham and this is my wife Steph. We bought the place from you, remember? Won't you come and join us on the terrace for a drink?'

Alice spoke no word but waved her stick again, even more fiercely, as if trying to fend off an attack. She said something to her driver who stepped in front of her and gestured officiously with his hands as if to push Alan back.

'The bloody little shit! How dare he do that to me on my own property. I say!'

'Leave it, Alan! It's not worth it. The poor woman's obviously nuts.' Alan stopped advancing on the pair, but he did not give ground.

'Well, I call it bloody rude.'

The two pairs stood facing each other. Alice was a good fifty yards from her but Stephanie was aware of two grey blue eyes, cold and hard for all their ancient wateriness, piercing her and almost compelling retreat. Yet she did not because by this time she was almost as indignant as her husband.

'It's as if she resents our being here,' she said.

'Why the hell should she? I bought it from her fair and square. The bloody nerve! Hi!' He started to advance again.

Alice spoke to the taxi driver who helped her back into the car. It reversed rapidly down the drive, almost hitting one of the gateposts in its haste to escape, and they were gone. Alan and Stephanie returned to the terrace but they had both been thoroughly unsettled by the incident, so Stephanie went indoors to start the supper.

Later that night when they were in bed, Alan said: 'I wonder if she'll come back again.'

'Oh, yes. I think so. She doesn't look the sort who gives up easily.'

'The bloody nerve!'

It proved hard for both of them to fall asleep. The night was warm and the window was open, letting in the sounds of a country night: owl hoots and the occasional shriek of a fox. The air moved around them in the darkness. Stephanie could not shake off the piercing malevolence of old Alice's glance, trying to find some fault in herself to excuse it. No, she could not, which made it all the more disconcerting. Suddenly there was a noise.

'God, did you hear that?'

'What?' said Alan, pretending to be more sleepy than he was.

'That sound. Like something falling. It might be Emma, or Sebastian.'

Stephanie jumped out of bed and went to the door, hesitating a moment before she opened it. She knew that noise. It seemed to her identical to what she had heard from the terrace on the first day they had come to The Crumblies. She came out into the passageway at the top of the stairs leading down to the hall. If anything had fallen down stairs the sound surely would have been muffled by the hessian stair carpet she had had installed.

'Emma? Sebastian? Is everything all right?'

All was still and absolutely silent. If anything, the silence was even more ominous. Alan emerged from the bedroom, having put on a dressing gown and slippers.

'What's all this about? Come back to bed, Steph.'

'Didn't you hear anything?' She peered into grey space. 'Emma? Sebastian?' Alan switched on the corridor light. Everything looked bleak and deserted.

Emma emerged blearily from her bedroom further down the corridor.

'Mum? What's going on?'

'I heard something that's all. Like something or someone falling. Didn't you hear anything? Where's Sebastian?'

By this time Sebastian had also come out of his room further down the passage: they were safe. There was no point in investigating further; that could be done in the morning, so the family returned to bed. Stephanie was relieved that Alan did not reproach her for causing an alarm. All he said was: 'Let's get some sleep.' And they did, eventually.

The following morning Stephanie looked for some explanation for what had happened. Her chief fear was that a part of the roof had collapsed, though it had not sounded like that. The noise had not come from above but from somewhere inside the house: she was sure.

At one end of the house was a small winding wooden staircase that led up to a door. This, Stephanie assumed, opened into an attic room, but when, in her first investigations of the house, she had tried the door she found it locked. Thereafter she had occasionally contemplated forcing the door or trying to locate the key, but other more pressing concerns prevented her. Besides, she felt a curious reluctance to investigate. This time too, she decided against it. It would have involved Alan, a hammer and chisel and much unnecessary fuss: the noise had not come from the roof.

She studied the ceilings—no cracks—the rooms and the stairs, finding nothing untoward, except . . . It really was too trivial.

At the bottom of the main stairs she discovered what looked like a pile of dust intermixed with fragments, no bigger than gravel, of something. There was no indication, though, that it had fallen from the ceiling, and it did not appear to be plaster or stone. She fetched a dustpan and brush and, on sweeping it up, became aware of a musty smell as of some kind of decayed organic matter, like old biscuits. This made her heart stop.

She recalled the *Crumblies* books that she had read to Emma and Sebastian when they were young, and somewhere from the back of her mind came a memory of an article she had read—or had it been a radio program?—about the origins of the Crumblies.

It all began as a childhood fantasy. Eleanor and Alice were the daughters of strict and intensely religious parents. The father ran a prosperous business making glassware but he was also a nonconformist lay preacher and a pillar of rectitude. His daughters escaped from their parents' puritanical regime by inventing the Crumblies, little biscuit people made out of dough supplied by their kindly cook and baked in the oven. (No dolls were permitted in the household, as being 'idolatrous'.) In the stories Eleanor and Alice subsequently wrote, the two sisters become Gerda and Matthew, a pair of orphaned siblings living with a tyrannical uncle who means them no good. The Crumblies, once baked, come alive and, surviving on biscuit crumbs supplied by Gerda and Matthew, engage in all kinds of mischief which infuriates and ultimately defeats the wicked uncle. Later volumes of the Crumblies saga recount Gerda and Matthew's adventures with these biscuity folk in all kinds of other circumstances and countries, but the house in which they live, known simply as 'The Rectory' continued to be a backdrop for many of their exploits. Stephanie could not help shuddering at the accident which had put what looked like a pile of stale biscuit crumbs at the foot of her stairs. It was a coincidence, of course, pure coincidence.

Stephanie put these idiotic thoughts behind her, and life went on. It was an idyllic summer so that she spent much time in the garden which, thanks to her and Jack Woodard's labour—with desultory assistance from Emma and Sebastian—was becoming a place of delight.

One day she and Jack had decided to make a start on the walled garden where Stephanie planned to grow vegetables, a lot of them, and become self-sufficient: the whole thing. It filled her with passionate excitement. Strange, she reflected momentarily, how such moments of thrilling enthusiasm never occurred indoors, always outside.

There was an entrance through a brick arch to the walled garden just below the terrace, on the south side of the house, but there was another way in via a door in the wall at its far end. Unfortunately, this door was locked with no key in evidence and, since the tool shed was situated just beyond, it proved necessary to find it. Stephanie consulted with Jack on the terrace.

'Miss Alice had that key, that I know,' Jack said. It was his first ever unsolicited reference to either of the Foljambe sisters. 'She were the gardener of the two.'

Stephanie was at once intrigued. 'Really, did she—?'

'Now, I seem to remember she kept some keys behind the scullery door. May be there we'll find him.' He began to make rapid strides towards the back door to the kitchen, Stephanie following.

'So Alice was the gardener?' she said, by way of opening an interrogation.

'That's right,' said Jack but offered no more.

The 'scullery', a small room off the large main kitchen, was not one of which Stephanie had as yet made much use, except to install a chest freezer in it. And there, on a hook behind the door were two large old keys on a loop of frayed string. One of them did unlock the door to the walled garden, the other, slightly smaller and less rusted, did not.

'I wonder what this other one is for,' said Stephanie, almost to herself, once the garden door had been opened.

'That I wouldn't know,' said Jack firmly and left soon after.

Stephanie's curiosity had been aroused by the fragment of information Jack had let fall. Now she was on fire and, though she experienced the usual dampening of her spirits on entering the house again, her eagerness did not cool entirely. Acting upon an instinct, she took the key up the stairs and put it into the attic door lock. It turned.

Before she opened it, Stephanie paused and contemplated the door whose chalky white paint had blistered and flaked off in parts, almost as if its surface had been scratched. She felt as if she were on a threshold, both literally and metaphorically. She could turn back or go forward. It was, for a moment, a delicately balanced choice, until something persuaded her that there was no choice at all: she had to go forward. She turned the handle and went in.

The space under the triangular roof was lit by two large north-facing dormer windows. There was an electric light hanging from the rafters but the bulb had gone. Just below the windows there was a table, a chair, a slanted drawing board, over which brooded an immense anglepoise lamp, with pens and brushes in jars, and an array of bottles containing coloured inks flanking the drawing board. So, this was Alice's studio where she had drawn The Crumblies.

When Alan and Stephanie had first moved into the house, all the other rooms had been rigorously stripped of every last stick of furniture; not so much as a rug or a free-standing bookcase was left, but this attic, for some reason, had been left intact. Were it not for the thick dust which smeared and shadowed every surface, it could have been left that very afternoon. There was even a half completed drawing on the board.

Stephanie went over and switched on the anglepoise. To her surprise the light worked.

THE CRUMBLIES

It was a drawing in Alice's familiar style of ink and wash on heavy paper. In it three gigantic figures, more than three times the height of humans were shambling among the smoking ruins of what had once been a country village. The sky above them was full of black clouds and a general air of apocalyptic dread pervaded the scene. A few small human figures were to be seen scattering in terror before the three monsters. The giants had big clumsy corrugated limbs and round heads like boulders, pitted and striated, with crude bulbous features and dark, crinkled currant eyes. They were Crumblies, swollen to twenty times their normal size—in the books they had never been more than a foot tall—and bloated with menace.

Stephanie stepped back in horror. Something had happened to these friendly, innocently mischievous little creatures in the mind of their creator. She glanced down and discovered that she was standing on a wooden floor covered with pieces of paper. She picked one up: it was a half-completed sketch of two Crumblies, one seemingly trying to gnaw the head off the other one. All the other sheets were sketches too. In another a Crumbly was wielding a club and pounding a fellow Crumbly to fragments. In another, perhaps the most strikingly realised of them all, a Crumbly stood at the top of a flight of stairs while another lay at the bottom in scattered shards, like a broken dinner plate.

Stephanie began to cough and retch. Her picking up of paper had unsettled the dust which now filled the air like a miasma, and there was a pervasive smell, not so much of decaying as *decayed* matter. She switched off the lamp and fled from the attic, almost tripping at the top of the stairs which led down from it.

When she had descended from above she found Sebastian and Emma having a violent quarrel on the landing. On seeing her they appealed to her judgement. Emma claimed that she had been standing at the top of the stairs when she felt two hands in the small of her back attempting to push her down them. She turned round but there was no-one there. The push had been

163

quite feeble so she had managed to maintain her balance and not fall, but she was still enraged. Quite obviously it had been a trick played on her by Sebastian who had quickly concealed himself before she could turn round. Sebastian protested his innocence, claiming that he had been listening to music on his headphones in his own room, where Emma had subsequently found him. Stephanie listened to both sides and concluded that Sebastian's defence was more than plausible, which infuriated Emma. Sebastian meanwhile made himself objectionable by talking loudly and scornfully about 'over-vivid imaginations'. (How like Alan he was!) Recriminations trickled on.

Alan had been out at golf that day, having just acquired membership of a nearby club, and seemed in a relaxed frame of mind on his return. Over a drink in the sitting room Stephanie told him about Emma and Sebastian's incident. Alan was silent for a while, unusually reflective, then, he said, characteristically: 'It's high time those two grew up.'

'And when they do,' said Stephanie, 'they'll leave us and we might never see them again.'

Once more Alan was silent, turning his wine glass around in his hands. Stephanie would have loved to have heard his thoughts. Most of the time she could read them with ease, but there were moments of enigma. Just then, through the open window, they heard a car on the drive. Alan leaped up and went to look.

'Hallo! I believe it's that mad old woman again.'

It was. The same taxi driver opened the passenger door while Alice Foljambe got out and stood on the drive. The moment she saw Alan and Stephanie at the window watching her she began to wave her stick threateningly at them, then suddenly she got back into the car which turned rapidly on the lawn and went back down the drive at speed.

'That mad old bitch!' said Alan. 'Well, at least we know she's still alive. You can't be haunted by the living.'

It was an odd remark. 'Oh, can't you?' was what Stephanie wanted to say in reply but didn't. Instead, looking at him intently, she said: 'You know something about Alice, that I don't, don't you?'

Continuing to gaze out of the window at the gathering dusk, Alan said: 'Only something one of the blokes at the golf club said. A local. Just that our Eleanor's fall down those stairs may not have been completely accidental. Probably just gossip. Bit of nonsense. You know what these local people are like. . . .'

Stephanie would like to have said: 'No, what *are* they like?' Once more she restrained herself.

'. . . Well, it's possible, I suppose,' said Alan. 'The woman's obviously doolally, off her trolley, several bottles short of a case of Cliquot.' Alan liked such phrases, even inventing his own sometimes. It was his one concession to the world of the imagination.

Stephanie smiled and said: 'When you're back at the bank during the week, I'd like to invite someone down to stay.'

'Oh. Who?'

'Well, I thought possibly Eric . . . ?'

Alan groaned theatrically. 'Oh, God! Really?'

Eric was Stephanie's half-brother: small, pale, unattractive, deeply religious, unmarried, in fact almost everything that Alan was not. He was the vicar of a church in North London, of distinctively Anglo-Catholic persuasion. Alan called him 'the bells and smells man' and sometimes 'the poofy vicar'. This last was probably inaccurate, Stephanie thought, as she had always regarded him as completely sexless, but you never knew. And what business was it of his? Alan, she thought, did not so much dislike as despise Eric, if this is not a distinction without a difference.

She said: 'He hardly ever gets away from that parish, and you know how poor he is.'

'Only because he gives practically all his money away to unjust causes. That man could bore the arse off a donkey.'

Stephanie had to concede that Eric was a bore, and he held some very silly views, notably on the status of women priests, but he had always been kindness itself to her.

'You'll only see him when you come down for the weekend. He is my brother after all.'

'Half-brother,' said Alan. But she could see that he was reconciled to the visit.

It was fortunate for Stephanie that Eric was of a distinctly ascetic turn of mind. She had managed to fit out a spare room at the end of the corridor, but it was very spare: just a camp bed, a chest of drawers with a reading light and a small rug on the bare boards. Meanwhile Alan had gone back to his bank in London, with the promise of returning at weekends for golf and fresh air, and Emma and Sebastian decided to follow suit. The novelty of the place had apparently worn off; and they wanted to see their friends in London. Stephanie wondered why she stayed behind. It was the garden, of course, and the need to welcome Eric for his little holiday, but something more: the urge to fulfil an unspecified task.

Before Eric arrived, she had two days alone in The Crumblies which were filled for her with restlessness. She had meant to work hard on the garden, but the weather was against her and Jack did not come. She tried to do things in the house, hang pictures that had not been put up, rag roll their *en suite* bathroom with sky blue paint as Alan had ordained, because it was 'rather smart', but always in these clean, lonely spaces she felt pursued by an anxiety that felt like guilt. More than once she heard that obstinately familiar sound as of a heavy weight falling down a flight of stairs, but at a distance, so that she could, if she chose, discount its significance. She did, but perhaps less easily dismissed were the strange little piles of decayed matter that she found around the house, often at the foot of the front stairs. She would hoover them up as soon as she saw them, trying not to seek an explanation for their presence. It did not help that the rain kept her indoors.

She did not sleep at night too well either, not because of noise, but because a great silence reigned in the hours of darkness. It was a close silence that seemed to absorb even an echo; it held secrets and the unutterable enmity of people who had refused to speak to one another.

However, on the third day she woke to find that the rain had gone and the sky was washed clean, and she had Eric's arrival to look forward to. Such was her eagerness to see him that she drove to meet him at Bracton Central station, a full twenty minutes before she needed to. When Eric arrived and stood smiling and plump on the platform with his anorak, his backpack, and a small old-fashioned suitcase of shiny brown leather, she thought how extraordinarily nondescript he looked. It was oddly comforting.

In the car driving back from the station, her brother kept up a stream of mild ecclesiastical gossip. Alan was right: he *was* a bore. The people and issues which he discussed might have been taking place on another planet for all Stephanie knew or cared about them. More importantly, what possible help could Eric be to her if his mind was taken up with such trivialities?

As they came nearer the house, Eric grew quieter and started to ask her about Alan and the children. Her replies, she reflected, may have been as dull and inconsequential to him as his talk was to her. On their arrival she gave him a tour of the house and garden, both of which excited much praise from Eric whose architectural enthusiasms were genuine enough even if they did not generally extend much beyond Butterfield, Buckton Lamb, Pugin, and other heroes of High Church neo-Gothic. It was only when he was confronted with the late Victorian staircase that he fell silent.

A MAZE FOR THE MINOTAUR

They enjoyed a simple supper in the kitchen, talking of memories which only had meaning for them. When these subjects finally evaporated, there followed a long, unembarrassed silence until Eric finally said: 'So, do you think you want to go on living here?'

Stephanie saw the futility of pretence. She said: 'I'm not at all sure.'

'Presumably that is why you asked me down here.'

'Only partly,' said Stephanie. Eric was not one of those people who took offence if you told him the truth. They said no more on the subject for the time being.

That night the house was full of noises again, not enough to force abandonment of all rational explanation but sufficient to excite unease. The following morning over breakfast Stephanie told her brother all that she knew about the Foljambe sisters and all that she had experienced. Eric listened without any expression of incredulity or even surprise.

'Of course,' he said, 'it is as possible to be haunted by the living as by the dead.'

'Do you think that is what it is?'

'I don't know, but I suspect that one of the sisters is at rest and the other is not. I understand little about the spirits of the dead, but I do know something about the guilt of the living.'

'Is there anything you can do?'

He shrugged his shoulders, smiling feebly. It was a gesture more of modesty than indifference.

Two days later on Friday evening Alan came down with Emma and Sebastian for the weekend. As usual the children teased and mocked Eric which he took with such complete serenity and good humour that they very soon desisted from boredom. Alan, on the other hand, did his best to ignore his brother-in-law altogether. He talked politics throughout supper with an aggressive dogmatism that even Stephanie, who was very familiar with his views, had not witnessed before. The mood of assertion communicated to Emma and Sebastian who began to argue about something that had happened in London involving a friend of theirs. Eric made no effort to intervene in the conversation; instead he watched with a kind of bemused curiosity. Stephanie was relieved when it was time to go to bed.

It was three o'clock when she awoke. She had heard the noise again. 'The fall', she had begun to call it: a single thump and then a succession of them, like a ragged fusillade. It punctuated the silence of the night. Stephanie lay rigid in her bed, her heart beating fast, but the silence that followed did not reassure her. She dared not get up. She felt she had only to lie very still and the thing—which was an illusion of some sort after all—would go away. When a noiseless minute had passed, she started slowly to untense. Then it happened all over again: the identical series of bumps dying away into an ominous silence. She froze and waited for it to stop. She did not switch on a light: the dark was preferable. She shut her eyes. There was silence once more. When, after a long three minutes, it began again, fury overmastered fear and she leapt out of bed.

In the grey light of the passage outside she not only heard it—louder this time—but felt it. The whole house shuddered, as if convulsed by the shake of thunder. She went to the top of the stairs from where the noise seemed to emanate, and clutched at the newel post to steady herself. The bumping sounds were now continuous, leaping over themselves, fugal, and Stephanie stood at their centre. She was numb now, neither furious nor fearful, but overwhelmed, possessed by the noise. She heard herself almost as if she were listening to another person, whimpering out a plea for it to stop, but it would not; it defied her. Then she felt something: hands in the small of her back trying to push her down the stairs. They were strong hands. Still clutching the newel post to stop herself from falling she twisted herself round and saw in the misty darkness the vague form of Alan, naked, expressionless, his arms reaching out and trying to propel her down the stairs. At that, her trance broke and she screamed.

Eric ran out of his room at the end of the corridor and immediately began shouting in his silly feeble voice: 'I say! No! None of that! No! Stop that now!' Stephanie almost laughed, but she was still struggling with Alan who seemed to take no notice of Eric's appeals. Eric meanwhile had realised that verbal protests alone were of no use.

'Stop that!' he said again, in a stronger voice as he came up to him. 'Wake up!' and he slapped Alan's face. By this time Emma and Sebastian had emerged into the corridor and were angrily demanding an explanation of the disturbance. Slowly Alan began to come to his senses. When he was fully conscious, he looked with dismay at the scene and fled back into his bedroom. It was only then that Stephanie realised that the falling sounds had ceased. Emma and Sebastian stopped protesting; Eric crossed himself: finally, Stephanie led the other three carefully down stairs to the kitchen. She put a kettle on the Aga and they had tea, saying little, and nothing of consequence.

Breakfast was a late and subdued affair, conducted mainly by Eric with a kind of bustling incompetence. When he, Alan, and Stephanie were alone, at about midday, he announced in a loud voice: 'I want you two to drive me over to this Home of Alice's. Meadowview, is it called? This afternoon. Two thirty, I should think.' Alan simply nodded his assent. He had not recovered fully from last night. Then Eric, declining any offer of lunch, went up to his room.

He reappeared at the appointed time in the hall wearing a suit of canonical black with a dog collar and carrying his little old-fashioned suitcase of shiny brown leather. He looked curiously businesslike. Stephanie drove, with Eric in front with her, and Alan slumped in the back. The only words spoken in the car came from the cool female voice of the Satnav directing them towards Alice Foljambe's new home.

They arrived at a large, rambling red brick house in its own extensive grounds. It looked substantial, reliable and ugly. They stopped on the gravel drive just in front of its large, glassed-in porch. Eric got out of the car with his little suitcase and told them to wait there. Alan scrambled out of the back and sat himself next to his wife in the front. Their hands touched. They said little.

It was almost three hours before Eric emerged from Meadowview. Stephanie and Alan saw a matronly figure, evidently the warden, shaking hands deferentially with Eric. She even appeared to be offering to carry his suitcase for him to the car, but he declined. Stephanie noticed that he was now wearing an elaborately embroidered purple stole over his black suit.

When he had climbed into the back seat of the car Eric said: 'I think she has peace now. But you never can tell.'

Alan and Stephanie both knew better than to press him for details. Stephanie started the car and once they had left the precincts of Meadowview she said to Alan: 'I still don't want to live there any more.'

There was a long pause before Alan said: 'Well, if we do sell, we'll probably get twice what I paid for it.'

For a moment Stephanie felt like hitting him; instead she laughed, and went on laughing, rather too long for comfort.

MONKEY'S

MONKEY'S

'The trouble with Soviet Russia,' said Straker, 'is too many chiefs and not enough Indians. That's what's wrong with Socialism in general: all very well in theory, but too many chiefs and not enough Indians. What you want is a small, well-educated, and of course benevolent, elite to run your country.'

Cavendish winked at me and said: 'You mean a Conservative government ruled by a cabinet of Old Etonians?'

'Well, yes.'

'Very sound idea, Straker. We must give it a go.' Cavendish was always amused by Straker's dogmatic pronouncements, and I had learned to be amused too because of my admiration for Cavendish. Very few people are good at finding themselves funny and Straker was not one of them, but he took Cavendish's teasing suavely, by pretending to be unaware that he was being laughed at. Cavendish had once said to me: 'Straker is destined to become one of those Tory grandees you hear so much about: those secret, hard-faced men who rule the country from smoke-filled rooms behind closed doors. Mark my words.'

I believed him, because Straker was well-connected, ambitious and, in spite of his opinions, far from being a fool. The fact that Straker did not, after all, trouble the history books may have had something to do with what happened on the day the above conversation took place. It is a possible explanation, I suppose.

On a perfect summer's morning in late June 1970 Straker, Cavendish and I were standing on 'Rafts', the name given to a complex of wooden boathouses and landing stages owned by Eton College. Across the river from us towered the stately grey form of Windsor Castle, crowning a steep rise overlooking the Thames. On that bright day it brought to my mind the 'many towered Camelot' of Tennyson's poem. If I remember rightly, the effect was enhanced by the fact that the royal standard fluttered from a mast high above us on the Round Tower, indicating that the Queen was in residence. Between us and the town and castle of Windsor, the river glittered in the sunlight, caressed by a slight breeze.

As I say, that is how I remember it. It is all very vivid to me, but that is no guarantee of accuracy. I have learned over the years to distrust memory, a necessary distrust. All the same, in the light of what has happened, I feel bound to record what I think I remember. I have marked the envelope in which you find this 'To be opened after my death', and it is up to you to do what you like with it. Burn it is my advice; burn it even before you read what follows.

That felt very odd: writing to an unknown someone from beyond a grave that has not yet, at the time of writing, been dug. So, enough of this! Let me just set down what I think I remember,

MONKEY'S

but please bear in mind: it may have been a delusion, or some sort of bad dream.

Straker, Cavendish and I were in our last half—term to the rest of you—at Eton. We had done our 'A' Levels, and our destinies at University or elsewhere were almost sealed. So, while the rest of the school did their end-of-half exams, or 'trials' as they were appropriately called, we could take our leisure.

That day we had decided to go down to Rafts and take a boat out on the Thames and row upstream to *Monkey's*, a little island in the river just below Bray. It was known by all of us as Monkey's, but its official name was *Monk's Eyot*. The story went that there had been a monastery on the site, but at the dissolution it had been donated to Eton College by Henry VIII in 'exchange' for some more valuable land nearer London. The site remained untouched until the 19th century when it began to be used by the school's rowers as a place where they could rest and refresh themselves before rowing back down stream to Rafts. A wooden clubhouse and a proper landing stage were built there in the 1920s. In the year 1970, the time I am talking about, there was a man employed to live on the island in the summer months and dispense refreshment to tired rowers. His name was Billy. It was a pleasant place, fringed with trees through which a path from the landing stage led to an oval lawn with the clubhouse, looking like an old-fashioned cricket pavilion, at one apex.

We expected nobody else to be on the island except Billy. In the afternoons on half holidays, the place would be teeming with boys and boats, but we were setting out in the morning, having obtained permission to be absent from 'boy's dinner' as lunch was called. We saw it as an adventure. The expedition had been suggested by Cavendish, not because he was a keen oarsman, unlike Straker who rowed bow in the school eight, but because he had a questing nature and an interest in unusual environments. A private island in the Thames was one such, I suppose.

We hired a 'gig', a leisurely, spacious kind of boat for two rowers sitting side by side and a cox in the stern. Straker insisted on steering. He pointed out that, being by far the superior oarsman, he would unbalance the rowing team and the boat would go round in circles, while as cox he could give us expert tuition in the art of oarsmanship. Cavendish and I accepted with a smile and without protest, but our first attempts at rowing after we had launched the gig away from Rafts were clumsy, and Straker got splashed several times.

'Feather! Christ! Don't you bastards even know how to feather?' He instructed us on how to slide the oar parallel to the surface of the water before dipping it in for the next stroke. After a while Cavendish and I began to be rather pleased with our efforts, though Straker remained critical. As we were passing Windsor race course on our left, we began to tire of Straker's dictatorial manner. We wanted to enjoy ourselves, so Cavendish decided to change the subject.

'So, here we are! Three Men in a Boat,' he said.

'I tried to read that book once,' said Straker. 'It turns out the three of them are all lower middle class. And that bit about the dead prostitute is just ridiculous.'

'Remind us about the dead prostitute. I'd forgotten her,' said Cavendish. But Straker would not; instead he continued to give us detailed instructions on how to improve our rowing.

A river cruiser full of trippers passed by, going downstream in the opposite direction. They waved at us. I waved back but Cavendish and Straker did not, so I stopped waving as soon as I became aware of their reticence.

'What ghastly people!' said Straker.

Cavendish said: 'How do you know they're ghastly people?'

There was a pause while Straker considered a reply as we ploughed on, to the creak of the rowlocks and the splash of oars. Eventually he came up with: 'A lot of time is wasted in life by not making snap judgements.'

Cavendish laughed. 'A typical Straker remark! I shall treasure it.'

After we had negotiated 'Locks' which was what we called Boveney Lock, the countryside on either bank of the river became more rural. I began to feel that kind of perfect exhilaration that comes to us rarely, but most often to the young and (comparatively) innocent. It was as if the glitter of the water and the insolently vibrant green of the trees that bordered the river had been made for my delight. I felt, I suppose, that sense of 'entitlement' which is so virulently condemned nowadays, but if it was so, it was of a fairly harmless kind. I began to hum the Eton Boating Song until Cavendish and Straker silenced me because it was 'not cool', which perhaps it wasn't.

It took longer than I expected to row from Locks to Monkey's but finally the little wooded island appeared in the stream. We moored our gig at the landing stage and stepped onto the eyot. It was approaching lunchtime and we were badly in need of refreshment.

Once we were off the landing stage we were protected from any prying eyes on the banks by a dense fringe of trees. On that bright summer day, the woodland felt as humid and intense as a jungle. No birds sang and Monkey's seemed deserted. Such was our carelessness that we had simply assumed that Billy would be on the island, but why *should* he be there?

We came through the wooded area onto the lawn that stood in front of the club house. It was a long low building clad in creosoted weather boarding with a veranda along the front. A clock over the central front entrance proclaimed it to be ten to one. Straker shouted for Billy, but no-one came. I suggested we should row a little further up stream to a riverside pub in Bray and get something to eat and drink there, but Straker was impatient. He seemed to believe that Billy had no right to be absent from Monkey's, the school island. He walked over to the clubhouse, Cavendish and I following. He tried the door and found it open.

'Billy must be here. It's unlocked,' said Straker. 'Billy!'

The whole place smelt of creosoted wood in the heat. It was a smallish, dingy area with a few tables and chairs, and a bar behind which an enticing array of bottled beers and soft drinks was displayed on shelves. Suddenly the place darkened even further. We turned and saw a huge figure framed by the open doorway.

'Hello! What are you lads doing, then?'

Billy was shirtless and dressed in nothing but a pair of baggy khaki shorts and plimsols. He was of middle height but broad-chested and carrying a fair amount of weight some of which hung pendulously over the leather belt that fastened his shorts. His face was bronzed and red from the sun, a great slab of a head in the middle of which his rather small features were gathered close together. Reddish curls clustered on the top of his head and glinted in the sunlight. I suppose he must have been in his late forties, almost the prime of life, but he looked like a monstrous baby. Even today, stripped of the snobbery of youth which looks on anything over thirty as physically unacceptable, I would be repulsed by his appearance.

'Hello, Billy,' said Straker.

'Oh, it's you, Mr Straker, sir,' said Billy who had recognised him as a member of the 'eight', and was accordingly deferential. 'What are you and your lads doing here? I wasn't expecting visitors.'

Straker explained laboriously, and Billy merely nodded, uninterested. The only other time I had been on Monkey's in the presence of many other boys on the usual half-holiday, he had exuded a kind of rough bonhomie and self-confidence, but on this occasion I detected a certain unease in his manner. In spite of this he was very accommodating. He set out a table and chairs on the lawn in front of the clubhouse and found some day-old sandwiches in his fridge for us to eat. We bought several bottles of beer off Billy whom we treated liberally with the same. He sat with us and talked, quaffing his lager straight from the bottle while we decorously poured ours into paper cups.

The slight furtiveness of his initial manner began to dissipate with the sun and the beer. He became expansive and talked reminiscently of his time in the army during the war. 'Those Jerrys, they were real bastards,' he kept saying. He claimed to have been present at the liberation of Belsen. In those days I was very credulous, but there was something formulaic about his description of the event that even made me sceptical that he had actually been there.

'Them Jerry guards. Them bastards. I just wanted to put them up against a wall and shoot the buggers. I would have done too if my sarge hadn't stopped me.'

At that moment we heard a faint banging and shouting coming from behind the clubhouse.

'What's that?' asked Straker.

'Don't you worry about it, Mr Straker,' said Billy. 'Just something I'm sorting out.' Billy's unease had returned, but he continued to talk volubly. He began to expatiate on 'what those bastard Jerrys did'. He went into detail; and now it was our turn to feel unsettled.

From the 'Jerrys' Billy's talk turned somehow to 'women' whose customs and characteristics, apparently, could be defined with equal ease. It was a hot day and I was not used to so much beer so I cannot say exactly how the transition occurred. He said many things which surprised us but which we, in awe of his experience, did not feel qualified to question. I glanced at my companions. Cavendish had a quizzical expression; Straker appeared actively amused. Billy was apparently very fond of women, but he thought they needed to be kept in order, and 'given a good hiding' once in a while. It was his view that they liked to be treated roughly, and to be given a good 'seeing to' on a regular basis. He then specified various methods by which this 'seeing to' might be applied. At this even Straker began to look doubtful: some of the ways were very strange and unpleasant. We tried not to picture the scenes. Billy said that relations with his wife had taken these forms and that their marriage as a result had been excellent for many years until she left him. He explained that her departure was the result of his having 'gone soft' on her.

In the end, I can only really attribute our lack of protest to the drink and because none of us probably had ever heard an adult talk like this before. During Billy's discussion of women we heard again the faint sounds of banging and protest coming from the direction of the clubhouse. Eventually the noise became so violent and anguished that Billy got up irritably, muttering that he had better 'see to it', and began to walk rapidly towards the clubhouse.

'What the hell is going on?' said Straker. He sounded indignant that the pleasure of that afternoon had been subverted by this strange interruption. Cavendish, more curious, less set in his ways, said: 'Let's see what all the fuss is about.'

Cavendish and I got up and set off, tracking Billy at a distance; Straker reluctantly followed us after a while. We saw Billy go round the clubhouse behind which, among the trees, were a number of sheds and outhouses. From the largest of these the noise was coming. Someone was kicking at the door and yelling. The voice sounded young and possibly male, but in my memory it had a quality that was not quite human, like the whine of a machine trying to simulate the human voice. The words spoken sounded English and full of swearing, but, like the language in a dream, not fully comprehensible.

Unseen by Billy ourselves, we saw him pause before the door of the shed which shuddered from the blows with which it was being assaulted from the inside.

'Hey, you in there!' he said, 'You little scumbucket! You cut that noise or I'll come in and give you the leathering you deserve.'

There was a silence, the shouting and the hammering ceased for about ten seconds, then it began again with renewed vigour.

'Fuck off, you old wanker!' the voice yelled. These were the only words I heard from it that were completely articulate, and even they did not sound altogether real, that is, coming from a real live boy. That is how I remember it, because, though my recollections of what happened are disturbingly vivid there are aspects of them which remain obscure.

Billy's reaction to the creature's insult was unnervingly calm and deliberate. He removed his leather belt slowly from around his waist. Fears that his shorts might ignominiously fall down were allayed by the way the waistband seemed to cut into his barrel of a belly. Billy slid back the bolt on the door of the shed and entered. The belt cracked and cries of pain, unnaturally high-pitched, were heard. I looked at Cavendish and Straker. Their expressions were blank but, like me, they appeared to be held to the spot. I knew that a supreme effort of will would tear me away from the sounds, but Cavendish and Straker did not move, so neither did I. Already we were beginning to feel complicit.

The cracking ceased and the cries had become muffled. Billy came out of the shed, bolting the door behind him. He was putting on his belt and adjusting his khaki shorts to conceal, not very effectively, his arousal when he saw us. Not put out by our appearance, he said: 'Oh, so you heard?' We nodded.

'Those little toerags, they swim over here and steal my lager beer. All those little vermin, they come from Monk's Lawn.' We looked blank. 'Over there—' He pointed to the Windsor bank of the river. 'Next to the old Bray Studios where they do them horror films. Monk's Lawn is like a Borstal or approved school, or what. The inmates there, they're the real horrors. Little bundles of evil, that's what they are; that's why they're sent there. They swim over here and they make bloody havoc with my island. One of them tried to set fire to the clubhouse. So, when I catch them, I give them a good hiding. That's what they should give them over there at Monk's Lawn, only they don't, the daft soft buggers. My leatherings don't do no good though. They keep coming back. I've caught this little nipper before. He's a right little shitbag.' He paused. 'Tell you what, lads, let's have a little sport, shall we? You young gentlemen wait here, while I get something.'

Billy went into the clubhouse, adjusting the belt around his waist. Straker, Cavendish and I looked at each other. Straker laughed nervously. I suggested we leave; Cavendish smiled.

'Billy is an interesting psychological study,' he said. 'Did you notice the erection? I think we should stay and see what he has for our further entertainment. We might find it instructive.'

That mixture of pomposity and mockery was entirely characteristic of Cavendish. You never knew how serious he was being. His manner was widely admired, but it was also annoying.

'It will afford Straker here, our coming politician, much valuable insight into criminal behaviour among the lower orders,' he added.

'Oh, belt up, Cavendish,' said Straker. For once I agreed with him: this was no time for satire.

Billy emerged from the clubhouse carrying a long coil of rope over one shoulder. He winked at us and put his finger to his lips. We watched as he unbolted the shed. Billy left the door open, but we did not follow him inside. We could hear him talking to what was in the shed and the noises made in reply suggested to us that Billy's prisoner was being gagged. It was some time before Billy came out of the shed with his captive, and I could see why. Its hands had been securely tied behind its back and attached to the long rope, and a rough hood, made, I think, from a large paper bag with holes in it, had been placed on its head.

You will notice that I use the word 'it'. I do this because, however hard I try, I simply cannot remember what the creature looked like. I assumed that it was male and adolescent, but I cannot be sure. I remember that it was smaller than I had expected and that the legs were bare and unpleasantly thin. But was the skin black or white? I cannot even be sure of that: the legs were possibly too caked in grime and mud to tell. I think I saw a little rivulet of blood trickling down the right leg, but I cannot be sure.

'You don't want to see his face,' said Billy, explaining the hood. 'It's like a little rat's face. You don't want to see that.' It was true: we didn't.

The captive began to make plaintive moaning sounds from inside the bag, but Billy jerked the rope sharply, and it nearly fell over.

'Hey! You! Pipe down, or I'll leather you again.'

'Are you going to let him go?' I asked.

'In good time, lad. In good time. But we're going to have a bit of fun first, aren't we, gentlemen? Teach this little article, a lesson, eh? All right, go on, then.'

He pushed the captive ahead of him until we reached the lawn in front of the club house. The sun beat down upon the enclave within the surrounding trees. All sound, except the faint rustle of leaves was excluded. We were cut off from the world on a private island where Billy was king and we were his courtiers. *Le roi s'amuse.*

Billy unwound the long coil of rope and shook it. 'Right you are, little horsy, away you go.' And he lashed the captive's back with the rope's end.

I expect the creature couldn't see very well out of his hood, because it stumbled forward and then fell. Billy jerked the rope.

'Run, you little beggar! Run!' The captive scrambled up and began to run off in the direction of the trees at the far end of the lawn while Billy paid out the rope. Cavendish sat down at the table on the lawn to consider the spectacle and I followed suit. Straker remained standing, enthralled, as we were, by the strangeness of the spectacle. I felt as if I had entered an alien world where the rules were different. If it was an illusion, it was a curiously satisfying one.

'I can see this becoming a new sport,' said Cavendish. 'What shall we call it, Straker? You are the sportsman among us. You decide.' But Straker pretended not to hear him; he was absorbed by the spectacle. Billy was urging his victim to run and then jerking him back once he had reached the end of the long rope. Slowly he was driving the captive towards the belt of woodland that fringed the island. Every time he pulled the captive back the creature fell and had to be got onto its feet again with cajolements and threats. There was a kind of savage comedy about it all, like a scene out of Beckett.

'Don't they remind you of Pozzo and Lucky?' said Cavendish, almost speaking my thoughts.

'What the hell are you talking about?' said Straker. He suspected Cavendish of trying to pull rank on him by means of literary references. He may have been right. He strode away from us towards Billy and the rope.

'I think our friend Straker is taking rather an unhealthy interest in the proceedings,' said Cavendish.

I said: 'Aren't we, as well?' and Cavendish fell silent.

Though we could not hear distinctly, it was plain that Straker was asking Billy if he might take over the reins. Billy seemed more than happy to relinquish the rope and watch. Straker took over with enthusiasm, urging the captive to run further into the woods, then jerking him back at the last moment with a shout of triumph.

Cavendish and I had been seated, but both of us rose as one after Straker's second go with the rope and began to walk in his direction. I am not sure whether it was curiosity or the concern that Straker was showing too much enthusiasm in his activities. I believe it was the latter. I hope so. Perhaps it was both. As we approached, we could see the captive in the trees frantically trying to free himself from his bonds while Straker was urging him to run. In his frustration Straker gave a sudden violent tug on the rope. The captive looked as if he was jerked off his feet and was flying through the air for a few seconds until the back of his head collided with a tree and he fell to the ground. Straker pulled on the rope again but could not stir it.

'Get up! Get up, you little shit!' Straker shouted. There was panic in his voice. The captive lay without moving at the foot of the tree. Billy, Cavendish and I ran towards the captive while Straker remained immobile. Coming nearer we saw blood on the ground about the body; there was blood too on a broken branch protruding from the tree. It would appear that the captive's head had collided with the branch; a deep wound in the back of the neck confirmed it. Billy knelt down to feel the body's pulse. The thing was very still; there appeared to be no breathing.

Billy said: 'Bloody hell, the stupid little fucker's dead!'

By this time Straker had joined us. He said: 'Christ!'

The body was lying face down, the bloodstained bag still partially covering its head. We turned it over and removed the bag, to reveal the face. The shock had been great already but, now, as I remember it, there was a further and even greater shock. The face was not quite human. It was covered in hair, the jaw protruded unnaturally, and the eyes, still open, were black: little round balls of polished jet. The face was like a monkey's: like one but not exactly. The skin, under the reddish-brown hair, was smooth, without the dense network of wrinkles you would see on a simian. The rest of the body, what we could see of it under the dingy shorts and T-shirt, was ambiguous too.

That is what I now remember. I have probed my recollections many times, particularly in these last few weeks and that is still what I see in my mind's eye. In my dreams—and I have often dreamed a version of what happened—I sometimes see a different face, just the ordinary pale face of a young boy in the throes of a terminal terror. Sometimes in my dreams the boy starts to breathe again, but in my waking memory the body lying there is still, silent, hirsute, and not quite human.

'Christ!' Straker said again.

After a long silence, Billy said. 'Right lads, there's only one thing for it. There's a couple of spades in that there shed. Go and fetch them.'

Cavendish and I raced off to get them. We said nothing: it was something to do. Anything was better than doing nothing. When we returned Billy and Straker had cleared a space a few feet from where the body had fallen under the trees, and we immediately began to dig.

One of us, I forget who, asked why we were burying the body there. Billy laughed and said: 'This is where all the bodies are buried.' Then seeing our stunned faces, he added: 'Only joking, lads, only joking!'

The four of us took it in turns to use the two spades, two of us resting for about ten minutes before taking over from the other two. It was hard work because the soil was criss-crossed with tree roots that we had to cut through, and Billy insisted that we dig a hole at least six feet deep. We did it in a daze of strenuous activity and sheer exhaustion, but it helped to take our minds off what had happened. Billy kept urging us to work harder and dig deeper. He seemed to take pleasure in our hot, sweating, tormented bodies under the tangle of trees.

At last it was done. There was the hole with watery mud seeping in at the bottom. Billy rolled the body with his foot until it tumbled into the grave. Filling in the hole seemed to take no time at all, though we were at great pains in the end to make it look as if the ground had not been disturbed at all. No-one was to know, except us four.

'There we are,' said Billy stamping down a slice of turf onto the grave. 'Rest in peace, you dirty little monkey.' Straker sniggered; Cavendish and I were silent. I think it was only then that the full enormity of what had happened came upon us. We hated what Billy had said, but we hated ourselves hardly any less. At least I did.

MONKEY'S

Very soon after, we were rowing away from Monkey's. Billy did not see us off. When we were several hundred yards downstream of the island, Cavendish said: 'We don't talk about this ever again,' Straker and I nodded and the rest of the row down-stream to Rafts took place in silence.

As far as I remember, none of us ever did mention what had happened to each other or to anyone else, so it is strange that my recollection of it—if it is a recollection—is so vivid in some respects. I do remember that for a week or so after the incident, I studied the local paper for the announcement of a young boy's disappearance, but there was nothing. That was reassuring in a way. Then came the end of the half, the end of our school life, and the beginning of another.

A few years later I read that the old clubhouse on Monkey's had burned down one summer night, and that Billy had perished with it. In its place now stands a magnificent new building which, in the Etonian vacations, hosts weddings, conferences and 'team building events'. As for me, I took the Civil Service exam from Oxford and went into the Home Office, retiring a couple of years ago with the regulation knighthood and O.B.E. During my time there I did once look up the file on a Young Offender's Institution called Monk's Lawn near Bray. It had been closed down due to some scandal or other, but the file was so heavily redacted that I got practically no information from it, which was something of a relief; so I left it at that.

Over the years, I came to believe that what I have recorded was an illusion, some sort of dream. Whether my so-called memories are an imaginary torment or a strategy, planned by my subconscious to protect me from a still more horrible reality, I have no idea. Such unanswerable questions should be dismissed from the mind, but they are precisely the ones which never are.

About a month ago Cavendish wrote to me. We had not been in touch for many years, and I have no idea how he had got hold of my address. It angers me now that he did. The letter told me nothing about himself, but simply informed me that Straker had committed suicide. It was done in a barn on his estate in Norfolk. Cavendish added the unnecessary detail that Straker had hanged himself from one of the beams, at the end of a long rope.

COLLECTABLE

COLLECTABLE

'She's very collectable, you know,' said the stall holder.

'Elsie Grace? Can't say I've heard of her.'

'Oh, yes. Big musical comedy star of the Edwardian Theatre. One of the most photographed women of her time. As they say, the camera loved her.'

When you are on a theatre tour, time lies heavy on your hands in the middle of the day. You might meet your friends in the company for a coffee, or perhaps lunch; you try to do some sightseeing. That day, in Norwich, back in 1972, I had seen a poster for an 'Antiques and Collector's Fair' in a church hall. I had suggested it as an attraction to some others in the company, but nobody seemed much interested, so I had gone by myself.

A MAZE FOR THE MINOTAUR

I had no intention of buying anything; I never do, but I sometimes succumb to temptation. On this occasion there was not much to interest me. Old topographical prints: no. Vintage vinyl jazz records: no. American horror comics in cellophane envelopes: no. Model railway accessories: oh, no. But then there was a stall packed with old postcards in transparent plastic sleeves, with a large section devoted to the theatre. This consisted mainly of postcard portraits, in black and white or sepia tones, of once famous actors and actresses, among whom the collectable Elsie Grace featured prominently.

For theatre people, such memorabilia offer pleasing moments of nostalgia for a time when employment on the stage was more regular and secure, but also some sad reflection on the transience of theatrical fame. Who was Elsie Grace? What happened to her? A star had faded from the firmament and the world was less bright because of it, but few had noticed its passing.

The face that confronted me in various demure but enticing poses was not quite the classic Edwardian beauty: those heavy, Venus de Milo features that were so much admired; the well managed curls, the confident, soulful gaze were not present. Elsie, when not showing off her profile, was looking at you with coquettish mischief in her eyes. The features, regular if a little thin were, as the French say, *piquant*. One of the postcards, a full-length photo, delicately hand-tinted with pink and pistachio green, bore the legend:

ELSIE GRACE AS 'MISS PHOEBE SUNBEAM'
IN 'THE PEPPERMINT GIRL'

There she was, head slightly lowered smiling up at you through her lashes and showing off her exquisite if well corseted figure. She was holding up her dress so that you could see, beneath a froth of white petticoat, her perfect legs up to the calf, sheathed in white silk stockings. One leg was thrust forward, in a dancer's pose, and the little feet were shod in gleaming white ballet pumps. That faded elegance and innocence had a charm for me that I could not fully explain. It reminded me, for some reason, of the lavender scented drawers in my grandmother's house where, as a very young boy, I first became conscious of a past that was not mine, but which, in some mysterious way, still lived.

That day I bought four postcards of Elsie Grace in different poses, including the one of her as 'Miss Sunbeam'. I was not sure what I would do with them. I had a vague idea of mounting the cards and putting them all in one frame as a set. I placed them in a desk drawer in my flat and forgot about them, for the time being.

The tour ended and I began to find myself perilously out of work. The savings I had made on tour dwindled rapidly and my agent had come up with nothing better than a few days on a commercial for shaving cream. I wanted some form of employment badly.

Then, in a pub, I met an actor friend called Max who was just about to start in a television series. After commiserating with my situation from the condescending heights of his own fast approaching prosperity, he mentioned that, thanks to his success, he was quitting a temporary job helping out at Kendall Hall 'a sort of Theatrical Old Folks Home', as he termed it, in Croydon. If I applied immediately to replace him, he said, he could 'put in a good word' for me. I swallowed what pride I had left and accepted his offer.

'Most of them are several sandwiches short of a picnic, but it can be interesting,' said Max. The long and the short of it was I got the job.

It is some fifty years now since I last saw Kendall Hall, yet I understand it still exists. Though I am almost at the age when I might be a candidate for its ministrations, I have no desire to renew the acquaintance. It is not that the six months I spent working there were notably unpleasant, though they were strange. I remember that time vividly, but as if the events that occurred hadn't happened to me, but I had read them in a novel or acted in them in a play. When you are in a long run, you can often later recollect very clearly what you did and said, and what others said to you on stage. You can recall what you felt too, even though those feelings were those of the character you played and not yours. That is how I remember Kendall Hall.

It had been built as a private sanatorium around 1900 and stood in its own quite extensive grounds. It was three storeys high and built of bricks the colour of dried blood. Along the ground floor façade ran a glass-covered veranda like a greenhouse through which you could see the desiccated blooms of elderly performers sitting and staring at the lawn and the plane trees beyond. To me, there was always something irreducibly grim about the place, even though some of the staff and inmates did their best to lighten the atmosphere.

My tasks were general: cleaning, working in the kitchen, making beds, wheeling tea trolleys and waiting at table. As most of the staff were female and, in those days, I was quite fit, I was summoned if any heavy lifting was required, or if any of the inmates had a fall, a not infrequent occurrence. My status as a 'resting' professional actor counted in my favour, since I could, as Mr Dibdin, the Hall's warden, put it, 'relate to the old dears'. This was true, to a certain extent, but many of the clientele of Kendall Hall belonged to the variety side of show business, as opposed to what those in variety called 'legit', or actors like me. These 'non legits', though they fascinated me, were, to some extent, alien beings.

Because I needed the money, I would often do nights at Kendall Hall, ready to help out if any untoward incident occurred. Very often nothing did, and I would sit through the night, in the staff room just off the entrance hall, bathed in silence, an oddly exhilarating experience.

COLLECTABLE

Occasionally the inmates (as I will call them) put on a show in the evening. One would tell ancient gags, another would belt out songs ('Any Old Iron' for some reason being a favourite), and there was a reasonably good magic act. The legits occasionally took part by reciting slabs of Shakespeare, or performing little sketches, but these were barely tolerated by the variety side and with good reason. You could tell that there had been talent, but what talent there was on display, like a very old suit of good clothes, was now threadbare, moth-eaten and coming apart at the seams. These evening sessions were not exactly enjoyable, but they were interesting in a melancholy way, and it was at one of these events that I first really noticed Mrs Vandeleur.

'Old Mrs Vandeleur', she was called by the staff because she was in her nineties and probably the oldest inmate. She was sitting at the back in a wheelchair and staring vacantly at the stage where an ancient comic with hideously elastic features was executing a slow and rather flat-footed tap dance. I looked away, unable to take this macabre performance any longer, and studied the audience instead.

Mrs Vandeleur was very white and withered, but her eyes, though empty of expression, were vividly blue, like those of a new-born baby. Unlike most of the older inmates she was not slumped in her wheelchair, but sat upright, though I could tell it was costing her an effort to do so. I wondered whether she had once been beautiful and concluded that she must have been, yet there was nothing in her features that could have told me. Age had not sharpened and clarified them, as it sometimes does, but rendered them indistinct and flabby. It was simply the way she held herself, with a distant, almost instinctive pride, that told me.

I noticed that her right knee was beginning to move up and down in time with the ponderous clacking of the performer's tap shoes. Otherwise there was not the least indication that she was paying attention to the act. Then her right leg kicked out, revealing, from under her night gown a small and perfectly formed foot in a white stocking. This movement evidently hurt because I saw a spasm of pain cross her face as she withdrew her leg. Thereafter she remained motionless, until the end of the dance, when she made a little gesture to the nurse behind her. This was evidently the signal for her to be wheeled from the room.

Later that evening I asked that nurse, whose name was Curdella, about Mrs Vandeleur. Curdella was a large young woman, smiling but serious, an active member of a nearby Pentecostal church. She once invited me to attend a service there and, though curious, I declined the offer out of anticipated embarrassment. Might I be invited to confess my sins, or speak in tongues?

'Oh, yes,' said Curdella. 'That Mrs Vandeleur, she's a strange one. You don't know what's going on inside her. She's very old. Someone told me she was a big star once, but that was long, long ago. She says she don't remember.'

'What was her stage name?'

'Well her Christian name is Elsie, though she likes to be called Mrs Vandeleur. But someone once told me. Elsie . . . something. It was a lovely name, that I remember.'

'Not Elsie Grace?' Quite unexpectedly and absurdly my heart was beating faster.

'Why yes! Grace! I knew it was a beautiful word. Like the Grace of God.'

'Has she been here long?'

'Ever since I've been here. But I believe she came from a private mental home. She'd been paid for by family, but when they didn't want to pay no longer and she was safe and quiet anyway, she came here. She don't talk much. It's like she's okay but she's not all there, if you know what I mean.'

I could not get it out of my head that I had actually seen Elsie Grace, and that only a few months before I had bought four photographs of her from a collector's fair in Norwich. I knew that all of us have a tendency to forge a meaning out of mere coincidence, but that did not stop me from speculating. I took the four postcards out of the drawer and put them in my pocket to take to work.

It was nearly a week before I encountered Elsie Grace again. Usually, for meals, she came down to the dining hall and sat at a table alone to eat. This was not because she had insisted on solitude, but because she was so silent and unresponsive that the others found it depressing to be with her. She did not appear to scorn her fellow inmates; she just seemed barely conscious of their presence. That hackneyed phrase that Curdella had used about Elsie being 'not all there', seemed to sum up her situation precisely.

On this particular day she was apparently not well enough (or willing?) to make it to the dining hall, so I was delegated to bring Elsie's lunch to her room on the second floor. I found Elsie sitting by the window and staring, with her customary vacancy, at the sunlit lawn below. She was, as usual, erect and did not appear to be in any physical distress.

The room was much like the others that I had seen, if perhaps a little larger. It was painted a dreary pale mushroom hue and there was only one picture on the wall, a faded, amateurish watercolour of some pansies in a vase, perhaps her own work. There were a few neglected-looking books on a shelf, but otherwise nothing to indicate a personality. Other rooms that I had been in were crowded with framed posters and memorabilia, and always several photographs or portraits of the inhabitants in the days of their glory. Elsie Grace had nothing.

'Hello, Elsie,' I said. 'I've brought your lunch.'

'Mrs Vandeleur!' she said. The voice had the quiver of old age, but was clear, emphatic, surprisingly deep. I had used the name 'Elsie' deliberately to provoke a response and had got it. While I arranged the lunch for her at a table by the window, I noticed that she was looking at me the whole time but without expression.

A MAZE FOR THE MINOTAUR

When I had finished, I said: 'I beg your pardon, Mrs Vandeleur, but you are Elsie Grace, aren't you?' There was a long pause before she replied.

'I was . . . I think . . .'

Then I made the decisive step. I took out the four postcards that I was carrying with me and showed them to her. She studied each one minutely with a puzzled expression, laying them in a neat pile on the table beside her plate when she had finished her scrutiny.

'Where did you get these?'

I thought I detected a flicker of anger in her eyes. I explained their origin.

'So, you are on the stage?'

'Yes.'

'You'll get nothing but misery out of it.'

I began to protest mildly.

'Nothing but misery,' she repeated. She swept the postcards onto the floor and, as I bent to pick them up, she began to examine her lunch, but without any visible enthusiasm. Having picked the cards up I decided it was time to leave her to her meal, but she stopped me.

'Young man!' She pointed a long trembling finger at her bookcase. 'The one with the torn . . . thing.'

'Dust jacket?'

She nodded. 'Mmm . . . Theatre . . .'

I saw the book she meant at once. It had a torn dust jacket, on which, over a colourful painted design of plum-coloured theatre curtains with gilded tassels and fringes was inscribed the title: *Our Theatres of Yesteryear*. The author was someone called Clarence Vane-Partridge, a name with which I was vaguely familiar. I had seen it on books I had found in my grandmother's house, works of nostalgia, celebrating the late Victorian and Edwardian stage.

'Page 113,' she said.

I opened it at the page indicated. Several paragraphs had been heavily underlined in blue pencil.

'Read it!' she said. I began to read. 'Aloud!' she commanded. I obeyed.

'Following *A Midsummer Maid* in the spring of 1906 came another triumph with *The Peppermint Girl*, this time with music by Ivan Caryll and Lionel Monckton. The programme had all the good old names on it, but there was a new one. Well, stars had a habit of being born at the Gaiety, perhaps this new venture would see the birth of a new star as well. It did.

'The part of Miss Phoebe Sunbeam was taken by one Elsie Grace. And was anyone more aptly named? It may have been a comparatively small and inconsequential role but Mr Monckton had written her a special number which brought the house down every night:

> I'm a fairy sunbeam
> Flitting through the trees
> Tickling the daffodils
> Floating on the breeze.

'Her voice was sweet, if small, but when she danced! It was not dancing; it was a piece of silvery thistledown floating in starlight. She did not touch the stage with her dainty feet, she was blown by the breeze, hither and thither. And then she kicked! Up went her leg, up went her little shoe, far above that golden head, without any visible effort, just as the wind might blow a spray of apple blossom or honeysuckle. And that kick knocked us all for six. Seldom has anyone so fresh danced so suddenly or so completely into the firmament of fame. In the space of a few days her face was to be everywhere, to gaze at us from magazines and from the innumerable picture postcards which we bought so eagerly to stick in our albums and send to our friends.

'All the stage-door Johnnies in London were at her delicate feet. Many were the baskets of flowers that ornamented her dressing room, some bedecked with precious gems and notes that read: "I just wanted these roses to see you!" '

When I had finished reading, she said: 'Words! Just words! I don't remember any of it!' The bitterness startled me. I wanted to pursue the conversation but she waved me away, pretending to concentrate on her lunch. When I came to collect it later, Elsie was asleep in her chair and the meal was barely touched.

After that I tried whenever possible to see and talk to her, but without much success. I don't think that she remembered me when I next saw her and when once I tried to address her as Elsie, she waved me away with that imperious gesture of hers. Thereafter she was always Mrs Vandeleur. I began to research her as far as I could. In the days before the internet, it was not easy. From an old *Who's Who in the Theatre* I gleaned the information that she had married a Thomas Vandeleur in 1913 ('no issue') and that thereafter her theatrical credits had dwindled, ceasing altogether in 1915; after which her life, according to the records, was a blank. The peak of her career would appear to have come with her debut in *The Peppermint Girl,* and, without exactly diminishing for several years following, not to have progressed. So many artistic careers have suffered the same trajectory, but hers seemed to me an extreme case.

One day when I was in a record shop which specialised in vintage discs and compilations of old recordings, I came across an LP entitled *Gaiety Glamour*. It had been made in the late 1960s and consisted in a remastered selection of early recordings of numbers from Gaiety Theatre musicals. On the back of the sleeve there was a list of about twenty tracks. Here among them was Gertie Millar singing 'I'm such a silly when the moon comes out', and George Grossmith Jnr with 'I say, Bertie, why do you bound?' —remembered now, if at all, because it features so memorably in Saki's 'The Open Window'. And here, yes, here, almost the last track, was: 'Fairy Sunbeam' (Lionel Monckton)

COLLECTABLE

from *The Peppermint Girl* (1906) by Elsie Grace. I paid the exorbitant price that was demanded of me and left with the record.

As soon as I had got back to my flat. I put it on the record player. The tune, like the words, was slight to the point of silliness:

> I'm a fairy sunbeam
> Flitting through the trees
> Tickling the daffodils
> Floating on the breeze. . . .

. . . but it was oddly memorable for all that. It evoked an era when trivial whimsy was not scorned or laughed at, but simply enjoyed. Once again I was conscious of that curious sense of nostalgia for a world I had never known: of audiences in evening dress, of champagne suppers at Romano's, of gaslit streets and 'carriages at eleven'.

Over the record's hiss and crackle, Elsie's voice was small and sharp, a little needle of sound, that pricked that early recording's grunting accompaniment. (In the days before electronic microphones refined the quality of sound, recorded orchestras consisted mainly of the more easily audible brass and woodwind sections.) After she had sung a verse and a chorus or two, there was an orchestral interlude, during which, one presumes, the listener could imagine her legendary ethereal dancing. The plodding brass did little to evoke it, but I thought I could picture the scene even to the moment when the shriek of a piccolo announced her famous high kick.

I listened to the track several times until the tune was playing over and over in my head whether I liked it or not, and I had no need of a recording. I wondered if I should take the record to play to Elsie. What would be her reaction? The idea was absurd. Who was I after all to do such a thing? A mere cleaner and handyman, an ex-actor: like Elsie now, I was a nothing.

A MAZE FOR THE MINOTAUR

A few days later I was on night watch. Curdella was with me in the staff room, a reassuring presence. While I read novels and biographies, she would study the Bible, earnestly highlighting passages in coloured markers, and consulting paper-backed commentaries. We would take it in turns to patrol the corridors, listening out for any disturbance or complaint from the inmates.

That night, at about 2 a.m., Curdella, who was more zealous in these activities than I, came into the staff room to announce that Mrs Vandeleur had had a fall and my assistance was required to return her to bed.

Elsie was lying on the floor in the middle of the room and appeared to be attempting to reach the door, though for what reason she could not say. She was making little inarticulate moaning sounds in which I could detect a word or phrase or two, the clearest of which appeared to be: 'Where am I?'

Curdella was as strong as I was, and, as Elsie was almost uncannily light, we managed to return her to her bed without much difficulty or injury to ourselves. Elsie remained placid during this operation and did not cry out with pain, from which we inferred that no bones had been broken.

Elsie's was a standard geriatric bed, the sides of which should have been up to prevent her from straying, but this, for reasons unknown, had been neglected.

'I will have to report that,' said Curdella, conscientious as always. There was a moan from the bed. 'What is it, darling?'

'I'm alone,' said Elsie. 'Don't leave me.'

'All right, Mrs Vandeleur,' said Curdella. 'I'll stay by you, till you get off to sleep.' Then addressing me: 'You go back down stairs now. I'll just sit here by the bed.'

'Not you! Him!' said Elsie, waving a finger in my direction. Curdella looked surprised and offended.

'You want *him* to sit with you, do you, darling?'

'Of course! And don't call me "darling"! You may go.' Elsie's voice was emphatic.

'All right, all right, Mrs Vandeleur. I go.' She turned to me. 'You okay with that?'

'Fine.'

'You ring if you need me. I'll be down there, praying for her.'

I nodded. She left the room, still hurt by the dismissal. When she had gone, Elsie said: 'Will you hold my hand, young man?' I took it. It was smooth and cold, like a piece of polished marble; the grip was surprisingly firm.

For a long time nothing was to be heard in the room except her breathing. I thought she would soon be asleep, but her grip did not relax. Curdella had left a dim light on in the room, and I could see that Elsie was lying flat on her back, eyes open, staring at the ceiling.

'Where am I?' she asked eventually.

'Kendall Hall.'

'What is that?'

'It's your home.'

'No. I have no home. Who am I?'

'Mrs Vandeleur.'

'Yes. Yes. But who am I?'

'You're Elsie Grace.'

'Am I? Why?'

There could be no answer; I was silent.

'Why? How?'

There was desperation in her voice. Clearly she was not simply going to fall asleep. Very gently I began to hum the tune of 'Fairy Sunbeam'. When I stopped, she told me urgently to go on. This time I began to sing the words of the chorus:

> I'm a fairy sunbeam
> Flitting through the trees
> Tickling the daffodils
> Floating on the breeze. . . .

And when I faltered, she completed it in the faintest possible voice, but in time and in tune:

> Leaping over lily pads,
> Sporting in the sun,
> Dancing on the dandelions:
> Oh, what fun!

And with the final words, her right leg gave a little twitch like a reflex action. Was this a ghost of the famous kick?

'You remember?' I said.

'Idiotic! "Oh, what fun!" Not fun at all.'

I tried to release my hand from hers, but she gripped it even more tightly.

'No. Hold on. I think I'm . . . Close your eyes.' I obeyed. 'Tell, me.'

Tell her what? Then, though my eyes were closed, I saw. I was standing in almost complete darkness, but looking down I could see a pair of small feet beneath a long white nightdress of the kind that Elsie was wearing. Looking up I found myself gazing into a long dark distance which, though almost without light, seemed to possess dimension; but whether that dimension was of space or time, I could not tell. These speculations passed through my head, but had little effect on my mind which was concentrated wholly on the experience. In the far distance, as if at the end of an immense corridor or tunnel, was a patch of light in which there was a confusion of movement and sound.

'Tell me,' she said.

I tried to describe what I was seeing.

'There's too much dark between. Make it come closer.'

She gripped my hand tighter and I concentrated. Whether I was moving closer to it or it was coming towards me I cannot say, but it did, though it was still diffuse. There were sounds randomly gathered, like an orchestra tuning up and the images similarly were fragmentary and superimposed. But it was a world with a distinctive tone and feel: perhaps not so much one orchestra tuning up, but several orchestras all playing different pieces of music by the same composer. I was beginning to distinguish some of the fragments: here was a row of footlights, then a chasm, then a row of white shirt fronts and bejewelled evening dresses. Almost as soon as these impressions became distinct, they started to fade while, simultaneously, Elsie's grip on my hand relaxed until it fell away altogether. I heard the faint sound of snoring and opened my eyes. Elsie was asleep. I laid her hand over her chest, tucked her in and left the room.

The following morning, Elsie was too weak to get out of bed. Curdella said that she would report it to the Warden of Kendall Hall and suggest that her next of kin be sent for.

'I think she is on the way out,' she said.

'Has she got a next of kin?'

'There is a great niece. She visited once, not for long. Nearly a year ago now. That's all I know.' She sighed. 'I just pray Mrs Vandeleur can accept Jesus as her saviour before the end.'

'How do you know she hasn't already accepted him?'

'Oh, no, not yet! I can tell. Oh, no!' She shook her head gravely as if speaking out of a deep well of spiritual experience.

Mr Dibdin, the Warden, an amiable but rather lazy man, evidently heeded Curdella's advice because a couple of days later a sage green Range Rover drew up on the gravel drive outside Kendall Hall. From it stepped the kind of woman you might expect to emerge from a sage green Range Rover: in her thirties, Puffa jacket, tweed skirt and pearls adorning the neck of a dove grey polo-necked jumper. Over her blonde hair was tied a colourful silk headscarf on which horseshoes had been printed in profusion. There were no black Labradors in the back of her car, but I guessed there might have been, had she been nearer to home than Croydon. Despite appearing to conform to a type, she was not unattractive, and she announced herself as Trish Hope-Duckenfield.

'I'm the great niece,' she said, by way of further explanation.

She had a brisk way of talking which suggested that her visit was one of duty rather than sentiment. I was selected to show her up to Elsie's room.

As we were going upstairs, she said: 'I gather from old Dibdin that Great Auntie Elsie is on her last legs.'

'We believe so.'

'Ah, well. About time she popped the clogs. You new here?'

'Sort of.'

'Well, glad you're doing the honours. Last time I was escorted by some Jamaican woman. Not that I've got anything against them, but she would keep banging on about Jesus. Had a funny name too. Cruella, or something like that.'

'Curdella?'

'That's it! I was mixing her up with *101 Dalmatians*. Loved that book as a kid. Is she still here?'

'Very much so.' I brought her to a stop in front of Elsie's room.

'Well, I think I may give her a miss, this time round, if you don't mind. This Elsie?' I nodded. 'Here we go! Family duty!' she said, then knocked and went in.

When she emerged about twenty minutes later, she was more subdued. 'Yes, definitely on the downward slope, I'd say. You were right to call me. Mind you, she didn't have much of a clue who I was. Thought I was her mother at one point, but that's par for the course. Still, she's had a good innings . . . Well, a long one, at any rate. Poor old Auntie Elsie.' She seemed on the verge of being upset, so I invited her down for a cup of tea in the staff room.

There she explained to me her connection with Elsie. She was no blood relation, being a Vandeleur by birth and the granddaughter of the brother of Tom Vandeleur who had married Elsie.

'We don't know much about her,' she said, 'except for ages we had to pay for her to be put up in an expensive private loony bin until she was moved here. I gather the marriage to Great Uncle Tom was not a huge success, to say the least. Can't entirely blame her. Great Uncle Tom was a bit of an S H one T, by all accounts. Never liked him myself. Even as a kid you knew not to go too near him, if you get my drift. Well, Auntie Elsie took to the bottle and went doolally, and Great Uncle Tom couldn't cope, so he bunged her in this private bin, and, when he died, we found he had got through almost all his money though he had had pots of the stuff. So, the rest of the family had to fork out for Auntie Elsie's keep which, as you can imagine, didn't endear. Added to which, I gather, she hadn't been exactly out of the top drawer. Something of a gold digger, I should imagine. Wasn't she on the stage, or something? Hence Kendall Hall.'

'As a matter of fact, she was quite a big star at one time.'

'Good God! Really? What was she in?'

'Musicals. Or Musical Comedy, as it was then called.'

'Musicals, eh? Well, that's not really our sort of thing. Don't really hold with that *Jesus Christ Superstar* nonsense and all those stupid American doo-dahs. No time for it. Mind you I did once go to *Salad Days*. Now that was quite jolly. My husband had been at Eton with Julian Slade, you see. Do you know *Salad Days?*'

I said I was familiar with it.

'Now that, I admit, was rather jolly. You seem to know a bit about this sort of thing. Was that the kind of musical Great Auntie Elsie was in?'

'I suppose . . . In a way.' How strange it would have seemed to me then had I been informed that within a few months of this first encounter I was to have a brief and passionate affair with Trish Hope-Duckenfield. Yet such improbabilities, after all, are what make life bearable. Even then, I had some respect for her sense of duty, if for little else.

When I shook hands with her beside the Range Rover that was to take her home to Hampshire, Trish was back to her normal brusque self: 'You'll let me know when she finally pegs out, won't you?' I said I would.

I was to learn that people who are dying often hang on for longer than you expect. That was the case with Elsie. She remained in her room and I would take her up her meals. Curdella had told Dibdin that I had established some rapport with her and, though there may have been some truth in this, there were days when Elsie barely acknowledged me. Her unclouded blue eyes were focused on distant objects far beyond the confines of her room. There was a look of search about her, but it was troubled and restless.

I had made a recording of *Gaiety Glamour* onto cassette tape and one day I brought it in to play for her. It was four in the afternoon and she was sitting up in bed listlessly sipping a cup of tea when I switched on the player. She paid scant attention to Gertie Millar, George Grossmith and the others, but when I turned over the tape and played her song, she was instantly alert. When it was over, she said 'Again!' and gripped my hand. I wound back the tape and played it once more. Her grip became tighter; instinctively I closed my eyes.

The stage was a dazzle of lights. The scenery was a woodland glade, delicately painted, like something out of Claude or Poussin, and across the footlights beyond the orchestra pit, the faint gleam of white shirt front and jewelled silk. I felt myself carried across the stage by the sweep of the strings in the orchestra, and something more intangible. It was as if the audience itself were lifting me by an act of collective will. I looked up to see a man in evening dress enter the prompt side stage box. He wore a top hat and a cape, and his eyes were on me, even as he closed the door of the box. Turning from it, still standing, he removed his hat and cape, and began to take off a pair of white kid gloves. All the while he was staring at me. Carefully he laid the gloves on the red velvet lip of the box and sat down, still fixed on me. He was dark and though not exactly handsome was imposing. He had a heavy black moustache and the lips beneath it were dark red. I felt myself held by his gaze, but still I floated, not dropping a step or a note. A quick glance behind me and I saw that the chorus too, even as they danced had noticed the man in the box and his eyes on me. A smile of conspiracy passed between them and me. I looked up at him and saw a flash of anger in his eyes.

'*. . . Oh, what fun!*'

There was a burst of applause, even a few cheers. He took the white rose from his buttonhole and threw it at my feet. I picked it up, put it to my lips, looked at him. There was a renewed surge of applause. I bowed and ran with light feet off stage.

There was a confusion of light and noise and I was coming out of the stage door. Boys, and some girls too, handed me little bunches of violets. I signed the postcards. At some distance he stood, under a street lamp so he would be noticed. The cloak, the hat, a gold topped cane, the white kid gloves. He made no sign, just looked with his great solemn dark eyes, as if he knew I would come to him. Then flowers, jewels; a table in a crowded restaurant; a ring with a diamond in it; champagne in a silvery bucket sweating with the cold; a cold church too, but full of light and orange blossoms. I was lying in a strange bed in a strange room. The man entered in a brocaded dressing gown; he closed the door, his eyes fixed on me. He paused, then turned and locked the door before advancing towards me. For a moment I felt his breath . . .

Elsie's grip relaxed. I heard her murmur something. I became aware of being myself again, but still I saw things, now vague and shadowy. I saw a door closing; I heard it slam shut and a key turning in the lock. Elsie's hand fell from mine. The dream, or whatever it was, faded. She was asleep. Some tea had spilled and I cleaned it up.

Later that day I played Elsie's song on the cassette recorder to Curdella. She listened to it gravely. I told her that it brought back memories for Elsie.

'Maybe,' said Curdella. 'but it is not a good song. There are no fairies, but there are devils. This is a devil song. Perhaps I will play her some of my gospel choir tapes. They are good songs.'

I understand she did play them to her but they were not well received.

I would often visit Elsie, even when there was no necessity, and always I would bring my cassette player because she demanded it. I had recorded the song so that it would play repeatedly. While I played it she would stretch out her hand to be held.

I saw things that perhaps I shouldn't have. I saw fragments of a life, not always in the order of their time. The dark man was always there with his great dark eyes, the stare either enraged, or full of the dead cold look of possession. The world began to spin around me. Sometimes Elsie would cry out and I let go of her hand but she would insist that I held her hand again. The scene darkened. It moved from the bedroom to the hall of a house: black and white flagstones like a chess board, a hat stand made from the antlers of a stag. Every time I advanced towards it, he would be there, turning the key in the lock. Then there were other hallways and corridors, colder, brighter, more clinical, but always doors shutting and keys turning in locks.

After these events she would be calmer, but she would often ask me to leave her with the cassette player. I left it with her permanently and I gave her the postcards too when she requested them.

Then there was one night. It was close and a thunderstorm brooded. I was in the staff room with Curdella on night duty. I noticed that she was frowning with concentration as she read her Bible, a sure sign that her attention was insecure. I had abandoned my book and was allowing myself to submit to the restlessness of the moment. When I glanced at Curdella, she became aware and looked up with an irritated expression.

'You know, *you* should be studying the Word,' she said.

I recognised this as the preliminary to one of those occasional theological discussions we had begun to have. They were never very fierce, even if they did not seem to me to achieve much, except to help pass the time. A faint flash was visible beyond the curtains, and a few seconds later we heard the murmur of thunder. Then came the hiss of rain. I felt a cold breeze from somewhere.

'Oh, Lord, what is going on?' said Curdella. I shrugged, determined not to submit to the unease we obviously both felt. All was quiet within.

Suddenly it was not. The door of the staff room blew open with a bang.

'Someone must have left a window open downstairs,' I said. It was a perfectly plausible explanation, but I was not convinced by it. We ran out into the hall where the front door stood open, flapping on its hinges. Beyond the door the falling rain became momentarily a bright screen of silver beads as another flash of lightning came and went with thunder at its heels.

We shut the door and bolted it.

'It should never have been left open,' I said.

'It wasn't left open,' said Curdella. 'Get real!'

Then the banging began. It came from upstairs, as if all the doors of all the rooms were opening and closing. We ran upstairs and began closing the doors, reassuring agitated inmates as we did so. On the second floor we saw something white lying in the corridor like a crumpled sheet.

She lay face down in her nightgown in the passage beyond the open door of her room. We turned her over. It was Elsie. Inside the room the cassette player was singing the Fairy Sunbeam song.

'Turn that off!' said Curdella. I waited till the number had ended with the curious shriek of the piccolo and its heavy final chord, then I went into Elsie's room and switched off the machine.

When I returned Curdella was cradling Elsie's body in her arms.

'She's gone.' As we stared at the calm, sleeping face, Curdella said: 'My lord! Now you can tell she was beautiful.'

I attended the brief service at Croydon Crematorium on behalf of Kendall Hall and the only other person present was Trish Hope-Duckenfield. Curdella had wanted to come, but illness prevented her. It was a desolate event, as these things are when the subject is unknown to the officiating clergyman, and barely known to those attending. It began at noon and was over by half past twelve. I felt something more needed to be done to mark Elsie's passing so, on an impulse, I invited Trish to have lunch with me at a small Italian restaurant in Croydon. At least we could drink a glass of Chianti to her memory, but when we got there Trish ordered champagne. And so began a brief, unregretted episode in my life which I remember now as if it had been a play and I a mere performer in it. Perhaps on my deathbed, like Elsie, I will reconnect. Who knows?

A few weeks later I auditioned for a part in a Pinero play at Chichester and got it. My understanding of the Edwardian idiom was particularly appreciated by the director, so I took my leave of Kendall Hall. Curdella, by this time a friend, gave me as a leaving present a copy of a book called *Path to Salvation* which I still have somewhere, unread of course; I gave her my record of *Gaiety Glamour* and the postcard of Elsie Grace in *The Peppermint Girl*.

In life Elsie had become a ghost, now she was one no longer. Once more she was the fairy sunbeam, to me and perhaps Curdella, if to no-one else. She did not even merit a mention in the obituary columns, but she was past caring. As I made my way down the drive, away from Kendall Hall for the last time, the sun was glinting through the green branches, and that idiotic little tune was repeatedly skipping through my brain.

>   I'm a fairy sunbeam
>   Flitting through the trees
>   Tickling the daffodils
>   Floating on the breeze.
>   Leaping over lily pads,
>   Sporting in the sun,
>   Dancing on the dandelions:
>   Oh, what fun!

Its hold on my mind was damned irritating, but a small price to pay for her release.

VIA MORTIS

VIA MORTIS

Recently, in *The Guardian*, I saw Nick Levkas mentioned as a possible future director of the National Theatre. I was not surprised, but it saddened me a little that we had lost touch. In the late seventies and early eighties when we were starting out in the profession, we had been close. Our careers had run on parallel lines for a while and then diverged; his, as a director, enjoying a markedly upward trajectory, mine, as an actor, not so much.

I had not seen Nick for at least a decade, though I had been to quite a few of his acclaimed productions. Several times I asked my agent to put me up for a show he was mounting, and once or twice I had even been bold enough to drop him a personal note, but there had been no response, not even so much as the offer of an interview. I took this to be the natural tendency of very successful people to sever connections with their less than successful past, so I decided to waste no time on resentment. Besides, though I remain 'on the books' as an actor, I had begun to achieve in other spheres.

Then, just over a week ago, I went to see a friend in a new play at Colchester, not far from where I live. It was a matinee, and I arrived at the theatre early to have a snack lunch before seeing the show. There were not many people in the theatre bar as I entered, but a tall, thin, grey-haired man sat at a table by the window with a coffee and a croissant. He was consulting a mobile phone, dressed entirely in black with a collarless silk shirt and a velvet jacket. Draped around his neck, a black silk scarf decorated with white polka dots offered some relief from this sepulchral uniform. It was a costume of calculated distinction.

Half a minute passed before a vague sense of familiarity turned into positive recognition. I decided it would be rude not to make myself known, so I walked over to his table. He had still not taken his eyes off the mobile when I spoke to him.

'Hello, Nick.'

When he first looked up, he seemed, for a moment, enraged by the interruption. Then his face underwent a transformation; one dictated, I suspect, more by politeness than pleasure.

'Good grief, it's Alan isn't it? Long time no see! What on earth are you doing here?'

I explained my presence. He nodded perfunctorily when I mentioned my friend in the cast. In turn, I asked him why he was there.

'Oh, some people are interested in a London production and may want me to direct it.' His manner was so off-hand and condescending that it angered me. I thought of apologising with a hint of sarcasm for disturbing him, but that would have been to exhibit weakness. I wanted to show him that I was out of his power and no longer needed him to give me a job. Unbidden, I sat down opposite him.

I said: 'I understand this play is all about nuns in Africa.'

'Yes. Rather a hot topic at the moment.'

'What? Nuns or Africa?'

'Both, I believe.' We laughed. The tension was eased: Nick seemed reconciled to my presence.

'So, Alan,' he said, leaning back in his chair, and surveying me with a critical eye like a headmaster with a former pupil, 'what have *you* been up to?' There was again, I thought, that slight note of condescension, the implication being that I would naturally know all about *his* activities, while mine were too obscure to have come to his attention. Perhaps I was being over-sensitive. I gave him a brief sketch of my recent life, and we went on to discuss the theatre in general. He spoke about the present scene with brisk authority, as if in command of everything there was to know about the subject, a characteristic of his with which I was familiar. It had been one of the keys to his success as a director that he always appeared to know exactly what he was talking about. Views other than his own were to be listened to politely, then dismissed.

Wishing to stem his rather didactic flow of information and opinion, I diverted the conversation to recollections of past times when we had worked together in an outfit called the Ruffian Theatre Company. He laughed when I first mentioned it, but nervously, I thought.

'Oh, my God! The old RTC!' The acronym began to be used late in the company's history when it became more established, and the novelty of its name had worn off. It was the RTC which had first made Nick Levkas a force to be reckoned with in the theatre; in spite of which he did not seem altogether happy that the subject had been raised. I kept my reminiscences light and amusing, but he was unwilling to join in the fun. He kept saying that he could barely remember anything about 'those days'. I felt frustrated, even a little hurt.

'But you must remember the time we went to Edinburgh for the Festival with *Last Man In*,' I said, 'and those two weeks at the Drumglass Chapel?'

I saw shock on Nick's face, covered almost immediately by a blank look. Then he said, in his usual, decisive way: 'No. No. That's all a complete blur, I'm afraid. So much has happened since then, hasn't it?' The three-minute bell rang. 'Well, we must be off to take our seats.' He stood up. 'Good to see you again, Alan.' He shook my hand formally and darted off to buy a program.

I did not see him in the interval, nor after the show. When I went round to visit my friend in the production, I told her that Nick Levkas had been in.

She said: 'So, it's true! I did hear a rumour he was in the audience. Someone told me he'd actually left in rather a hurry, just before the end. What was all that about?'

Some days later, an envelope containing a picture postcard was forwarded to me by my theatrical agent. The image was a striking black and white photograph of Lon Chaney as the mad, vengeful clown in the silent film of *He Who Gets Slapped*. On the reverse was written:

'Good to see you, looking so well, mate, after all these years. You mentioned Edinburgh and *Last Man In*. Well done for bringing up the subject! I suppose I can understand why you did, but don't try to be in touch again. No offence, but let's call it a day, eh? Best. Nick.'

I was shocked. There was something decidedly unbalanced about his rejection of our former friendship. That use of the word 'mate' was uncharacteristic. He had, it is true, come from quite a poor background, but, when I first knew him, he had done his best to eradicate all traces of his origins. It was as if, once more, he had forged for himself a fresh personality and was trying to burn newer boats. But why had he bothered to write at all? And there remained the mystery of why my mention of Edinburgh had triggered such a violent reaction.

I tend to feel very ashamed of things which, at the time, I barely notice I have done or said. It is my moral blindness that most upsets me. Therefore I felt guilty, even though I could not quite work out what my offence had been.

I had not mentioned Edinburgh out of malice, but simply because it had come into my head as one of the most memorable events of my association with Nick. Perhaps, at the back of my mind, there was a certain curiosity to see how he would react to something in our past which I still remember vividly. When he said he had completely forgotten it, I had taken his words literally, but this was clearly not the case. Something at Drumglass Chapel had affected him even more deeply than it had me.

ೞ

Nick and I had been at drama school together and when we came out and were struggling to find work, we decided to start our own theatre company to make a name for ourselves. That is to say, Nick decided and I was his first recruit. The name, Ruffian Theatre Company, was of course Nick's idea and derived, I think, from the fact that our first major production was Joe Orton's *The Ruffian on the Stair*. We were both very ambitious, but Nick was the more dynamic character. I, having inherited some money, was able to finance the venture to some extent, especially in its earliest phase. In those days, there were plenty of fringe venues around London where we could perform our work; the difficulty always was to get the public to come and see us, but we began to acquire a certain reputation. Nick was generally the director and I one of the main actors and there was a floating population of performers whom we recruited mainly from drama school friends.

A MAZE FOR THE MINOTAUR

Then, in the summer of 1979, Nick wrote a play which he believed was going to transform our fortunes. It was called *Last Man In*. We rehearsed it and put it on for two or three nights at a couple of fringe venues. It went well, but Nick believed it could go much further. It was early July when Nick proposed that we should take it to the Edinburgh Fringe for the Festival in August. I said that it was far too late to find a decent venue for the show, but Nick was determined. Within three days he had rung me up to say he had found a theatre for the first two weeks of the Festival. I saluted his enterprise and asked how he had managed it.

'It's a new venue,' he said. 'Just opened for the Festival. Called the Drumglass Chapel Theatre. It's a disused church of some kind, owned by the Council and leased out to this live wire called Kirsty Wang.'

'Is she Chinese?'

'No, she is not Chinese. Don't interrupt. Not as far as I know. I've only spoken to her on the phone. She has a Morningside accent and talks like Miss Jean Brodie, but she's very keen on really cutting edge, radical young theatre. That's why I was able to persuade her to take us on. That, and the fact that she's got a late evening slot free. We will be one of four shows in the theatre every day during the Festival.'

Further questions from me were dismissed or answered perfunctorily. It would not be quite true to say that I was swept away by his enthusiasm and dynamism. I had many reservations, but I recognised Nick as an irresistible force, and even agreed to stump up some cash to pay a deposit on our 'slot'. I learned a little more about our future venue as we prepared for the journey north.

The day's performances at the Drumglass Chapel were to start in the afternoon with *Gas-Oven Gertie!*—a musical about the Holocaust. The title and subject matter were intended to provoke outrage, and did so, together with a good deal of useful publicity. However, those who went to it in search of a healthy

224

dose of moral indignation, or challenging ambiguity were disappointed. It was mostly worthy and a little sentimental, with a few cautiously signalled jokes. The music was pleasant enough, though.

The evening's program began with *The Means and the Ends*, one of Bertolt Brecht's lesser-known and, it must be admitted, duller plays. As such, it was billed, naturally enough, as 'Brecht's neglected masterpiece'. In addition, very late at night, a well-known actress was doing a one woman show about Rosa Luxemburg, but that was to be expected. In those days of early Thatcherism and radical dissent, an Edinburgh Festival rarely went by without someone performing a one-woman show about Rosa Luxemburg. We were given use of the stage from half past nine to eleven thirty, between Brecht and Rosa Luxemburg, perhaps in a misguided bid to inject some light relief into the program.

Our play, or rather Nick's, *Last Man In,* was set in a cricket pavilion in the Home Counties. Two young drifters, Deena and Finchy, the former an addict and part-time prostitute, the latter a drug dealer, are camping in it out of the cricket season. Into this milieu comes Charles (played by me), the young upper-class secretary of the cricket club, on a routine inspection of his club's pavilion. Deena and Finchy appear at first to be intimidated by him as he threatens to call the police and have them evicted, but the tables are turned and they begin to menace him. The end of the play sees Charles trussed and blindfolded, in nothing but his underpants, a gibbering wreck, and possibly about to be killed.

It was a play about class, power, sexual ambivalence and menace, not uninfluenced by Harold Pinter but, as Nick always insisted, 'more raw'. The humour, of which there was, happily, a decent amount, was certainly Pinteresque.

Though I enjoyed playing such a substantial role I had realised that, as in life, it is always more emotionally exhausting to play the victim than the aggressor. That was one of the reasons why I rather dreaded a two-week run of the play in Edinburgh.

The company had been lent a small flat for the run by some acquaintance of Nick. This involved sleeping on floors and sofas for the rest of us while Nick laid claim to the one bedroom. But we were young.

Having arrived in the morning by the overnight train from London, we, that is Nick, myself, with Carol and Tim, the two other actors in the show, dropped our bags at the flat and went straight to the theatre. There were two days before the festival began and our opening performance.

Drumglass Chapel was situated not too far from the centre of things just across the Leith from the castle and hard by Dean Cemetery. My first sight of it rather lowered my spirits, as do most Scottish ecclesiastical buildings. It was a substantial but somewhat squat edifice of gothic pretentions built entirely of red sandstone and granite, the colour of dried blood. The central perpendicular style doorway had recently been given a coat of bright scarlet gloss paint. No doubt this had been designed to cheer it up, but it looked to me like a mouth of Hell.

The door was unlocked, so we entered. The entrance hall was built of the same dried blood sandstone. A screen of dark polished oak separated the hall from the main body of the chapel beyond. It had been sunny outside but the interior was only dimly lit by the gothic windows with leaded panes of thick greenish glass. On one wall a wooden panel was inscribed with a list of 'Ministers' of the chapel, and the beginning and end dates of their periods of office. The last name, 'Jabez McCreel' had '1939-' written after him, but no termination date for his ministry. A large, framed sepia photograph of a man with a chin beard but no moustache hung beside the wooden panel. A label on the frame proclaimed the sitter to be the same Jabez McCreel. It was a severe ecclesiastical face with a long thin mouth and fierce little eyes. (I have always associated moustacheless beards with religious fanaticism, maybe because they seem to me to represent such a wilful abnegation of aesthetic allure.) The picture gave the impression of dating from rather earlier than 1939, perhaps the turn of the century, but I was the only one of my company who paid the least attention to such mysteries.

I think we had arrived in the expectation of being greeted, and were rather disconcerted by finding no-one about. Nick, as always the first to act, sighed with exasperation and pushed open the double doors which gave access to the main body of the building.

Above us was a gallery with benches running round three sides of the chapel. In the main body of the hall chairs were stacked up around the sides, but there were no pews. At one end was a raised wooden stage on which had stood a pulpit, now removed. In the middle of the stage was a long table of polished oak with bulbous legs. I guessed that this was a relic of the chapel's religious past, a 'Lord's Table' on which communion was celebrated: the low church apology for an altar. At the back and to one side, behind a low wooden screen, was a harmonium. In the gallery a lighting console had been set up, while, from metal gantries across the ceiling, there hung a substantial array of lights.

'Wow!' said Nick. 'Great space!' The rest of us agreed that it was indeed a 'great space' because that was what one was meant to say in those days about any environment in which one was privileged to act. I had my reservations. There was no way of knowing the nature of the services conducted here in the past, but to me the place still reeked of religious oppression. The fierce eyes of Jabez McCreel had made an impression on me.

'Glad you like it!' said a voice. We turned and saw a large, square-shouldered woman in her early thirties, with long lustrous black hair and a fair amount of copper-coloured jewellery. 'Hi, I'm Kirsty Wang.' It was, as Nick had observed, a clear-cut Morningside accent.

Her skin was pale, her eyes as dark as her hair, suggesting partly Asian origins; but what I was most aware of was the strength of her personality. Though well-built she was far from fat and by no means unattractive, even if I felt personally immune. Nick came forward and shook hands with her. I sensed an affinity between them. People with a mutual interest in power often enjoy an instant rapport: how long that lasts will depend on circumstances. I noticed that Kirsty, while paying little attention to Tim and myself, gave Carol a brief but hard and suspicious look which was cautiously returned with similar intent. I knew that Carol suffered from a deep, almost slavish admiration for Nick, but had no idea if it had been taken any further.

Kirsty began to show us round the chapel, addressing all her remarks to Nick. I was impressed by her enthusiasm for 'the space' as it was insistently referred to, but did not altogether share it. The hall was spacious, and, having been built for sermons, hymns and liturgies, did not have the best acoustic for naturalistic speech. There was a reverberant echo which varied considerably, depending on where you stood on the stage. When I mentioned this, Kirsty said that the problem could be rectified by the use of screens. Nick frowned at me as if to imply that my objections did not show the right spirit.

Other misgivings I did not share, because I knew they would be dismissed out of hand. In the dark polished wood and ensanguined stone, in the vagrant echoes, in the absence of any decoration, even in the form of carved texts or stained glass, I detected a note of puritan rigidity, almost of menace. It was fanciful I knew, even as I sensed it, but I felt it nonetheless and it would not leave me. On an impulse, Carol sat herself at the harmonium at the back of the stage and tried out a few chords. The sounds that emerged were like tormented groans.

'Please don't touch that!' said Kirsty, and Nick gave Carol a warning frown.

VIA MORTIS

We passed from the hall into a passage leading to the dressing rooms, once a vestry. This was lit by only a few small, opaquely glazed gothic windows. It was as if everywhere in the building, contact with the outside world was to be kept at a minimum. On one of the walls of the passage was a framed photograph, identical in size and arrangement, to the one of Jabez McCreel in the entrance hall. This time it was of a woman and bore the legend.

Mizpah McCreel
'And she shall prophesy the Day of His Wrath.'

The face carried a certain resemblance to Jabez, but more because it reflected a similar cast of thought than any particular feature. There was a stony rigidity about the set of the mouth and the jawline, but in the eyes there was the far look of the visionary.

I asked Kirsty whether she was Jabez's wife.

'Sister, I believe,' she said, and seemed surprised, even rather offended by the question. At that moment I thought I could detect in Kirsty a look of Mizpah: the dogmatic, the enthusiast. It prompted me to enquire further about the Chapel and its history. When Kirsty spoke, it was almost as if the words came out of her involuntarily in a fluent monotone, like a well-practiced but rather bored tour guide.

'It was a Protestant millenarian sect, an offshoot of the Seventh Day Adventists, or some such. Apparently Jabez and his sister had worked out that the world was going to end in 1939. Something to do with numerology and the Book of Daniel, and Revelations, of course. The usual thing. Then 1939 came and the Great Disappointment, as it was called, when the world didn't end. A lot of followers drifted away. Well, Jabez and Mizpah did their calculations again and came up with the idea that 1939 was actually not the end of the world but the beginning of the reign of the Antichrist, Hitler being the Antichrist naturally. Or it may have been Stalin. I forget. So far so good, but then they prophesied that the Reign of the Antichrist would last for forty years until he was finally defeated in a great battle and then the Last Things would happen. Well, the Antichrist, whichever it was, went under rather sooner than expected, and there was another Great Disappointment. Some people clung on, but Jabez and Mizpah died and the place was sold. The new owners neglected it in the hope that it could be destroyed and an office block put in its place. But the council wouldn't have it, and eventually took it over. Then this year I managed to get a lease with a grant. So here we are.'

'You seem to know all about it.'

'Yes. Actually, my mother was a Jabezite, as they were called.'

'Really? So, did you—?'

'Right. Dressing rooms. You want to see those, I expect.'

Her interruption was so abrupt that I did not need a warning look from Nick to halt my questioning. But I could not help recollecting that it was 1979, the end, according to the McCreels, of the reign of the Antichrist, but also the true beginning of the end.

We saw the dressing rooms which were adequate; we met Dave who would do our lighting, and supervise the stage management. Kirsty took us briefly into her office where we were introduced to a girl called Imogen who handled bookings and publicity. She was a pale blonde, dressed in black jeans and a T-shirt which accentuated her spectral thinness. As we came out of the office, Tim murmured to me:

'That's *Anorexia Nervosa*.'

'You seem to know everyone,' I said. Carol giggled. Kirsty, who was walking ahead of us with Nick must have heard. She turned round and gave us a reproving look.

Thereafter, in private, the three of us would refer to Imogen as 'Ann'. Childish, I know, but it made for a bond between us.

Nick did not share in the joke, and this, I now see, was the first of the rifts in our relationship.

Nick seemed exhilarated by his choice of theatre. Tim and Carol expressed enthusiasm, as did I when called upon to do so, but an inner and seemingly irrational uncertainty would not be appeased. Kirsty told us that that night, there was to be a party in the Chapel to mark its opening as a theatre and we were all invited. There would be some refreshment, but the bringing of a bottle was advised.

While Tim, Carol and I returned to the flat, Nick remained behind to talk to Kirsty. After fixing a scratch lunch for myself and the others, I wandered around Edinburgh. The art gallery for some reason was shut so I climbed the steep, narrow streets that led up to the castle. It was a bright day, but windy. Already eager actors were out everywhere, publicising their forthcoming attractions. In the course of my wanderings, I was accosted by several people dressed as clowns with fixed greasepaint grins smeared onto their faces. One of them was on stilts and seemed almost as tall and menacing as the dark tenements that flanked my way to the Castle Mount. As he stood over me in the narrow street, I was returned to a childhood when shadowy relatives and well-meaning friends of my parents would loom above me and ask how I was enjoying school. The clown stooped to hand me a leaflet. It was for *Gas-Oven Gertie! The Outrageous Holocaust Musical at the Drumglass Chapel!* I began to feel there was no escape.

Later that day we ran through the play in the flat with Nick, then, rather later than we had planned, set out to attend the celebrations at the chapel. I carried with me a bottle of Spanish Merlot—that was what it said on the bottle—the only reasonable-looking wine I could find at the off licence and tobacconists where we made our purchases.

It was dark when we arrived at Drumglass Chapel. The scarlet doors were open and from within came the thump of amplified music. The chapel was illuminated by green floodlights which gave the red sandstone façade a sickly indefinable colour, like putrefying flesh. The shadows cast by its gothic ornamentations were pitch black; dark green lights glittered in the leaded panes of the windows.

Inside, all was noise. Two vast speakers stood like black monoliths on either side of the stage where a band of sorts was playing. It was the age of punk, and the band's name, Groin Strain, was emblazoned in blood-red gothic letters on its members' black T-shirts. There were about a hundred people in all. We mingled. I saw Nick talking to Kirsty in a dark red sparkly outfit by the makeshift bar where I had deposited my bottle of Merlot. It was almost immediately taken away and emptied into a vast cauldron of 'punch' on whose foaming surface floated slices of orange and lemon, but not before I had used it to pour myself a glass of unadulterated wine. I began to talk to a girl with hair dyed a shiny bright blue. She was in the Brecht company and told me that she was 'really into theatre'.

Out of the corner of my eye I caught sight of Imogen from the theatre office. Her skeletal limbs were encased in a bright green Lurex jumpsuit, which made her look like a giant tropical insect. She was dancing on her own, close to the band, a look of rapt concentration on her white face. A shifting kaleidoscope of coloured lights illuminated the stage where, beside the band and its paraphernalia, rather incongruously, the Chapel's 'Lord's Table' stood, an isolated relic of the building's religious past. I wondered why it had been placed in such a prominent position.

The playing of Groin Strain gave way to a kind of impromptu cabaret. Someone told jokes, another did a magic act; several people attempted to sing with the band. The only act which I remember distinctly was the last one in which Imogen performed a dance on the table to the rhythmical backing of Groin Strain. Her moves were supple and sinuous: eroticism was suggested but somehow negated by the stony-faced impersonality with which she performed. She was watched in an attentive but bemused silence. No-one whistled, or called out, or applauded while her shiny green limbs wrapped themselves round the bulbous table legs and she worked her meagre body up and down them, until she ended by performing the splits on the table top.

This finale was greeted with a storm of applause, and some cheers, more I think from relief that her unnerving performance was now over than anything else.

Immediately following this, Kirsty walked briskly onto the stage carrying a microphone and what looked like two large dusty sheets of cardboard. These she placed on the table and proceeded to make a speech of welcome which was punctuated by whoops of enthusiasm from the audience. She told us how the Drumglass Chapel had just acquired 'a new and vibrant identity' and how we were all a part of it. (Loud cheers.) She added that the Chapel's oppressive and destructive past was ended and consigned to 'the flames of history'. It was an odd phrase, but I guessed it signified something because, immediately following it, she made a beckoning gesture. Onto the stage, to more loud cheers, came Dave, her stage manager and electrician. He was wearing a leopard skin patterned robe, making him look like one of those lamp-stands in the shape of Nubian attendants that were once so fashionable among the rich and tasteless. He was carrying a large stainless-steel dish of the kind used to pass round sandwiches at municipal functions.

He placed it on the table while Kirsty held up the two pieces of cardboard, so that I could now see what they were. She had removed the sepia photographs of Jabez and Mizpah McCreel from their frames. She placed them on the steel dish, still holding them upright so we could see their faces while Dave set light to them with a small blowtorch. A great roar of approval went up from the crowd. Within seconds the McCreels were engulfed in flames. Kirsty let go of the pictures, raising her hands above her head as she did so in a hieratic gesture; Dave followed suit.

Someone set up a chant of 'Burn in Hell! Burn in Hell!' It was taken up by others and accentuated by a heavy percussive beat from Groin Strain's drummer. This was too much for me so I left the hall. Outside on the steps of Drumglass Chapel the Edinburgh night was pleasantly cool. I drained the glass of Merlot which I still had with me. I was not quite sure why I had been so violently impelled to leave: some atavistic sense of propriety, I suppose. I sat down on the steps and was joined after a few minutes by Nick.

'Anything the matter?' he asked. He sounded more indignant than concerned.

'Just the heat—and the noise,' I said, almost immediately ashamed of my dishonesty.

'Your exit was a bit conspicuous. Quite a lot of people noticed.'

'I don't believe in Hell.'

'What's that got to do with it?'

I shook my head. Nick sat down on the steps with me.

'Well, you haven't missed much,' he said. 'Almost as soon as you'd left, something went wrong with the sound system. There was the most godawful noise and then the amps just packed up. Groin Strain is furious. It's their equipment, you see, and they alone are permitted to destroy it.'

The following night—the day before the Festival officially began—was to be our technical dress rehearsal, the first time we were able to perform in the theatre. Unfortunately, because on the eve of the Festival rehearsal time in the theatre was at a premium, we were booked in with Dave the lighting man to do our 'tech run' between two and four on the morning of the day we opened.

The only person who did not appear to be unhappy with this arrangement was Dave. Like many theatre technicians, Dave was very competent and amenable, but appeared quite uninterested in the theatrical product itself. His easy confidence and indifference were assisted by a regular consumption of weed, and a mild herbal aroma accompanied him wherever he went.

Our play had few lighting cues but adjustments had to be made to the positioning of some of the lamps. Nick, as in all things theatrical, had a very precise conception of what he wanted. This involved shifting a large scaffolding tower on wheels around while Dave on top of it adjusted the lamps that hung from the gantries across the ceiling. Nick sat in the gallery at the lighting console, directing proceedings, while Tim, Carol and I moved the tower. We began to be very tired of Nick's meticulous instructions. It was past three in the morning, and we simply wanted to rehearse the show and go to bed.

Nick himself was becoming impatient, but more with the technical inadequacies of the theatre, and its inability to give him the effects he wanted. As we were moving the tower yet again, we heard him mutter: 'Come on! This stupid place! This stupid, sodding chapel!'

A strange sound, like a groan was heard, not human but somehow in imitation of a living human. It seemed to come from the harmonium, but wherever it came from it distracted us, so that, in the act of turning the scaffolding tower we moved it too quickly for the wheels at its base to adjust.

I remember vividly that long, slow moment when we realised that the back wheels of the scaffolding tower were off the ground and we had lost control of it. It remains an image in my dreams to this day. The tower began to tilt, gradually at first, then with increasing speed. Tim, Carol and I let go of the falling structure and scattered, calling up to Dave as we did so. We saw him take in the situation with preternatural calm, then, just before the tower crashed to the ground, he jumped clear of the platform on which he stood and rolled away. The scaffolding hit the floor with a clanging sound which seemed to echo round the hall for an age after the fall.

'What the hell, do you think you're doing?' Nick shouted from the gallery, more irritated than concerned.

Dave, who was the first to recover his composure, called up to him: 'It's cool, bro. No bones broken.' That night considerably revised my views on cannabis.

I cannot remember exactly when we got away from the theatre in the morning but I know that a green and yellow dawn was well into the sky when we emerged. The streets were still empty, apart from a milk float which we stopped to purchase a couple of pints. None of us wanted to talk about what had happened. I knew that if I so much as mentioned that my dread of the theatre had been greatly magnified by the incident, Nick would have been scornful. I sensed, though, that he had not been unaffected.

It is often said in the theatre, though usually without much truth, that a difficult dress rehearsal makes for a good first night. In this instance, however, it turned out to be true. The shock and exhaustion produced by those traumatic early hours in Drumglass Chapel had perhaps forced on us that fierce, monomaniacal concentration needed to bring off a successful first performance. For once the intense, oppressive atmosphere of the chapel worked in our favour. At the end of the show Nick came to the dressing room, accompanied by Kirsty who brought with her a bottle of Australian sparkling wine. She appeared to be more exultant than Nick and watched him closely as he handed out carefully qualified praise to the cast, announcing that he would be giving notes the following morning in the theatre. Kirsty informed us that a critic from *The Scotsman* had been in that night, rather as if this had been secured through her particular expertise. I seem to remember us going off to a pub, or a club or an Indian restaurant, that Kirsty and Nick joined us for a while, then left together.

The following morning there was a review in *The Scotsman*, and it was enthusiastic. I have a vague recollection of the words 'stark', 'vibrant', 'searing' and 'disturbing' being used, and they were all good ones to find in a review in 1979. My own feelings were mixed, as they always have been towards criticisms of any description, especially when they are couched in such modish terms. Were the reviewers sincere in their appreciation, or were they merely bending to the fashion of the day? I tried to put such thoughts from me and rejoice in our success, because, as each day passed, the review—whose encouraging adjectives were now pasted across our posters—and word of mouth were steadily building the audiences.

Whenever I entered that blood-red mausoleum of a theatre in the days following, I still experienced a lowering of the spirits, and there were some objective reasons for this. There were tensions between the companies. Though our own tiny ensemble was comparatively immune, we were conscious of a certain resentment from the others because our show was the only one to have received unequivocally good notices.

The companies of *Gas-Oven Gertie!* and *The Means and the Ends* were perpetually at war. Both were comprised of a dozen or so performers, and, as they shared (with us) the same smallish dressing rooms, there were disputes between them over allocation of space for costume racks, make-up, wigs, personal props and the like. There were even mutual charges of theft. *Gas-Oven Gertie!* was accused by *The Means and the Ends* of not vacating the dressing room quickly enough after the end of their show, while *The Means and the Ends*—according to *Gas-Oven Gertie!*—was guilty of barging in on them before they had had a chance to change. The Rosa Luxemburg actress was not cantankerous, merely depressed. Her audiences were scant, and *The Scotsman* had suggested that her one-woman Rosa Luxemburg was not nearly as 'challenging' as the previous year's Rosa. A general air of fractious discontent pervaded the theatre.

Other factors, rather less understandable, played their part in the atmosphere of malaise. There was, for example, the question of the harmonium. A number of complaints had been made that it emitted sounds at odd moments. This was thought to be impossible because someone needed to know how to operate the 'patent mouse-proof pedals' to produce any sound at all. The casts of *Gas-Oven Gertie!* and *The Means and the Ends* nearly came to blows when the one accused the other of sabotaging them by sounding the organ during their performance. It was eventually established that none of *The Means and the Ends* company was in the theatre at the time, but suspicions remained.

I myself heard it once at the end of one of our shows, a long bass note, almost like a growl of a beast, but not one of flesh and blood: something with rusty iron and rotting wood for lungs. I was the only one who heard, so I said nothing about it. The noise had, however, aroused my curiosity.

It was early one morning, a few days after I had heard the sound. I needed something from the dressing room and Imogen from the theatre office had let me in. She always appeared to be there, though what she did in the office all day was anyone's guess. I thought, though, that I detected a look of slight relief on her thin face that I was disturbing her solitude.

'I won't be a minute,' I said.

'Fine. I'll be in the office if you want me.'

I went to the dressing room and fetched the book I had accidentally left behind the night before. When I came out, the chapel was silent. No sounds penetrated from the street outside. Imogen's office door was shut, but I could hear no typing or telephoning from within. It was then that it occurred to me that I should take a closer look at the harmonium.

At the end of the chapel, between the stage and the back wall there was a semi-circular way, like an ambulatory in a medieval church. It was only from this passage that one could gain proper access to the harmonium which was guarded from the stage by a low wooden screen. One went up a little staircase on the left of the harmonium to arrive at the bench and the console. I mounted the steps, sat down on the bench and studied the instrument. It was in a terrible state. The 'patent mouse-proof' foot pedals were flat on the floor and could not have generated any air; many of the ivory covered keys were cracked and some had lost their skin altogether. The wooden frame was worm-eaten, and crumbling away. I pressed one of the keys by way of experiment: a faint asthmatic cough was the response. It reverberated through the chapel for rather longer than it should have done.

I rose from the bench, intending to leave the sinister enclave, but as I did so, I noticed that there was another set of wooden steps to the left of the harmonium. They were identical to the ones by which I had ascended to get access to the console, but they led nowhere. They appeared to have been created merely for the sake of a symmetry invisible to all except the harmonium player. On the lowest step, enclosed by the high wooden back of the instrument an inscription in Roman capitals had been carved into the polished wood.

VIA MORTIS

It meant 'the way of death', or perhaps 'the road of death'. What was that about? I decided that my exploration must end.

Coming down into the dried blood passage and making my way to the entrance, I felt no better. The feeling of oppression, enhanced by the inscription on the step that went nowhere—and why in Latin?—had not left me.

Something glinted as I passed by on the way to the front entrance. I stopped and saw that the frame that had held the photograph of Mizpah McCreel had been put up again. There it was restored to the wall with its glass and its rough wooden backing, but no picture in it. I wondered at this as I scrutinised myself, darkly mirrored in the glass. It reminded me of Dr Dee's polished obsidian 'scrying stone' in the British Museum.

I was so absorbed by this vision of my anxious face that I started violently when I saw a reflection of something pale flitting past my shoulder. I turned and was confronted by Imogen who had come up behind me so silently that I thought for a moment she was a ghost.

'Sorry,' she said. I looked at her carefully for the first time. Despite her paleness and awful thinness, there was something likeable about her. She seemed to have no guile, and none of the urge to power that I had detected in Kirsty. No doubt there was a wound behind her anorexia, but it did not seem to be a fatal one; perhaps it was even a source of strength.

I asked what the frame was doing there.

'Kirsty put it up. I think she wants to put something in it.'

'Not another picture of Mizpah McCreel?'

A hint of a smile twitched her lips. 'Oh, no! Maybe a poster or something. She hasn't decided yet.'

'I see.' I wished her a nice morning and went on my way, faintly conscious that Imogen was staring after me. Or perhaps I was vain enough to believe she was. I forget.

By the end of the first week our audiences had increased but those for Rosa Luxemburg had dwindled to such an extent that the actress concerned decided to leave, thus forfeiting the deposit she had made on her second week. Nick announced this to us on the Monday evening, so we had no opportunity to sympathise with Rosa, or bid her farewell, because she had already gone. Kirsty was standing beside him as he told us. I got the impression that she was there to intimidate us, to prevent us asking questions or even making comments. In any case, Kirsty and Nick left before any discussion could take place. The rest of us, I think, felt relieved that the actress's agony was over, and perhaps too that we were no longer under pressure to vacate the dressing room quickly after the performance. I was ambivalent. I had been vaguely comforted by the fact that our company was not the last to leave the theatre at night, and I guessed that my fellow actors may have felt the same. During that week we usually contrived to leave the theatre together after the show. The subject was not discussed, but it became an unspoken rule. There was one night, though, when that did not happen.

Nick had become more detached from us as the run progressed. This was to be expected. He was establishing contacts, drinking with producers in the Festival Club at night, talking to media people and theatre critics. I noticed that he was confiding less in me than he had been, and was occasionally away from the flat where we were staying at night. Though I did not see him often with Kirsty I sensed that they were an item because whenever I saw him in the theatre it was always with her.

On the Tuesday of the second week Kirsty came to our dressing room to tell us that she would be away for two days and would be leaving the office in the hands of Imogen. She was looking harassed, having spent the afternoon, I gathered, resolving yet another acrimonious dispute between *Gas-Oven Gertie!* and *The Means and the Ends*. Nick, who was standing beside her as she made this announcement, added:

'So, try to keep out of trouble while she's away, guys.' I noticed again that tone of condescension mingled with matey familiarity which was increasingly becoming a feature of his personality. I became aware that Nick might possibly be some sort of participant in Kirsty's absence. A glance at Carol told me that she too suspected, but we did not discuss it.

As we were leaving the theatre after the performance, I glanced at the empty picture frame in the passage. The glass barely reflected us but I thought I saw some kind of subtle movement in its dark interior. Was that a face? A face with firm set ascetic features, and a glittering fanatical stare? No. It was an illusion, so we passed on and left the theatre. Imogen followed behind turning off the lights as she did so and locking the gothic double doors of Drumglass Chapel.

I was not as careful of my health then as I am today, and would eat anything without much thought for its nutrient value. Tim, Carol and I had begun our fortnight in Edinburgh by cooking most of our meals in the flat. By the second week, a certain lassitude had set in and we had resorted to take-away meals or eating in cheap restaurants and cafés. This, in addition to the quantities of alcohol we consumed at the Festival Club, was bound to take its toll. It did so for me after an Indian takeaway, the remains of which I unwisely finished off for breakfast on the Thursday morning.

The consequences, which had been festering for most of the day, only became acute towards the end of our performance of *Last Man In*. I felt that I was suffering some sort of retribution for the careless lifestyle I had been leading. Guilt has always come naturally to me, but I could not help feeling that my quasi-ecclesiastical surroundings had enhanced this natural predisposition. The result was that, when the performance was over, I found myself confined to the lavatory while my fellow actors reluctantly (or perhaps not so reluctantly) took their leave of me.

At some point I must have blacked out, because the next thing I knew I was still in the back stage lavatory, and in darkness. Tim and Carol had presumably left the theatre without warning Imogen of my continued presence, and she had left the building after throwing the mains switch.

At first, I was strangely calm. The ache in my stomach had left me; I felt drained and empty with a dry mouth and a slight headache, but no sensation of nausea. The blackness was complete, but my other senses were alert. I groped for a light switch but it did not work, as I had expected. The silence was all-enveloping. I felt my way into the dressing room and to a chair.

Because I was completely deprived of sight, the possibility that I had gone blind did occur to me, but it did not seem likely. I felt my eyes. Nothing hurt, but I had no other proof. I even entertained the wild idea that I was dead.

It seems very odd to me now that such a possibility had taken hold over my mind, despite its absurdity. I was inside my body, my sense of touch functioned, I heard myself cough, so hearing was unimpaired. No, I was not dead. The afterlife could not be as banal as this: merely a lightless replica of the real world. I almost smiled at my own thoughts.

I sat for some time in the dressing room in the complete dark, afraid to move beyond it. It was possible that some entrance to the theatre was unlocked, though how I could find it was going to be a problem. At every moment inertia seemed the most desirable option, while at the same time I knew I must move. Eventually I felt my way to the door and opened it.

It seemed at first as dark in the passage outside, but I began to see patches of less impenetrable blackness. Death was still in my mind, and it somehow gave rise to the bizarre thought—one which seemed to come out of nowhere—that I was undergoing a kind of rehearsal for death. Perhaps it was not so strange, my being an actor, and considering the play I was in, but I wondered at it. It surprised me as much as the images that well up from my subconscious in dreams. It was like coming into your own house and finding a stranger sitting on your sofa.

I crept forward, trying not to jolt my brain into any more harrowing thoughts. But they kept coming. *Via Mortis*. The Way of Death. That was why I was possessed by these tormenting notions. No. Stop! I must find the front door and see if I could get out.

I doubted, even if I found a door, that it would open. Imogen was too conscientious for that. Perhaps this was what death was. You were still conscious, but you were shut in somewhere in the dark, deprived of nearly all sensation, knowing nothing except that hell was empty, and empty miles of dark air lay before and behind for all eternity. But then, what would be the point of rehearsing for this? It would only increase your fear, not your preparedness. Fear is the most primitive of emotions; it had evolved to save you from death by heightening your senses, not to fill you with despair.

A MAZE FOR THE MINOTAUR

The noise at first came almost as a relief. At least it distracted me from these thoughts. To begin with, I could not identify it. It sounded like muttering or scuffling, from within the building, but at a distance. It was so faint and indistinct that I wondered whether it was just another trick my mind was playing on me. It seemed to vary. There were bouts of silence, then something like laughter, then a faint chant of some kind—was it two voices or one?—then a conversation which became more animated. I could hear no words, but it could have been an argument. It gathered intensity and venom: a high-pitched cry, thin and strangulated, and finally silence again. But there was no silence for me because I could hear my heart banging against my chest. I must find a door.

I found none. I blundered against cold granite walls but could feel no wood. I had no idea where I was. Darkness filled the space around me, vast as a starless night sky, confining as a coffin. Occasionally the blackness was disturbed by vagrant shreds of greyer matter, no sooner seen than evaporated into gloom. Then a great roar. It was the harmonium and I must have been very close to it. Someone or something had played a chord on it, the most vicious, least harmonious I had ever heard. All the works of Berg and Schoenberg were infantile, sentimental pipings compared with this one lost chord.

The noise rang in my ears for what seemed like minutes after it had been sounded, shattering all thought and meaning. It was while I was beginning to recover my senses that I saw them.

I knew them from the photographs which had been ceremoniously burnt at the theatre's opening. Like their photographs, Mizpah and Jabez McCreel appeared to me in monochrome, their features faintly outlined in silvery grey. Their long thin mouths were agape, their eyes open, but both eyes and mouth appeared to be veiled by a thin skein of grey gauze, like a cobweb. Their arms waved, as if to threaten, but the gestures were so feeble and futile that they excited only pity. It was purely the strangeness which created terror, but this was bad enough. Then they began slowly, arthritically, to dance.

I watched transfixed until something within shut down all consciousness, and saved me from anything more.

Imogen found me the next morning just before ten, lying on the entrance mat just inside the front door of the chapel. She stirred me gently into wakefulness with her foot. I looked up at her and she stared down at me, unreproachful but curious. She seemed to me in that moment refreshingly normal.

'And what happened to you, laddie?' she said in her crisp Scottish voice. I explained my history as far as the blackout on the lavatory, but no further.

'You haven't seen Kirsty, have you?' she asked. 'She was supposed to meet me here this morning.'

I shook my head.

'Are you all right? Can I get you something?'

'Oddly enough, I don't feel too bad, but I am incredibly hungry. Is there somewhere near here where one can get breakfast?'

Imogen took me round the corner to one of those cafés that used to be called (with some reason) a 'greasy spoon'. I ordered a fried breakfast, as unhealthy as only a Scottish greasy spoon could make it; Imogen declined food and settled for a cup of milkless tea.

I apologised for what had happened, but she had decided to shoulder the blame. 'I should have checked more thoroughly before locking up,' she said.

I said, rather fatuously: 'No harm done.' But it had been, for once, the right thing to say. Any tension there had been between us was gone.

I asked her how she came to be working at the Drumglass Chapel Theatre. She told me that she had known Kirsty as a girl when both had been taken regularly to the Chapel, because Kirsty's parents and Imogen's grandmother had been Jabezites. I pressed her for further details about the Chapel and its doctrines, but Imogen was unwilling to oblige. She only said: 'My Gran got out in the end, but she didn't hate them. At the end they were pathetic. Pathetic, but still dangerous. You can't kill the dead.'

The cryptic finality with which she said this seemed to forestall further discussion, so I offered her a piece of buttered toast instead. It was the least harmful element of my meal. She took a tentative nibble.

'Thank you,' I said involuntarily. She almost smiled.

'Ah, there you are!' said a voice from the doorway of the café. It was Nick. As usual, he gave the impression that we had somehow kept him waiting. He looked pale and tense, and was carrying a copy of *The Scotsman*. I thought at first he was the bearer of bad news, so apparently did Imogen.

'Have you seen Kirsty?'

'No. No. Why do you ask?' He seemed on edge. 'No. Look!' He threw *The Scotsman* on the table. 'We've won a Fringe First.'

That, in those days, and for all I know still is, a considerable accolade. So, we finished our Edinburgh run with glory and good audiences, but, even so, I was glad to leave Drumglass Chapel.

Kirsty did not reappear, and I heard later from Imogen that the police had made enquiries. She became a missing person, but, having no close relatives and few concerned friends, the case was soon dropped.

Following the Edinburgh success, our company performed *Last Man In* in London, once more to some acclaim. On the back of it I got a small part in a rather dull television series about a bank, and Nick was offered an assistant directorship at the Royal Court. We barely saw each other after that, and very soon not at all, until Colchester.

It was only yesterday that I received Nick's postcard through the post. His strange message and the image of Lon Chaney, the sinister clown in *He Who Gets Slapped*—bringing to mind those ubiquitous clowns in the Edinburgh Festival streets—are now inextricably linked in my mind. Then this afternoon I had a call from Carol. We were always on good terms and had kept in touch with each other after Edinburgh. She had married and moved to Devon. We exchanged Christmas cards; I had even become godfather to one of her children, but it is still something of a coincidence that she should call me today.

'Hello, Alan. How are things? Have you had a visit from the police?'

'What!?'

'I just have.'

'But why?'

'Well, you know they've found Kirsty Wang's body?'

'Good God! No! After all these years! When did this happen?'

'A couple of weeks ago. Oh, Alan, don't you ever read the papers or watch the news? You are *so* out of touch.'

'I live in Suffolk.'

'That's no excuse.'

She told me that Drumglass Chapel was at last being pulled down to make way for a block of luxury apartments. The foundations, when exposed, revealed a labyrinthine network of underground passages and chambers, in one of which a corpse had been found lying on a table. Though almost forty years had elapsed, the dry atmosphere in the chamber had preserved the body in a mummified condition. It was quite rapidly identified as the body of Kirsty Wang, missing since the 17th August 1979. A violent and possibly homicidal end was suspected, as the hyoid bone in her neck was found to be fractured in two places. One newspaper, Carol told me, had included the curious detail that the underground passages had been accessed by a carefully concealed entrance beneath the harmonium in the Chapel. It was known only to a very few select devotees of the millenarian sect known as the Jabezites. According to the report, the passages had been used for a kind of ritual initiation known as 'The Second Death', said to be modelled on the rites of Eleusis in Classical Greece. This, given the Jabezites' origins in nonconformist Christianity, seemed to me unlikely, but I let it pass.

'So what did the police ask you about when they came?'

'Just general things about the plays at the Chapel and when she disappeared. And, of course, I had to tell them about Kirsty and Nick.'

'What do you mean?'

'Well, that they had a thing going. Surely you knew that?'

'I suspected. But you're positive about that?'

'Oh, yes. I actually saw them together. You know. At it. On what you insisted on calling "The Lord's Table" as a matter of fact. It was all rather horrible because you know I fancied him like mad at the time.'

'I rather gathered that.'

'Well, of course, afterwards he would barely speak to me. And no chance of him ever giving me a job again.'

'Par for the course. So they'll be talking to Nick?'

'Bound to.'

'And me.'

'Almost certainly. What are *you* going to say?'

'What *can* I say? I have nothing to say really.'

That was not quite true. It is rather that I have no idea what I am *going* to say, if I am interrogated. I can predict nothing, not even that Nick will become Director of the National Theatre, though his appointment has now been announced. I have begun to feel sorry for him.

A Cabinet of Curiosities

A CABINET OF CURIOSITIES

No. 1
THE SLEEPING PORTRAIT OF MONKSHOOD HALL

Portrait of Sir Granville Cavernham by Sir John Millais RA

Monkshood Hall in the county of Wiltshire has for a little over three centuries been the home of the Cavernham family. It has now acquired an unwelcome notoriety thanks to the strange phenomenon which was observed shortly after the present occupants, Sir Sydney and Lady Cavernham moved in. Sir Sydney became heir to the property and the baronetcy when his uncle Sir Granville Cavernham 'the Bachelor Baronet' died without legitimate issue. Sir Granville had lived with his mother Lady Cavernham at the Hall until she died of asphyxiation in somewhat opaque circumstances. His portrait, which hangs above the fireplace of the Red Drawing Room, is the work of Sir John Millais and excited much admiration when it was first exhibited at the Royal Academy in 1893, the year of its subject's death. Before long Sir Sydney and his wife began to notice the singular fact that, during the hours of darkness, the eyes of the late Baronet in the portrait appeared to be closed, but in daylight hours the eyes were open again.

Portrait of Sir Granville Cavernham by Sir John Millais RA seen in the hours of darkness

Watch was kept upon the portrait by Sir Sydney and his guests, but, though the phenomenon always occurred at about the same time, the actual moment when the portrait closed its eyes was never observed. The distinguished scientist Henrik Bohemius, Professor of Analytical Chemistry at the University of Tübingen, was called in. He suggested that the phenomenon was due to the variable refractive values of some pigments in different lights, but this did not explain the fact that the portrait always closed its eyes at roughly the same time at night, regardless of the condition of the light. A less scientific explanation was provided by the domestic staff. It was said by some of the servants that, after his mother's death, Sir Granville never enjoyed a restful night. They often discovered that his bed had not been slept in and he was occasionally to be seen pacing the leads on the roof of the hall. Sir Granville, they thought, was taking in death the sleep that he had not enjoyed in life. Whatever the explanation, the phenomenon of the 'sleeping portrait' attracts a great deal of unwelcome attention from the idle curious, and has caused Lady Cavernham so much vexation that her own sleep has been severely disturbed. One night loud cries were heard proceeding from her bedroom. On arriving there from his adjoining chamber Sir Sydney discovered his wife in a state of some anxiety and complaining that someone had attempted to smother her with a pillow, but, despite extensive searches, no intruder was discovered. Lady Cavernham is now said to be staying at a private institution in Mentone. We wish her ladyship the speediest of recoveries.

Monkshood Hall, Wiltshire

A MAZE FOR THE MINOTAUR

No. 2
TEMPORARY DISAPPEARANCE OF A SCHOOL

Greybridge Priory School, Dorset

One of the more unusual incidents of this eventful summer has been the temporary disappearance of a well-known public school in Dorset. Greybridge Priory has been, since its foundation by the Knights Templar in the early fourteenth century, an educational establishment with an unblemished reputation and a fine tradition, both sporting and academic, which is being well maintained to this very day by its headmaster the Rev. Dr. A Walford-Bocock.

No premonitory sign of the curious occurrence of June 3rd had been given. It is true that in the previous term, one of the boys, Hittering Major, had been accidentally buried alive, but he made a full recovery and nothing untoward happened thereafter. When the event occurred the school was empty apart from the school porter, the matron, a Mrs Dugdale, and the entire fourth form who had been kept in writing lines as punishment for an unfortunate prank involving the School goat. It was also rumoured that the Science Master, Mr Magnus, was in the building, conducting an alchemical experiment of his own devising, but this has been vehemently denied, by Mr Magnus, and we have no legitimate reason to doubt his word.

The rest of the school was keenly watching a first eleven cricket match between Greybridge and Thurnley Abbey on the Upper Playing Field. At about three in the afternoon a curious sound was heard, like a muffled explosion followed by a prolonged whistling sound. The entire school was seen to have vanished, and the match had to be abandoned with Greybridge on the verge of inflicting an innings defeat upon Thurnley.

The same scene, shortly after the school's mysterious disappearance.

Of the school buildings only the foundations remained, and some of the cellars. In one of these, the wine cellar, a third former, Fenshawe Minimus, was discovered. According to his own account he had been locked in there by the geometry teacher, but he was unable to throw any light on his school's strange disappearance. It is fortunate for us that the Headmaster was able to contact our artist who came down to sketch the scene the very next day, for on the day following Greybridge School reappeared as suddenly as it had vanished.

All had been restored as before including the fourth form and Mrs Dugdale, though the school porter had unaccountably lost the use of his left leg. No-one, unfortunately, could give any account of the forty-eight hours in which they had been absent. One curious phenomenon, however, was noticed: the ears of the fourth form boys were decidedly larger than they had been before the incident, and there has been a marked improvement in their scientific and mathematical skills.

'No such improvement, however, can be detected in my fourth form's Greek and Latin construe,' remarked Mr Sathan, the Classics master, with his customary genial humour. 'Their ignorance of the dative and the weak aorist still requires condign correction!'

Hittering Minor (IV Form) after his reappearance (note the curiously enlarged ears).

No. 3
MRS MIDNIGHT'S ANIMAL COMEDIANS

Handbill for Mrs Midnight's Animal comedians at the Royal Surrey Theatre, 1838

The recent reopening of the Royal Surrey Theatre in Clerkenwell has been the occasion for much general rejoicing among the citizenry in that region of London. The building had been a virtual ruin since its destruction by fire fifty years ago. It has briefly housed a chair factory, but no-one seemed willing to restore its fortunes as a playhouse until the advent of the celebrated actor Mr R. Thurston Mandeville. Last month he inaugurated the newly refurbished Royal Surrey by reviving one of his most acclaimed roles, that of The Reverend Archibald Talbot in the popular drama *His Wife's Honour*.

However, the first night, which should have been a gala occasion, was marred by a number of unfortunate and inexplicable incidents. Mr Mandeville seemed not to be his usual confident self and at several points in the action was at a loss for words. Other performers found themselves uttering curious involuntary cries resembling those of savage beasts. At one point the leading lady Miss Davidge was seen to crawl across the stage on all fours for no discernible reason, and at the close of the third act Mr Mandeville, during that affecting scene when he forgives his erring wife, suddenly began to devour a basket of wax property grapes. The curtain mercifully fell before the audience could witness the distressing spectacle of the distinguished actor being violently ill. He and his company could find no explanation for their extraordinary conduct.

It would appear, though, that some weeks earlier an elderly actor, Mr Hope Spettigue, had approached Mr Mandeville with a warning about the theatre. When asked to explain himself he was heard to mutter something about 'Mrs Midnight's Animal Comedians', but his remarks were dismissed as the ravings of a senile and disappointed thespian.

Following the first night, enquiries were made into the cause of the fire that had destroyed the Royal Surrey half a century before. In those days novelty performances by trained animals were still popular with an unsophisticated public. One of the most notable of these troupes was 'Mrs Midnight's Animal Comedians'. The night before the fire they were giving their celebrated rendition of *The Idiot of the Alps* at the Royal Surrey. The two principal performers were Bertram, an ape and Esmeralda, a highly intelligent greyhound. In one famous scene, acting entirely upon musical cues from the orchestra, Bertram the ape would leap across a chasm and climb the walls of a castle to rescue Esmeralda. On this particular night some demon had entered into Bertram—always a temperamental creature—and instead of rescuing Esmeralda he bit her head off.

A CABINET OF CURIOSITIES

So inflamed was the audience by this disgusting spectacle that there was a riot and the theatre management requested 'Mrs Midnight', in reality a Major Digby Crust who always appeared on stage in feminine attire, to terminate the engagement forthwith. Major Crust was so enraged by this summary dismissal that he responded by setting fire to himself and his entire menagerie at the Royal Surrey, thus occasioning its total destruction.

During rebuilding workmen had discovered human and animal bones among the foundations of the theatre. These have since been buried and the disturbances have abated somewhat.

Lovers of the Dramatic Art will be pleased to learn that Mr Mandeville has made a good recovery after these stressful events, but will never again allow property fruit of any kind to adorn his stage settings.

'My wife's honour for a Bishopric! I scorn your offer, Wimbledon!' *A touching moment from* His Wife's Honour. *From left to right: Mr Plinge as Lord Wimbledon, Mr Mandeville as The Reverend Archibald Talbot, Miss Davidge as Elsie Talbot. Note the property grapes on the table.*

No. 4
A CAUTIONARY TALE CONCERNING BEARDS

Dr Ezekiel Renton MD

Dr Ezekiel Renton MD was a well known figure in the medical world and beyond for the cures he effected through his celebrated 'biscuit remedy' and his patent 'iridescent lozenge'. Shortly before his tragically early death he had completed his major work on Transmigratory Therapy which he believed was to transform the world of medicine. His theory was that certain sicknesses could transmigrate from a sick body into a healthy one where they would be defeated by the 'positive energies' of the body. These energies, Dr Renton believed, could even survive death.

However evidence for these theories has proved elusive and their progress in the world of Science has been further impeded by the good doctor's sudden death in a strange boating accident.

His funeral was attended by many grateful patients a number of whom donated money towards the erection of a suitable funerary monument or mausoleum. In it his embalmed body was placed in a lidless satin lined casket.

A CABINET OF CURIOSITIES

The Interior of Mr Renton's mausoleum.

The sole key to this edifice was placed in the hands of Dr Renton's relict, Mrs Maria Renton, a lady who had recommended herself to the good doctor by the singular beauty of her person and character. Mrs Renton remained after her husband's death devoted to his memory, to such an extent that she was frequently to be seen entering the mausoleum of an evening and not emerging from it until the following morning.

Mrs Maria Renton

These visits became more frequent, to a degree which many began to think less than entirely wholesome. Moreover, it had been noticed that Mrs Renton was developing a growth of facial hair, which is only recognised as proper to the female sex among the lower orders or circus performers. Its colour and luxuriance was remarked on as being strangely similar to that of her late husband. Indeed it was believed by some that Mrs Renton had adopted a false beard out of reverence to her dead spouse, an allegation that the devoted widow strenuously denied with threats of legal action.

Her rescue came in the form of her cousin Lady Pettifer who took her away from these melancholy scenes for a six month tour of Australia and other remote outposts of empire. She returned utterly without any hirsute appendages and her complexion unblemished.

However, Mrs Renton has not remarried, believing—perhaps with some reason—that a more fearful indignity even than facial hair might descend upon her if she did.

Mrs Maria Renton shortly before her restorative trip to the colonies (note the facial hair).

No. 5
THE REV ARTHUR GASPORT AND HIS DAEMONOGRAPH

The Reverend Arthur Gasport

Those of us who know the Reverend Arthur Gasport as the celebrated 'Sporting Divine' who once scored a century for Cambridge University with Greek New Testaments strapped to his shins in lieu of the more conventional 'pads' may be interested to know that he has other unusual pursuits. His interest in Angelology derives from the time when, at the age of six, he beheld an angel seated on the parapet of Harpenden Water Tower. Since that time one of his principal ambitions has been to communicate with these celestial creatures.

Early experimentation with phonographic equipment proved fruitless and, in one instance, positively dangerous. Gradually, by trial and error Gasport devised an engine which would obtain writings and images from the spirit world. A prototype of his 'spiritual telegraph', as he then called it, was built and patented to the astonishment of many men of science who had been extremely sceptical about the venture.

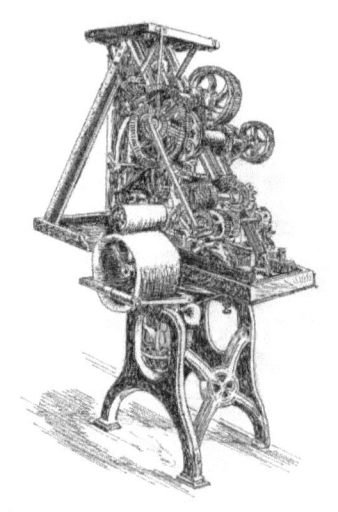

The Reverend Arthur Gasport's patent Daemonograph. (Note the spacious 'manifestation platform')

To his surprise, the Reverend Gasport discovered a reluctance among angels to make use of his remarkable machine. No such reticence is to be found in the demonic quarter of the spiritual realm and he has received many lively communications from several demons. Some of these messages and designs have been unwelcome, because of their extreme savagery or impropriety, but on the whole a degree of civility has been maintained.

Such has been the success of his invention that in recent months the Reverend Gasport has had attached to it a platform for actual physical manifestations. One of the most complete of these has been that of a minor demon from the fifth circle of Hell by the name of Gakorkos who has taken up temporary residence with the ingenious clergyman-inventor.

'I recognise that Gakorkos is a Demon,' says the Reverend Arthur Gasport, 'and therefore conventionally believed to be beyond the reach of Divine Redemption, and confined to everlasting tribulation and darkness, but he is capable of civilised intercourse, and will take sherry, if it is placed in a bronze chafing dish and mingled with a little human blood. I have discouraged his devotion to music, as he has but a poor voice, and his skills on the mandoline are indifferent. To distract him I have been encouraging Gakorkos to practice with me in the nets and he has proved to be a fearsome fast bowler.' The Reverend Gasport hopes to introduce him into his amateur cricket team the 'Ecclesiastical Occasionals' next season. 'We may make an English Gentleman of him yet,' remarks the genial cleric.

Gakorkos, a poor player of any stringed instrument but a 'demon bowler'.

THE ARMIES OF THE NIGHT

THE ARMIES OF THE NIGHT

I

16th April 1936
Whenever Nathan Brady was summoned to the office of Mr J. Edgar Hoover he felt nervous. An atmosphere of power and menace, assiduously cultivated by Hoover himself, surrounded the Director of the FBI like a force field, and it threatened even Brady who had never suffered its ill effects.

It so happened that Brady was one of 'the young men', as Hoover liked to call them, who had found favour in his eyes. Tall, well-dressed, handsome, Harvard educated, daring in his actions, observant and yet discreet in his reports, Brady met with Hoover's approval in almost every respect, except perhaps for his literary and artistic leanings. Mr Hoover regarded an over-pronounced taste for literature and the arts to be, as he termed it, 'being too clever by half'. What precisely he meant by this is uncertain. After all, *could* you be too clever by any sort of fraction, however vulgar, if you worked for the FBI?

Despite his apprehensiveness Brady knew better than to knock hesitantly at the Director's door. A sharp double rap was met almost instantly by a characteristically staccato 'Come!' from within. Brady entered.

Brady sometimes wondered, without naturally ever voicing his wonder, whether Hoover had taken a leaf out of Signor Mussolini's book. Like *Il Duce*, Hoover had had his office built on the grand scale, calculated to intimidate the visitor, with a huge desk at one end of the room opposite the door. It stood on a dais so that anyone, whether seated or standing before the Director, would have to look up. Mr Hoover was somewhat self-conscious about his lack of inches, and wore built-up shoes.

The floor was of polished black marble relieved by a fine Turkish rug or two. To Brady's left as he looked down the room were bookcases filled from floor to ceiling with gilt-tooled, leather- bound volumes that the Director would never open. To his right three tall windows looked out onto Washington and the Capitol Building, gleaming like a wedding cake in the spring sunshine. On the wall behind Hoover's desk was a full-length portrait of himself, left hand tucked napoleonically into his double-breasted jacket, looking even more menacing, and rather more *soigné* than its subject who crouched beneath in shirtsleeves behind a battery of telephones, intercoms, and neat stacks of paper. He was a squat, squarish man with round slightly protuberant eyes that seemed to penetrate the soul of whatever came within their range. *The face of a power worshipper, if ever I saw one*, thought Brady who did not himself pay homage at that particular shrine.

'Come in, Brady,' rasped Hoover in a tone that implied *approach the presence, if you dare.* 'Take a seat, young man.' He waved him to an uncomfortable looking Chippendale dining chair that had been placed some five feet in front of Hoover's desk. 'I've read your report. How in hell did you get to know about this in the first place?'

He held up a rather undistinguished looking octavo volume. It was hardbacked with a white dust jacket on which was printed in grey lettering the words SHADOW OVER INNSMOUTH and below it the author's name: *H.P. Lovecraft.*

'I take an interest in this kind of literature, sir,' said Brady. 'I have read some of this man's work before. In *Weird Tales.*'

'*Weird Tales*! You, a Harvard man, read *Weird Tales*!'

'We all have our faults, sir,' said Brady, instantly regretting his levity; but the Director did not seem to notice. Perhaps it was just as well that J. Edgar Hoover, like most power addicts, was a stranger to irony and humour.

'Do you play golf, Brady?'

'No, sir.'

'Then, take it up. That's my advice to a young man like you. It's a decent open-air kind of pastime. Takes you out of yourself. *I* play golf, Brady.'

'I'll bear that in mind, sir.'

'Take up golf, young man. Don't mope around reading trashy books all day. Still, in this instance, I'm very glad you did. You realise this darned book is potentially a thousand tons of high explosive just waiting to blow our asses off?'

'That's why I have brought it to your attention, sir.'

'Well, Brady, you did a good thing there. Consider yourself commended.' It was not a particularly gracious phrase, but it was the highest accolade that Hoover ever offered his subordinates, and that sparingly. 'You say in your report that only two hundred copies of this thing have been issued?'

'That is correct, sir.'

'Well, you must make darned sure there are no more published. And I want every available copy destroyed, if possible. Without attracting undue attention naturally.'

'I have already taken steps to ensure that, sir.'

'Good man. Good man. Shows initiative. I like a young man with initiative, Brady. But you can take a thing like initiative too far. It's like the game of golf. You can try to hit your ball all the way to the green in one, and land yourself in a bunker—'

'Yes, Mr Hoover.'

'—Or a goddam lake. . . . So who is this sonofabitch Lovecraft anyhow?'

'He is a writer, impoverished, something of a recluse. Comes from an old New England family. Not very well known, though highly thought of by a small circle of admirers. Divorced, lives with an aunt, somewhat eccentric.'

'Is he a Commie? A Bolshevik sympathiser?'

'Very much not, sir, I understand.'

'Well, that's something anyhow. Is he a fag?'

'I don't believe so, sir.'

'Not a Commie fag. That's encouraging. So how in hell does this guy know about Innsmouth? I thought we had well and truly buried that, and now this cock-a-mamy sonofabitch comes up with his book that spills all the beans.'

'It *is* supposed to be fiction, Mr Hoover.'

'I know that, Brady. Do you take me for some kind of a dumb-ass?'

'No, Mr Hoover!'

'But fiction is only a fact disguised as a lie. You know who said that?'

'You, Mr Hoover?'

'Correct! Note it down, Brady—'

'I will, Mr Hoover.'

'In this case very thinly disguised. What's this guy's game, Brady?'

'I don't know, sir.'

'Then find out, goddammit!' Hoover banged the desk with his fist in the manner approved by all men of power. 'And find out what else he knows. You never know, he might be useful to us.'

'Have I your permission to go and interview, Mr Lovecraft, sir?'

'Yes goddammit, but be discreet about it. You know we are literally sitting on a goddam volcano at the moment. If it blows, our asses are toast. Literally toast!'

Brady, being a Harvard man, deplored the misuse of the word 'literally', but he understood what the Director meant. He nodded agreement.

'So get to it, young man,' said Hoover. The interview was at an end. Brady rose and went to the door. Before he reached it there was one further instruction from the man behind the desk.

'And get yourself some golf clubs, young Brady!'

23rd April 1936 (from the diary of H.P. Lovecraft)
A young man called Nathan Brady has written to me. He claims to be an admirer of my work and wishes to discuss it with me. A Harvard man, I note with approval. Well, I will see him. I feel thoroughly out of sorts and I am, as usual, plagued by ailments mostly of the gastric variety, and perhaps he may bring cheer to my benighted existence. Another bad night full of visions. Auntie Annie tells me she heard me cry out in my sleep, though what I said she could not make out. 'It was some awful foreign or negro tongue,' she informed me. I wonder if I have the courage this time, or the energy to translate my dream into story. My nightmares are a plague, an alien infection; I am convinced of it.

I found myself in of all places a theatre. Sometimes my dreams are confused. It was a new theatre and they were still excavating its nether regions while on stage a rehearsal was in progress. A whole line of 'hoofers', as I believe they are termed, in their rehearsal clothes were thundering away in their tap shoes to the accompaniment of an upright piano. I couldn't make out the words, but I know they were inane. As for the music, it was some vile jazz-infected negroid muck that banged its way into my brain and now won't come out. Those odious jungle rhythms! They stayed with me as I seemed to descend below the stage and into the depths of the theatre where workmen were excavating so as to put in machinery for a revolving platform for the dancers. (How I knew this was so, I cannot say.) I saw them stop as they dug and listen for a while. Below the chattering of the stage piano and the clattering of metal shod feet that battered out the rhythm of their tawdry dance came another sound, darker, deeper, still more primitive than the music above and yet almost, though not quite, in step with it. The sounds were like a boom, an echo from beneath, as if the very earth were responding to the shallow travesties of dark rites from above. I saw the workmen stop, hesitate, wipe their grimy faces, look for a moment with astonished terror at each other, then resume their labour.

And then it was as if I had descended further into the earth than they, and had entered into a vast space, like a long gallery, barrel-vaulted and illumined by the pale eldritch light emanating from some fungoid growth on the walls. These walls were cunningly built of vast cyclopean blocks of masonry that might have seemed rudely antique, but for the subtle precision with which they were locked together. Moreover, upon them had been carved many runic signs and bas relief sculptures of figures, monstrous, shambling and piscine: hideous to behold. Yet I was enthralled by the cunning with which the carver had limned them as if from the life.

Then I heard the sound as of a thousand marching feet, yet not like the boots of soldiers, nor yet the rhythmic fusillade of those 'hoofers' from above. The sound they made was a kind of thousand fold slap as if a myriad great splayed or webbed feet were stamping onto smooth rock through a thin integument of standing water. They seemed to come nearer, and their hastening was a doom laden terror to me, and as they came they let out cries, piercing and hideous, yet clearly discernible above the monstrous rhythmical din of their approach. One cry in particular was borne in on me.

'*Rghyyeloi fo Xhon! Rghyyeloi fo Xhon!*' And it seemed as if I knew by some dreadful instinct what these horrid intonations signified. It was '*The Armies of the Night! The Armies of the Night!*'

Nearer they came and nearer, by which time I was half conscious that I was dreaming and must needs shake off the surly bonds of sleep to rid myself of this mounting terror. I felt like a diver who realises belatedly that he has gone too deep and must struggle upwards, almost despairing that he may reach the surface, gulping for air where none exists. I shook the thunder from my brain and gasped. Almost it seemed I was sinking back into that unspeakable subterranean cavern, then with a final lung-tearing, heart pounding effort I broke the surface of wakefulness and found myself panting and sweating in my narrow bed at 66 College Street, Providence. More than ever does it seem a blessed haven and a refuge.

Yet for a long while those terrible cries still echoed through my brain: '*The Armies of the Night! The Armies of the Night!*'

I had barely dressed and made my toilet when Mr Brady was knocking at the door of Number 66. My visions had completely shaken the thought of him from my mind; so that my usual punctiliousness was confounded. I showed him what courtesy I could in my distracted state and he reciprocated. He seems a most gentlemanly fellow with the clean-cut Aryan features of which I approve. His clothes were enviable, evidently the work of the best tailors in Washington whence, he tells me, he hails. I asked him his occupation and he replied somewhat nebulously that he worked for the government, though in what capacity he would not specify. However, all misgivings that I might have had evaporated when he offered to take me to luncheon.

I told him that there was an excellent hostelry nearby where for $2 a very decent noontide repast was to be had. Moreover, I added, I was not a drinker and never had indulged in the kind of libations with which many of my fellow scribes seek to stimulate their genius. My muse is solitude and the dreadful blessing of dreams.

My new friend Mr Brady seemed somewhat dismayed at the prospect of taking luncheon at the *Providence Temperance Hotel and Coffee Rooms* which is the establishment I favour, but thither we repaired, and, having reconciled himself to my modest requirements, Mr Nathan Brady proved to be a most delightful companion. I must say he is gratifyingly well acquainted with my *oeuvre,* as I may term it, but he asked a number of questions whose import I could not entirely fathom. . . .

24th April 1936. Extract from FBI Report from agent Brady
. . . Mr Lovecraft has been most communicative. He is a good and fluent talker and, as far as I could make out, an honest one. In the light of what he told me, however, this may be questionable. He was certainly well informed about the Innsmouth incident; accounts of events at Dunwich and Red Hook conform with and may even exceed the very confidential information that we possess. Using what tact and discretion I could, I tried to find out precisely how Mr Lovecraft had gained access to this knowledge. Though he made reference to certain printed or manuscript sources, including the *Necronomicon,* of which we were led to believe there is but one copy and that in the library of the Miskatonic University under lock and key, Mr Lovecraft claims that his understanding of certain events derives from dreams or 'visions' as he sometimes calls them. This may or may not be the case, but it would seem that Mr Lovecraft is in possession of valuable insights. I recommend that an agent remain in regular contact with him. I suggest myself for this task if only because I

have already established cordial relations with this source and a new and inexperienced contact might arouse suspicion.

I attach an invoice for expenses. The bill for the meal at the *Providence Temperance Hotel and Coffee Rooms* amounts to $4.75, including a 25¢ tip. The meal itself, foul beyond description by the way, came to exactly $4 but Mr Lovecraft demanded several extra cups of coffee, under which influence he talked, as he would say, 'volubly'. . . .

5th May 1936
'Well, Brady,' said the Director. 'I have read your report. I like it. You're a smart kid. I gather you've been seeing this Lovecraft character on a regular basis. The guy who lives with his aunt?'

'Yes, Mr Hoover.'

'There's no funny business going on between this guy and his aunt is there?'

'No, Mr Hoover. I have seen the aunt and the possibility seems vanishingly remote. In any case, I believe Mr Lovecraft is largely asexual.'

'A sexual? What sort of a sexual? A homosexual?'

'No, Mr Hoover. Just no sex at all.'

'Then why not say so? You want my advice? Don't mess with sex. If you don't mess with sex, sex won't mess with you. Note that down, Brady. And you think this stuff Lovecraft is giving you is on the level?'

'It certainly tallies with the reports we've been getting through from other quarters. And in some cases he anticipates them.'

'Anticipates? How?'

'He claims that he dreams them.'

'Dreams? Brady, is he levelling with us? Or is he giving us the phonus balonus?'

'He has been accurate so far, but we have a way of testing his veracity, Mr Hoover.'

'Never mind that. I just want to make sure somehow he is on the level.'

'Well, Mr Hoover. He has been talking to me recently about some disturbances beneath a theatre which seems to be a Broadway theatre in New York. It would appear that according to him that this is the site of the next intrusion of these—phenomena...'

'Yes, yes. I get it.'

'Now we have yet to have any report of this from other sources, so I suggest we investigate this to see if—'

'I got it! We investigate this, and if it turns out to be true we know our guy is on the level and not the phonus balonus. And we get to burn these dam bums before they get really dangerous. What do you think of my plan, Mr Brady?'

'I think it is excellent, sir.'

'It *is* excellent, Mr Brady. And I am appointing you to investigate. You leave for New York tomorrow. Young man, allow me to let you into a big secret which on pain of having your ass diced and then fried on the hot plate you will keep under your Stetson. I am forming a secret body of men to combat this new threat which I am to call the Human Protection League, or HPL.'

'How very appropriate, Mr Hoover—'

'Appropriate, my ass! It's the right thing to do, for America, Brady. And when America's ass is on the line, J. Edgar Hoover is there to defend that ass at all times. I am appointing you, Nathan Brady, as agent number one of the HPL and you will be directly answerable to me alone together with my Assistant Director Mr Clyde Tolson. Is that clear, Brady?'

'Yes, sir!'

'Good man! You want to know something, Brady? The Commies are at the bottom of all this somehow. I've got a feeling in my water. You mark my words. This is a plot masterminded in Moscow to undermine our American way of life.'

'I'll bear that in mind, Mr Hoover.'

Most agents knew that the Director could under no circumstances be contradicted. If he said anything with which they could possibly agree, they replied with a smart: 'Yes, Mr Hoover, sir!' If the Director, as he was prone to do from time to time, made a remark so wild and fantastical that a self-respecting agent needed to distance himself from it, the response would be: 'I'll bear that in mind, Mr Hoover.' But the Director, for all his faults, was a shrewd man, and one could never be certain that one's evasion had not been noted and filed in that voluminous and vindictive brain of his. Like the Bourbons, Mr J. Edgar Hoover very seldom learned anything, but he forgot nothing.

'Oh, yes. It's the Commies all right. Brady—I'm going to call you Nathan—'

'Thank you, sir.'

'And you can go right on calling me, Mr Hoover. Nathan, I want you to nail these Commie bums for me. Nail them! See my secretary Miss Gandy in the outer office. She will furnish you with all the requisite travel passes, weapons certificates and expenses forms. Nail those goddam bums, Nathan!' Hoover's fist banged emphatically on the tooled leather surface of his bureau, and with that the interview was at an end.

In the outer office Miss Gandy was at her desk, a large, pleasant middle-aged blonde woman, puffy and powdery and wreathed in smiles. She appeared to know exactly what Brady required before he even asked for it.

But the room had another occupant. A tall man stood silhouetted at the window, gazing out towards the Capitol building. At first he seemed to take no notice of Brady, then he turned and advanced towards him. Brady noticed that, as he did so, Miss Gandy's manner became at once more flustered and more formal. He immediately recognised it to be Hoover's Assistant Director, Clyde Tolson. They had never met before but Brady knew him by sight and reputation. He was a good-looking, impeccably dressed middle-aged man with a fishy eye and a glacial smile.

'Ah, Mr Brady, isn't it?' Brady thought Tolson was going to put out one of his hands to shake; instead he clasped them behind his back. It was as if he was out to disconcert his subordinate.

'Yes, Mr Tolson.'

'I hear you are a coming man in this Bureau, Brady.'

'Thank you, sir.'

'Oh, don't thank me, Brady. For that you must thank our Lord and Master, J. Edgar, eh?' And he winked conspiratorially. Brady sensed that this was a trap, and that if he responded with too much familiarity he would be rebuffed, so he merely bowed his head. Tolson seemed both gratified and frustrated by Brady's ritual submission. As he came closer, Brady caught the distinct smell of peppermint on his breath. Was it to disguise the alcohol perhaps?

'Yes,' said Tolson almost in a whisper, 'A coming man, but—a word of warning, young Brady—don't try to come too far.'

At that moment the door of Hoover's office opened a fraction and the familiar rasping voice was heard.

'Is that you, Clyde? Get your ass in here. I want you!' Tolson looked furious for a second then disguised his rage with a sickly smile and went in to his 'Lord and Master'.

Brady and Miss Gandy heaved a sigh of relief at almost exactly the same moment and smiled at each other in mutual sympathy.

II

6th May 1936 (from the diary of H.P. Lovecraft)
I am become a martyr to dyspepsia. Aunt Annie wishes me to see a doctor, but I have no wish to commit myself to the costly and generally futile ministrations of the medical profession. However,

the other day I found a bottle of *Dr Ogmore Van Bogusteen's Patent Gastric Preparation* in the secret drawer of my *escritoire*. It may be rather old, but my esteemed grandfather Whipple Phillips always swore by it. Well, I took a tablespoon full of the greyish glutinous liquid for my stomach ache yesterday afternoon. At least, I think it was yesterday and the afternoon—I cannot be positive on that—but whenever it was, it did wonders for the pain, despite tasting like the pus from a diseased reptile. Shortly after taking it, however, I fell into a deep sleep, then, waking of a sudden at some remote hour of the night or the morning, I lay on my bed incapable of motion but without any discomfort save a certain mental agitation at my incapacity. Having lain like this for I do not know how long I began to dream. 'Yet 'twas not a dream neither,' or if it was, it was such a dream as I have never had to this intense degree, and I am a man prone to such things. It was more like a waking vision. I seemed to be fully conscious throughout my reverie and was able to reflect on my being an unwilling witness to the events I must describe. It was as if I were a prisoner in my own body, trapped, unable to move so much as a finger and yet able to see and hear with a distinctness that rivals or even supersedes my current awakened senses.

I am back in the basement of that infernal theatre again. The workmen I had seen before are having an altercation with some men. These men are all wearing dark double-breasted suits with a wide chalk stripe and those vulgar two-toned shoes. One of them has a knife. They are swarthy of complexion and I have no doubt they are of Italian extraction and 'hoodlums': dago vermin from the lowest stews of Naples or Palermo. One of them has a missing finger, the other a pencil moustache so thin it looks like the gash from a knife. I can hear their voices but cannot tell what they are saying, even though I suspect it is English, of a kind, and not some greasy foreign tongue.

In these visions, I am endowed with a supernatural understanding, yet the language I understand is not my own, but a deep remote tongue that comes from the stars, a language of aliens.

It seems to me that the workmen and the hoodlums are in some dispute over working conditions and pay and that the hoodlums are threatening them. All but one of the men maintain some defiance in the face of threat and eventually down tools and leave the basement where they have been working. The one who remains behind is a young man, tall, but not very well set up, and he seems fearful. Perhaps, I divine, he has a wife and young children to support and cannot afford to leave, much as he might like to. When the others are gone the hoodlums give this man a cursory nod, as if they approve his conduct, but also secretly despise him for it.

The young man continues to work. He is wielding a pick axe to the floor of the basement when there comes a rending and cracking sound, and then the sound of large pieces of masonry falling down a deep chasm. The man surveys his handiwork and sees that a large black hole has appeared in the floor at which he had been hacking. He stares in wonder at it, then, seizing a lantern he lies on the ground next to the hole and shines the lantern into the black depths. I cannot see what he sees but something makes him drop the lantern accidentally down the hole.

Then I see the man in a quandary. He hesitates. Finally, he takes another lantern and gingerly descends into the darkness beneath the floor. It seems that in my vision I follow him. The sense of dread is now magnified and palpable, but I cannot escape. My body is trapped, held in a vice by my own paralysis.

He climbs from the floor above down an uneven slope of rubble and debris at the bottom of which lies the lamp, now extinguished. I see him stop several times during his cautious descent to listen. His features are taut and white. The man reaches the bottom and is in the long barrel-vaulted chamber or passage that I have seen before. Its walls are slicked with a dampness from the green lichen that spreads over it like a disease. On it are incised signs whose meaning I cannot fathom and carvings in bas relief of monstrous ichthyoid forms whose heads sprout long and fibrous tentacles and whose vast saucer eyes look out at me even from the stone in which they are graven.

He stoops down to pick up the lamp, and, as he crouches, he looks round in wonder at his surroundings. He starts at a single sound, like that of a large splayed foot stamping in a puddle, innocent in other circumstances perhaps, but hideously disconcerting here and now. He calls out hesitantly and such is the strangulation that his nerves are causing him that his voice is a shrill pipe in the throat. The voice is answered by a deep boom, and then terror absolute and unadorned seizes the wretch.

He turns and, abandoning both lanterns, begins to scramble up the rubble incline towards the floor above. In his terror and desperation he begins to slide and stumble amongst the fallen masonry. He cannot get a firm grip; his hands are slicked with sweat. I watch paralysed, unable to move or even cry out. I am present in his agony and at the same time I know that I am miles away.

It is pitiful indeed to watch a man so abject with terror, but this is nothing to what happens next. As he struggles helplessly among the sliding scree, trying to gain some purchase and reach the floor above, dark shapes are seen moving in that subterranean chamber. I do not see one of them whole—mercifully I am spared that!—just a limb here, the misshapen outline of a head, a tangle of lank, coarse hair. Their shapes are anthropoid, but neither are they wholly human, their skin being hard and squamous, like that of a reptile. I sense that the creatures are of both sexes with perhaps the females predominating, for they are the ones who now surround the workman, pawing and caressing him with their powerful scaly arms. Their fingers are long and prehensile but are webbed together by a translucent skein of skin. It is hard, thankfully hard, to see clearly in the subdued light, but it seems to me that the hue of their flesh is vilely iridescent, like a slick of oil on stagnant water.

Then all at once they pounce and engulf him. He gives a despairing cry and for a moment it is as if I am one with him, suffocating under a sea of slimy, scaly possessing flesh. I am struggling now to escape not from my body but from his. All goes dark and I hear again the voices pounding against me.

'*Rghyyeloi fo Xhon! Rghyyeloi fo Xhon!*'

'*The Armies of the Night! The Armies of the Night!*'

Then I am lying on my bed, every item of clothing on me soaked in sweat. I know I am once more in Providence, but what day or what hour it is I cannot say. There is daylight, of a sort, to be seen through my curtains.

I had barely recovered from this hideous adventure when there was a knock at the door. It was my new acquaintance Mr Brady come to pay a call. Fortunately by this time I had found myself a fresh shirt and a reasonably clean collar, so that I was 'clothed and in my right mind' when I answered the door, but he could see that all was not well.

Mr Brady was most solicitous. He took me out to dinner—Yes! It was the hour of the evening meal!—but not, alas to the *Temperance Coffee Rooms*, but to the *Arkham-Biltmore Hotel* where he had a couple of highballs—not, it goes without saying, available at the *Temperance Coffee Rooms!*—before we both partook of a sumptuous repast which was a little too much for my delicate digestion. He asked me to describe my dream (or vision?) in the greatest detail and I was happy to oblige. He seemed highly gratified by my account though I cannot quite fathom why. Is he perhaps an aspiring writer looking to plunder the resources of my perfervid subconscious? This seems to be the only probable explanation.

At all events, his pleasure in my society seems to know no bounds and he asked me if there was anything I could do for him. I immediately said to him that I would be much obliged if he could secure me some more bottles of *Dr Ogmore Van Bogusteen's Patent Gastric Preparation* as my local pharmacy seemed unable or unwilling to sell me same.

At this Mr Brady looked somewhat shocked. Did I not know that Dr Van Bogusteen's *Preparation* had long ago been proscribed as it contained various highly narcotic substances? I said I did not care as it was the only thing that relieved my stomach problems of which I gave him a comprehensive, indeed exhaustive summary. He took my 'organ recital' very well, considering, and asked me if I had seen a doctor. I replied that I had not. He seemed perturbed and said I should do so at once, and that his 'Bureau' would defray any expenses, then, immediately correcting himself, he said he would do so personally. I really cannot fathom this young man; but then, as my literary friends keep reminding me, an understanding of human nature has never been one of my strengths as an artist or as a man.

A further oddity occurred, for when I happened to mention that the vividness of my visions of late may have been due to my ingestion of Bogusteen's *Preparation*, he immediately said that he would 'see what he could do', but he also insisted I should visit a doctor. We took our leave most cordially. I cannot help liking Mr Brady. He is obviously a gentleman, even though he appears to work for a living. What precisely is the nature of that work, I have yet to discern.

7th May 1936
The first thing Brady did after checking into his hotel on West 54th Street was to call up his friend Charlie Chin. He and Charlie had been star pupils together at the Harvard Law School and an immediate friendship had been formed which despite the fact that Charlie was a New Yorker and Brady was based in Washington, had endured. After Harvard Charlie went back to New York to help run his father's very successful string of Chop Suey joints in the Broadway area. Brady, whose family had lost everything in

the Wall Street Crash and subsequent Depression, needed to earn money fast and so joined the FBI straight from graduation. Very soon Charlie, whose energies were prodigious, had, in addition to running the Chop Suey establishments, set up a law firm on Broadway, specialising in show business clients: theatre contracts, copyrights and the like. He had immediately written to his friend Brady offering him a partnership. Brady, who had begun to find his work at the FBI engrossing, had reluctantly declined but not without the warmest expressions of gratitude to his old friend Charlie.

They met, that evening, in Sardi's. Both men were delighted to see each other again, Brady noting that his old friend looked the very image of prosperous contentment, but it was not long before Brady came to the point. He wanted to know if Charlie—whose store of show business gossip had always been prodigious—had heard about any trouble going on at a theatre which was under construction or renovation.

Charlie Chin leaned back on his banquette and looked at Brady with an anxious, puzzled look on his face. It was unusual for Charlie to look anything other than completely at his ease.

'You wouldn't like to tell me exactly what all this is about, Nathan?' he said.

'It's an FBI matter. We've heard some rumours. I'm afraid I can't be too specific.'

'All right, Nathan, but you're going to go carefully aren't you?'

'Okay, so what have you got, Charlie?'

'Ever heard of Micky "The angel" Buonarotti?'

'I am familiar with his reputation. We have him on file.'

'Well, then you know he is not a man to be messed with. Sometimes just known as Micky Angel. So called because he was once an altar boy in the church of St Ignatius in the Lower East Side and looked angelic. Once. Then came puberty and he joined his uncle Joe "Claw Hammer" Buonarotti, so called because—

well you get the picture. Joe specialised in liquor importation and extortion and young Micky Angel learned his trade quickly and developed it to include prostitution, numbers rackets, you name it. He is now one of the most notorious and powerful hoodlums in all New York. My advice, Nat, is on no account to seek acquaintance with this guy. He has a way with a sawn-off that is in no way gentlemanly, and his close associates are no longer choirboys either.'

'So? Where does the theatre come in?'

'Micky Angel is an empire builder. He is always acquiring businesses and property—legit or illegit, it makes no difference to him. Well, one of the properties he acquires is a run-down old theatre on Broadway called the Roxy Palace and he is in the process of restoring it and putting on a swanky show there mainly for the benefit of his current doll, a Miss Billie Bernard, a Broadway hoofer with ambitions to be a star.'

'So?'

'So, they have completely renovated the stage area, including putting in a revolve and a hydraulic system under the stage, but there is a problem. The builders and workmen he has hired are refusing to work down there. Micky throws threats and money at them in equal measure and still they refuse, and many, including Micky, natch, are beginning to suspect that Leo "The Artichoke" is at the bottom of it all.'

'The name is not familiar to me, Charlie.'

'That has been till now your good fortune, Nate. His full name is Leo "The Artichoke" Vinci. He is a big hoodlum and the only one maybe who can make Micky Angel still look like an altar boy.'

'Why "The Artichoke"?'

'Believe me, Nate, you do not want to know.'

'So?'

'So, in the first place Leo runs a fashionable nightery called The Garden of Allah which is just a block away from the Roxy and does not take too kindly to Micky Angel setting up an even classier establishment on what he considers to be his *terroire*. And second of all Miss Billie Bernard used to be his doll and used to sing and dance at The Garden of Allah. Well, then these guys start turning down well-paid work in Micky's theatre and won't give no clear reason. Then a couple of nights ago something else happens.'

'Tell me, Charlie.'

'This is only rumour, mind, and I had it at third hand, so you didn't hear it from me, and anyway the details are so hazy . . .'

'Yes, yes! Well?'

'Some guy who's still working at the Roxy disappears. Just vanishes. And while he's working in the building. Honestly, that's all I know.'

Brady shivered. It may be that Lovecraft's vision had been accurate. It was a thrilling and decisive moment, but something in him wished he had been wrong.

After a pause, Brady said: 'So how do I find out more, Charlie?'

'I suppose you will not take my excellent advice and have nothing to do with this?'

'Charlie, I took an oath to the flag and to J. Edgar.'

'You always were such a boy scout, Nate. All right then. My advice then is to hang around Mindy's, the restaurant. It's where all the show people go, it's cheap and if you don't prefer chop suey as you should, the food's not half bad. And you know how show people gossip. There's bound to be someone in from rehearsals at the Roxy. Make yourself out to be some kind of an agent—a theatrical agent, I mean, not a G Man, for Christ's sake! Or a newspaper man. Most show people have an inordinate and misplaced faith in agents and newspaper men, until they become old and cynical, so pick on the young ones. You never know, you might find it amusing. You look like you need some recreation.'

'And you won't tell me why this Leo guy is called "The Artichoke"?'

'My lips are sealed. Have a cognac.'

8th May 1936 (from the diary of H.P. Lovecraft)
My dyspeptic condition is no better and I am running out of Dr Van Bogusteen's *Preparation*. Ever since my vision, the phrase 'the armies of the night' has been echoing through my head like some execrable tune by Messrs Gershwin or Berlin. Well, having nothing better to do by way of editing or writing I decided if I might try to see what it signified. Among the volumes bequeathed to me by Grandfather Whipple was an ancient and battered copy of Dr Dee's translation of the *Necronomicon* (1598). It is, alas, incomplete and in some respects inaccurate, but I have been denied access (as has everyone) to the only copy of the more comprehensive and accurate Latin version by Wormius (from which in any case Dee derived *his* version) at Miskatonic. Well, enough of this pedantry! Following a minute perusal, I did come across the following:

> It is written that the Old Ones shall lye a-dream till certaine awakenings shall happen. Then they shall mingle with mortals —perforce, or by the debased and willing subjection of some —and bring forth a race accursed, a half-broode. And these shall be called the *exercitus noctis* or armies of the night, or, in their owne blasphemious tonge: *Rugelloi fo Ixion* [as usual Dee, never having heard the language spoken, has transcribed it innacurately]. And they shall rise up from beneath the earthe and smite all in their pathe, and though many perish, they cannot be subdued till one shall perform the three Voorishe Invocationes under the protectioun of the Hand of Glorye.

The *Hand of Glory*, I understood. It is an ancient magical instrument made from the severed hand of a condemned man, but the 'Voorish Invocations' I could not fathom. I knew that the

Wormius *Necronomicon* contained a section at the end (which Dee had not translated) on ancient Voorish magic, so perhaps the invocations were there. But the Miskatonic *Necronomicon* was no longer available to scholars such as myself. Long years ago I was briefly granted access to their copy, but, alas, I only took a cursory glance at that last section because it was in some form of code. No doubt that was why Dee made no attempt to translate it, though he was a friend of Trithemius and something of an expert in cryptograms.

My friend Mr Brady called on me. He expressed great interest in my researches and asked me some detailed questions about the possibility of gaining access to the Miskatonic Library in order to examine the Wormius *Necronomicon*. He seems to have some ulterior motive in wanting all this information from me which I cannot fathom. Still, he is a gentleman and treats me like a gentleman, and that is a rare thing.

He gave me the name of a physician whom I should see for my gastric problems, telling me that I had no need to trouble over the expense as he and others who admired my work had arranged for all bills to be paid. He also gave me a bottle containing a liquid which, he told me would have much the same effect as Bogusteen's *Preparation*. I have tried it and it does, but it is not nearly so foul to the taste as the *Preparation*. For some reason, this is rather a disappointment; my Puritan blood runs deep.

9th May 1936
When Brady got to Mindy's he sat himself at a table near the wall so he could watch all comers and goers. He ordered a coffee and a plate of ham hock and sauerkraut which, he was told, was Mindy's speciality. It was six o'clock which was about the time that most Broadway players come in from rehearsals, or to catch something to eat before doing a show. Brady watched the clientele with the fascination of the born observer as they came in and

out, insisting on their favourite tables, or, eyes wandering, looking for a friendly face: the almost famous who made a grand entrance to attract attention, and the already famous who tried desperately to avoid it.

Brady was on his fifth cup of coffee and Mindy, the proprietor, was beginning to eye him unfavourably when a group of chorus girls came in and sat themselves in the booth next to Brady's. They exuded, life vitality and laughter and it seemed to Brady that they were taller than the average hoofer. Brady was struck in particular by one of them, darker than the rest with jet black shingled hair, a golden skin, high, aristocratic cheekbones and wide smiling eyes. A slight Southern drawl permeated her Brooklyn accent. They began to gossip about the show they were rehearsing and much of it, suffused with giggles, was incomprehensible, but then he began to hear odd fragments of conversation which interested him.

'So what's with this revolving stage?'

'They've stopped working on it.'

'For Micky Angel? That's bad news for them. What's the beef?'

'Someone said the smell. Like a million-year-old dead fish. Haven't you caught it even in the dressing rooms? And it's worse down there. Much worse.'

'So there's a smell down there. So can't they wear masks or something?'

'And then this guy who's working down there just vanishes. Young guy and all. With a wife and kids. And Micky goes ape.'

'Why, it's not the poor guy's fault. Maybe he just—I don't know. . . .'

'No. But Billie says, Micky thinks it's The Artichoke at the bottom of it!'

'Jeez! Keep your voice down, Ellie. You don't know who might be listening.'

Suddenly a blonde, bubble curled head appeared above Brady's stall.

'Excuse me, sir. But might you be earwigging on a private conversation. If so, please desist forthwith or you might get a sock in the kisser.'

Brady remained calm. 'That would be regrettable, Miss—?'

The blonde who, in spite of herself seemed favourably impressed by what she saw introduced herself as Lisa Bolt. The others were also introduced by name including the dark girl who was called Miss Ellie Jackson. Brady bowed formally and told the girls that he was Nick Carraway of the *New York Sun*.

'But I assure you, ladies,' he said, 'That I will regard anything you say as off the record.'

'Oh, yeah!' said Lisa. 'I've heard that one before.'

'Aw, give the guy a break,' said Ellie. Brady caught a smile that was echoed in her eyes.

'*You* give the guy a break, sister. I'm off home to give my kitty his *tuna au naturelle*. Are you coming girls?' The others apart from Miss Ellie followed Lisa Bolt who was evidently a leader of women. The one left behind was neither leader nor led, and Brady registered the possibility of a kindred spirit.

'May I join you?' he asked.

'It's a free country.'

'I hope so, Miss Ellie,' said Brady seating himself opposite those smiling brown eyes. 'My view, for what it's worth, is that the jury's still out on that.'

'My! A newspaper man *and* a philosopher. I've never met one of those before. Or are you a newspaper man, Mr—what was it?—Nick Carraway? A swell literary name that. Now where could I have read it before?'

Brady had reached a moment of decision: to trust or not to trust. He plunged.

'You are working at the Roxy Palace?'

She nodded. 'And you?'

'Nathan Brady FBI. I'm very pleased to meet you, Miss Ellie Jackson.'

Ellie had little more to add to the information Brady already had about the situation at the Roxy Palace, but she promised him that she would observe. She admitted that she had been troubled by what had happened and that the place 'had a bad feel about it'. To lighten things Brady ordered two dishes of Mindy's famous apple pie and asked her about the show.

Ellie explained: 'It's a musical called *Zip Ahoy!* It's about this guy called Johnny Saint who's an inventor, like poor but honest, that stuff. And he's soft on this doll, right and she's like a big star called Dorita Sunshine, or Sonnschein, only she's not Jewish or nothing. And she's a great doll because she loves Johnny even though he's poor and stuff and this guy Johnny invents this zip fastener, see. Only it's a great zip, like a million times better than the ordinary zip and he's going to make a whole lot of potatoes from it. Only there's this Ritzy gangster, called Rocco "The Slasher" Golstein—but he's not Jewish neither, he's kind of Jewish Italian—so he blackmails Johnny and steals the formula and he says he's not going to give it back or nothing unless he can have Dorita and Johnny says nuts to that, but Dorita she wants to save his invention 'cause she really has the hots for him and wants to be his ever loving wife and that, so she says she don't love him no more and they all get on this ship where Dorita is singing in the cabaret and there's this big mix up over some missing pearls which end up in Johnny's cabin so he is arrested and put in the sneezer on board. But there is this doll on board called Ruby Emerald and she's a jewel thief and Dorita recognises her and threatens to tell the cops and put *her* in the sneezer unless she steals back the zip and anyway it all ends happily. And I'm a hoofer in the chorus and understudy for Ruby Emerald who is played by Miss Billie Bernard, Micky Angel's doll.'

'I see.'

'Sounds a bit of terrific, huh?'

'I hope Billie Bernard is prevented from playing Ruby Emerald so I can see you in the role.'

'Don't you wish that on me, Mr FBI. Micky Angel will not be pleased if Miss Billie Bernard is stopped from being a big star which is what this show is all about. Anyway, Billie is an okay broad and I would never wish harm on her.'

'Can I pick you up after rehearsals tomorrow?'

'You may, Mr Brady.'

'Thank you, Miss Ellie. I'll be outside the stage door.'

III

11th May 1936

'You seem to have done well, young man,' said Hoover. 'And this informant of yours. Miss Ellie Jackson. Is she to be relied on?'

'I am sure of it, Mr Hoover.'

'Hmm. She is, however, a woman, Brady. And a woman, Brady, is always a woman. Note that down.'

'I'll bear it in mind, Mr Hoover.'

'The next thing is to gain access to the theatre.'

'I am working on that, Mr Hoover.'

'Good man. Now this stuff about the three invocations and the Hand of Old Glory.'

'Hand of Glory, sir.'

'Hand of Old Glory. What are we doing about getting hold of them?'

Brady explained the difficulty of acquiring the invocations without access to the Miskatonic library; and getting hold of the severed hand of a condemned criminal also presented problems.

Brady added: 'But all this is just superstition, Mr Hoover. In an old book.'

'Don't knock old books, young man. They may be old, but they can sometimes give you the low-down, such as the saying:

'There are more things in heaven on earth.' Do you know who said that?'

'I think it was Hamlet in—'

'A great American called Buffalo Bill said it. Not a lot of people know that.'

'No, sir.'

'We need to get hold of one of these Hands of Old Glory. It may be, as you say, the phonus balonus, but we need to make sure. So we got to find the severed hand of an executed criminal. Am I right?'

'Yes, Mr Hoover.'

'And it's got to be fresh, I reckon. Let me just check out who's coming up for the hot squat.' He pressed a button on his intercom and spoke into it. 'Miss Gandy, will you bring in a list of the folks who are going to the electric chair in the coming fortnight?'

Brady heard a faint: 'Right away, Mr Hoover!' And surprisingly soon Miss Gandy was in the office with a neatly typed list which she laid on Hoover's desk before leaving the room, casting a quick friendly smile in Brady's direction as she did so. Hoover studied the document.

'Huh, so there's Machine Gun Willie Biggs down in Idaho, but he's got a mother who'll kick up hell if we take the body. These mothers of condemned criminals are the pits. Officially we need consent from the jail and the prisoner and the relations to get hold of the body. Then, there's Velma Van Horn, but just maybe she didn't hack her husband to pieces and feed him to her pet 'gator, and her uncle's a Congressman. Could be a reprieve for the broad. . . . Steve "Slugger" Jones. . . . No. He's got God, so he won't buy it—Wait a minute! Here's Obadiah Willums in Sing Sing. An old guy: cut off his wife's head with a pruning hook because she yacked too much. He's got no-one who cares about him, least of all the relatives who get the farm. He might just say yes. We tell him the FBI laboratories want his body for studies in the Brain of the Superior Criminal or some such balonus. That might hook him. Now where is he due to meet Old Sparky? Sing Sing on the 13th! New York State. We're in the money, young man. Ever been to Sing Sing, Brady? I'll get Miss Gandy to arrange a visit as soon as possible.'

11th May 1936 (from the diary of H.P. Lovecraft)
When Mr Brady called yesterday I was able to tell him I had seen the Doc he recommended. Apparently he was already acquainted with the results of my examination, and had made provisional arrangements for me to go into hospital to undergo further tests and possibly an operation. I protested in the strongest possible terms at this intrusion into my personal affairs. Mr Brady listened patiently to my outburst, then remarked quietly that my continued health and well-being was his greatest concern. He told me that all expenses for my treatment and operation would be taken care of, but before that could happen, he would ask one favour of me. I told him to name it.

'I would like you to help me to break into the Miskatonic library and steal the *Necronomicon*,' he said.

My utter astonishment can without difficulty, I presume, be imagined. I asked him in crudely vernacular terms what his 'game' was, and he, as the vernacular also has it, 'came clean'.

After he had explained, it took several minutes for me to regain my customary coolth and composure. So the visions were real! My dismay that I had been something of a dupe these last few weeks was mitigated by Mr Brady's sincere admiration for my work. And, after all, I am a patriot and my respect for that great American Mr J. Edgar Hoover knows no bounds. It would seem that I am to become an *ex officio* G man! Mr Brady enjoined on me the utter secrecy of this mission which not even Aunt Annie must know about. I agreed.

Last night my visions took me back to that accursed theatre. Brady was there and in mortal danger. I tried in my dream to cry out to him to be wary, but no sound came. I await news from him with trepidation. For all his underhandedness he is, like me, a gentleman and I can't help liking the fellow.

12th May 1936
As Hoover had correctly surmised, Brady had never been to Sing Sing. He had interviewed prisoners in other jails, but never one of the condemned on Death Row. The prison governor seemed most anxious to assist and asked Brady to convey his best regards to 'Mr Hoover'. Brady found this degree of courtesy often to the point of obsequiousness among officials where J. Edgar Hoover was concerned and wondered if the Director 'had something on' the governor. It was usually the case.

As he led Brady through a succession of metallic passages and locked doors, he said: 'You'll find Obadiah Willums a queer sort of guy. I reckon he's positively looking forward to the chair. Why does the Bureau want the body, by the way? If you don't mind my asking.'

'Our forensic laboratories are conducting a number of highly advanced scientific experiments on brains which will enable us to identify the criminal mind almost from birth in the future.' Brady was astonished and ashamed at his ability to come up with his sort of nonsense.

'Really? Really? Modern science is a wondrous thing, sir. That's most interesting. Mr Hoover is a truly great man.'

'He is indeed, sir.'

'But I wouldn't say Willums is exactly a criminal, more like crazy. He told me that this kind of weird creature came out of the well in his yard and told him to snuff his old lady. I reckon he ought to be in a booby hatch rather than Sing Sing, but he won't have it. He says he's sane and he wants to go to the chair, but if he really wants to sit in Old Sparky he *must* be bughouse.'

'Mr Hoover is particularly interested in the criminally insane.'

'Well, okay then. Mr Hoover is one hell of a great guy. And you be sure to tell him I said so.'

'I certainly will, sir.'

'And if he—or you—ever want to come down to see an execution with Old Sparky at work, you only have to ask. You will be most welcome.'

'Thank you, governor. That is very generous. I am sure Mr Hoover will appreciate the offer.'

'I sure hope he does. Well, here we are. Death Row. You'll notice I have just had everything repainted. Cerise pink. My wife Florine chose the colour. It's part of our humane policy to make things feel kind of homey here. I'll hand you over now to the Reverend Mortice, our Death Row chaplain. He does a great job here with the prisoners, saving their souls and such.'

The Reverend Mortice was a small, round, smiling individual with the manner of a practiced receiver of confessions, like a solicitor with extra unction. As he led Brady to the interview room, he smiled at the guards in the corridor and spoke to each by their Christian names and waved to all the men in their condemned cells.

'I have a great love in my heart for Obadiah,' he told Brady, 'but, sadly, I cannot get him to repent. If only they repent then they can go straight from that chair of death into the life eternal of paradise. It's the free gift from the Lord to all us sinners. But if they will not repent then they must go to Hell. It gives me great distress to think of any of these poor souls in a place of eternal torment. Perhaps *you* can persuade him to repent.'

'I think that's your job, reverend. I am here to—on another mission.' Then, witnessing the crushed look on the Reverend Mortice's face, he added: 'I'll do my best.'

Mortice beamed. He opened the door of the interview room which was painted the same hideous shade of cerise pink as the corridor. It reminded Brady of flayed flesh. 'Someone to see you, Obadiah.'

A little wizened, bald old man in dungarees sat rigid and upright at a table. He glanced with scorn at Mortice, but showed mild interest in his new visitor. He did not speak until the chaplain had left the room and then he fixed Brady with a disconcertingly mild gaze.

'You can see me, son,' said Obadiah Willums, 'but I ain't going to say no more. Tomorrow I'm going to meet Old Sparky and we'll get along just fine.'

In quiet respectful tones Brady stated the purpose of his visit which was for Willums to sign a paper giving consent for his body after execution to be handed over to the FBI for 'research'.

'Search?' said Willums. 'Search for what? You won't find nothing save bones and a bit of old gristle. What's the use of searching for that?'

'Well, in that case, that is what we will find out, Mr Willums.'

'You folk are the darndest fools. Still, ain't no concern of mine. But I done nothin' wrong, son.'

Brady looked at Willums enquiringly. A miscarriage of justice would complicate matters beyond measure.

'Oh, I killed the old beaver all right. Cut her head clean off.' Brady heaved an involuntary sigh of relief. 'Nice and neat too. But I had to, son and I don't regret it, no, sir. The Old One tells me to.'

'The Old One?'

'Yes. The Old 'Un. Ain't you heared of the Old 'Uns? You college educated boys don't know nothing, do you? Up Dunwich way where I lives, you get the Old Ones. They comes up from under and speak to you, not in words like other folk but like light through the brain. And they smell like thunder, and sometimes you see them and sometimes you don't, but you sure know when and where they've been. For they come with all Hell in their wings which they stretch up to the stars from where they come a long way back. My grandaddy spoke with them and taught me to speak with them too. And we had an Old 'Un specially ours and he lived in that there old well in our back yard. And every Midsummer Eve we'd lay flowers on the well and throw a cow down there or maybe a couple of hogs, but mostly a cow, hogs being too vallable. And the Old 'Un'd come up and maybe show himself or maybe not, but my wife Martha she never see'd him because she didn't hold with the Old 'Un, being in with the Holy Joes up the Baptist Chapel. And she called the Old 'Un all kinds of names like Old Moloch, and Beelzebub and Satan's Brood and such, and the Old 'Un took it till one day he says to me: 'Oby'—that's what he calls me, see—'Oby, that old lady of yours don't like me, nor you, nor your hogs, and she ain't no use any more. You give me her head; I'll see you right.' So that's how it come about. And so one night close to the end of summer when the whippoorwills were a'screaming in the dusky air, I picks up my pruning hook and I snips her head and I throw it down the well to the Old 'Un. And the Old 'Un goes Boom! And up comes a smell like thunder and all the whippoorwills stop their screeching and a great peace comes down on the earth. And later comes the po-lice and all and they find Martha sitting upright on a kitchen chair with the gurt old Bible open at the fifth chapter of Matthew in front of her on the table, but no head to read it. So here I be. And you can do with my old body what you like because Old Sparky he's going to take my soul right back down to the Old 'Un where I belong.'

There was a silence in the room when Willums had finished speaking. For a full minute Brady hardly dared move. Then slowly he took out a pen and passed it across the table with the paper for Willums to sign while the old man hummed gently to himself.

'What do you think I've ordered for my last meal, son?' said Willums suddenly.

Brady shook his head.

'Pork!' And he chuckled with delight. 'I've always kept hogs, see, since I were a young shaver. I was known for my hogs, so I'm going to have pork. Best darned meat in the whole world, pork. That's one reason why I had to kill my old lady. The Old 'Un told me she didn't respect my hogs no more. I couldn't have that, so I got out my old pruning hook—Not a gun. I don't hold with no guns, ever since my Daddy shot off his foot chasin' a bear—and I sliced off her mean old head neat as you like. So I'm going to have some nice fat pork with a bully piece o' cracklin' before I sits me down in Old Sparky. Do you think you can fix me that, son for sure? Nice piece o' cracklin'?'

'I sure can, Mr Willums.'

'Then I'll sign your paper. Anything more I can do for you, son?'

Brady, who felt unaccountably sorry for Mortice, gently hinted that Obadiah Willums would make the chaplain very happy if he repented of his crime.

'But I don't repent it, son,' said Willums. 'I'm darn glad I sliced off her mean old head. She was all dried up like a stick with not an ounce of juice left in her. That Old 'Un had the right of it.'

'But you could *say* you repent, couldn't you, Mr Willums? Just to keep Reverend Mortice happy. You don't have to *mean* it.'

Willums was silent for a while, considering this, then he slapped his thigh and let out a yell of laughter.

'My! If that isn't the durndest thing I ever heared of! I'll give him repentance, the old coyote! I'll lead that smirking, psalm-singing preacher man in a square dance he won't forget, no sir! And inside, me and the Old 'Un will be laughing fit to bust. Here's your paper, son. Signed and sealed. Darn me! That's the biggest laugh I've had since old Great Aunt Thirza fell into the grain silo and drownded herself in corn!'

As he left the interview room, Brady could still hear Obadiah Willums chortling to himself. In the corridor he met Reverend Mortice who heard the noise and looked at him enquiringly.

'He is sobbing over his sins,' said Brady. 'Give him a few moments. I think you'll find him ready to repent.'

'Bless you, Mr Brady,' said Reverend Mortice, a wide smile splitting his round face. 'And Praise the Lord! Today you and Mr Hoover have saved a soul for Paradise!'

It would have been inhuman of Brady not to feel a little ashamed: still, the body of Obadiah Willums, condemned murderer, now belonged to the FBI.

IV

13th May 1936

Brady's seat at the Roxy Palace Theatre was some way towards the back of the circle, but he had a good view. It had been kind of Miss Ellie Jackson to secure him the complimentary seat. He looked down into the audience. Most of the men, like him, were wearing black tie and dinner jackets, though a few people in the boxes were in white tie and tails. Among them, Brady was astonished to see his own director, J. Edgar Hoover with his faithful assistant Clyde Tolson. Brady noted, with something of the innate snobbery of the well-favoured, that a white tie did not in any way diminish Hoover's air of squat brutishness. But his *farouche* appearance was as nothing to the man in whose box they were evidently guests. A huge man, mightily built though not grossly fat, stood behind them smiling proprietorially on the proceedings. He was florid in his complexion and his black curly hair, sleekly oiled, was abundant. His features, apart from a calamitously broken nose, were still classically regular and Brady could just imagine that he might once have been a handsome, even a pretty youth, though more Murillo urchin than Botticelli angel. For this, as Brady knew from consulting the photograph in his remarkably slender FBI file, was Micky 'The Angel' Buonarotti. But what were the Director of the FBI and his assistant doing in his box? Brady decided to dismiss this puzzle from his mind as the conductor, to a ripple of applause, took his place and the overture began.

THE ARMIES OF THE NIGHT

Brady was no connoisseur of musical comedy but he judged that *Zip Ahoy!* might well be a hit. It was certainly cheered and applauded enough to give that appearance, though Brady knew that it was the Broadway critics who would have the last word. The numbers were perhaps a little too big and brassy for his rather over-refined taste, but whenever the chorus came on his attention was instantly drawn to Miss Ellie Jackson. Her golden skin and lustrous eyes marked her out. Was it just his own personal preference? She certainly danced superbly, with a lithe and natural grace, and Brady thought he could pick out her voice among the others: lower, smoother, silkier. She had one line to say and it got a laugh. Was he falling under her spell? Given Mr Hoover's less than advanced views on race, it was a dangerous thing for Brady to do. Brady dismissed the thought from his mind: theirs was a purely professional relationship, he told himself, albeit friendly.

He made a note too of Miss Billie Bernard who played the part of Ruby Emerald the jewel thief. It was a showy part with one or two good numbers and Billie Bernard had made a fair fist of it, he supposed. She danced well but her voice was a little thin and her personality didn't run to much.

While the audience was filing out Brady made his way towards the pass door to the stage at the right hand end of the circle. Ellie had told him that she would leave it unlocked. Once through Brady found himself on a metal walkway above the stage where, behind the fallen curtain, he could look down on the heads of the cast still milling and hugging. Brady waited until they dispersed and only stagehands were present, moving scenery into place for the start of the show the following night. Unobserved he moved across the walkway and through a second pass door into the upper dressing room corridor where the chorus lived.

On one of the doors Brady knocked and asked for Miss Ellie, opening it a fraction to do so. Presently she slipped through the door and came out into the corridor.

She had her hair up and wore a long white silk dressing gown, tightly belted to show off her exquisite figure. Though she was out of make-up and *en deshabille* Brady thought he had never seen anyone look more glorious. She gave him that warm generous smile that could melt an iceberg a league away.

'Thank you for those lovely flowers, Nathan. All the girls in there think you must be my beau.'

'I hope I am your very, very good friend, Miss Ellie.'

'You see that door at the end of the corridor? That's the wardrobe and nobody will be in there till six tomorrow morning earliest. I had a key copied. Here. Now you go in there and lock yourself in. I'll make sure I'm one of the last to leave and I'll knock on the door three times to let you know it's clear. But you watch yourself. Micky Angel don't like anyone creeping round his theatre, specially not the FBI, I guess. Are you packing a rod?'

Brady opened his jacket to reveal a Colt automatic neatly tucked into a leather holster strapped close to the left side of his ribcage.

'My!' she said. 'It doesn't show with your tux buttoned at all!'

'I told my tailor to make allowances,' said Brady, a little self-consciously. 'What are you giggling at, Miss Ellie?'

'Oh, nothing! Just that for a G Man, you really are quite sweet.' And she kissed him on both cheeks. Brady blushed. 'Remember. When you're done with the snooping, I'll be at the show party at Sardi's all night.'

'I'll try to get there.'

Ellie blew him a kiss and tripped back into the dressing room. Brady heard whoops from the other chorus girls as she did so and he rapidly made his way to the wardrobe room at the end of the corridor.

Brady did not have long to wait before he heard three sharp raps on the wardrobe room door, but he did not immediately come out, and it was as well he didn't. Soon after he heard footsteps coming down the corridor and the door being tried. Fortunately he had locked it, as Miss Ellie had suggested.

Twenty minutes later he emerged to find the theatre apparently deserted and in darkness. He nevertheless moved silently, having taken care to put crepe on the soles of his patent leather pumps. He came down two flights of stairs, hearing and seeing nothing, but when he came to the stage level, he heard a noise coming from one of the star dressing rooms. He crept closer and found an alcove from which he could hear unobserved what was going on.

'No, Micky, no!' said a high, slightly nasal voice which Brady recognised as belonging to Miss Billie Bernard. 'I will not come to your ball. I know when I'm not wanted. I was lousy tonight and I know it.'

'But, honey, you were great! I did all this for you.'

'I know, Micky, I know. And I'm grateful believe me. But I just can't take it. Aw, Micky just leave me.'

'You are coming to Sardi's, doll. I said so.'

'Let me go, you big ape!'

Brady heard sounds of a struggle, then a grunt from Micky and a scream of pain from Billie. He peered out of his recess, darting back just in time to avoid being seen by Micky who emerged from Billie's dressing room nursing what looked like a scratch on his right hand. Brady saw him turn a corner and then, beyond Brady's line of sight, begin to speak in muffled tones to some person or persons.

Brady heard the words: '. . . and see she shows up' from Micky, followed by a 'Yeah, boss,' which was echoed by another. Then Micky left, slamming the stage door behind him. Meanwhile a sound of sobbing was coming from Miss Billie Bernard's dressing room.

Brady was just about to emerge from his hiding place when two large men came round the corner and walked purposefully towards Billie's dressing room. Their faces were shapeless and pockmarked: one of them had the little finger missing from his left hand, the other a pencil moustache so thin it looked like the gash from a knife. Incongruously they were immaculately costumed in midnight blue dinner suits with wing collars and black bow ties.

They paused before Billie's dressing room door and knocked.

'We've come to take you to the party, Miss Billie,' they said.

'Scram, you great lunks!' screamed Billie from within. 'I'm not going for you or anyone!'

'Boss's orders, Miss Billie,' said Pencil Moustache.

The one with the missing finger who seemed, if possible, even more brutish than his companion mumbled: 'Boss's orders.' Then they both entered Billie's dressing room.

Presently Brady heard scuffles and screams and the smashing of glass followed by the heady odour of cheap scent. A bottle of perfume had been thrown. Brady wondered if he should intervene, but this was not what he was here for. Besides, it sounded as if Miss Billie Bernard could look after herself. Then there was a further crash and Billie came bolting out of her dressing room. She wasted precious seconds trying to lock the two mobsters in her dressing room, but they forced the door open, pursuing her down the corridor past where Brady was concealed. Billie tried to dodge through the door to the stage but they blocked her way. There was now only one possible route of escape, the staircase down to the understage, and this she took with Pencil Moustache and Missing Finger in close pursuit. Brady decided to follow at a discreet distance. Billie was screaming, the two hoodlums bellowing: it was a primitive scene.

Brady followed them down to beneath the stage where he was just in time to see Billie take an unwary step and half slide, half tumble down a ragged hole in the floor of the basement. Pencil Moustache and Missing Finger followed her down more carefully, using their cigarette lighters to see where they were going.

Brady came to the edge of the hole to watch the descent of the thugs at a safe distance. He had a flashlight but would not use it unless absolutely necessary. He could hear the hollow echoes of Billie's screams and the splashy echo of her footsteps as she wandered blindly in the spaces below.

As soon as Pencil Moustache and Missing Finger had reached the bottom of the hole and had set off in rather hesitant pursuit of their quarry once more, Brady started his own climb down into the depths.

The first thing he became aware of on reaching the bottom was the smell. It was ancient and putrid and fishy. The atmosphere down there was not, as he had expected, close. There was air coming from somewhere, almost like a breeze, but the odour it carried was all decay and death. The walls Brady touched were mostly smooth and clammy, though in parts it felt as if they were covered with coarse wet hairs: some sort of moss or weed, he presumed. The weed was faintly bioluminescent, and of a greenish grey colour, like a vast hirsute glow worm.

Brady risked a quick flash of his torch and what he saw astonished him. It was as Lovecraft had described. He was in a vast barrel-vaulted corridor with smooth walls, some of them masked with the coarse subterranean growth he had felt and seen. Other parts of the wall were damp and naked but intricately carved, either with lettering which Brady identified as Runic in character, or with grotesque bas relief sculptures. He had no time to examine them because ahead of him Pencil Moustache turned round uttering the words—'What the—!'—but Brady immediately snapped off his torch.

Ahead of him the two thugs had other things to occupy their minds. Brady saw them halt and hold up their flickering lighters to stare around them. The vaulted gallery had debouched into a wide, almost circular chamber from which numerous passages wound off like tentacles from the head of a monstrous beast. They evidently could not tell which way Billie had taken, and were dazed by the awesomeness of the structure that they encountered. The roof of the space was conical, like the beehive tombs of pre-classical Greece, and every inch of the smooth cyclopean masonry with which it was built was covered in carvings of strange and hideous creatures coupled with what looked like astronomical charts featuring constellations and planets.

Brady came up close to the two men unobserved and watched as they stared in horror and wonder at the chamber they had entered. For a moment there was complete silence, then a scream was heard coming from one of the tunnels that led out of the space they were in. It was Billie.

Pencil Moustache and Missing Finger had some discussion as to which was the tunnel from which Billie's voice had come. Eventually Pencil Moustache overruled Missing Finger and plunged down one of them, the latter following, disgruntled. Brady thought he rather favoured Missing Finger's decision but decided to follow them at a discreet distance.

As soon as Brady entered the tunnel, he was aware of a thicker, more oppressive atmosphere, the fish corpse odour now so powerful that he could hear the two hoodlums ahead of him choke and retch. Brady conserved his strength and took shallow breaths. The two men began to call out: 'Miss Billie! Miss Billie!' trying vainly to sound conciliatory, but nothing except the hollow echo of their cries was to be heard.

Then came another sound. At first it was no more than a pulse in the earth that could have been mistaken for the thump of Brady's own beating heart. Rapidly it grew louder and began to boom like the vibrating skin of a vast drum. Pencil Moustache and Missing Finger were still moving forward ahead of him, but slowly, tentatively. Now the booming sound was accompanied by the splashy patter of splayed feet advancing over puddles. There was a curious hissing noise before Brady heard Pencil Moustache say: 'Son of a—!' Then things began to happen rapidly.

There was a swishing sound and Pencil Moustache was swept off his feet by something like a giant arm. Missing Finger pulled his gun and started firing indiscriminately until the clip of his magazine was exhausted. Brady switched on his torch to witness a scene of such horror that for a few seconds he could do nothing but look.

Pencil Moustache was being held aloft by a giant arm or tentacle and he was either dead or unconscious but his eyes were wide open and staring. Most of his right leg had been torn off and was being devoured by a host of creatures, half human, half piscine and of unimaginable hideousness. Meanwhile Missing Finger was bellowing and struggling among a roiling mass of creatures.

Above it all a half human voice cried out triumphantly, *Rghyyeloi fo Xhon! Rghyyeloi fo Xhon!* And it was taken up by many more: *Rghyyeloi fo Xhon! Rghyyeloi fo Xhon! The Armies of the Night! The Armies of the Night!*

Brady considered intervening, but it looked as if Pencil Moustache and Missing Finger were doomed and perhaps not to be much missed. He would be better employed trying to rescue Miss Billie Bernard. He switched off his torch and ran back down the tunnel towards the central hall. As he did so the dreadful bellowing of Missing Finger stopped in mid scream.

When he reached the hall, almost without thinking he darted down the tunnel from which he and the late lamented Missing Finger had thought Billie's screams were emanating. Losing all caution, he switched on his torch and ran calling out 'Miss Billie!' as he went. The passage became narrower and Brady noticed that it was now constructed from homely brick. He heard what he thought sounded like a muffled human cry. There was a right-angled corner which Brady turned without any precaution, his torch flashing over the rough brickwork as he ran. He did not even draw his pistol. Then, before he saw him, he heard a man say: 'Stand right where you are!'

Brady halted, cursing his own recklessness. He shone his torch directly ahead and saw a big man standing in a blade of light made by a half open doorway. In his right hand he held a revolver which was pointed directly at Brady. His left arm encircled the frail form of Miss Billie Bernard who struggled feebly in his grasp and the massive left hand was clamped tightly over her mouth.

'You better come with us, punk,' said the man, a vast Chinaman, almost as wide as he was tall, 'unless you're looking for a gut full of lead.' Brady was not, so he followed instructions and preceded Billie and the Chinaman through the door and up a narrow flight of stairs. From somewhere he could hear the sound of laughter and a very capable dance orchestra in full swing. Brady felt the almost irresistible urge to ask the Chinaman if he knew his good friend Charlie Chin, but felt this was neither the time nor the place. But he did ask where they were. They were not in the Roxy Palace, that was for sure.

'You dumb or something?' said the Chinaman, 'This is The Garden of Allah, and I am taking you to see the boss, Mr Leo Vinci.'

'Oh, you mean Leo the—' Brady just restrained himself from uttering the dreadful word 'artichoke'. 'Mr Vinci. Yes, of course.'

'And,' added the huge Chinaman, rather superfluously, Brady thought, 'Mr Vinci will not be very happy to see either you, Mr Smart-Ass or Miss Billie Bernard!'

V

14th May 1936 (early hours)
The office of Leo 'The Artichoke' Vinci was situated at the top of the building which contained his highly fashionable nightclub The Garden of Allah. It would not, however, be true to say that the aforementioned establishment owed any of its success to Mr

Vinci. It had been bought, for a very reasonable sum, from the club's original proprietor and creator who had got into difficulties with Vinci and been made, as they say, 'an offer he couldn't refuse', Mr Vinci, however, was not a man to deny himself credit even if it was undeserved and he made sure that everyone knew that he was The Garden of Allah's sole director and that the excellence of its orchestra, the refinement of its food and liquor, and the slenderness of its chorus girls' legs were all down to him. His office was the epitome of what was considered in his world to be sophisticated modernity. Whatever was not chrome plated was gold plated, and the elegance of his *moderne* furniture was only matched by its discomfort. Behind his desk a portrait of Vinci by the artist of the moment, Tamara de Lempicka was a miracle of popular cubism and shameless flattery.

He himself was not a thing of beauty, even though Tamara de Lempicka had done her best to imply it. She had certainly caught the angularity of the man. He had an abominably long, thin face which had been likened by no less a person than Miss Dorothy Parker to 'two profiles stuck together'. His nose was a beak; his lips were exiguous. That narrowness of aspect reminded Brady, when he first came into his presence, of his new friend Lovecraft; but this was a demonic version of the lantern-jawed sage of Providence, Rhode Island.

The Chinaman had been right. Vinci was not pleased to see them, though Brady doubted whether the man sitting opposite him and playing with a dangerous looking steel letter opener was ever pleased to see anything except his bank balance.

'I found these guys in the basement,' said the Chinaman.

Vinci was enraged. 'Haven't I told you, Hang, never to let anyone go down in that goddam basement!'

'But, boss, they didn't come from The Garden, they came in some other way.'

'What! Is this true?'

'It's true,' said Brady.

'And who in hell are you?'

'Nathan Brady, FBI,' he began to reach for his badge, but as he expected, was stopped.

'Keep your hands away from your pockets, punk!'

'Very well, then, Mr Vinci. If you or your assistant reach into the right hand outside pocket of my jacket, you will find my authority.'

'Do it!' said Vinci to the Chinaman who extracted the badge and threw it onto the desk in front of Vinci.

'So, Mr FBI,' said Vinci, lacing every syllable with sarcasm, 'you expect me to be impressed.'

'Not impressed, but perhaps better informed.'

Vinci's eyes narrowed. 'Would you like to tell me how in hell you got here?'

'It's very simple. I was following this young lady here. Miss Billie Bernard.'

'Yes, I know her name, thank you, Mr FBI. We know each other well, do we not, Miss Bernard? Have you come back to me, then, Billie, begging for forgiveness? Have things gone sour between you and that hulking great sonofabitch, Micky Angel? Is that your game?'

Billie, released at last from Hang's debilitating grip, began to show spirit. 'Listen, Leo,' she said. 'I know I was your doll once, and I know you are pretty mad at me for throwing you over for a sap like Micky Angel, but that is not here nor is it there. And how I got here, I do not truly know and who the hell this G man is and what he is doing shnozzling around after me I know not neither. Now, will you kindly release me from your extremely classy joint? I have a party at Sardi's to attend following the premiere performance of a show named *Zip Ahoy!* at the Roxy Palace with which you may not be entirely ignorant.' And with that she began to march confidently towards the door of Vinci's office.

'Not so fast, sister!' said Vinci. 'At this moment my betsy is pointed at your ass which is a very fine ass as asses go and would not benefit from being rearranged by the insertion of lead.' Billie halted. She knew Vinci well enough to sense that he meant business. She turned round to see that Vinci's revolver (pearl-handled and gold plated) was indeed pointed directly at her nether regions.

'Aw, Leo,' she said, 'it is truly touching that you still have my best interests at heart.' Vinci, a stranger to irony, did not smile.

'Park your ass, doll and lay off the gabbing till I tell you to gab.' Billie sat down in the chair to which Hang had motioned her with a flick of his Colt. 'Now I want to know how in hell you got here and where you came from or I shall loose Mr Hang on you with some methods of persuasion that you will not like.'

Brady explained that there was a route from the basement of the Roxy Palace to the basement of The Garden of Allah which had been discovered and that he had followed Miss Billie Bernard there. He did not think it appropriate to mention the part played by Pencil Moustache and Missing Finger, or their unhappy fate.

'And why were you following Miss Billie?'

It was a question that Brady had been expecting and dreading. 'That is a confidential FBI matter and no business of yours, Mr Vinci.'

'Oh, no? And suppose Mr Hang makes it relevant, punk?'

'Mr Hoover would not be happy with you, Mr Vinci. And when Mr Hoover is not happy consequences follow.'

'Oh, yeah! And if you end up in the East River wearing the concrete overcoat, who's to know?'

'Mr Hoover would know. He knows enough already and he always gets to know everything in the end. I will give you plenty of five to seven on that. I can only guarantee your safety if you let me go unharmed.' This was, of course, as Mr Hoover might say, *the phonus balonus*, but it seemed to impress Vinci. Like most people of a criminal persuasion Leo Vinci was superstitious, and had bought into the myth of the FBI's omniscience.

The proprietor of The Garden of Allah considered a moment, then spoke. 'Okay, Mr Wise Guy. I'm going to let you go, but you do exactly as I tell you. You go to Micky Angel and you tell him that I have got Miss Billie Bernard and that she does not go on tonight or in any show ever unless he comes and does business with me. We will meet in a friendly way and our people will be carrying the minimum of weapons. And I expect his answer by tonight. I am done with Mr Buonarotti muscling in on my territory. First he steals my broad, then he builds his theatre a few blocks away, then he comes at me from under my building. This is not the action of a guy who used to be a buddy. Micky and I grew up together. Hell, we used to run a whorehouse together! Best goddam whorehouse in Brooklyn too! Together we buried 'Feet' Macorquodale alive for singing to the cops about the Hoboken bank heist. Now he's in cahoots with your Director. What's his hold on the guy? Why does he not share it with me? Where is comradeship? Where is loyalty and honour? Where is the old pals act? It is all gone. I tell you, Mr FBI, this country is taking the A train to Hell. Now get your ass out of here.'

'Do I have your assurance that Miss Billie Bernard suffers no harm?'

'You do, but she stays in my keeping until Micky Angel gets his ass over here and starts talking business. And no FBI in on the act. Capeesh?'

Brady, who was a linguist, indicated his understanding with a nod and was released.

14th May 1936 (later that morning)
It was fortunate, Brady reflected, that Mr Hoover had been at the first night of *Zip Ahoy!*, because it might mean that he was still in New York. This proved to be the case. A phone call gave him the information that he was at the New York FBI building in

downtown Manhattan and by ten o'clock Brady was standing opposite him in the Director's office. With Hoover was his assistant, Clyde Tolson, watchful, enigmatic, and cold.

Brady gave them an edited, but, he hoped, credible account of the events of the night before. He was listened to in silence.

'Well, young man,' said Hoover, 'we have ourselves a situation. Mr Buonarotti is as far as I know a man of good standing in this city—'

'I understand that you and Mr Tolson enjoyed his hospitality last night.'

Hoover stiffened; Tolson glared. Brady had taken a risk, but he had wanted to gauge their reactions. Vinci's remark about Buonarotti's 'hold' on Hoover had impressed him.

'Mr Brady,' said Hoover, 'I did not ask you to interrupt while I was speaking.' The coldness was evident but he was clearly on the defensive. 'A lot of nonsense in this city is talked about so-called Mafias and organised crime. There is no such thing. There are just criminals. There is no organised crime. There is no "Mob". Do you understand, Brady?'

'I'll bear that in mind, Mr Hoover.'

'Mr Buonarotti is a businessman in good standing; he owns a theatre which is under threat from these communist rats. There is your organised crime if you like. Now, I know nothing of this dispute he has with Mr Vinci. That is not FBI business, but this dispute should be resolved. After all, Mr Vinci is also a businessman, though I am not personally acquainted with him. Your task, Mr Brady, is to give Mr Buonarotti every assistance in ridding himself from these commie bums. I do not want to know how you do it, but you will do it. It will be a test for you. Do I make myself clear?'

'Absolutely, Mr Hoover. I have your permission to act on my own initiative then?'

'You do, Brady. You may hit your approach shot any way you like so long as you get your ball in the hole. Do you have a plan?'

'I believe I do, Mr Hoover.'

'Well, don't tell me about it, just get a going and kick some ass. And, Brady—?'

'Sir.'

'By the time you get back to your hotel room, a parcel should have arrived for you. Special delivery from Sing Sing. Via our laboratories. Understood?'

'Understood, Mr Hoover,' said Brady. Out of the corner of his eye he noticed Tolson look enquiringly at the Director. Evidently he had not understood; there were some things that Hoover kept even from his closest associate.

The rest of that morning and the afternoon Brady spent mainly with Mr Buonarotti who, after an initial explosiveness, proved most accommodating. He also made other arrangements. The last task on his list, and not the least important in his eyes, was to see Miss Ellie Jackson, who took the news he had to give her with a kind of sober level-headedness, neither fearful nor exultant, which only enhanced his admiration for her. Then she too had her preparations to make.

They met again only shortly before curtain up on the second night of *Zip Ahoy!* in which Miss Ellie was to take over the leading role of Ruby Emerald owing to the indisposition and absence of Miss Billie Bernard. As the overture was playing, they stood together in the wings.

'Miss Ellie,' said Brady looking into those wonderful eyes, 'I want you to go out there and come back a star.'

'You honestly think I can do it, Nathan?'

'I *know* you can, doll.'

'Oh, Nathan! You called me, doll! How thrillingly ungentlemanly of you!'

'I am now going to *do* something ungentlemanly,' he said and kissed her full on her soft lips. 'Now go out there, Miss Ellie, and knock 'em dead!'

And she did. Watching from the back of the stalls, Brady felt immense pride, but also something else: deeper, more primitive, and, somehow, purer. Hoover would not have approved; but to hell with Hoover. Miss Ellie Jackson came back a star.

Later that night, having congratulated Miss Ellie on her superb performance, Brady went down to the basement beneath the stage where he was presently joined by Micky 'The Angel' Buonarotti and what seemed at first like a dozen musicians for they were all carrying instrument cases. However their pin-striped suits and two-toned shoes were not particularly musicianly, and their features would not have suggested to a casual observer the subtlety and sensitivity of the musical mind. Brady was hardly surprised, when the men began to open their cases, that none of them contained a violin, or even so much as a trombone.

'Okay, you guys, listen up,' said Micky Angel. 'This dude here is Mr Nathan Brady. He is a G Man—' There were murmurs of faint disapproval as Brady stepped forward, revealing himself to the assembled hoods. 'But don't you give him no lip, see. I can vouch for him. He is a regular guy and he is on a special mission from my very good friend Mr J. Edgar Hoover to help us get that sonofabitch Leo the Artichoke who has nabbed my doll and done other goddam lousy things that no decent guy like you gentlemen here would speak of let alone do.' At this the assembled men looked at each other with a surprised complacency and some began to burnish the barrels of their Tommy guns and sawn-offs with handkerchiefs. 'Now we are going to conduct a raid on this lousy sonofabitch and teach him a lesson in honour, because this roach is also trying to muscle in on my territory by building a tunnel under the Roxy and hiring a lot of bums to scare the pants off my employees. Mr Brady here tells me that Leo the Artichoke has got these lousy bums up in some goddam scary costumes, like fish or some such, so don't you go running off saying you seen a ghost or any of that crapola. Hell, you are Americans, and proud of it, so just go right ahead, do your duty as citizens of the land of the free, and fill their lousy guts with a bucketful of lead. Gentlemen, let's go down there and kick some ass!'

This rousing speech received a muted cheer. Then Brady said: 'This way, gentlemen, but tread carefully!'—and led the way down into the subterranean chambers of the Old Ones. Micky Angel with his army of mercenaries followed, and if Micky Angel was a little surprised that Brady did not advise his men to keep silent and stop flashing their torches around, he did not voice his misgivings. During their long and complex interview Brady had managed to inspire confidence: it was one of his gifts.

The men could not help looking round and wondering at the monumental architecture that surrounded them. Brady explained that the galleries in which they were walking had probably been built as water conduits by some of New York's very earliest inhabitants.

'You mean, like redskins?' asked one of the men incredulously.

'Very likely,' said Brady shortly. He was becoming increasingly nervous. The plan he had devised was beginning to look more and more foolhardy. He held up his hand for silence.

Faintly at first but becoming louder by the second they heard a rhythmical booming sound that echoed through the underground chamber like the throb of a heartbeat. This began to be accompanied by strange half human cries which even Brady who had heard them before found troubling. He could just make out the words—if they can be called words.

Rghyyeloi fo Xhon! Rghyyeloi fo Xhon!

'Forward, but steady as we go, gentlemen,' said Brady who surprised himself by not sounding fearful or hesitant. They had come almost to the vaulted circular chamber with its numerous passageways leading off it, and as they did so the tension increased. No-one spoke, and all the men were checking their ammunition. Brady's torch began to make out vague shapes waving and shaking in the distance. He told the men to dip their

THE ARMIES OF THE NIGHT

torches until they got to the opening. Confident as he sounded, he realised that from now on he must rely on improvisation. A faint grey green light came from the lichen which bearded the slabs of masonry that lined the gallery walls. Brady drew his automatic from its holster and felt for the other weapons at his disposal. The booming became louder, as did the slap and rustle of great wet feet. Now they were in the vaulted space. Brady flashed his torch into it and the others followed suit.

Nothing could have prepared them for what they saw. A great roiling mass of organic life stood before them. The shapes were a grotesque parody of the human, the skin glaucous and scaly, the eyes saucer-like and the gaping mouths crammed with needle teeth embedded in grey flesh with mucous strings of slime hanging from them were beyond description hideous. The beasts stared at their human adversaries. There was a moment of motionless stunned silence as each side contemplated the other. Brady saw the men recoil, not least at the hideous corrupt stench they gave off, but they steadied themselves and began to aim their weapons. Micky Angel was the one to break the silence.

'Hell! Those are some crazy costumes, all right! I always knew The Artichoke was one mean sonofabitch, but this is booby hatch time!' There was another short pause during which all considered this profound reflection, then Micky said: 'Okay! Let 'em have it, guys! Right in their ugly kissers!'

The sound of gunfire in that vaulted, confined space was all but deafening. The whole cavern was ablaze with the flare of Tommy guns and the angry flash of the double barrelled sawn-offs, no sooner discharged than reloaded and blasted again. Brady shot off a clip from his automatic and then withdrew from the front line to observe better and decide on tactics.

The creatures were falling under the storm of bullets, it was true, and they seemed to have no weapons with which to retaliate, but there were so many of them, and they seemed curiously, flabbily, resilient. Even when they had fallen, a part of them seemed to stir and grope forward towards their killers. But the men did not falter once they had begun. The creatures seemed to react slowly but they were staggering towards the line of firing men, stumbling over their fallen comrades, dull but undeterred. Micky's line of defence did not break but it began to fall back.

Meanwhile Brady was reloading and considering his next step when he felt a touch on his arm. He started violently and spun round to find himself staring into the lovely shadowed face of Miss Ellie Jackson.

'Good God what are you doing here, Ellie? Go back at once! This is no place for you!'

'I Iell, no! And what gives you the right to tell me what to do, Mr Brady? I came here to help rescue Miss Billie and that is what I will do, and the hell with you!'

'Okay, Miss Ellie, but as you may have noticed things are getting kind of hairy round here. Are you armed in any way? Have you packed a rod?'

'Have I packed a rod? Is the Chief Rabbi Jewish? You bet your sweet ass I've packed a rod, and I can shoot straight. I come from Harlem, remember?' The automatic she removed from her stocking top was an elegant piece, and so was her stocking top, but there was no time for that.

'Very well, Miss Ellie. Keep close to me and watch your back.'

'What the hell are those?'

'The Armies of the Night. I'll explain later.'

Micky Angel's men were still firing and still bringing down the creatures but there were so many of them and they kept coming, scrambling over the bodies of their kind whose limbs still twitched and struggled. Two of Micky's men had exhausted the supply of ammunition for their sawn-off shotguns and were using knives.

'You see that passageway opposite you, Miss Ellie, that's what we need to aim at to rescue Billie.'

'My God! You mean we have to climb over those bodies?'

'*You* don't have to. You can leave now.'

'I don't quit.'

'Then keep with me, and make every bullet count.'

'Nathan! Behind you!'

Brady turned and saw a group of the mutant creatures shambling towards them from the long gallery. If there were more of them Micky and his men would be surrounded and that would be the end, however many they killed. There was only one thing for it.

'Okay, Ellie,' said Brady. 'You hold them off with your rod while I do this.' From the inside of his pocket he drew a thin object wrapped in brown paper, about the size and shape of the baguettes they sold at the French *boulangerie* in Spring Street, Lower Manhattan.

'Hell, what's that?'

'Keep them off with your rod, sister. If this doesn't work, we're sunk. Aim for their eyes.'

Ellie began firing and made every shot count. As the creatures fell, they made a strange hissing sound as if air was escaping from their bodies, but still they twitched. Brady tore the brown paper off to reveal the object.

'Christ! What is that,' said Ellie, as she plugged another assailant.

'The hand and forearm of Obadiah Willums, wife murderer,' said Brady. It was indeed, a withered hideous thing, rigid and stiff as if desiccated, but it was an authentic Hand of Glory as stipulated by the *Necronomicon*. 'It is a traditional magical instrument which makes any person or persons who hold it invisible.'

'Baloney!'

'Quite possibly, but it's our only hope just now. Now I need a steady hand so I am going to hold this up and give you my lighter. Now all you have to do is to light each of the fingers. They have been prepared with a mixture of tallow and human fat so they should light easily.'

'What the hell is this?'

'Please! Just do as I say! This is our last chance!'

Without further discussion Ellie took the lighter and applied the flame to the top of each finger in turn as if to a candelabrum. From each finger shot a pure flame of bright emerald green. Brady made Ellie grasp the withered arm with him and held it aloft.

'Behold!' he shouted. 'The Hand of Glory!'

The effect was almost instant. The creatures who had been advancing on Ellie and Brady stopped in their tracks with something that looked like bafflement on their subhuman faces. Brady and Ellie had the sense of being surrounded by a slight mist through which they could see but which formed a barrier between them and the outer world. One of the creatures, more enterprising than the others, began to grope his way into the mist. He had almost touched the hem of Ellie's skirt when, with her free hand, she raised her automatic up to the beast's head and fired. The head exploded into a starburst of glaucous slime. The other creatures immediately turned tail and ran off howling.

Meanwhile Micky's men were slowly being overwhelmed. Two men were down and one was being strangled by a hundred scaly arms. The sawn-off shotguns had been abandoned as firing pieces due to lack of ammunition and were being used as clubs. The men with Tommy guns were eking out their last rounds sparingly. Micky's depleted mercenaries were on the retreat.

Then, suddenly a burst of gunfire. Out of one of the tunnels brandishing Tommy guns came six men who immediately began firing on the mutant creatures. They were followed by Leo Vinci languidly holding his pearl-handled Colt revolver in his right hand, while with the left he occasionally fed his mouth with a lighted Havana cigar.

This sudden incursion with new ammunition was too much, even for the hordes. With strange grunts and exhalations they began to retreat down various tunnels. Brady heaved a sigh of relief. His plan had succeeded, and his message to Leo the Artichoke that Micky Angel was planning to invade his territory with a whole lot of his actors dressed up as fish-like creatures to scare him had got through.

The last of the wholly alive members of the Armies of the Night were gone and the firing ceased. Across the vaulted hall in which lay a sprawling hideous mass of quivering subhumanity two groups of men faced each other. Micky with his ten still able men, though seriously short of ammunition, against Leo Vinci with his six, slightly more adequately equipped.

'So,' said Vinci, 'Mr Buonarotti. We meet again.' In his mouth Vinci's cigar glowed and faded, glowed and faded like a wicked winking eye.

Micky said: 'Where's Billie, you punk? You've got my doll, and I want her back.'

'Not so fast, lunkhead. What are you doing dressing bums up in stupid fish costumes and coming on my territory?'

'*Your* territory! Baloney! And don't pretend that those fish men are my bums, because they're your bums. I don't need no fish costumes to protect myself.'

'Are you calling me a liar, you sonofabitch?'

'You bet your ass I'm calling you a goddam liar, Artichoke!' There was an audible gasp from Vinci's associates, and a similar reaction from Micky's. This was followed by an impressive silence before Vinci spoke.

'You just called me Artichoke.'

'Sure I did . . . Artichoke!' Another gasp.

'Nobody calls me Artichoke, and lives. The last guy who did that is asleep in the East River with a very big rope around his guzzle.'

'Well, Mr Arti-choke,' said Micky very deliberately. 'I am about to prove the exception.'

'Don't be too sure of that, Micky Angel, you big fat sonofabitch!'

Then it all happened in what seemed to Brady and Ellie like a split second. Vinci had begun to raise his pearl-handled revolver rather languidly, but Micky, who was holding his automatic in his jacket pocket, fired from the hip four times into Vinci's torso. Vinci collapsed then Micky took the gun out of his pocket (now pretty much destroyed by the blast) and emptied the last two rounds into Vinci's convulsing body.

Vinci's men looked at him in astonishment, then one of them started firing, missing Micky who had dodged behind his men to reload, but hitting one of the foot soldiers. Then a battle began between between Micky's ten men and Vinci's six. Vinci's had the advantage at first because they had more ammunition and fire power but soon this position was reversed when Micky's men charged their opponents and the struggle became hand to hand. Fists flew; knives flashed.

'Come on, Ellie, now's our chance to get Billie. If we can reach that tunnel over there, that should take us to her.'

'But we can't get past all these guys beating the hell out of each other.'

'We can if we use the Hand of Glory. They won't see us. It's worked so far. Do you want to save Billie or not? This way!' And with both of them still grasping the Hand of Glory they began to skirt the battlefield. Whether it was the magic or the intensity of the struggle between the two gangs, nobody took any notice of Brady and Miss Ellie Jackson as they edged round the strangely carved walls of cyclopean masonry towards the tunnel. Having reached it, they ran through it. As they did so the Hand of Glory began to gutter and, with some relief, they both, with one mind, let go of the thing. Then they were hurrying through the door and mounting the staircase that led to Vinci's office.

THE ARMIES OF THE NIGHT

At the top of the stairs, before they burst in, Brady took out his automatic. Ellie followed directly behind him. In the office they found Billie trussed and gagged in one of Vinci's most elegant and uncomfortable chairs. Behind her stood Mr Hang holding a revolver which he pointed directly at Brady.

'Drop the rod and put up your dukes,' said Hang. Brady did as he was told, letting go of the automatic and raising his hands in the air. No sooner had he done so than he heard a bang by his right ear which temporarily deafened him. Then he saw a blood red flower unfold in the centre of Hang's forehead as he dropped heavily to the floor like a sacrificial ox. Miss Ellie had fired her automatic from behind him over Brady's shoulder.

'Good shooting, kid!' said Brady, his right ear still singing.

The next moments were spent untying and ungagging Miss Billie Bernard. The first thing she said when the gag was off was: 'Hell! What kept you?' Then she gave vent to a torrent of colourful language aimed at no-one in particular. It was strange to see it come from someone who, despite her long ordeal, was still coifed and pearled and gowned for a very classy first night party in Sardi's that was long over.

At length she calmed down and began to study the huge bulk of Mr Hang, lying face down on Mr Vinci's fine Bokhara rug.

'Is the Chink a stiff?' Billie asked.

Ellie prodded Hang's bulk with an elegant foot. 'The Chink's a stiff,' she said.

'Where's The Artichoke?'

'He's a stiff too,' said Brady. 'Micky Angel plugged him.'

'Well, Hallelujah for that!' said Billie. 'Listen, kids, I owe you for this. Anything I can do for you, say the word.'

'Well, to begin with,' said Brady, 'You could tell me why they call Leo Vinci "The Artichoke".'

'Don't you know? Jeez, I thought everyone knew. So, Leo Vinci is much enamoured of a doll called Nancy Spider who is a hoofer at The Garden of Allah. This is some time before I became Leo's doll, so this is ancient history, right? And Vinci, as you know, is not a guy who takes kindly to any other guy taking a peek at a doll he regards as his, but Miss Nancy Spider in no way sees herself as any guy's exclusive goods. So along comes this dude called Artie "The Ant" Millstein. And do not ask me why he is called "The Ant" because you do not want to know. And he is a handsome dude and has plenty of potatoes, whereas Leo, though he too has plenty of potatoes, is no oil painting, except that oil painting be by Miss Smart-Ass Lempicka. Well Artie and Miss Nancy start taking peeks at each other and the next thing you know they are holding hands at a table in The Garden of Allah between floor shows. So Vinci he gets mad at this, but rather than blasting Artie with a sawn-off like a normal guy, he gets all subtle. Perhaps he wants to keep the right side of Miss Nancy. Well, he invites this Artie to supper at Luigi's to discuss, as he says, a matter of business, and Artie goes all unsuspecting. Well, at Luigi's, as you may know, the speciality is a codfish cooked in the South Italian style with a tomato sauce. So they order the fish, then Vinci and two of his loyal colleagues who happen to show up, force the speciality *de la maison* down Artie's throat, bones and all, with the result desired.'

'He makes *Artie choke* to death?'

'You got it. And one and all, excepting everyone who knows of course, thinks it is by natural causes that Artie "The Ant" puts on the wooden overcoat.'

'Well, thank you, Miss Billie.'

'It is a pleasure, Mr Brady, to enlighten such a well-educated and high-toned dude such as yourself. Needless to say, when Mr Vinci's new sobriquet gets around he is not best pleased for Leo "The Artichoke" Vinci is not by nature a guy with a big sense of humour. And now he is no more—God rest his soul—plugged by my ever-loving Micky Angel. Listen kids, I am busting to split from this lousy joint. If I don't get out of this goddam wet ball-gown and into some very dry Martinis eftsoons, I will go apeshit.'

VI

20th May 1936 (from the diary of H.P. Lovecraft)
I write this from my comfortable bed in the Curwen Memorial Hospital in Arkham where I am currently undergoing tests and sundry examinations for my ailments. Aunt Annie seems content that I should be here, for of late I had been, as she put it in her demotic way, 'looking rather peaky'. This is hardly surprising given the severe physical and spiritual ordeal I have lately undergone.

Three days ago, Mr Brady called on me and asked me if I had considered the matter of purloining the *Necronomicon* from the Miskatonic Library. I told him I had, but that it was a venture both morally dubious and fraught with risk, whereupon he replied that no venture was morally dubious nor too risky when the very safety of the United States of America was at stake. As a patriot I saw the force of his argument; as a gentleman, I sighed but assented. After some prolonged discussion we settled upon that very night as the time for our adventure. I protested that I was not in a fit condition for an escapade of this nature but he insisted I accompany him, for only I could identify the volume in question and knew precisely where it was to be located in Miskatonic's labyrinthine bibliotheke.

A gibbous moon was riding high in a firmament laced with silver cloud as we drove in Mr Brady's Packard through Arkham County towards the Miskatonic University. When we reached Dunwich, Brady stopped the car and offered me a slug of Bourbon from his flask. I declined, for I never touch intoxicating liquor, but asked if he had any of Dr Bogusteen's *Preparation* on him. He said he had not and that, besides, we needed to keep all our wits about us for the coming venture. As we went over once

A MAZE FOR THE MINOTAUR

again our strategy, I heard the whippoorwills making their eldritch cries in a nearby brake. Having concluded our deliberations, we proceeded on our way, arriving at the outer limits of the Miskatonic campus at a quarter after midnight.

The gates of the campus had been locked for nigh on two hours and there was a high wall surrounding the whole, but Mr Brady had come well-accoutred with grappling hooks and a rope ladder, in addition to carrying on his back a haversack containing other tools to facilitate breaking and entering. Despite these useful adventitious aids, I found the climb over the high flint wall arduous, and needed encouragement, sometimes amounting to threat, to complete the task. We descended into a belt of trees on the other side of the wall whence we could see but not be seen. I myself had selected the spot where we might scale the walls undetected and Mr Brady commended me on my excellent choice of location.

Before us, glaucous under the pale moonlight, lay a great expanse of grass, sometimes used, I believe, by the alumni for football and other recreations. Beyond it reared the gaunt and Gothick edifice of the famed Miskatonic Library, looking ancient, monastic and somewhat eerie in the lunar effulgence.

I had warned Mr Brady about the guard dogs which roamed the campus at night, ready to apprehend the intruder or the errant sophomore. He said he had anticipated their possible intervention, but, fortunately, there seemed to be no evidence for their being in the vicinity. Nevertheless, we proceeded with caution, crossing the football field on swift but silent feet. Arrived at the foot of the library, I directed him first to the alarm bell on the wall of the building. With an agility that astonished me he climbed the rusticated masonry on the lower courses of the edifice, and, by clinging to the wall with one hand, with the other he succeeded in cutting the wires which attached the bell to the system within. Back on the ground he took from his haver-

THE ARMIES OF THE NIGHT

sack what he told me was a 'jemmy', with which he forced open one of the library's casement windows.

We found ourselves, by an irony which did not escape me, in the 'Law' section of the library. There we crouched under one of the tables and, with the aid of a flashlight, consulted the rough sketch map I had made of the place. We thought it best to proceed, as far as possible, unlit by artificial light, and, though the moon was not full, its illumination via the great Gothick windows was enough to help us on our way. But the library is vast and the way to the *Camera Librorum Prohibitorum* where the *Necronomicon* was kept, long and involved. Many was the time we had to stop in the protecting shadow of a wall of books to consult the map with the aid of our torches. A library by day or well-lit is to me the most welcoming of places, but in the dark of night it assumes an aspect of menace. Several times I fancied I heard the tread of furtive feet behind me, but I dismissed this as idle imagining and pressed on, though I noticed Mr Brady once or twice cast a hasty glance behind him.

At length by devious ways and by descending several flights of steps into the vaulted cellarage of the library we arrived before a low Gothick doorway of heavy oak bound with iron on which the following was inscribed:

C. L. P. [for *Camera Librorum Prohibitorum* or,
'Chamber of Forbidden Books']
STRICTLY NO ENTRY EXCEPT BY EXPRESS PERMISSION
OF THE PRINCIPAL AND GUARDIANS

The arch which formed the doorway had as its keystone a grinning head of such menacing and malignant appearance that we were both taken aback and around it was carved the following inscription:

Cave, Quaesitor, Custodem Enim Super Hanc Portam Posui

The inscription, translated means: *Seeker, beware! For I have set a guardian over this doorway.* Of what nature the guardian was or whether this was a mere idle threat we did not pause to consider, but neither the inscription nor the carved keystone had been present on my last visit to the library.

From his haversack Mr Brady took a curious metal instrument which, he told me, had been developed in the FBI laboratories, but which looked to me like a version of the old skeleton key. This he applied to the lock which after several tentative turns yielded and the door swung open.

The small vaulted chamber that revealed itself to our torchlight looked at first like a kind of mausoleum. It was windowless and painted black. On all walls were shelves housing a number of ancient leather-bound volumes as well as several iron-bound muniment boxes, no doubt containing loose manuscripts. What gave me something of a shock, I must own, was that in the centre of the room was a small wooden table covered in a red velvet cloth fringed with tarnished silver thread, and on the cloth reposed a heavy volume bound in black and heavily corrugated leather. I recognised it at once as being the Miskatonic's copy of the *Necronomicon*. It was as if the book itself had been expecting us.

Latent feelings of terror and misgiving which had been present with me as soon as we entered the building, suddenly became urgent. I turned round to see the door of the chamber beginning to swing shut. I hurled myself upon it, anxious beyond reason that it should not close upon us and managed just in time to interpose myself between the door and its frame. My slender body felt that it was being crushed; yet the air was close and still, and I could feel no trace of a breath of wind which could account for the door's movement. Brady picked up the volume, thrust it in his haversack and then, with me forced the door open. Once we were through it closed with a deafening clang and we were horrified to see two heavy steel bolts descend vertically from either side of the keystone and settle themselves over the door. Had I let it shut Brady and I would have been immured.

It was then that something like a panic seized us both and we began to run. Brady, being now burdened by the considerable weight of the book on his back, could go no faster than I. Several times we had to stop reluctantly to catch breath and in those dreadful moments the silence was punctured not only by the gasping of our exhausted lungs but also a strange pattering, rustling sound as if someone or something were in pursuit. Sooner than we would have wished we felt compelled to run on. Several times we lost our way among the dark and brooding stacks which compounded our terror.

At last we reached the law library and the open casement. Through the great Gothick windows we could see wind-driven clouds racing across the moon, sometimes obscuring it entirely and plunging the law library's great hall into Stygian darkness. The pattering sound came closer, and was in the hall as we scrambled our way to the open window.

We had reached the window when Brady in a moment of absurd folly turned round and shone the torch back into the obscurity of the library. It caught a whitish object. I saw it for barely a second but the memory of it will remain with me till the day of my death and—who knows?—beyond. It was roughly human in shape and monstrously tall. The head, like the body was featureless and entirely composed of what looked like scraps of paper or parchment on which signs and sigils had been inscribed. The thing was forever shifting and turning as if a whirl of wind were keeping it in shape. On it came, rustling dreadfully and intent on some nameless harm. Brady turned me about and bodily pushed me through the casement.

I collapsed in a heap outside. Meanwhile I saw him pick up a sheet of paper from one of the desks, squeeze it into a ball, light it with his lighter and then hurl it at the oncoming spectre. It burst into flames and only then did Brady follow me through the window.

We began to race across the playing field towards the belt of trees and the wall, but our peril was not over yet. I heard the barking of dogs and then I saw, galloping over the grass towards us, the shapes of several massive hounds, bull mastiffs by the look of them. They gained on us rapidly but we managed to reach the belt of trees. Brady shouted to me that I should climb the wall first while he held off the hounds, but I said I was too weak to climb by myself and needed to be hauled up from the top of the wall. The dogs were almost on us and I also saw several human figures hurrying towards us in the distance.

One of the animals, outrunning the others, leapt upon us but Brady struck it on the nose with a densely folded copy of *The Arkham Observer*, upon which it slunk away whining. The rolled-up newspaper, he later informed me, was a sovereign remedy against aggressive canines, a stratagem he had learned during his boyhood in Maine.

Brady climbed up the wall and tossed his rucksack containing the book over the other side. Then he told me to take hold of the rope that was hanging down and he would drag me up. I caught the rope but just then I felt a sharp pain in my ankle. It had been seized in the jaws of one of the mastiffs. I shook it off, losing my shoe in the process. Brady by this time was pulling me steadily up the wall, but then another of the hounds leapt up and seized hold of the seat of my pants. I was, perhaps fortuitously, wearing a pair of particularly old pants—and nearly all my garments are somewhat threadbare—so that the cloth ripped easily and the mastiff fell to earth with nothing but a piece of old tweed and a few minor abrasions on my posterior for his pains.

At last I was pulled to safety and sat for a moment atop the wall while the dogs yelped and barked beneath it. I looked across to the library and saw to my horror that the interior was illumined by a sheet of yellow flame. Then Brady was enjoining me to hurry. I climbed over the other side of the wall and dropped onto the soft turf beneath. Then, bruised and panting, my lower garments in a state of hideous disarray, I staggered over to the Packard whose engine Brady had already begun to stir into roaring life. The next moment we were speeding away from the Miskatonic along the midnight roads of Arkham County.

21st May 1936
That morning Miss Billie Bernard had invited Brady and Miss Ellie Jackson over to her apartment (lavishly paid for and equipped by Micky 'The Angel' Buonarotti) for cocktails. Neither Brady nor Miss Ellie were in the habit of drinking dry Martinis at such an early hour but they thought it churlish to make their reservations known. After her ordeal Billie had been off sick from the production of *Zip Ahoy!* but she had summoned them to announce that her absence from the show would become permanent and that Miss Ellie Jackson, formerly the understudy, was now confirmed in the part of Ruby Emerald. As the show was now a popular and critical success with Miss Ellie in the role, not even Micky Angel had raised objections.

'Micky has asked me to be his ever-loving wife,' said Billie, 'and I have agreed. He may be a big sap, but he's my big sap. As for the show business, you can keep it, and I hope it keeps fine for you, Miss Ellie. Me, I am going to have six kids, and make cupcakes and become a member of the Manhattan ladies sewing circle. Hell, I might even start going to church, for Micky Angel is very big on the Pope whom he regards as a regular guy. Though how the Pope sees Micky Angel might be not quite so dandy. Mr Brady, I wanted to thank you properly for your rescue of me from the clutches of The Artichoke, and as a token of my thanks I am giving you this which may help you in your further career. I obtained it from my ever loving Micky Angel who does not know that I have, and if you ever breathe a word to him or anyone that I have I will personally use you for target practice, and though no Annie Oakley like Miss Ellie here, I am also no beginner with a betsy.'

She handed him a thin brown Manila envelope which Brady immediately put in the inside of his jacket pocket. When he had done so Miss Ellie took hold of his hand and squeezed it. He squeezed back.

'You have my word I will not split on you ever, Miss Billie.' said Brady.

Billie smiled on them both. 'You may now kiss the bride,' she said.

22nd May 1936
The train had just left Pennsylvania Station, New York, bound for Washington when Brady, alone in a compartment, opened the envelope. It contained two glossy full plate photographs. One of them, a flash photograph, showed Mr Hoover wearing a sparkling sequinned ball-gown (oddly similar to the one Miss Billie had been wearing on the night of her abduction), an elaborately curled blonde wig perched on his toad-like head. As female impersonations go it was unconvincing in the extreme; Mr Hoover's customary swarthy scowl was the antithesis of feminine charm. The second seemed to have been taken clandestinely through a window, but it was quite clear enough for Brady to make out Hoover, still in his ball-gown, engaged in a very intimate act with his Assistant director, Clyde Tolson who was *not* wearing a ballgown, or anything else, for that matter. Brady shuddered at the thought of ever having to make use of these striking pieces of evidence, as no doubt Micky Angel had, but he decided to keep them safe. Along with the purloined *Necronomicon*, they would be put in a very secure place indeed.

The photographs did have one almost immediate effect on Brady. When, later that day, he knocked on the door of Hoover's office in Washington D.C., Brady did so without even a trace of nervousness or apprehension. Having heard the word 'Come!' he entered directly and found Hoover standing by the window staring out at the Capitol Building. Brady could not help, just for a second, reclothing him in his mind's eye in that sequinned ball gown and grotesque wig. When Hoover turned towards him, he must have noticed some change in Brady's manner because he took a step back, then mounted the dais where his desk stood.

'Ah, Brady. Good man.' His tone was slightly hesitant; it might even have contained a touch of obsequiousness. 'So,' he went on, 'we nailed those commie bums, but you know and I know that it doesn't stop there. You are agent one of the HPL and I want you to help me to recruit a whole bunch more. We've got one hell of a fight on our hands, have we not, Mr Brady?'

'We have, sir!'

'Good man! You've got spunk, Brady, and I like a man with spunk. Have you any further suggestions for recruits, then?'

'Just one at present, Mr Hoover.'

'I'm listening, Brady.'

'Mr Lovecraft, sir.'

'Lovecraft! That cock-a-mamy sonofabitch! You want *him*!'

'He has been very useful to us so far. Just now he is undergoing an operation at the Curwen Memorial Hospital in Arkham. It is for cancer, but we are hopeful of a successful outcome. If that occurs, I suggest that we relocate him to a safe place where he can continue his invaluable researches. He has yet to decipher the three Voorish Invocations, but given time, he will do so, and that may prove invaluable in our fight. Meanwhile I propose the hospital makes out that he has died and he disappears from the scene.'

'And this Lovecraft guy agrees to this?'

'He suggested it himself. It appeals to his reclusive nature. His Aunt Anne will be suborned and we will, of course, supply him with all the comforts and resources he requires, but he is not a man of extravagant tastes.'

'You seem to have got this all worked out.'

'I apologise, Mr Hoover, if I have over-anticipated your intentions.'

'Well I was going to put forward something on those lines myself, so consider yourself pardoned, Brady. Mr Lovecraft can become officially HPL Agent Number 2.'

'An excellent idea, Mr Hoover.'

'It *is* an excellent idea, Brady. These excellent ideas come to me all the time. That's why I am the Director. Bear that in mind, young man. Now about the Roxy Palace, you're sure those commie bums—armies of the night, or whatever they call themselves—have been eliminated.'

'For the time being.'

'Consider yourself commended, Brady. You hit a hole in one there. You and your lady friend who seems to have helped out. What was her name? Ellie?'

'As a matter of fact, sir, Miss Ellie Jackson and I were thinking of getting married.'

'Well, I can't stop you, Brady. And at least it shows you're not a goddam fag. But if I were you, I'd take up golf instead. You can't do both golf *and* marriage in my experience, and golf's one hell of a lot easier to get right.'

'Thank you for the advice, Mr Hoover, sir. I'll bear it in mind.'

A TARTAREAN CENTURY

A TARTAREAN CENTURY

Author's note

This collection marks the fact that, with this volume, over a hundred of my stories have been published by Tartarus Press in eight volumes. Grateful thanks are due to Tartarus for having done so with such flair, equanimity and dedication to the highest standards.

'Coruvorn' first appeared in *The Silent Garden, A Journal of Esoteric Fabulism*, (The Silent Garden Collective in 2018).

'A Maze for the Minotaur' first appeared in *Soot and Steel, Dark Tales of London* (Newcon Press 2019).

'Shadowy Waters' appeared in *The Far Tower* a collection of stories in celebration of W.B. Yeats (The Swan River Press 2019).

'The Old Man of the Woods' first appeared in *The Pale Illuminations* (Sarob Press 2019).

'The Crumblies' first appeared in *Crooked Houses*, a volume of haunted house stories (Egaeus Press, 2020).

'Collectable' was first written for and appeared in *Strange Tales: Tartarus Press at 30* (Tartarus Press, 2020).

'A Fragment of Thucydides' was written for a volume intended to mark the hundredth birthday of the distinguished ancient historian G.L. Cawkwell. Though he did not quite make his century, it was published in a posthumous tribute volume entitled *George Cawkwell of Univ* (Godage and Brothers 2019).

'Monkey's' was published in *Terror Tales of the Home Counties* (Telos Publishing 2020).

'The Wet Woman' and 'Via Mortis' come virgin to the volume.

The section entitled *A Cabinet of Curiosities* represents work in a lighter vein. 'The Sleeping Portrait of Monkshood Hall' first appeared as 'The Sleeping Portraits of Monkshood Hall' in *All Hallows #42* (October 2006). All four of the others first appeared in *Madder Mysteries* (Ex Occidente Press, February 2009).

The novella 'Armies of the Night' was written for the second volume of, *The Lovecraft Squad* subtitled *Waiting*, published by Pegasus in 2017.